PAYDIRT

Paul Levine

ALSO AVAILABLE

THE JAKE LASSITER SERIES

TO SPEAK FOR THE DEAD: Linebacker-turned-lawyer Jake Lassiter begins to believe that his surgeon client is innocent of malpractice...but guilty of murder.

NIGHT VISION: Jake is appointed a special prosecutor to hunt down a serial killer who preys on women in an Internet sex chat site.

FALSE DAWN: After his client confesses to a murder he didn't commit, Jake follows a bloody trail from Miami to Havana to discover the truth.

MORTAL SIN: Talk about conflicts of interest. Jake is sleeping with Gina Florio and defending her mob-connected husband in court.

RIPTIDE: Jake Lassiter chases a beautiful woman and stolen bonds from Miami to Maui.

FOOL ME TWICE: To clear his name in a murder investigation, Jake follows a trail of evidence that leads from Miami to buried treasure in the abandoned silver mines of Aspen, Colorado. (Also available in new paperback edition).

FLESH & BONES: Jake falls for his beautiful client even though he doubts her story. She claims to have recovered "repressed memories" of abuse...just before gunning down her father

LASSITER: Jake retraces the steps of a model who went missing 18 years earlier...after his one-night stand with her.

STAND-ALONE THRILLERS

IMPACT: A Jetliner crashes in the Everglades. Is it negligence or terrorism? When the legal case gets to the Supreme Court, the defense has a unique strategy. Kill anyone, even a Supreme Court Justice, to win the case.

BALLISTIC: A nuclear missile, a band of terrorists, and only two people who can prevent Armageddon. A "loose nukes" thriller for the 21st Century. (Also available in a new paperback edition).

Visit the author's website at http://www.paul-levine.com for more information. While there, sign up for Paul Levine's newsletter and the chance to win free books, DVD's and other prizes.

Table of Contents

"*When the One Great Scorer comes to write against your name;*
He marks—not that you won or lost—but how you played the
game.*"
—Grantland Rice

"*Just win, baby!*"
—Al Davis

PART ONE

Losing It All

-1-

A Rebel Without Balls

Bobby Gallagher had it all. A beautiful, savvy wife he adored, a whiz kid son who amazed him, and a high-profile, high-prestige job that his law school classmates would have sued their mothers to land. So what the hell was wrong?

I bend the rules until they break. I use my degree as a license to warp justice and perpetuate frauds. I'm a lawyer who's lost his moral compass and doesn't know how to find it.

He pondered these thoughts while sipping margaritas. After the third drink, he reached a conclusion. He would change his life.

But how, without giving up all the perks that come with my job as a professional prick?

Bobby was reclining on a wooden chaise lounge on his father-in-law's patio, an expanse of flagstone shaped like the Texas Panhandle and nearly as large. The patio jutted from the rear of Martin Kingsley's weekend ranch house, a rustic building the size of several football fields in the Hill Country southwest of Dallas.

The margarita was heavy on tequila and light on lime, just as Bobby liked it. Just as singer Peggy Lee liked it when she guzzled the first one ever poured, according to local legend, in a Galveston bar fifty years ago.

My life has become a Peggy Lee song. "Is that all there is?"

Bobby caught sight of Kingsley, sending him deeper into a funk.

My host, my boss, my father-in-law. Mein Fuhrer.

Kingsley owned pro football's Dallas Mustangs, which he liked to call "America's Team." Today, Kingsley wore a white chef's hat and a shimmering black suit with silver shoulder piping and a string tie, as he supervised a dozen cooks who were roasting corn-fed turkeys—plump as country parsons—on a brick grill the size of a factory furnace. White plumes of smoke swirled in the clear November air, carrying the aroma of dripping meat and savory spices, whipping up appetites, adding to the holiday mood.

Bobby doubted that the Pilgrims ever imagined Thanksgiving the way Kingsley celebrated it. Turkeys stuffed with corn tamales, venison picadillo, walnut bread pudding with rum sauce, all prepared by Dallas' finest chefs. The nouvelle Texas cuisine was far from Kingsley's hardscrabble roots of hog jowls and black-eyed peas, Bobby knew.

The Thanksgiving feast was held one day late because Kingsley's Mustangs were busy on the holiday making mincemeat out of the Eagles. All of the team's higher echelon employees and their families were here, herded down from Dallas across cypress-lined rivers, through the bigtooth maple forests aflame with autumn colors. Bobby and the other front office folks came by bus. Traveling by chartered jet to a private airfield were the on-the-field folks—the agile, mobile, hostile young men who each Sunday wore knickers and plastic hats and crashed into each other with felonious intent at ferocious speeds. They all headed to Kingsley's ranch house known modestly as *Casa del Conquistador*. It was one of the man's possessions, along with his Dallas mansion that resembled a Southern plantation, his private jet, various oil and gas exploration companies, extensive real estate, two refineries, and, of course, his prize football team.

And me, too. He's got clear title to my sorry ass.

Bobby considered his father-in-law to be both the most giving and most demanding man he had ever known. After Bobby married Christine, Kingsley made him general counsel of the team, though his credentials were thin. The two men constantly clashed, Bobby balking at Kingsley's insistence that he zealously defend the players from the law, the league, ex-wives, and creditors.

No, strike that, Your Honor. We haven't "clashed." I'm too chicken

3

shit for that. Kingsley gives orders. I whine my lawyerly dissent. He orders again, louder, and I comply. I'm a rebel without balls.

When it came to the Mustangs, Kingsley instructed Bobby to follow the rule coined by the late Al Davis, owner of the Oakland Raiders.

"Just win, baby."

Earlier that week, Bobby had again followed that simple instruction. He walked Buckwalter Washington out of the courthouse, beating an assault and battery charge. He didn't win with courtroom theatrics, but rather by quietly suborning perjury. Bobby listened as his chief witness took the redundant oath—the truth, the whole truth, and nothing but the truth – then told a lie, a whole lie, and nothing but a lie.

Under Bobby's questioning, the witness, a bar patron, swore that Buckwalter didn't clobber the obnoxious Tennessee Titans fan. The poor fellow simply toppled over in a drunken stupor, banging his head.

The team's security consultant—nice name for a bag man— had paid the witness in cash, insulating Bobby from criminal responsibility, but not from corruption of his soul.

Thinking about it now, stewing in the juices of his self-loathing, Bobby knew he was trapped. Owing Martin Kingsley so much, how could he stand up to him?

Attack his father-in-law's character? Hell, Kingsley wasn't a bad man, at least not by robber baron standards. He had clawed his way into money and power and used both to buy a big kid's toy, the Mustangs. He adored his daughter and grandson and blessed his son-in-law with a dream job.

So what am I complaining about? Why not just do what I'm told? Everybody compromises, right?

Bobby spotted his wife, Christine, slipping out a rear door of her father's sprawling house, headed his way with a pitcher of pale-green margaritas. The house was a constructed of cross-hatched logs and was intended to look both historic and western, but in fact, was designed by a Boston architect and built in the 1990's for six million dollars. The fireplace was made of multi-colored river rock and was large enough for a man to step into the open hearth without stooping, large enough to consume an ungrateful son-in-law, Bobby figured.

She offered to refill his glass, and he didn't say no. On this cool day, with the tangy scent of pine trees mixing with pungent mesquite smoke, she wore a Dallas warm-up suit and running shoes. Holiday attire gave way to more practical outdoor wear in the Kingsley household, especially with the touch football game to come before dinner. "You've been so quiet all day," she said, sounding worried, "and now you look depressed."

"My job has no social utility," he blurted out, surprising both of them.

"Would you rather still be in the P.D.'s office, defending penniless criminals?"

"Penniless criminals, wealthy criminals," he said. "What's the difference?"

Christine ran a hand through her blond hair, which was pulled straight back and revealed a widow's peak and smooth, high forehead. Her eyes were greenish gold, cloudless as a spring day, and crinkled with laugh lines. Her lips were delicate, peach toned, and expressive. He thought she was even more lovely at thirty-six than a dozen years earlier when they met.

Christine, you could have done better. You could have snagged a man who was smarter, richer, better looking. And honest. How do I even merit such a woman?

Bobby stood an even six feet, had shaggy brown hair and deep brown eyes. Women did not run from the sight of him, but they didn't exactly throw their thongs at him, either. At thirty-nine, his stomach was starting to turn soft from too many cocktail parties and too little racquetball. Bobby always saw himself as not bad looking, not a bad lawyer, and not a bad guy.

I define my life by the absence of negatives while Christine is the epitome of superlatives.

She was competent at everything she tried. Phi Beta Kappa

in college and a track star, too. Running cross country might have given her some of that calm confidence, that steadiness and stamina, Bobby thought.

He could not imagine life without her.

Christine ran the Mustangs' marketing department with smooth efficiency, helped their son Scott with his Latin homework, routinely beat Bobby at tennis, and also found time to run the Kingsley Center, a shelter for abused women. Bobby never knew anyone who juggled so many flaming batons each day and then looked high-society gorgeous in a slithery cocktail dress at night.

"You're having a mid-life crisis." Her voice soothing, her eyes compassionate. "I didn't expect it for a few years, but we'll just deal with it now."

No crisis too challenging great for the great problem solver.

He took a hit on the drink, hoping the liquor would melt his pent-up frustrations. "Chrissy, I don't know how to deal with it, because I'm trapped. If I quit and go into private practice, I'd be starting from scratch."

Below them, down a set of flagstone steps from the patio, Martin Kingsley, minus his chef's hat, was barking orders at workers who were finishing the yard lines on the perfectly groomed football grass. Irrigated and fertilized, the field was a re-creation of Mustangs Stadium except the logo in the end zone here said, "Kingsley's Mustangs." Children clung to footballs and chirped happily, running and turning somersaults on the soft grass. Bobby caught sight of their eleven-year-old son Scott tossing a ball with the children of the assistant coaches. Adjacent to the field, team executives in shorts and running shoes mingled with players near the portable bars, working up their courage for the game.

"It's so hard for me to relate because I love my job," Christine said.

Another difference, Bobby thought. You love your father, too.

"But if that's what you want to do, Bobby – start over – I'll understand."

"I knew you would."

"Hey, Ro-ber-to!" Bobby looked up to see Craig Stringer, the veteran Dallas quarterback with the TV anchorman smile. "You gonna warm up your throwing arm?"

"That's what I'm doing," Bobby replied, hoisting his glass.

"Better be on your game, because the MVP gets to kiss the boss' beautiful daughter."

Stringer gave Christine his best crinkly eyed, pearly grin, and Bobby indulged in the pleasurable vision of an opposing linebacker crushing the QB's throat with a forearm shot. Stringer thought he was so irresistible he could get away with anything, including sleeping with half the Mustangs' Cheerleader squad, and telling every Shari, Sandi, and Sunny that she was the only one. Or, in Stringer's Georgia drawl, "the onliest one, ah swear."

"Craig, you're an outrageous flirt," Christine said.

"I'm the quarterback," Stringer tipped his ball cap to the lady and ambled off.

"I don't like the way he's always sniffing around after you," Bobby said.

Christine laughed, and a smile rippled across her face like a breeze across a lake. "Oh, Bobby, I think you're jealous!"

They both watched as Stinger ran the cocktail party version of a slant route , cutting sharply across the field directly toward cheerleader captain Shari Blossom, who was standing at the bar.

A trio of Mexican guitarists strolled by in full mariachi costume. They were playing *"Besame Mucho,"* in which a lover begs to be kissed.

"Do you want to talk more about it, Bobby? Your job."

He itched to tell her the truth about Buckwalter Washington and all the other players he'd gotten out of trouble by breaking the rules. He wanted to confess he'd used the law, money, and her father's influence to become everything he hated about sleazy lawyers.

But what would she think of me? She has a blind spot to the old bastard's failings, but would she be as forgiving of mine?

"It's hard to explain," he said.

"Do you want me to talk to Daddy?"

"No!"

He said it too harshly, and Christine eyed him warily. In a dozen years, they almost never raised their voices to each other. "I'm sorry, Chrissy, but I have to fight my own battles. I'm going to do it. I'm going to tell him we've got to clean up the franchise, do things the right way."

"Okay, but be diplomatic. Don't butt heads with him."

"I won't," Bobby said. "His head is a lot harder than mine."

-2-

Man as Beast

Poor Bobby, Christine thought. He didn't understand business. He didn't understand what it took for a man like her father to build from the ground up. Sometimes, she felt she had to mother Bobby even more than their son Lovable as a floppy-eared puppy, her husband was a grown man who still needed protection from the world.

And from Daddy.

Daddy mistook Bobby's decency for weakness, and Bobby considered Daddy's ambition to be rapacious greed. Both men were far more complicated, she knew, and both had extraordinary qualities.

How can I make peace between them?

Lately she'd been charting Bobby's moods like a meteorologist watching tropical storms. Something was bothering him, and he wasn't talking.

She headed down the flagstone steps to the field where the guests dipped corn chips into smoked tomato salsa and nibbled pickled jalapenos while sloshing icy rivers of margaritas. Her co-workers greeted her with a dozen "Howdys," and "Hidys," as she glided by, avoiding the cocktail party chatter about the big win over the Eagles yesterday. Several players and their wives stopped her momentarily to wish Happy Thanksgiving. White-uniformed waiters skated by with platters of hor d'oeuvres. Inside a huge tent of Dallas silver and blue, other servers were preparing tables for the coming feast. Christine approached the tent, heard a commotion inside, and stopped in the open entranceway.

What she saw froze her. Nightlife Jackson, the team's All-Pro wide receiver, was angrily shouting at a young woman, wagging a finger under her nose. Her face twisted in terror, the woman lurched backward – one step, two steps, three shaky steps – but he pressed forward, staying in her grill. Staying in her face, screaming. "Fuck you want, woman! Fuck you want!"

Nightlife's dark round, cherubic face usually was composed in a playful smile, but now, unaware of Christine's presence, he was snarling, the veins on his neck thick as cables and throbbing with every heartbeat.

"I don't want *you!* I'm goin' home."

Christine recognized the woman as Nightlife's girlfriend, a flight attendant named Shaina.

"You ain't going nowhere, bitch!" Nightlife yelled.

"I'm goin' home and don't bother callin'!"

She turned and Nightlife grabbed her by the shoulder and spun her around, his biceps straining against the sleeve of his silver Mustangs t-shirt. "Give me those car keys, 'ho!"

"Lemme go!"

Changing tactics, he lowered his voice to a seductive whisper. "C'mon now, sweet meat. Do what Daddy says."

He tried to pry open her hand, but she resisted, screaming as Nightlife bent a finger backward.

"Wilbur!" Christine shouted, using Nightlife's given name and moving toward him. "Let her go!"

Nightlife spun around, startled. "This don't concern you, Ms. Gallagher. Me and Shaina's just jaw jacking. It ain't nothing."

"Help me! He's breaking my bones!" Shaina yelled, her voice keening into a high-pitched wail, her beaded corn rows flailing as she tossed her head. Her eye make-up was streaked over her cheeks tinging her cinnamon skin a sooty charcoal.

"Shut up, Miss Thang!" Nightlife yelled.

"Let her go!" Christine ordered.

"Bitch shamed me in front of the team, and she's—"

"His whore's here!" Shaina bawled. "He had Tyrone Wheatley

bring her, but I know Nightlife's doing her when I'm off flying."

"Don't be stupid!" Nightlife hollered.

"You're stupid!" she screamed back. "You're so stupid you leave your fly open just to count to eleven."

She tried to twist away but Nightlife grabbed her arm and yanked it behind her back, then wrenched hard, pressing the back of her hand against her shoulder blade.

"Ow!"

"Give me those car keys!"

Christine moved closer. "You do not lift a hand to a woman, Wilbur Jackson. You do not hurt a woman, ever!"

Nightlife turned to Christine, his eyes flaring with such fury that she staggered back a step on wobbly legs.

"The fuck you doing, woman! This ain't your fight!"

"If you don't let her go right now, I'll have my father suspend you.

"Fuck that! I'm your meal ticket, rich girl and this 'ho ain't nothing."

Nightlife's face was a searing mask of violence. For a moment, Christine was sure he would hit her. Her vision blurred, and his features mutated into something barely human. He became a horned beast, a goat-man, and then finally something else altogether. Something – someone – from her past. As Nightlife balled his fist and glared at her with eyes as hard as steel spikes, she saw the face that still haunted her nightmares. She girded herself and chased away the memory.

"Don't be a fool, Wilbur. I can end your career."

"The fuck you can, woman. You're just the team bling and don't even know it."

"Try me."

With a look of utter disgust, he released Shaina and turned to leave. "Shee-it, you women stick together like flies on shit."

Christine put her arms around the young woman and let her sob. "He's not worth the tears, Shaina," Christine told her, remembering her own past, "but someday you'll find someone who is."

-3-

Daddy

Christine was late for the game because she had stopped to see her father in his macho den. It was a place of dark leather sofas and tobacco humidors, red Mexican tile floors with Navajo rugs, rough-hewn knotty pine walls mounted with crossed swords and rifles used in the defense of the Alamo. On the wall behind her father's desk, the head of a wild boar, fangs exposed, greeted her with a macabre smile.

She found her father standing at a reading table. He was a ramrod straight Marlboro man who looked younger than his sixty-seven years. He stood six feet-three—taller in his ostrich cowboy boots—and was a fit, rangy one hundred ninety-five pounds. His skin was a leathery parchment from too much West Texas sun in his youth, and his deeply set blue eyes looked out from under bushy white eyebrows. He had let his trademark long hair go silvery white, sweeping up at the neckline. He did not discourage sports writers who compared his looks—and actions—to Buffalo Bill Cody.

Christine had intended to tell her father about her encounter with Nightlife, but something stopped her. At first she thought she was afraid what her father would have done to his All-Pro receiver. But upon further review – as the replay officials say, it might have been just the opposite.

So what if Nightlife had beaten his girlfriend? So what if he had frightened Christine?

Her father wouldn't suspend his star player. She could almost hear him.

Now Chrissy, it's part of their culture, and you best not stick your nose into any of my players' personal affairs.

Bobby might exaggerate her father's flaws, but he was right about some things, she thought. Daddy was obsessed with winning and the glory that came with it. Overlooking his best player's sins would not be all that difficult. Christine felt a sisterhood with Shaina and every other woman who knew the terror of a man's fist. But her father, with no connection to Shaina, no stake in her life, would be insensitive to her pain.

"I need to talk to you about the Kingsley Women's Shelter," Christine said, after they said their hellos.

"That again?" He leaned back in his black leather judge's chair and propped his boots on the mahogany desk. Breaking into a crooked grin, he exhaled a long whistle, then spoke in his West Texas twang. "Christine, darlin', I'm trying to get to the Super Bowl. I don't have the time or inclination to get involved with those problem women."

"*Abused* women, Daddy."

"I know. I know. But my point's still the same. I got bigger catfish to fry."

"The Super Bowl isn't everything, Daddy."

"Sure it is! It's the American way. Winner take all. When the final gun sounds and the music stops playing, one guy goes home with the girl, and the other guy's singing the big dance blues."

"Is winning a football game more important than saving a woman's life?"

"Depends on the woman," he said, cracking a smile to let her know he was only semi-serious.

"We need another ninety thousand dollars for roof repairs," she said.

He let out another whistle. "If I keep giving money away, I won't have a pot to pee in. Hell, I won't even have a window to throw it out of. Sometimes I wonder if you realize the value of a dollar."

"I realize the good it can do when it's well spent."

"I guess I look at money differently. After my old man lost

13

everything, we were so poor the roaches had to eat out or go hungry."

That was part truth, part amiable fiction, she knew. True, her grandfather, Earl Kingsley, went from poverty to riches and back to near-poverty again, but there had always been food on the table.

"All that oil and gas in the ground but we couldn't afford any for the car," her father went on, rehashing family folklore. "I filled up my old man's Ford with the help of a West Texas credit card. Do you know what that is, Chrissy?"

"A rubber hose."

"Right! We'd just siphon it out of the banker's Buick. Only time in my life I ever got anything from a banker without signing enough papers to choke a horse."

Christine let him ramble on, telling tales she'd heard dozens of times. Her father always had to bleat and paw the earth for a while before giving in. While he blathered, she planned her strategy. She wouldn't tell him about the panic-stricken women who would be forced back into the streets or worse, into the homes of men who brutalized them. He couldn't relate to women, so she'd make it personal for him.

"Remember the great publicity when you opened the shelter. Pictures in the paper, TV interviews."

"Sure. It was damn near worth the half million you talked me out of."

"Well, give the ninety thousand now and hold a press conference challenging all your Ashbrook Country Club pals to each match it. Get enough to endow the Shelter so we don't need to do this again."

"Hey, I like that, put the squeeze on those cheap bastards."

"It'll make the local news for sure, probably the NFL pre-game show on Sunday."

He chewed over a thought for a second, then said, "Done deal."

Christine smiled to herself. Now, if she could only teach Bobby how to handle her father. He wasn't that difficult."

-4-

Razzle-Dazzle

"C'mon Dad, put a spiral on it," Scott Gallagher urged, as a wobbly pass fluttered over his head.

Bobby was looking at the world through a tequila haze as he warmed up, tossing the football to his son on the freshly lined field. Scott wore a tattered Penn State jersey, number twelve, because it once belonged to his father.

Twelve was a quarterback's number, but Bobby Gallagher never played a down at that position in college. He held the ball for the kicker. With a weak arm and slow feet, he was third-string quarterback at Shanahan High in Fort Lauder-damn-dale. A walk-on at Penn State, his good hands and keen concentration made him a natural for the sport's least appreciated position: the holder on field goals and P-A-T's.

Three years and he never bobbled a snap. Repetition and focus. Consistency, the quiet confidence that coach Joe Paterno admired. Even now, Bobby could visualize the ball rocketing back to him from between the center's legs. Hundreds of snaps in practice, each time Bobby catching the ball with thumbs together, bringing it down smoothly, tilted ever-so-slightly toward him, simultaneously spinning the ball so the laces faced away from the kicker's foot, leaving a left index finger on top, and tucking his right hand into his crotch, out of the kicker's way.

The snap! The ball's down. It's up...and go-oood!

"Yo Dad, I've drawn up some plays," Scott said, whipping out a sheet of paper filled with x's and o's. Scott was a towheaded, wiry 11-year-old with his mother's delicate features and an endless fascination with numbers. He did logarithms for fun and never understood why his father couldn't convert centimeters to inches in his head. Bobby looked at diagrams of intricate pass patterns and double reverses and shook his head. "We've got wives and kids playing who think a quarterback is a refund, and you're giving me all razzle-dazzle plays."

"C'mon Dad, don't bone out on me. We can score with the flea flicker. You hand off to me, I'll dive into the line like it's a running play, then lateral back to you, and you'll hit Mom slanting across the middle."

Bobby laughed. "Sure, why not? A family flea flicker. I love it, kiddo."

&

Bobby's team was already two touchdowns behind when Christine arrived at the field. She had tied her blond hair back in a ponytail, and in her warm-up suit and running shoes, she looked like a college coed.

"Hello gorgeous!" Bobby greeted her, his spirits improving. He was in running shorts and a faded sweatshirt advertising a barbecue joint. The air was filled with the sweet smells of freshly cut grass, mesquite smoke, and roasting turkeys.

The game was being played with the casualness of a fraternity's coed volleyball match. A few Dallas players were distributed to each team but mostly just provided mischievous encouragement or heckled each other. Craig Stringer quarterbacked the opposing team, tossing soft floaters to the civilians and kids. Had he thrown with the same velocity he used in a league game, the ball would have ripped through the webbing of some accountant's thumb and broken his glasses.

"Mom, hurry up!" Scott shouted. "We need you." He turned to his father who was returning to the huddle with a motley, disorganized team consisting of his son, three women from season ticket sales, a guy from public relations, one Mustangs Cheerleader, and two reserve linebackers whose competitive fires were limited to a struggle for the cheerleader's attention.

"Dad, let's try the flea flicker now," Scott urged in a whisper.

"Okay, explain it to your mother."

"Mom, lemme show you this. We're gonna razzle-dazzle them."

"Really?" she said, smiling. "That's what your father did to me a long time ago."

A moment later, Bobby's team was lined up in a raggedy formation that neither Vince Lombardi nor Joe Paterno ever envisioned. Hunched over the ball was cheerleader Shari Blossom, chosen to play center on the theory that she distracted the opposition when her breasts tumbled out of her top. The tall blonde was in full uniform, white short-shorts, bare midriff, exposing a flat stomach. In her white boots and silver-starred bolero vest, Shari was the ideal Texas girl-woman, eternally worshiped by Bubbas in the lower deck.

Playing tailback was Scott Gallagher, an eleven-year-old math wizard. His mother was split to the right as a wide receiver, and his father was barking signals. "Hut, hut, hut!"

On the third count, Shari wiggled her rear and whisked the ball between her legs, bosom atwitter. Standing a few yards back in the shotgun formation, Bobby took the snap on one skittering bounce and handed the ball to Scott who started for the line of scrimmage, then suddenly stopped and flipped the ball back to his father.

Christine played possum, just hanging out along the right sideline as if admiring the dandelions. Suddenly, with a burst, she dashed 15 yards straight down the sideline, then cut hard, slanting left across the middle. Her defender, an overweight account exec in promotions, was left standing along the sidelines, dazed and confused.

Bobby watched Christine break open in the middle of the field. The defense was in disarray, some of the linemen tagging Scott, thinking he still had the ball. The only defender near Christine was Nightlife Jackson who'd never moved from what would have been the free safety's territory in a real game.

Bobby let loose a decent spiral, leading Christine, allowing her to run under it, ball and receiver meeting at a precise geometric point down the field. Bobby watched as several things happened at once.

Christine looks over her shoulder to spot the oncoming ball...
Nightlife takes two steps to his right, directly into her path...
And stops...
He never raises his hands, never goes for the interception.

The ball was thrown slightly high, and Christine leapt for it, watched it settle into her hands, then turned just in time to see Nightlife blocking her path.

What's he doing? Look out, Chrissy!

As she landed, she tried to pivot, but her left knee buckled underneath her, and the sickening *pop* was audible across the field.

The bastard! Why did he do that? He could have moved out of her way and just tagged her.

Christine sprawled to the ground, crying out in pain, the ball ricocheting off her hands and toward Nightlife who picked the interception out of the air just before it hit the ground.

Ignoring Nightlife who sprinted past him for a touchdown, Bobby raced to his wife and bent down over her, holding her by the shoulders, sensing from her cries that it was a serious injury. She twined her fingers through his, clenched his hand and moaned.

"Oh Chrissy, don't move," he said. "We'll get help."

Scott appeared near tears. "Does it hurt bad, Mom?"

Christine gritted her teeth through the pain and tried to shake her head, but Scott wasn't buying it. "Do something, Dad!"

"Doc Joyner's in the house," someone said, referring to the team physician.

Bobby swept Christine up in his arms and carried her toward the house, passing Nightlife who was doing a funky celebration dance in the end zone. Rage whistled through Bobby like the West Texas wind. "What the hell kind of defense was that, Jackson?" Bobby demanded.

Nightlife threw up his hands in mock surrender. "Hey, lawyer man, chill! I never touched her."

"You purposely blocked her path! She tore up her knee to avoid hitting you."

"Hey, it's a tough sport, but it wasn't my fault."

"You son-of-a-bitch!"

"Bobby, just get me inside," Christine pleaded.

"Not done with you, Nightlife."

"Whatever you say, lawyer man."

Furious, Bobby carried his wife up the steps and into the house, his son trailing alongside.

"My hero," Christine said softly through her tears. "You've rescued me again."

"Too late, this time. My armor is rusty and my steed a step too slow."

She nuzzled his neck. "Promise you'll never let me down."

"It's a promise." Bobby believed his words. Never thinking he could blow it so completely. Never imagining he could lose her love, his career, and even his son on one day of dreadful luck and impulsive choices.

"You seldom, if ever, find an athlete who is a criminal. He is essentially a good boy, a good sport, and a gentleman. He adheres to the word of God and the Golden Rule, both on the field and off."
—Vince Lombardi

-5-

How 'Bout Them Mustangs!

Nine days later...

Bobby sat next to Christine in the back row of the owner's suite in Mustangs Stadium. Her bandaged left knee was propped on a pillow on an adjacent chair, and she swallowed a Percocet every two hours. She'd come out of surgery ready to go back to work, though it would take months for the torn ligaments to heal.

Now, Bobby and Christine watched Dallas taking on Washington. Bobby held Christine's hand and shot glances at his son Scott in the front row of the suite huddled with Martin Kingsley, who kept a rolled up game program gripped fiercely in one hand, a pair of binoculars in the other. The boy and his grandfather were inseparable on game days. They spoke football jargon to each other between plays, high-fived after Mustangs touchdowns, strategized at halftime, and hugged when the final gun signified a victory. In these moments, Bobby almost felt warmth for the man who made his life so difficult.

If he loves his grandson, he can't be all bad, right?

"Blitz, blitz, blitz!" Scott yelled.

"Got him! A sack!" his grandfather fired back, smacking his grandson affectionately on the shoulder. "Good call, Scott."

Christine barely paid attention to the game. She was speaking rapidly into one of the many phones, explaining to an angry sponsor that his upper deck sign would be visible on TV again, as soon as stadium security tore down the homemade banner inadvertently obscuring his invitation to the Durango Saloon. Christine's spirits were upbeat as usual, even though her bandaged knee throbbed.

There was a stir in the suite as Dallas intercepted a pass and took over the ball at midfield. They trailed 10-7 early in the second quarter and needed a win to take over first place in the division. In the stands, the hometown fans began pumping up the volume.

"Did you make dinner reservations for tonight or did you forget?" she asked Bobby.

"Forget our anniversary? I remember the day we met. The Mustangs wore gray; you wore blue."

Christine smiled and nodded toward the front row where Scott was cheering. "Someone's having a good time."

"Scott's as addicted to the game as your father. Last night, I caught him devising a power rating to beat the point spread."

They watched Stringer complete a deep pass down the sideline, and the cheering echoed through the stadium. At the bar in the rear of the suite, someone watching the game on TV shouted, "First and ten at the twenty-one!"

"So where are you taking me for dinner?" Christine asked.

"To a candlelit dining room between our kitchen and the den."

"You expect me to cook?" She shot a look at her leg.

"Not you, me. I thought you'd be too uncomfortable in a restaurant."

She gave him an affectionate squeeze. "You're right. Thank you, darling. So what's for dinner?"

"Your choice. Snapper in white wine sauce or hamburger on the grill?"

"Why do I think I should order the burger?"

"Because I know how to make it?"

She laughed, and Bobby turned back toward the field where Stringer took the snap and backpedaled, side-stepping a blitzing linebacker.

"Nightlife's open!" Scott shouted from the front row.

"Hit him, Craig!" Kingsley yelled.

"Touchdown!" someone else cried out.

The stadium erupted in deafening cheers.

Bobby derived more pleasure watching his son enjoy the

moment than from the play itself. Scott whirled toward his father. "Didja see that, Dad?"

Bobby gave his son two thumbs up.

"How 'bout them Moo-tongs!" Kingsley yelled.

"Awesome, Grandad!" Scott replied, and the two exchanged high fives.

It was a family joke. When still a toddler, unable to pronounce "Mustangs," Scott told his grandfather that he loved the "Moo-tongs." The name stuck and was even picked up by the Dallas sportswriters.

Bobby turned toward Christine who was waiting, puckered up. Another tradition, along with barbecue on Friday nights and church on Sunday mornings. When the Mustangs scored, so did he, with a long, lingering kiss.

As their lips touched, he felt the familiar surge of warmth run through him, and in that moment, he made a decision to live by.

I can put up with old Daddy-in-law. I won't do anything to jeopardize what I have.

A moment later, before their lips separated, the phone in front of him rang, a discordant jarring that rocked him out of his mellow mood.

ᴄ⁊

Bobby picked up the phone as the clock ticked off the last few seconds of the first half. Dallas was ahead 14-10, but Bobby was oblivious to the score, indifferent to the future of the team. As the Assistant District Attorney spoke to him, Bobby felt feverish and his head throbbed.

A warrant had just been issued charging Wilbur "Nightlife" Jackson with sexual assault.

"Date rape, if you want to call it that," Larry Walters, the A.D.A. told him on the phone. "Name's Janet Petty, a cocktail waitress at the team hotel, single mother with a two-year-old at home. Nightlife invited her up to his room after her shift. They

23

smoked some weed, drank some tequila. She told him she had to get home to her kid. He grabs her at the door, drags her to the bed and—"

"Star fucking groupie," Bobby said, playing defense lawyer, saying his scripted lines, repressing what he feared was true. "C'mon Larry. She went to a player's room at one a.m. and got stoned. It'll be her word against his on consent."

"She's got two broken ribs and assorted bruises to prove it, plus she passed the polygraph this morning," Walters said. "Did I mention she holds two jobs, goes to community college and sings in her church choir?"

Damn, a nightmare victim.

"Kind of ironic, isn't it?" Walters asked. "You lock up your players in a hotel to keep them out of trouble, and look what happens. Hey Bobby, you don't need coaches, you need jailers."

Walters wanted to know if Bobby would surrender his client in the morning for a quiet booking and immediate bond hearing, avoiding the media circus. Nightlife would be on the street within ninety minutes. The wheels of justice are well greased for the rich and famous.

"Yeah, I'll have him there," Bobby said. "And thanks, Larry."

"Don't mention it. By the way, I'll expect four playoff tickets by hand delivery."

Bobby hung up and slipped down to the first row. Crouching next to Kingsley, Bobby was a humble supplicant, whispering the bad news. Kingsley reached into his pocket and pulled out a thick wad of hundred dollar bills in a silver and turquoise money clip.

"Take care of it with the woman," Kingsley said. "Let her know there's more where that came from. Get a final number from her and do the paperwork tonight. You'll want her signature on a release before some contingent fee shyster gets to her."

Bobby looked up at Kingsley from his catcher's crouch. Now was his chance. If ever he were going to stand up to the man, this was it. But then, hadn't he just promised to play it safe? Didn't he owe it to Christine and Scott? Waves of conflicting emotions tore at him, and he reached one inescapable conclusion: he lacked the balls to do what was right..

"You know the drill, don't you, Robert?" Kingsley asked.

"Know it? Hell, Martin, I invented it."

-6-

Bagman

Bobby drove to the hospital with Kingsley's wad of cash bulging uncomfortably in his pocket. He felt disembodied, numbed, as if under an anaesthetic.

I'm to blame for this. I'm the one who got Nightlife off the first time.

Was this his penance? Was a wrathful God bringing him here to lance the boils that festered on his conscience? He felt weak, as if his spine were made of leaves, wet and mushy from the rain. He tried to rationalize.

It's my job, dammit! If it weren't me, it would be someone else.

His thoughts turned to his boss. What was Kingsley thinking now? Surely not about the woman sedated in a hospital room. No, only whether the Mustangs hang tough for another win. Back-slapping along the sidelines as the last seconds tick away, then some quips for the sportswriters.

The nurse's station was deserted, the staff huddled at the end of the corridor in the visitors' TV room. Bobby heard the familiar background noise of the football game. IV's and bedpans could wait; the Mustangs were on the tube.

Bobby could feel his pulse quicken as he let himself into Janet Petty's room. She seemed to be asleep. Her eyes were nearly swollen shut, and a spot of dried blood stained a bandage at the corner of her mouth. An African-American woman in her early twenties, she probably was attractive when her face wasn't swollen from a beating.

Bobby's legs felt heavy as logs, and his breathing became so labored, he worried his exhalations would wake her. Looking at her, battered and bruised, his heart thundered in his ears, as if beating itself to death in some rocky cavern.

"Are you a doctor?" Janet Petty asked through parched lips. Her eyes had opened, tiny slits in the swollen flesh. "Because if you are, I'd just as soon have one who's not wearing a Mustangs shirt."

"I'm the lawyer for the team," Bobby said, taking on the role he despised.

Her laugh was a parched and humorless cough. "The D.A. said you might come around. I'm not gonna sign anything, so you can just go talk to my lawyer."

I have a job to do, so do it!

"I'm not here to get you sign anything," he said. "The team management simply wishes to assist you in your current situation."

"I don't have a *situation*! I've been beaten and raped."

Bobby reached into his pocket and withdrew the wad of hundreds, crisp as fresh kindling. Surely, somewhere on the planet, he told himself, was someone who was sleazier, scummier, more reprehensible than his own miserable self.

"Isn't that what lawyers do, Bobby? Make excuses, settle cases, get people off?"

Maybe it is, Chrissy, but once I pictured myself as Atticus Finch, standing tall for justice...and look at me now.

He started peeling off the bills, letting her see Ben Franklin's picture, trying to whet her appetite.

"The D.A. told me not take any money from you," she said.

"No obligation," Bobby told her. "We just thought you could use some spare cash for babysitters, food, doctors' bills. Then, when you're feeling better, we could bring some paperwork by."

Jesus Christ, how did I sink to this?

"No way," she said. "You talk to my lawyer. He'll be by later."

"Lawyers," Bobby said, rolling his eyes. "I hate to say it, but sometimes my brethren just slow things down, muck things up."

"I'm in no hurry," she said, shifting her position on the pillow, wincing with pain.

Beaten but proud, refusing to be buffaloed by the fistful of hundreds. "The D.A. told me he'd done it before."

"What?"

"Nightlife. That he raped another girl, but that it never got into the papers. Had I known, I never would have gone up to his room."

Bobby started to say something about everyone being innocent until proven guilty, but he bit off the words like a strand of thread.

"Did you know about it?" she asked.

Bobby sucked in a breath but stayed quiet, his own silence bearing down on him like a tombstone.

"Of course you did." She propped herself on an elbow, grimaced as if someone had just lodged a dagger between her ribs, then sized him up. "You're his lawyer. You're probably the one who hushed it up, aren't you?"

"I..." He wanted to say he was only doing his job, but it sounded so pathetic, he swallowed the thought.

What kind of a job was that? What kind of a man am I?

"How do you sleep at night?" Her swollen eyes filled with tears. "What do you see when you look in the mirror?"

Engulfed in misery, he put the money back in his pocket. "I want to help you. I really do. Forget who I am, or what I came here to do. If there's anything I can do to help..."

"Put your client behind bars."

He wanted to tell her it didn't work that way. *The system, you know.*

"I can't." Feeling empty.

Janet Petty turned her head toward the wall and spoke so softly Bobby could barely make out the words. "After they gave me the sedatives last night, I dreamed about that animal. He was biting me and clawing me, dragging me down and soiling me..."

"I'm sorry," Bobby said, his voice dry as burned paper. "I am so very sorry." His pity extended to both of them. He stepped closer to the bed and reached out for her arm, but when he touched her clammy skin, she recoiled and screamed.

"Get out! Get out of my room!"

She frantically reached for the buzzer, her face twisted in pain, and Bobby fled, fighting back tears of his own.

-7-

A Gutless, Spineless, Soft-Bellied Shyster

Bobby wound his way through the bowels of the stadium, working his way toward the locker room where a cacophony of sounds echoed off the walls. The game had ended half an hour earlier, a Dallas victory, as if that mattered in the grand cosmic scheme.

Reporters circled players, jamming microphones into their faces, pleading for grunted tidbits of wisdom. The floor was slick with sweat and shower spray, littered with soggy towels and wads of tape. Filthy uniforms were flung into laundry carts. An occasional victory whoop was heard, as the players celebrated defeating Washington, their long-time rivals.

Bobby waited until the reporters edged away from Nightlife, having asked the same question a dozen different ways. Bobby was constantly amazed at how complicated the sports writers tried to make a game that was essentially blocking and tackling, throwing and catching.

"Hey, whas-up, 'Meanor?" Nightlife asked him. The nickname, "Misdemeanor," which always bothered Bobby, infuriated him now. A former defensive back had coined it after Bobby convinced a judge to reduce an attempted murder charge to simple assault.

"We have to talk," Bobby said.

"Talk's cheap, but Nightlife ain't."

Nightlife looked at Bobby with innocent, doe-like dark eyes. He had a child's face and a slightly buck-toothed smile that only made him seem even more boyish and guileless. Bobby considered him a narcissist and pathological liar.

"Hey man, you're not still pissed about your old lady, are you? Wasn't my fault." He was naked except for a white towel wrapped around his midsection. He was shorter than Bobby, one of those quicksilver wide receivers with explosive strength and Olympic speed, a gazelle who darts across the middle unafraid of being crushed by ornery linebackers who outweigh him by fifty pounds. If not for his highly developed pecs and trapezoids that seemed to connect his shoulders directly to his head without need of a neck, Nightlife would have resembled a teenage camper headed for the bunkhouse showers.

"That's not it," Bobby said, grabbing him by the arm and dragging him toward an adjacent room where the offensive unit held its meetings. The room resembled a lecture hall with writing-desk chairs, a raised stage and a blackboard covered with "x's" and "o's."

"I'm here about Janet Petty."

"Never heard of her. She want an autograph?"

"She says you already tattooed her."

Nightlife's features were expressionless, his eyes bored.

"Last night, your room," Bobby said. "She claims you raped her."

"Hey, lawyer man, do I look like I gotta force 'em?" He cocked his head, pointed with both index fingers to his presumably innocent face and showed a smile that was more of a wink, a nudge in the ribs.

"You tell me. This is the second time around."

"Shee-it! Old story, 'Meanor. Bitch complaining 'cause I tossed her out, didn't ask her number. She was moaning and groaning last night but feels used and abused in the morning."

"Jackson, don't bullshit me. I'm your lawyer. The woman has a black eye, a split lip, two broken ribs, and contusions on her inner thighs."

"Nightlife got a tool like an anaconda. Maybe she got bruised

31

trying to ride it."

"I said, don't bullshit me! We went through this before with the perfume counter clerk."

"Right. How much is this one gonna cost me?"

"How about five to ten in Huntsville?"

"That ain't funny."

"Neither is rape." Bobby's headache had spread down his neck and he hunched his shoulders like a bear. "I should never have gotten you off the first time."

"What!" Nightlife jammed the heel of his hand into Bobby's chest. It was the same move he used to separate himself from a defensive back, a short push that disguises the power behind it. Bobby winced and took a step backward.

"Your *job* is to get me off!"

"No, my job is to make the state prove its case."

"If it's her word against mine, how she gonna prove it?"

"Did you rape her?" Bobby shouted. His legs felt unsteady and he knew his face was reddening. "Did you rape Janet Petty?"

"I did that 'ho better than she ever been done, then I came out here today and won the game. People pay good money to see me catch the ball and boogie in the end zone. They don't care who I fucked or how I fucked her."

"Did you rape her!"

The player's shrug seemed to say, *what's the big deal.* His mouth was twisted into a mask of scornful derision. "Maybe she said to stop, but Nightlife was past the point of no return."

"You ought to be put away." Saying it with more sadness than anger.

"And who's gonna do it? You, 'Meanor? Your wife's got bigger balls than you."

"I'm going to talk to Kingsley."

He turned, but Nightlife grabbed his shoulder. "You do that, lawyer man! You tell the King. He knows who totes the mail, and it ain't you. I pay your salary! I am the main attraction and you're just an usher for the show."

"You have an inflated opinion of your own worth."

"Mr. K. thinks my worth is eleven million dollars a year plus performance bonuses."

"When I talk to him, he may decide you're more trouble than you're worth."

"If you had eyes up your ass, lawyer man, you still couldn't see shit! You don't have the power to touch me. You're a bitch just like that 'ho from last night."

Bobby stepped close to Nightlife, invading what trial lawyers call the personal zone. He'd never lean over the rail and breathe on a juror this way, but just now, Bobby ached to get in Nightlife's face, and they stood nose-to-nose. Bobby knew the athlete could flatten him with one punch, but it didn't matter.

"Okay tough guy!" Bobby yelled. "We know you can beat up cocktail waitresses and perfume clerks. What about me? You want some of me?"

"Shee-it!" Nightlife said, mocking him. "Aren't you the guy who gives the lectures to the team every year? 'Some night you're gonna be in a bar, and some fool's gonna jack you up, challenge your manhood. But men, you gotta be the ones to back down, you gotta be the ones to say no.'" He cackled with laughter. "So, 'Meanor, I'm saying 'no' to sticking my Nikes so far up your ass, you're gonna have swooshes coming out your ears. I did my job today. Now you go do yours!"

Holding onto his towel with one hand, Nightlife turned and walked back to the locker room.

❧

On his way to the parking lot, Bobby concluded that his client was right.

Nightlife knows my job better than I do. My job is to protect the corporate assets. To wheedle and cajole judges, to obfuscate, confuse and muddy the issues. To warp illusion into truth and polish dung into gold. His job was to set Nightlife free so he could abuse some starry-eyed young woman all over again.

He felt untethered, floating free in a dark cold space like a lost astronaut, caught between what he knew was right and what he was paid so handsomely to do. For years, he'd longed to cleanse his soul. How low had he fallen? He wanted to change, but how? Did he even have the courage to take on his father-in-law? In the battle for his soul, had he already surrendered the prize?

"Have you a criminal lawyer in this burg?"
"We think so but we haven't been able to prove it on him yet."
—Carl Sandburg, "The People, Yes"

-8-

The Road to Ruin is Paved with Foie Gras

As sensitive as a swallow to a change in the wind, Christine had been concerned about Bobby's shifting moods for the past several months. But as hard as she tried, she still couldn't figure him out. Did he hate his job or hate her father? Was he insecure when measuring himself against Daddy?

Oh Bobby, don't you know I love you just the way you are?

She sat at the vanity mirror in her dressing area, brushing her blond hair, now loosened from its clips. She wore a peach-colored silk bathrobe and her knee was throbbing. The pain pills made her groggy, but she forced herself to focus on what Bobby was saying. She sensed that the tides of change were about to sweep Bobby in some new, uncharted direction, and it frightened her. He had always been so dependable. No drinking bouts with the guys from the office. No affairs. Now he seemed lost and needed her support more than ever.

Listening to his mournful monologue, Christine quickly realized he wasn't just having a case of mid-career blues. When he came out of the locker room, there was something different about him. A seething anger, seemingly directed at himself.

"I'm responsible," he had told her, pacing in their bedroom after midnight. "If I hadn't gotten Nightlife off, he'd have gone to jail, and this never would have happened. Now he thinks he can get away with anything, but why shouldn't he? I'm the one who enabled him."

She measured her words like a baker with the sugar. "You're too hard on yourself, Bobby. You keep looking for perfection in the world and in yourself."

She'd always accepted Daddy's explanations about the players' antics. They were easy pickings for the media and for women setting them up for lawsuits and extortion. At heart, the players were just a bunch of fun-loving, God-fearing, hard-working boys. But Daddy had fiddled with the truth, she knew.

Sometimes, in the car, she listened to radio talk shows, where callers attacked the team's character with nasty jokes:

Q. What's another name for a Texas Crime Ring?

A. A Mustangs huddle.

Q. How do you get 45 Cowboy players to stand all at once?

A. Will the defendant please rise?

"I know how you feel about violence against women," he said, after a moment.

Do you ever! You knew it the moment you charged into my life.

The thought brought back a memory, and it send a spidery shiver up her spine. The blurry outline of another man's face came back to her then, the image she had seen when Nightlife seemed ready to strike her. It was Lowell Darby nearly a dozen years earlier.

The spoiled youngest son of a Fort Worth banking family, Lowell was fifteen years her senior. Handsome, single, rich, the perfect match, her father told her. Only after their high-society engagement party did she discover he was also a passive-aggressive alcoholic with bipolar disorder. Given to binges, Lowell would become sullen and depressed. He rose from the abyss of his own self-pity by attacking those he loved, or more accurately, those who loved him. It began by pushing, then slapping, then a fist to the stomach. Even drunk, he was careful enough not to leave any marks.

"Why do you make me do this?" he would cry, smacking Christine across the room.

At first, Christine thought it was her fault. If only she were more caring and less demanding, if only she thought of him first, if only this, if only that...

One night, she was working late, alone in her Mustangs Center office, when Lowell staggered through the door wearing a disheveled tux. Had she forgotten their date for the symphony or had he forgotten to tell her? It didn't matter. He shattered a vase against a Remington sculpture of a cowboy on a bucking bronco. He slapped her, raising a welt on her cheekbone, then shoved her across the office where she fell, knocking a computer monitor to the floor.

"I only do this because I love you!" Darby shouted, as he pulled her head backward by the hair. She fought him off, clawing his face with her fingernails and screaming.

In the corridor, headed toward the parking lot, the new associate in the general counsel's office heard the commotion and burst through the door, finding Lowell clutching her throat, squeezing the life out of her. She blacked out and never saw what happened, but when she came to, the lawyer was scooping her up into his arms. Lowell lay moaning on the floor, blood spurting from a broken nose, three teeth missing from his predator's smile.

"Are you all right, Ms. Kingsley?" Bobby Gallagher asked, carrying her gently toward the door.

She looked up at the shaggy haired young man with warm, sad eyes, placed her head on his shoulder, and said, "I am, now."

To this day, two of Bobby's knuckles carried a scars from Darby's canines.

In the mirror, she could see Bobby behind her. He had just stepped out of the shower and was toweling himself off.

"It's not your fault, Bobby. Now we know what a thug Jackson is. But two years ago, how could you have known? You played by the rules and did your job."

She could hear him exhale as if he had started a word, then changed his mind. "Didn't you, Bobby?"

"I paid an investigator twenty thousand dollars to find an alibi witness."

"That seems like a lot for..." She felt her hairbrush stop in midstroke and she turned to look at him head on. "You mean you paid for false testimony."

She tried to make eye contact, but his gaze wouldn't meet hers. "My P.I. found a limo driver who claimed he was driving Nightlife on a club-hopping tour and never lost sight of him all night. No perfume clerk, no hotel room, no rape."

"And it was false?"

"All I know is that the driver's memory improved with each thousand dollars, and by the time of the final draft of the affidavit, his statement was so convincing that Nightlife was never even charged. No messy trial, no bad publicity. The prosecutor practically apologized for our inconvenience."

"You never told me," she said, looking at her naked husband. He had started going soft around the middle, and now, his shoulders slumped. She wanted him to say more. She loved him, but even after all these years, she still didn't know exactly what made him tick. Why was he so difficult to reach?

"Does Daddy know?"

Bobby's laugh was empty and humorless. "He gave me the cash for the payoff. Your father regards his players' criminal charges as public relations problems, not moral issues."

"Don't do that, Bobby. Don't shift this to him. We're talking about you. What else have you done?"

"Everything dear old Daddy wanted me to."

"Then confront him directly. Anything else is cowardly."

Bobby blinked twice as if a flashbulb had startled him. Immediately she regretted what she had said. "I'm sorry, Bobby. I didn't mean that you're—"

"No, Chrissy, you're right." He lowered his head, and his voice was barely a whisper. "I'm afraid of your father. I owe him so much I don't know how to stand up to him, and I blame him for my own weaknesses."

"Talk to me," she pleaded. "Tell me everything."

"'What shall it profit a man,'" he said, his eyes distant and unfocused, "'if he shall gain the whole world and lose his own soul?'"

She stared at her husband as if she did not know him. He was not one to quote Scripture. He seemed to be disintegrating before her eyes. "How have you lost your soul, Bobby?"

He didn't speak, didn't seem to be able to form the words.

"I'm not just your wife," Christine said. "I'm not just the mother of your son. I'm your best friend, Bobby."

"Locked up in the marketing office all day, you've been insulated from a lot of what's been going on."

"I read the papers. I know we've been embarrassed. And I listen to you after you have a second martini on a Saturday night, and you start whimpering that you're going to quit your job and join the Peace Corps."

"Now you're mocking me."

"I'm not! I'm trying to draw you out of your cave. I'm trying to get you to talk about your feelings. What is it you've done or think you've done?"

Men! Why do they have such difficulty expressing their emotions? Other than anger, that is.

He sat down on the edge of the bed and stared at the floor. When he finally spoke, his voice was parched. "I've paid witnesses to leave town and others to testify about events they never saw. I've fabricated drug tests and suborned perjury. I've carried piss for your father."

"What?"

"I've peed into bottles and switched urine samples with half-a-dozen players. As far as the league knows, the Mustangs have no drug problem but suspiciously high cholesterol."

"Oh, Bobby," she said, feeling his humiliation. "Why didn't you talk to me before?"

"I've repressed it. I convinced myself how wonderful life was because I love you and Scott so much. I even like some of the work. But the fixing and cheating is eating away at me. And now, this! There's a woman in the hospital, beaten and raped, because of me."

Christine used a cane to stand up at the vanity table, then

hobbled over to the bed, sitting down next to him. His eyes were red and puffy, and sitting there, naked, he looked like as vulnerable as a lost little boy. She put her arms around him and stroked the back of his neck. She would do anything to breathe life back into him. This was the man who had saved her from an abusive man, who fathered her son, who teased her and made her laugh. "Don't you understand that I love you no matter what? This only brings us closer together. Your problems are mine. Your pain is mine. We can work through this."

She held his hand as they talked, felt the warmth of him. This is what marriage was all about, she was sure. Bonding in times of crisis.

"If you want me to talk to my father, I'll—"

"No, Chrissy. This is my battle. I'm going to handle it myself."

"Fine. But don't threaten Daddy," she cautioned. "That doesn't work with him. And don't just stake out the high moral ground. You need to give him business reasons for every decision."

"I'm not crawling on hands and knees to kiss his ring. I'm through being afraid of him."

There was an edge to his voice that frightened her.

Oh Bobby, how can I protect you?

She worried that he was too undisciplined and impetuous to confront her father. When directly challenged, Daddy always lashed back.

"What are you going to do, Bobby?" she asked.

જી

Bobby took inventory before answering, tallying the bounty of his life. His wife and son, of course, and a deep love for them both. Then, the material items. A gorgeous home with a lap pool, a Jacuzzi, and a tennis court. A garage shielding his Lexus and Chrissy's Mercedes from the Texas sun. An expense account and pension plan. Cocktail parties and business lunches and a closet full of expensive suits.

For years, he had been stuck in a web of finely spun gold. The road to ruin is paved with foie gras, he concluded. The pursuit of victory—on the field, at the ticket window, in the courtroom—had become paramount. Corruption was the handmaiden of success. He had gone along, handing up his balls along with his self-esteem. A man can rationalize almost anything.

Hey, this is the big leagues. This is the way the game is played.

Tonight, he had stood fifteen minutes under the scalding water in the shower but could not scrub himself clean. He heard terrified screams in the roar of the faucet, saw the face of an anguished woman rising from the steam. With those visions still etched in his mind, a plan began to form.

He would reclaim his manhood. Maybe he'd lose the material possessions but he'd still have what mattered most to him, the love and tenderness of his wife and son.

"I'm going to take a stand," he said. "I'm going to change my life."

"Do it," Christine said, reaching out to stroke his cheek. "But remember, it's my life, too."

PAUL LEVINE

"The Cowboys are America's Team. Dallas has the babes, the glitz, the uniforms. The Cowboys are the American Dream."
—Tony Kornheiser, sportswriter

-9-

An All Pro Quid Pro Quo

This was the day, Bobby Gallagher vowed, he would reclaim his soul. He would confront his father-in-law and climb out of the shallow grave of corruption and despair he had dug for himself.

Okay, let's put a lid on the melodrama. I made a deal with Martin Kingsley. I do whatever the hell he wants, and he overpays me for it.

Most lawyers for pro football teams are paper pushers, laboring over player contracts and sponsor deals.

Not bagmen, dishing out cash to witnesses.

"Keep my players off the docket," Kingsley had ordered, more than once. The idea was to deep-six cases before they ever reached the courthouse door.

The lawyer as Fixer. But today I'm putting a stop all the sleazy tricks.

৩

Ordinarily, Kingsley was the first to arrive at the Mustangs' Valley Ranch headquarters but on this morning—the day after the victory over Washington—Bobby was waiting in the anteroom at 5:35 a.m drinking black coffee from a mug he had carried in the car. Bobby had been unable to sleep and had nowhere else to go. Christine was knocked out, purring contentedly under a haze of pain killers. Kingsley seemed both surprised and pleased to see his son-in-law in the quiet of the early morning. He greeted Bobby him with the satisfied smile of a man who owns a large chunk of God's green earth.

"Helluva game, wasn't it Robert? Now, bring on the Bears. Say, did I congratulate you and Christine on your anniversary?"

"We received your gift, Martin. Thank you. It was very generous."

Damn. How do you confront with the man who just gave you first class tickets to Maui and a fully paid hotel suite? It had seemed so easy rehearsing the speech in the car, but now...

"No need to thank me," Kingsley said. "Hell, it's a selfish gift. I love Hawaii, and I'll have a suite just down the hall from you. Nothing more I'd love to do than celebrate with my family."

He winked at Bobby. The trip was one week after the Super Bowl, so Bobby had no doubt what celebration his father-in-law had in mind.

They walked together down the corridor, Bobby matching strides with the long-legged Texan. Kingsley wore his trademark black suit with silver shoulder piping, a matching gray tie, and black ostrich-skin cowboy boots. He was vital and strong with a crushing handshake and a charming personality when he chose to use them. He also could be ornery as an old mule.

Bobby took a deep breath and tried to relax. He had never confronted Kingsley before. In every major disagreement, Bobby had always backed down. Today, he vowed, it would be different.

Don't worry, Chrissy. You'll be proud of me when this day is out.

ᘓ

Listening to Kingsley re-live the glory of the victory over Washington, Bobby let his mind wander. How had he even gotten here? For years, he thought that the passive act of holding a ball for someone else to kick was the only thing in the world he was perfectly competent to do. He was rejected by every law school in Florida but finally secured a spot at a small college in Dallas whose accreditation was pending. He got a job pouring tar on roofs during the day and studied law at night. Even now, he could remember the choking fumes of the tar on a hot Texas day, his skin darkened by the sun and singed by drops of the boiling black liquid.

Bobby graduated from law school with what he liked to call "low honors." He got a job in the public defenders' office in Dallas and discovered he had a knack for trying cases. In his second year, he handled a case that would change his life.

"The bastard spit beer on my girlfriend," his client had told him.

"Whereupon the defendant did strike the victim on or about the head with a deadly weapon, to wit: a pool cue."

Or so said the indictment against his client.

Bobby thought it hurt his case that his client had assaulted a Dallas Mustangs defensive lineman with the pool cue. The players were still in their demi-god phase. But Bobby was masterful in closing argument, railing about the "mountain of reasonable doubt." When the jury came back with a big fat Not Guilty, Bobby was interviewed on local TV as a rising star in the local courthouse, and the next day, the new owner of the team called. "They tell me you know how to talk to a jury without polishing your words so shiny you could skate on 'em," Martin Kingsley said. "C'mon out to Valley Ranch. I'll buy you lunch and pick your brain."

Bobby didn't need to be asked twice. Kingsley gave him a tour of the training facilities, then began asking questions about a player who had been set up for a cocaine purchase by an informant.

As he listened, Bobby realized that he was auditioning for a job. Associate counsel, maybe work his way up to vice president for legal affairs and general counsel. Prestige, money, a fun job. Better than the hard tile floors and green metal desks in the P.D.'s office.

Bobby ran through the usual advice of attacking the credibility of the snitch, who almost certainly had a criminal record, of getting the jury upset that the cops are using scumbags to make their cases, of pleading entrapment.

"But none of that will work," Bobby said.

"So what the hell would you do?" Kingsley demanded, impatiently.

"I'd want to know who the judge is," Bobby said. "Is he a football fan? Judges are just like everybody else once they take off their robes and step down from the bench. They want to rub shoulders with celebrities and get close to the action. You'd be surprised how much mileage you could get out of a few hor d'oeuvres and some skybox seats."

Kingsley's smile stretched across his face. "Do you like cigars?" he asked, opening a wooden humidor on his desk.

At first, Bobby genuinely admired the man who was to become his boss and later his father-in-law. The charismatic Texan could be warm, generous and giving. What Bobby only realized much later was that every gift—paying off the house mortgage, the Mercedes at Christmas—came with a price.

An All Pro quid pro quo.

Martin Kingsley required unwavering, unquestioning loyalty. A willingness to follow orders without so much as a "why," "but," or "maybe."

When Bobby was hired, Kingsley was still in his honeymoon phase with the news media and the fans. He gave great interviews, allowing himself to be quoted on every subject from the length of the cheerleaders' short-shorts—"Bubba ain't paying to see no Vestal Virgins"—to his players' taunting, flaunting, swaggering style—"It ain't braggin' if you kin do it." He was country with a wink and a nod.

Slick as owl shit as they say west of the Pecos.

But the charm soon gave way to something never seen at press conferences and cocktail parties, the cold-blooded pursuit of victories and profits at any cost.

☙

Finally, Kingsley asked why Bobby had come around so early. They were settled into the plush office, decorated in silver and blue and large enough for a decent down-and-out pass. Bobby glanced at the Super Bowl memorabilia lining the walls and wondered if he'd ever see them again.

"Nightlife Jackson," he said, evenly.

"Ah yes." Kingsley propped his cowboy boots on his desk. "Is that taken care of?"

"I wanted to talk to you first."

"Make sure bond is arranged before going downtown. I don't want him to sit in jail and miss practice."

"That's not what I wanted to talk about. It's more complex than that."

"Set a meeting with that P.R. woman we used when Buckwalter busted up that tavern. Get your investigator to find out if the woman's ever cried 'rape' before.'. Let me know when a judge is assigned to the case. If it's Wilford Adams, I'll call the old bastard myself. If it's one of those young Turks, you'll have to orchestrate some dog and pony show."

"That's not what I had in mind," Bobby said. He gripped the chair and tried not to fidget. He felt a rivulet of sweat streaking down his temple.

"No? What's your strategy?"

"Martin, this is a great opportunity to do something right, to take a stand on principle."

"I don't follow you."

"We can win without him."

"What are you talking about?"

Bobby felt jumpy, as if his chest were filled with fluttering birds. "Let's use the morals clause in his contract to cut Nightlife from the team. Make a public statement. You won't tolerate immoral behavior. From now own, the players must adhere to principles and values. Zero tolerance for violence against women, drug abuse, or criminal conduct of any kind. You'll clean out all the thugs and lawbreakers."

A moment of dead silence sucked all the air from the room. Kingsley looked at Bobby as if he were speaking some strange, foreign language.

"Cut Nightlife Jackson? Is that what you're saying?"

"We'll be setting an example for the league and for all the kids who look up to athletes. We'll let the whole country know you've got to be a good citizen to play for the Mustangs."

Kingsley swung his boots to the floor and leaned across his desk toward Bobby, fixing him with a look as vicious as a pit bull guarding a bone. "Nightlife would be signed by another team in an instant. We'd face him in the playoffs, for Christ's sake!"

"No one will sign him because he'll be in jail. I plan on pleading him guilty."

"The hell you will! What's gotten into you?"

Bobby wasn't sure what to say. His seduction and corruption had occurred slowly, the drip from a faucet that eventually overflows the sink. After a moment, he said, "I took an oath, Martin, but I never heard the words."

"What the hell does that mean?"

"Last summer, we took Scott to Washington," Bobby said. "We did the Smithsonian, the White House, all the tourist things. I went to the Supreme Court. Hell, I'll never argue a case there, but I wanted to see it. On the front steps are these two marble statues, one representing justice the other law. I started to believe the words carved in the marble."

"What words!"

"'Equal Justice Under Law.' The blindfolded lady with the scales, the whole nine yards."

Kingsley ground his teeth and his craggy face knotted up like burled oak. When he spoke again, his voice cut the air with the hiss of a swinging scythe. "Lady Justice is a whore who can be bought and sold. A good lawyer bends Lady Justice over his desk and fucks her up the ass."

"That's pretty much what Nightlife Jackson did to Janet Petty."

"Just get down off your high horse and fix this thing. Christ, by now, you should know your job."

"Nightlife's a menace. He raped that perfume clerk two years ago, and now he's done it again. It's our fault, Martin. Yours and mine. We're as guilty as he is."

Kingsley stared a long, hard moment at his son-in-law, his eyes dead and cold as stones in a mountain creek. "My fault?" Disbelief in his voice.

"We could have put a stop to it. We could have helped put him away."

"This woman the other night, this barmaid, went back to the hotel room with him, didn't she?" Kingsley asked in a cross examination tone.

"Yes, but she didn't consent to having sex. He beat her up."

"Maybe she liked it rough," Kingsley suggested. "Women these days..."

"He raped her!" Bobby shouted. It was the first time he'd ever raised his voice to his father-in-law, and he felt his hands tremble. "He told me so! He laughed about it. You want to hear about the drugs, the young girls he gets to his hotel room half blitzed, how he humiliates them, dirties them."

Kingsley's ice-blue eyes narrowed and he thrust his chin upward at a pugnacious angle. "For Christ's sake, Robert, get your priorities straight. Your job is to protect the good name of this franchise."

"Not any more." Bobby shook his head. "It's time to do what's right, Martin. He's got to own up to what he's done, and so do we."

"We?"

"Both of us, Martin."

"Why, you piss ant!" You want to start looking for a real job in this economy?"

"No matter what happens to me, I'll make sure the truth gets out."

"Let me give you some Texas advice, young man." Kingsley's voice was low, his features as hard as granite. "When you're standing chin-deep in manure, you're best to keep your mouth shut."

Kingsley's rage sizzled from every pore, like cold butter dropped on a hot skillet. "I have a dossier on you, fellow. I could get you disbarred, tarred, feathered, and strung up like a nine-point buck on the first day of hunting season. And don't think just because you're married to my daughter I won't do it. She's my blood, not you. You're the hired help."

A delicious feeling coursed through Bobby's veins. He no longer felt fear. Now, he was indestructible. With each insult, he grew stronger, with each threat, braver. "Do what you want to me, Martin, but you mess with the justice system, I'll bring you down."

Kingsley stared hard at him, the fury burning like coal in his eyes. "You ungrateful piece of shit. I made you what you are today."

A derisive laugh exploded out of Bobby. "Right, Martin. You made me a cheap carbon copy of yourself. But I'm a lousy you. I can't lie, cheat, and steal and still smile all the way to the bank. I can't be the biggest phony in town and still sleep at night."

Kingsley moved quickly for a man his age. He was out of his chair and around the desk before Bobby could stand. He grabbed Bobby by the shirt collar and yanked him to his feet. Their faces were jammed together, and Bobby could smell the coffee on his breath. "You've got ten seconds to apologize and get the hell back to your office or I'll thrash your hide before firing you."

Bobby felt lightheaded and giddy. He laughed, which seemed to infuriate Kingsley even more. "What's so damn funny, you jackass!"

"You are, Martin. You're a bully and a blowhard, and you don't scare me."

"You self-righteous son-of-a-bitch!" Kingsley shoved Bobby into a shelving unit. Trophies tumbled to the floor, and a football-shaped crystal ornament shattered on its first bounce.

Bobby rebounded from the shelves, his knees buckling. When he regained his balance, his vision was filled with the sight of Kingsley's fist coming toward his chin. He slipped his head to the right, and the punch grazed his temple. Instinctively, Bobby threw a punch of his own, but it was a looping right hand with too little power behind it.

"You swing like a girl!" Kingsley taunted him, assuming a boxer's pose with a left hand lead, standing straight up like some bare knuckled-champion from the Nineteenth Century. "C'mon girlie. Let's see what you've got."

All the pent-up frustrations ignited a fire inside Bobby. He wanted to hit Kingsley, wanted to scar him, wanted him to feel the pain of Janet Petty. He snapped out a left jab that caught Kingsley on the cheekbone and rocked him backwards. Kingsley responded with a left hand of his own, but Bobby blocked it. They bobbed and weaved a moment in imitation of countless prizefighters, and then Bobby flicked a straight left that glanced off Kingsley's forehead.

Before he could follow up, Kingsley dug a short right hook into Bobby's gut. Bobby gagged and stepped back, bending at the waist, sucking for air.

"You're soft!" Kingsley ranted. "You've got the belly of a sow."

Bobby hunched his shoulders, lowered his head and barreled into the older man. He knocked Kingsley backwards, and they toppled onto the desk, then slid to the floor amidst overturned files and fluttering papers. Bobby bear-hugged Kingsley who flailed away at him, unable to get any power into the short punches, but finally loosening Bobby's grip by gouging both thumbs into his eyes.

Pain shot through Bobby's skull as he scrambled to get to his feet. Blinking furiously, he turned toward Kingsley, afraid he was about to be sucker punched. Instead, Kingsley was reaching into a desk drawer. A second later, he pointed an ancient long-barreled Colt .45 at Bobby. The gun looked like a cannon and was shaking visibly in Kingsley's hand. If Kingsley's trigger finger twitched, Bobby feared he'd have a hole the size of a fist in his chest.

"You're not going to shoot me, Martin."

"Not today, maybe. Today, I'm just gonna—"

"You can't," Bobby said. "I quit."

-10-

The Piano Player in the Whorehouse

Bobby stormed out, making one stop on his way to the parking lot, liberating a bottle of Jack Daniel's from the antique sideboard in his own office. He got into the Lexus, drove to a donut shop, and then to the stadium, empty except for three workers repairing the artificial turf. Bobby carried his bottle of bourbon and bag of cream-filled donuts into the stands and climbed to the upper deck, shaded by the partial roof.

He sat there for hours, working it over in his mind. He had taken a stand on principle. But was that enough? Would that salve his soul? As the amber liquid warmed his insides, the more grandiose his plans became. He would write a book disclosing the evils of corporate greed, the sham of the justice system, the hypocrisy of the league. He would lecture at great universities, offering himself as a witness to society's failings. He remained sober long enough to realize that his fantasies were self-indulgent meanderings.

He was out of a job. Or was he? Christine would try to salvage the situation, have the men shake hands and make up.

What should I do? How can I do what's right for me when it might not be right for Chrissy and Scott?

All he knew was that he couldn't go back to the status quo.

His secretary called him three times on the cellular, telling him that Larry Walters, the prosecutor, was trying to reach him. Probably wanted to know when he would surrender Jackson. It didn't feel as if he'd quit his job. Nobody knew about it except Kingsley and him. Just after noon, as the sun peeked through the hole in the stadium's roof, the phone rang again.

"Bad news," the Assistant District Attorney said when Bobby answered.

"Is there any other kind?" Bobby said.

"Janet Petty got her hands on a bottle of sedatives and attempted suicide last night."

"Oh no. Oh God no." The news jolted him out of his boozy haze. He felt like a tree that had been struck by lightning, his limbs splintered, his trunk blazing with pain. His mouth, at first tasting sour from the bourbon, now seemed filled with ashes.

"She's gonna make it, though she'll have a five-alarm headache when she comes to. And brain damage can't be ruled out. This pretty much complicates the bond hearing, and I didn't want to sandbag you when you brought him in."

"I won't be bringing him in," Bobby said. "I come to buy Nightlife, not to represent him."

෬

Christine hobbled into the kitchen and was unpacking the takeout Thai cartons when she heard Scott call from the den.

"Daddy's on TV!" he cried out, excitedly.

It had been a long day, and she hadn't seen Bobby since he left the house early that morning. She had still been on the fringes of sleep, but she remembered him leaning down and kissing her. What had he said?

I love you, Chrissy. No matter what happens, I love you and pray that you'll always love me.

Or had she dreamed that? Just before noon, she had buzzed his office to see if he wanted to grab lunch, but his secretary said she hadn't seen him. Chrissy tried her father's office, but he had been tied up in meetings with Nightlife Jackson's agent and a crisis team of P.R. experts.

Now she walked into the den, licking her fingers, tasting the garlicky sauce of the chopped pork Nam Sod. Suddenly, everything was wrong. Scott had tears in his eyes. Bobby's face filled the entire screen, a microphone under his chin. He was sweating, an unruly tousle of brown hair falling into his eyes, which leapt from side-to-side.

"The Dallas Mustangs aren't American's Team, they're America's Most Wanted," Bobby thundered. "They're coke-sniffing, bar-busting bullies, bums, and rapists."

"All of them?" a reporter asked.

"Of course not. But enough for loyal fans to question why they put up with criminality, immorality, violence against women, and a general disregard of the rules the rest of us must live by."

Omigod, no! Bobby, don't do this!

From out of camera range, a flurry of questions were shouted. "What about Nightlife Jackson?"

"He's a dangerous, brutal, multiple rapist who should be put away," Bobby said. "He'd be in jail now if I hadn't suborned perjury in his first case."

A gasp went through the throng of reporters who then buzzed with more questions, but in the babble, the words were indecipherable. Bobby reached into a briefcase and pulled out a stack of documents that he began handing out to the reporters who fought for their copies.

"I've prepared a list of cases in which my actions were unethical and numerous incidents involving the players that were covered up," he said.

Christine's breath caught in her throat. She felt as if hot knives had pierced her heart. For a moment, her anguish was so intense, it was if the man she was watching—the man she loved—had died in front of her eyes.

Oh, Bobby. You think you're baptizing yourself in purifying waters, but you're drowning, and there's nothing I can do to save you.

"Why's Daddy talking that way?" Scott asked. She rushed to his side on the sofa and wrapped her arms around him, trying to shield him from harm.

More shouts, each reporter clambering to grab the sword Bobby would dive onto next. He ignored the pack of jackals and continued on his own. "I've bribed witnesses, used political influence, and violated every one of the Canons of Ethics and a few more that were never written down."

"What about Martin Kingsley?" someone asked. "Did he know?"

Christine held her breath.

No Bobby! Please!

"I was the piano player in the whorehouse," Bobby said, "but he called the tune. I never did anything without his express approval."

Christine fumbled for the remote in a crevice of the sofa, found it, and clicked off the TV. She sank to the floor, her legs crossed beneath her. She felt numb, anaesthetized.

How could you do it? How could you do this to Scott and to me?

In that moment, she knew that their lives would never be the same, and the numbness gave way to the lacerating white heat of anger.

PART TWO

The Reluctant Bookie

"If the Super Bowl is the ultimate, why are they playing it again next year?"
—Duane Thomas, former Dallas Cowboys running back

-11-

Bookmaker and Son

Two years later—Friday, January 27—Miami

Were the hell was the Cantor?

Bobby had been calling for three days, but the old bookie had disappeared, and no one could find him. Bobby had checked the Lincoln Road cigar store that was the front for the Cantor's bookmaking operation. Closed. He'd checked the dog tracks, the jai-alai frontons, and the good seats at the Panthers and Heat games. No sign of Saul (the Cantor) Kaplan.

He'd asked some of his own betting customers, Murray Kravetz, the sportscaster, Jose de la Portilla, the chef, and Philippe Jean-Juste, the Santero priest. Nobody had seen the little man with the turkey-wattled neck.

Now, at the wheel of his old Lincoln limo, Bobby was headed toward Calder Race Track with Scott by his side. Maybe the Cantor was at the track. Where the hell else would a bookie be on a cool, clear Friday afternoon when bettors believe the future is as bright as the Florida sun?

"What if Mr. Kaplan didn't lay off the bet and the Mustangs covered the spread?" Scott asked, as they crawled along the Palmetto Expressway behind a rumbling garbage truck.

Bobby gripped the steering wheel with sweaty palms and fought off a queasiness in his stomach. He hated to admit it, but he was a lousy bookie. Scott, a sixth grader, could pick the ponies better than he could and knew more about beating the point spread in football.

"Don't even think about it," Bobby said. "Vinnie LaBarca would make sushi out of me."

How the hell had he gotten into this fix? So much had happened so quickly. Back in Dallas, he'd lost his job, his wife, and his ticket to practice law in a matter of months. He thought he'd had a heart attack, too, but the doctors said the piercing chest pains were stress-related.

Returning home to South Florida, he found there were few job opportunities for a disbarred mouthpiece. He got his chauffeur's license and worked off hours for Goldy Goldberg, an aging bookmaker, who eventually turned over a piece of business. Then, just four days earlier, Bobby had logged the biggest bet of his short, unspectacular career as a reluctant bookmaker.

On Monday morning, when Las Vegas made Dallas a seven-point favorite over Green Bay in Sunday's NFC Championship game, a mobster named Vinnie LaBarca had stopped at Bobby's sidewalk table at the News Café. He was in his mid-forties, short and stocky, with a square head that looked like a cinder block on his sloping shoulders. He wore a gray Armani suit over a black t-shirt and looked disdainfully at Bobby's plate of yogurt and fruit.

"Can you handle six hundred large?" LaBarca asked.

Bobby wasn't sure he'd heard correctly. LaBarca usually bet a couple thousand per game, but nothing like this.

"Six hundred thousand dollars?" Bobby whispered. It was a sum that demanded the respect of a hushed voice.

"Yeah. I'll take the Mustangs minus seven. Can you handle it?"

I can't even handle a new transmission for the Lincoln. I can't handle the rent or my son's tuition.

Bobby's pulse quickened with equal measures of excitement and fear, as if he were walking a tightrope over a fiery pit. This was his chance to get out of debt and to fight for his son. How could he insist Scott stay with him in Miami half the year if he couldn't even afford the boy's schooling? He was being eaten alive in the court proceedings, but this could change everything. If he could get the tuition paid, he could show the judge some stability.

"I got it covered," Bobby shrugged, trying to sound street smart. "Six hundred large on Dallas minus seven over Green Bay."

LaBarca studied him with a gaze the wolf reserves for the sheep. "I've only been stiffed once by a bookie."

"Yeah?"

"I sliced him up, used the pieces as chum off the stern of my Hatteras."

"I get it, Vinnie. I've got no intention of becoming shark bait."

Later, when LaBarca had left, Bobby called the Cantor to lay off the bet. There was no chance of attracting anywhere near enough money on Green Bay to balance his own books. The ideal situation, Bobby had learned quickly, was to book an equal amount of action on both sides. With a "splitter," the bookie was assured a profit because he charged ten per cent vigorish on the bets his customers lost, but paid only the amount of the bet itself when the customer won. So a customer risks a hundred ten dollars to win a hundred, while the bookie risks a hundred to win a hundred-ten. The cautious bookie isn't betting at all. He's simply matching opposing bettors and taking what amounts to a broker's commission. By balancing his books, he can never lose. When Bobby booked a few thousand dollars on each game, it wasn't difficult to lay off a little here, a little there, and get splitters on most of the games, eliminating risk, earning his vig. But six hundred thousand dollars! No way.

When they had met earlier in the week, the Cantor had agreed to take it all, maybe spread around pieces to other bookies in Tampa and New Orleans.

"What do you want from it?" the Cantor had asked, eyeing Bobby suspiciously. He was nearly eighty, a small man with parched white skin who always dressed in a seersucker suit and polka dot bow-tie.

"Eighty per cent of the vig, forty-two thousand dollars."

"You *gonif!* You got nothing at risk."

"Once you balance the books, neither do you," Bobby responded. "It's just a question of dividing the profits."

"What a *holdupnik!* I'll give you sixty-per cent of the vig, thirty-six thousand, not a penny more."

"It's a deal."

Was it ever! Win or lose the bet on Dallas, as long as the Cantor's books were balanced, they'd pocket the vigorish on the losing bets. But Bobby hadn't heard from the Cantor since Monday afternoon. If he hadn't come through, if he hadn't laid off the bet, if no one was backing the huge wager...

If, if, if.

Just thinking about it tightened his chest as if a hand clenched at his heart. If the bet hadn't been laid off, Bobby would be standing naked, a bettor himself, putting everything at risk. The bet could bankrupt him several times over.

No, a bet that could get me killed!

A shudder ran through him like a sudden gust across still water. He tried to chase the thought away with sheer will power, telling himself the Cantor must have laid off the bet, then hopped over to the Bahamas for the week. He'd said it was a done deal. Hadn't he?

ᔓ

Bobby longed to pass the garbage truck but doubted the limo could handle it. He'd bought the old clunker from a dusty car lot in South Miami. In the Miami heat, the radiator was exhaling puffs of steam. The exterior had been midnight blue at one time but now was a splotchy gray-green and, with its dings and dents, looked like a survivor of a meteor storm. The leather upholstery was dry and cracked, and the suspension sagged, but it was good enough for teenagers headed for the prom, Brazilian tourists on a budget, and out-of-town salesmen trolling the strip clubs.

"If the Cantor didn't lay off the bet, there might be a bright side," Bobby said. Looking for a silver lining in the shit storm of gray clouds.

"What's that, Dad?"

"I could win the entire six hundred thousand if the Mustangs don't cover."

"Plus the vig," Scott went on, knowingly.

Bobby smiled. At thirteen, Scott had grown into a lanky, cute, towheaded kid at the stage between adorable childhood and wise-ass adolescence.

"Right. Six hundred-sixty-thousand with the vig," Bobby said, wistfully. "No more polishing this old wreck limo every Saturday afternoon."

"Hey Dad, you only polish the right-hand side."

"That's the side the customers get in and out of," Bobby said, wondering if the limo would overheat before they got to the race track. It struck him then, just how far he had fallen. "Does it bother you that your Dad is a chauffeur?"

"No way! It's kind of cool. Most of the kids at school, their Dads are doctors, lawyers, or brokers. Total drudges."

"I don't mind driving, either. It gives me time to think."

And to listen. Husbands who cheat on their wives, brokers who churn their clients' accounts, employees who embezzle. His customers treated him as if he weren't there, and sometimes Bobby felt invisible.

Blame it on the chauffeur's uniform, the no-wrinkle polyester black pants with the silky stripe, the cheap white shirt and dark tie pulled up tight, and of course, the *coup de grace,* the cap, which creased his wavy brown hair and made his ears look like catchers' mitts. It all screamed "working class guy." Women looked right through him and men acted as if they expected him to carry their luggage. Which, of course, he did. Still, it was better than being Martin Kingsley's errand boy, better than toting his garbage to the curb and calling it roses.

"So what do you think, Scott? Hypothetically. What are Green Bay's chances of covering the spread and making us rich?"

"Fogetaboudit!" Scott called out. "Green Bay will be hurtin' for certin'."

"You sure?"

"I hate to tell you, Dad, but the Mustangs will win and cover the seven."

"You're their number one fan," Bobby said. "I can't rely on you to set the point spread."

"Sure you can. I used my computer to manage the strength indicators. If you look at scoring margins against teams with winning records, you'll see that—"

"Okay, okay, but I didn't have a choice. I had to give LaBarca what he wanted. That's why I needed the Cantor to lay off the bet just so I could pick up a sweet piece of the pie."

The Cantor. Where the hell are you, anyway?

Bobby's cellular rang, startling him. He eased the old Lincoln limo onto the berm of the road and looked at the display: *"Private Call."*

"Hello," he said, picking up.

"Bobby, there you are!"

His heart seized up at the sound of her voice.

"Where have you been?" Christine asked. "I've been leaving messages."

"Chrissy! I've been meaning to call you."

Regret stabbed at him like blades piercing his skin. How he missed her.

"Mr. Montgomery called from the school again," she said. "Scott's tuition hasn't been paid."

"Got it covered," he said, just as he had to Vinnie LaBarca. In truth, nothing was covered. His life was a series of uncovered bets and unpaid bills. "I'm going to pay the first semester and second semester in one lump sum."

"Bobby, you know Scott's transferring to Berkshire Prep for the second semester."

"No," he said, refusing to acknowledge what the Texas judge ordered over his objections.

"I'll be paying for everything," Christine said.

"It's not the money, and you know it. I don't want Scott shipped off to some boarding school fifteen hundred miles away."

Bobby was getting a headache. The limo belched out fumes and sputtered its discontent. The race track was ten minutes away, and cars whizzed past, kicking up dust.

"It's the only way to maximize his potential," she said.

"How, by taking him away from me?"

"No Bobby. You're a wonderful father."

"Then why do it?"

"We've been through this," Christine said. "Scott's off the charts in math. He needs a special environment to nurture him."

"We could nurture him. Together."

"We're not going to rehash that," she said with a sigh. "And what we're doing now, splitting the school year between Dallas and Miami, is crazy. The shrinks all say so."

"Then give me full custody."

"Dammit, Bobby. Can you write a check to the school or should I do it? I don't mind advancing you the money if—"

"Whoops, going through a tunnel," Bobby said, scratching his fingernails across the mouthpiece. "Losing you."

No, strike that. Lost you.

He clicked off, eased the car into gear and headed for the race track.

"Dad, I don't want to go to some skanky prison for math geeks."

"You won't have to."

"'Cause I like hanging with you, Dad."

Bobby walked a fine line as a divorced father, trying not to interfere with Scott's relationship with his mother while battling to influence how the boy was raised. It wasn't easy, not against the strong-willed Christine and her belligerent father. Bobby never doubted that Martin Kingsley loved his grandson. Scott was his flesh and blood, the only child of his only child. Unlike his material possessions, however, Scott was no longer under Kingsley's control, and that must have rankled the old man. The fact that Scott loved his Dad and emulated him must have been a prickly burr under Kingsley's saddle.

The bastard hates me more than he despises Democrats, taxes, and the Washington Redskins.

Bobby's mind drifted back to that day in front of the cameras two years ago, the day that flipped his life over like a tortoise onto its back.

"What were you thinking?" Christine had demanded when he came home, his accusations filling every living room in Dallas. "After all my father's done for you, this is how you repay him! Where's your loyalty?"

"Where's your heart?" he replied. "Is it with your father or with me?"

"Is that an ultimatum? Are you forcing me to choose between the two of you?"

To Bobby, it should have been a simple choice. He was the man she loved, the father of her son. Her father was corrupt and tainted everything he touched. Couldn't she see that?

"I'm divorcing you," she said, each word crackling like a rifle shot. Her

eyes glistened, but her voice never wavered, and her spine stayed straight as a spike.

-12-

Something Ain't Kosher

Father and son passed the Homestretch Café and climbed the steps to the grandstand. It was a glorious sun-baked Florida day of blue skies and steady breezes. Still, Bobby was out of sorts, and he popped antacids to calm his knotted stomach.

Where's the Cantor? Why the hell hasn't he returned my calls?

Bobby was desperate to know that he wasn't on the hook—a grappling hook—for six hundred thousand. Then he could enjoy the afternoon with his son. He wanted Scott to smell the sweet saltiness of the horses in the paddock, then treat the boy to some stone crabs in the Turf Club, maybe sneak him into the casino to play the one-armed bandits.

But the real reason they were here was to find the Cantor.

Where the hell is he?

Why is he ducking me?

Bobby had started to worry on Tuesday morning when the Vegas oddsmakers moved the line half a point. Then Dallas was favored by seven-and-one-half. The half point, he knew, was to prevent the game from being a "push," in which the bet is canceled if the final score falls right on the point spread. At seven points, there'd be a "push" at 14-7, 21-14, 24-17, and a bunch of other common scores.

Bobby hoped that the movement didn't also signify a ton of money being bet on Dallas, so that the oddsmakers would have to keep adjusting their lines to balance the books. Wednesday brought more bad news, as the line jumped a full point to eight-and-a-half. Then, yesterday, it crawled up another half point. Now, Dallas was favored by a startling nine points.

If the Cantor hadn't moved quickly, he never would have been able to lay off the mobster's bet—Dallas as a seven point favorite. Bettors wanting to take the favored Mustangs today had to give the bookies nine points, not seven. To a savvy bettor or bookie the two-point swing was monumental. No one would take Green Bay today with only a seven-point cushion when he could get nine. Bobby prayed the Cantor had laid off the bet early in the week.

∾

Once in the clubhouse, Bobby asked all the regulars if the Cantor had been around, but nobody had seen him all week.

With Scott at his side, Bobby walked toward the parimutuel windows. They checked the barber shop and the rest rooms, the shoe shine stand and the hot dog vendor, even the shop selling authentic horseshoes, ingrained with dirt. They ignored the mile-and-an-eighth allowance race going on below them, the bettors whooping from the grandstand.

As the horses were jitterbugging into the gate for the next race, bookmaker and son headed for the concourse, Bobby's thoughts wandering toward Dallas. Sometimes he wondered what life would have been like if he'd stayed. Lunches at the Mansion on Turtle Creek, drinks at the Stadium Club. He'd still have Chrissy. The family would be together. Why hadn't he just sucked it up and played Kingsley's game?

Because I just couldn't.

But what had he accomplished? He'd lost his wife and impoverished himself. Nightlife Jackson was still playing, Kingsley having hired a slick attorney to do what Bobby wouldn't. Faced with embarrassing questions about her past sex life, harassed by the news media and wanting to leave Dallas, Janet Petty dropped the case for a small cash settlement.

If I had to do it all over again, I would. If only I could have gotten my freedom without losing Chrissy.

Bobby and Scott walked along the concourse where bettors lined up at the windows clutching Racing Forms, like Bibles, in sweaty hands. Still no sign of the Cantor. Bobby was fighting against an edginess that buzzed inside him like a bee against a window.

They paused at a refreshment stand so Scott could order a Cuban sandwich—roast pork and ham with cheese and pickles on white, crusty bread—while Bobby scanned the area, looking for the Cantor. They walked past the fifty-dollar window, the bell ringing, bets closing, aged bettors scurrying back to their seats, cigars clamped in teeth, stubby pencils tucked behind ears.

They watched a stakes race, Bobby at first ignoring Scott's pleas to let him bet on the one-eight perfecta, then avoiding the boy's told-you-so smirk when the combination paid fifty-six dollars. Then they headed down to the paddock.

He popped three more antacids into his mouth, but still, he felt as if hamsters were running a treadmill in his stomach. Not only did Bobby fear for himself, he felt he had let down his son. If he couldn't pay the bills, he'd lose joint custody and the boy's grandfather would have even greater access to Scott. The bastard would try to mold Scott into younger version of himself.

Bobby looked toward Scott, his heart aching with love. The boy's dirty blond hair radiated in the afternoon sun as he stood on the paddock railing, leaning toward a jittery bay which could have been descended from wild mustangs.

"Hey Dad, isn't that Mr. Kaplan?" Scott pointed to a far corner of the paddock where a shriveled little man in a seersucker suit and a Panama hat watched the horses prance through the moist soil.

"Saul!" Bobby called out. The Cantor looked up, made eye contact, then gingerly slipped between the rails of a fence and disappeared into the open door of a stable.

What the hell!

Bobby took off, vaulting the fence, shouting back at Scott. "Wait here!"

He caught sight of the Cantor, waddling more than running, ducking out of one red-paneled stable and into another. "Saul!

Stop!" Bobby called after him.

Bobby ran through the open door of the stable, horses filling stalls on either side of an earthen walkway. Flies buzzed, and the air was tangy with horse sweat and horse droppings. A chestnut mare kicked at her stall, and an Indian red stallion across the way responded with a plaintive whinny. But the Cantor was neither seen nor heard.

Bobby hurried between the rows of stalls, peering into each one, scratching the noses of several horses. He was near the end when a pile of straw seemed to move inside a stall occupied by a large seal brown horse with a jet black mane and tail. The door to the stall was slightly ajar.

Bobby grabbed a pitchfork from against the wall and entered the stall, sidestepping a mound of droppings. Gently, he pushed the pitchfork blades into the straw pile. "Saul, I'm going to feed you to the horses and any leftovers go to Vinnie LaBarca's sharks."

"Ow!" Suddenly, the Cantor, Panama hat still weirdly in place, burst from the straw pile, spitting dust and expletives, his Adam's apple bobbing like a cork in the ocean. "You *momzer!* It's not bad enough there's rats in here, you gotta stab me, you *nogoodnik!*"

"Why are you hiding from me?" Bobby demanded.

The old man blinked from behind his thick eyeglasses, looking like an owl aggravated at being awakened by the sun. "Because I'm not a brave man."

"What's that supposed to mean?"

The Cantor calmed down and looked dolefully at Bobby. His face was speckled with age spots, and he was barely above five feet, even in his elevated alligator loafers. His sparse white hair was matted with straw, and his wattled neck quivered. "You know why they call me the Cantor?"

"I don't know. I figured maybe you went to seminary, or whatever you call it."

"Yeshiva? Not me. I'm the Cantor because every time I'm arrested or subpoenaed, I sing like it's Yom Kippur. Like it's *Kol Nidre*, I sing."

"What are you saying?"

"Once the line moved, I couldn't lay off your six hundred dimes, and I've been afraid to tell you. I like you Bobby, so I couldn't look you in the eyes and tell you that I let you down. And now, I'm scared to death Vinnie LaBarca's gonna make you into chopped liver."

Bobby tossed the pitchfork into the pile of straw, and the brown horse whinnied. "*You're* scared? What about me?"

"What I can't figure out, why'd LaBarca place a bet like that with a little *pisher* like you? For that kind of money, why didn't he go straight to the sports books in Vegas?"

It's a question Bobby had asked himself, but he thought he'd figured it out. "You bet that kind of money out there, they withhold taxes, report it to the IRS. He wanted to go incognito, that's all."

"Yeah, maybe." The Cantor removed his eyeglasses and dusted the lenses with his shirttail. "But all week long, the line keeps moving and I keep asking myself, 'Why did Vinnie LaBarca come to Bobby Gallagher, whose ex-father-in-law just happens to own the Dallas Mustangs?'"

"Okay, Saul, tell me."

"I don't know Bobby, but if you ask me, something ain't kosher in Dallas."

-13-

Living Large

Saturday, January 28—Dallas

Martin Kingsley drummed his lacquered nails on his mahogany desk and scanned the financial reports in front of him. Attendance figures, quarterly revenues, annual projections, income from local radio and network television, even sales of nachos and salsa. Revenue up a healthy thirteen per cent. But expenses...expenses were killing him.

Signing the free agents last year, then re-signing the veterans ready to bolt, gave him highest payroll in the league. Kingsley's file cabinets were stuffed with players' contracts so complex it would take a room full of Philadelphia lawyers to figure out how he was circumventing the salary cap, if not outright violating it.

The financials showed he was losing buckets of money on America's Team. But to hell with it! It's worth every last dollar, he told himself. They were just one win away from the Big Dance, the Super Bowl, and he could feel the atmosphere at Valley Ranch crackling with anticipation. Tomorrow was the NFC championship game, and his senses tingled with an electric buzz.

Damn, it's a fine day to be alive and be a Texan.

He'd had his annual physical earlier in the week, and the doctor pronounced him a remarkable specimen for his sixty-seven years. "You've got the heart of a lion and the prostate of a teenager." His long mane of white hair was brushed straight back, and today, wearing a tailored jet-black suit coat with silver piping, he felt vigorous enough to spar a few rounds in the gym or rope and brand some ornery livestock.

He considered himself a man who had damn near everything. There was only one missing element needed to fulfill his life.

I gotta get me a Super Bowl ring...the biggest, brightest Texas-sized ring they ever made.

All his energies were directed toward that one goal, and his assets were being drained for it. If they beat Green Bay tomorrow, they'd be on the threshold. But something else was gnawing at him, distracting him. The unfinished business of Robert Gallagher. It should have been finished two years ago. He'd crushed the little turd into dust and expected him to blow away like a West Texas tumbleweed. Would have too, if Christine hadn't agreed to that asinine split custody deal.

What a damn fool settlement! With Judge Bonifay—my golf partner for Christ's sake—we could have stripped the bastard of all his rights to Scott.

He still fumed thinking about it, Christine playing King Solomon with his grandson. He'd warned her there'd be trouble. Now, the shyster was refusing to return Scott from Florida and send him to boarding school. This time, he'd take care of Gallagher his way. Kingsley toyed with telling Christine his plan, then decided against it. She was too sentimental, too weak where the son-of-a-bitch was concerned. But she'd know soon enough, and when it was over, there'd be a barbed wire fence—or "bobwire" as they say hereabouts—between Scott and his loser father.

Kingsley shot the French cuffs on his custom-made shirt and glanced at his watch. No Rolex or Piaget. This was a solid gold number shaped like a Mustangs helmet and encrusted with diamonds. Two smaller versions of the helmet were fashioned into cufflinks.

Nearly noon. The plane was scheduled to leave for Green Bay in an hour. But it could wait. It was, after all, his own Gulfstream 5,.the silver and blue "Point After."

"Let's cut back expenses," Christine had told him in their breakfast meeting that morning. Filled with pride for his little girl, he watched her expertly dissect the financials.

"You're a one-man oil shortage, Daddy. Why in the world do you need a jet with a five-thousand mile range?"

"Who knows, darlin', we might play an away game in Buenos Aires."

"I'm serious. If the bankers knew how cash poor you are, they could call your loans and wreak havoc."

"I'll let you and the accountants worry about it," he said. "I'm more concerned with beating Green Bay."

"Please don't brush me off like that. You get the monthly statements. You know what I'm talking about."

Yeah, he was leveraged to the brim of his handmade Stetson. While he could throw lavish parties with flowing champagne and mounds of imported caviar, he also gave express instructions to hand out pay checks after the banks had closed on Fridays.

"Once we re-finance, we'll be fine," he told her. He knew he was still paying the price for buying the team years before for a wildly inflated sum. Then, he'd poured millions more of borrowed money into improved facilities, salaries, and promotion.

Christine patiently went over the spread sheets, explaining that going to the Super Bowl would *cost* him money, the travel and entertainment expenses exceeding the payoff. "Especially the way you entertain, Daddy."

But what the hell? Winning is what it's all about. He'd let her figure out where the money would come from.

Over coffee and cinnamon buns, he listened as Christine kept leading him through the columns of numbers, endless digits revealing growing liabilities that piled up quicker than manure in a corral.

"Living large," he told her, "is important to my image. It's expected. It's what I'm all about."

"Maybe you could live a little more economy sized," she suggested gently.

Kingsley watched her, thinking of the resemblance to Dolores, his wife, who had died in a car accident at thirty-nine. Christine had the same fair skin, and with her blond hair pulled back, the same high forehead and widow's peak. Her green eyes were tinged with gold and seldom revealed what she was thinking. He'd raised a fine daughter and he'd raise a fine grandson, too, especially once he got that crackpot ex-son-in-law out of the picture.

"Did you see the P.I.'s report on your ex?" Kingsley asked.

She frowned, wrinkling her nose just as she had done when she was five years old. "I'm hoping we won't have to use it."

"Not use it? It's a godsend. Gallagher wants primary custody, and he's become a bookmaker! A disbarred lawyer turned bookie! Hell, the judge will laugh him out of court."

"Bobby's willing ton continue joint custody. He just doesn't want me to send Scott away to boarding school, that's all. Bobby's afraid they'll lose the bond they've formed."

"Good!" Kingsley banged a fist on his desk. "Scott doesn't need to bond with a common crook."

"Daddy, Bobby loves Scott very much and Scott adores him."

Ah, his sweet daughter was smart and beautiful but with little street smarts. He had shielded her from so much. Christine didn't know what it took to climb so high. Corners must be cut, deals made, hands dirtied. To win, you can't play by any rules except your own.

"Maybe there's a way we can work this out with Bobby so we don't have to go to court," she said. "I've even had second thoughts about the boarding school myself."

"Nonsense! Scott's a genius. All the tests show it, but his genius is untapped. If he hangs out at race tracks and bookie parlors, he'll be stifled, frustrated. He could end up a weirdo, living alone, collecting bottle caps and railroad schedules."

"You're being overly dramatic." She glanced toward a framed photo of the three of them—son, mother, and grandfather—standing under the goal posts at the old Texas Stadium. The photo was five years old, and Bobby had been cropped out of the shot, just as he'd been deleted from her life. A hole in the photo, a hole in her heart. "I just don't want to hurt Bobby any more than I already have."

"Hell, you've been too kind to him." He didn't like the wistful look in her eyes. "Has he been trying to contact you?"

"The usual. Flowers, cards, candy, even a crate of Florida stone crabs."

Kingsley harrumphed his displeasure, but he'd already known it. At the end of each day, he reviewed the security desk logs, scanning the names of every visitor to the Valley Ranch complex and reviewing the receipts of all deliveries. When it came to running a tight ship, Captain Queeg could take lessons.

"Daddy, don't worry. I won't make the same mistake twice."

"I know you won't, honey."

He was pleased that Christine was dating Craig Stringer. Hell, he'd set it up. This time, he vowed, Christine wouldn't let her heart rule her head. He'd help her lasso Stringer and bring him into the barn.

Stringer was a fine choice as a husband and future V.P. of operations of the team. He was a war horse of a quarterback, playing his last season, just ambitious enough to want to please his boss without wanting to kick him off the throne. The amiable fiction would be that Kingsley had turned over operations to his new son-in-law, the handsome, well-liked former All Pro quarterback. But Kingsley would still call the shots, and Stringer would be a well-paid martinet who would enjoy better relations with the Commissioner's office than his boss ever had.

⁓

How can I get Daddy out of debt and out of my personal life?

Both questions plagued Christine. Despite his bluster and bombast, despite trying to convince the world that he owned half of all creation, her father's finances were a disaster. Here she was sitting in his office, trying to get him to tighten his belt, and there he was spouting off about "living large."

Then there was her personal life. She just wanted peace. No

private investigators, lawyers, or judges. She yearned for an end to the hostilities with Bobby and an end to their fight over custody and schooling of Scott. She knew her father was up to something in the lawsuit, but she didn't know what. He kept so many things from her. Still, she never doubted his love for Scott or for her.

If Mom had lived, maybe it would be different, but without her—without anyone— it's so hard to get Daddy to butt out.

She knew Bobby was broke. She knew he was humiliated over his disbarment, and her heart ached for him. But maybe Daddy was right. Maybe it was better to have Scott away in boarding school, rather than spending half his time in Miami with Bobby, subjected to God-knows-what influences. Though he meant well, Bobby sometimes showed poor judgment.

Either way, with Scott in Miami for six months or boarding school for nine, it would still be hard on her. She was guilt stricken and lonely when Scott was away. Sure, she'd fly to Miami every other weekend, or Bobby would bring Scott to wherever Dallas was playing, but still...she felt hollow and anguished in the stillness of her home without her only child.

I had a husband and a son. Now, no husband, and sometimes it feels as if I have no son, either.

Often, arriving at her empty, dark house after late meetings in the office, she carried her take-out Chinese cartons straight up to bed and cried herself to sleep. Her last thoughts were of Scott and Bobby and how she missed them.

Yes, Bobby, I miss you, too.

Ever since the nightmare of Bobby's televised press conference, Christine had felt torn between the two men, the conflict cleaving at her heart.

Maybe she should change her life, get away from her father. She considered leaving the team and starting a company on her own. Hey, she had an MBA from Wharton and a dozen years of business experience, but as the boss' daughter, she was treated with too much respect on one hand and not given enough credit on the other. She needed to make her mark. Her father kept talking about grooming Craig Stringer to be the general manager of the team, but would he, really? She doubted that Daddy would give up control until they carried him out of the office, boots first. And even if he did turn over operations to Craig, what would change for her? She'd go from daughter of the old boss to girlfriend – or wife – of the new one. In her heart, she knew she could do a better job than either of the two men.

"How are you and Craig doing?" her father asked when they finished going over the finances.

"I don't know, Daddy." Evasion was simpler.

"It's a perfect match," he said. "You have the same interests. You can talk football with him, and he can talk business with you. You both love horses, and you're both great riders. You want another child, and the Stringer gene pool looks damn good from my skybox."

"Daddy, please don't treat me like your prize heifer."

He steadied his gaze, his blue eyes cool as coins. "Can you give me one reason why you shouldn't marry Craig Stringer?"

"I don't feel enough when we kiss."

"Romance doesn't last," he said, shaking his head. "Security, common goals, commitment, and loyalty, that's what marriage is all about. Craig's a great catch and you know it. He's a good man."

"He's vain and a born womanizer."

"He's over that phase, darlin'. When he started seeing you, I made it damn clear he couldn't run around with any more cheerleaders or models, or I'd hang his balls from an old hickory tree."

"Daddy, I'm a grown woman, divorced with a child. It's not necessary to stand at the door with a shotgun."

He barked a laugh and said, "You get much older without marrying, I'll have to wound a man just to get you a husband."

-14-

The Ghost of Mustangs Past

After Christine left his office, Kingsley packed his attache case for the flight to Green Bay. He felt the electric buzz of anticipation that always started the day before a game.

He was juiced. Hell, this is what he lived for.

My daughter, my grandson, my team. My cup runneth over.

His mind was focused on the shiny image of the Commissioner's trophy, the prize for the Super Bowl champion, when he heard a disturbance coming from his outer office. The door flew open, and Molly, his secretary of twenty-five years, tried to block the way of a tall older man who pushed by her.

"But you don't have an appointment!" she protested.

"I don't need an appointment," grumbled the man. He wore a baggy, wrinkled brown plaid suit, pointy snakeskin cowboy boots, and a white shirt with a string tie and turquoise clasp. His head was shaved bald, and he held a brown Stetson at his side. He was taller than Kingsley but sparrow thin, his neck layered with loose skin, as if he'd lost considerable weight. His left eye was milky white and unfocused. His most striking feature, however, was the line of purple scar tissue that covered the left side of his face from his cheekbone to his forehead, stopping just below his shaved scalp.

"What the hell..." Kingsley rose half way out of his chair. "Who are you?"

"You haven't forgotten your ole pardner, have you Martin?" the man said, his voice rattling like gravel down a metal chute.

"Ty?" Kingsley's voice quaked with uncertainty and fear. "Is that you?"

"Hell, no, it's the ghost of Mustangs past."

☙

Kingsley offered Houston Tyler a bourbon, and his old partner didn't say no. Seated in a plush leather chair, he tossed down the amber liquid, swallowing with painful gasps.

"They cut up my throat," he said.

"I heard," Kingsley said, nodding solicitously.

"Took out a tumor the size of a golf ball. Guess I should be glad it wasn't a football." His laugh was dry and hoarse, like a dog coughing up bone splinters. "I don't blame you for not recognizing me. I look like shit."

"What's it been, Ty ten years?"

"Thirteen years, two months, and three days."

Kingsley winced and cursed himself. He'd been cavalier about it. To a man in prison, time is measured as precisely as gold on a jeweler's scale.

"Got the parole last week. Guess they needed the bed for someone more dangerous."

Kingsley nodded. What do you say? What can you say to a man who went to prison instead of you?

"I want to thank you for helping Corrine," Tyler said. "She told me you had your personal doctors taking care of her, and they were mighty nice."

"It was the least I could do," Kingsley said.

"Yeah Martin. It was."

"I was sorry when I heard you'd lost her."

A heavy silence settled over them. Kingsley thought Tyler resembled an old mutt that had been kicked too often. Just when you think he had all the fight knocked out of him, he would lunge for your throat. There had always been a menace to Houston Tyler, a threat of violence just beneath the surface, but now, scarred and defeated, he appeared even more dangerous. As if prison had stolen his heart but not his claws.

He'd once seen Tyler pick up a man by the shirt collar and thrust him into the blades of a ceiling fan in the midst of a barroom brawl. He'd fought with his fists, with knives, and once, with a pick axe in the oil fields. But Tyler had been twenty years younger and forty pounds heavier then. With some partners, you worried about lawsuits and double dealing. With Tyler, you worried he would shatter a long-neck on the edge of the bar and gut you. There was a dual nature to his personality. He was so honest you could shoot dice with him on the phone, and so violent you'd be afraid to cheat him.

Houston Tyler's good eye swept over the office, taking in the photos of Kingsley with various celebrities, the trophies, the signed footballs with the white-painted scores of various triumphs. A chunk of a goal post sat in one corner, mounted on a brass pedestal like some post-modern sculpture. His gaze stopped on a Stairmaster in the corner, and he looked as puzzled as a caveman staring at a locomotive.

"You bought the team just after I went away, didn't you?" he asked.

"A few months later.'"

"Right after you'd bought out my interest in Ty-King Oil. Bought it damn cheap, as I recall."

Kingsley saw where Houston Tyler was headed and didn't intend to go along for the ride. "There was no market for your stock. After the accident—"

"What *accident*? The jury said it was a criminal act, and that I was the criminal."

"That was a horrible wrong, Ty. Tragedy compounding tragedy, but you know how it was then, the news media, the politicians, all crying for blood. If I could have done anything, I would have."

"Oh you did plenty. You stayed out of harm's way."

"I had a company to run, our interests to protect."

Tyler cleared his throat, the sound of sandpaper on wood. "I did a lot of reading in prison, Martin. History, classics, that sort of thing. Did you know you can't find Hitler's name on one document sending the Jews off to the death camps? He had plausible deniability on all his crimes against humanity."

"Surely you're not comparing me to—"

"Your name wasn't on one piece of paper that tied you to maintenance at the Texas City refinery, but you were behind every move. The Board of Directors laid off six hundred full-time employees and ordered the hiring of unskilled part-timers, but it was your doing. The plant manager reduced safety training, but that was at your direction. You put me in charge of day-to-day operations, but you vetoed new pumps because of the costs. You got fat off the profits, fat enough to buy yourself a football team, and what did I get?"

"Ty, if there's anything I can do, just tell me."

His milky white eye stared off into space. "When the pump blew and the line ruptured, the men ran. Who could blame them? For eleven dollars an hour, you shouldn't be turned into a cinder. I went into the thick of it, closed the valves with my bare hands and have the tattoos to prove it."

He held up his hands. His palms were covered with scar tissue and the imprint of a wheel. "I was standing in three feet of burning crude. My rubber boots melted onto my feet."

"I know, Ty. You're a hero, not a criminal. You saved lives. If it hadn't been for you, a hundred men would have been killed instead of seven."

"I like to think you would have done the same thing."

Kingsley kept quiet.

Tyler's smile was a jagged blade. "I know you, pardner, like I know the price of crude."

"Ty, we haven't been partners since you went away. The Board demanded that you divest yourself of your shares."

"Damn convenient for you," Tyler said, "that Board members you picked would vote that way."

"I thought I was helping you out," Kingsley said, knowing Tyler wasn't buying it. Hell, why would he? Kingsley had been a vulture, picking at his partner's bones. "There was no market for a minority share of the company. If I hadn't bought it..."

"My stock gave you control," Tyler said. "You paid me two million dollars for thirty per cent of the company and sold the whole shooting match for ninety-eight million in cash, your down payment on a shiny new toy. The Mustangs. You leveraged yourself into the high cotton by sucking my blood dry."

"I don't think that's a fair characterization, Ty. Not fair at all."

"So here you are, rich enough to air condition hell, and I'm broke," Tyler said, bitterly.

"What about the two million? What about your savings?"

"Gone! Gone to lawyers and fines and Corrine's medical bills. That's why I've come to see my ol' pardner. Oil's in my blood, Martin. My granddaddy was in Beaumont in 1901 when Spindletop blew sky high. Your Dad and mine were partners for twenty-five years and you and me for eighteen more. Now, you don't just take that away from a man, do you pardner?"

"What are you saying, Ty? What do you want?"

"My share! Not even all of it, not even a fraction of what would make up for what I've been through, but enough to get me by 'til my bones turn to dust. Five million dollars, Martin. For Christ's sake, you can take that out of petty cash."

"Everything I have is tied up in this team," Kingsley said. "I mortgaged my pecker and liened my balls to buy the team."

"Bullshit!"

"It's true, Ty. I'm asset rich but cash poor."

"Martin, don't treat me like I just rode into town on a load of watermelons."

"I swear. Even if I wanted to help you out, I—"

"No helping out! No charity! You owe me. I want five million two weeks from Monday, the day after the Super Bowl."

"Ty, be reasonable. There's no cash."

"Don't be a-peeing on my leg, Martin."

"Look, we can work something out. A job, a company car, maybe some stock options in the team."

"I had a job! And as for your stock options, the only pieces of paper I want from you better have Ben Franklin's picture on 'em."

"Ty, I don't have—"

"Get it!"

His voice reverberated throughout the office, bouncing off the wood-paneled walls. It was the old voice, a bass drum, as if he'd willed himself back in time before surgery, prison, and eternal grief. The sound sent shudders of fear through Martin Kingsley, the dread compressing his chest like a vise.

"And if I don't, Ty. Then what?"

"What do you think?"

Kingsley twitched like a fish on the line. When he spoke, his voice was barely a whisper. "You'll go public, tell where all the skeletons are buried. You'll disgrace me."

"You think I'll call a press conference like your son-in-law? Yeah, I read all about that. Not my style, Martin." He drew an embroidered white handkerchief from his suit pocket and dabbed at his wet lips, then got to his feet. "Martin, there's nothing more dangerous than a man who doesn't have anything, who doesn't care anymore. I've been stripped bare. I've got nothing to lose."

"What then, Ty? If you're going to threaten a man, lay it on the table. If I don't pay you, if I can't pay you..."

Tyler leaned over Kingsley's desk, bracing himself with his scarred hands on the fine, polished wood. "I'll do to you what was done to me. I'll burn you, Martin. I'll burn you 'til your flesh smells like pork barbecue on a Sunday night. I'll scald you 'til blisters turn you into a leper. I'll melt the skin right off your face and burn your hands into stumps, and when I'm through with you, even your own daughter won't recognize you, and your grandson will run away in fear. So don't fuck with me, pardner!"

Houston Tyler turned smartly in his cowboy boots and left the office before Kingsley could say another word.

Martin Kingsley sat motionless for a full minute, forcing himself to remain calm, to think rationally, though the fear left him with the taste of rusty steel in his mouth. He was not a man given to panic. His sense of control compelled him to push back the dread. But fear is not irrational, he thought. There are times when nothing is more damn sensible than to fear the coyote that would chew at your heart.

When he finally stood up, he finished packing his case for the trip to Green Bay, all the while ticking off the conclusions he had reached. First, Tyler was deranged, and it was futile to attempt to reason with the man. Second, Tyler would not hesitate to torture or kill him. Third, he had to find a way to pay Tyler, and if that task seemed impossible, Kingsley reminded himself of his first two conclusions.

"Losing is worse than death."
—George Allen, former NFL head coach

-15-

Love Without Limits

Saturday, January 28—Miami

Never let them see you sweat.

Bobby and Scott sat inside the old rustbucket limo as it was dragged through the car wash. Bobby stared at the water streaming over the windshield, trying to clear his mind and steady his nerves.

He would have to remain calm. He would use logic and reasoning to convince Vinnie LaBarca to let him off the hook, to cancel the bet on tomorrow's game. In his mind, Bobby rehearsed his plea.

"I can't pay off the bet if you win, Vinnie, so what's the use of holding me to it?"

As the car jerked along, suds pouring over the car, Bobby vowed not to show his fear. Not to LaBarca and not to Scott, either. If he did, the boy would try to help him. A father's job is to care for his child, not the other way around.

Before becoming a father, he never knew he had the capacity for such love. But now, just thinking about Scott sometimes brought tears to his eyes. It was a love without limits. He once tried to quantify it, but the closest he could come was to realize that he would pass the ultimate test of love: he would take a bullet for his son. Without blinking, without thinking. Simple as that.

Scott had his mother's serene sense of logic. If the boy knew the extent of his father's problems, he'd plug all the facts into that computerized brain of his and come up with three alternative plans with predicted probabilities of success.

So different from me.

Bobby was self-aware. He knew he was impetuous and emotional. Sometimes, he envied Christine's imperturbability in the face of crisis. Other times, he found it irritating. Either way, he figured Scott was better off inheriting his mother's cool tranquility rather than his own mercurial nature.

Bobby had set up the meeting with Dino Fornecchio, LaBarca's bodyguard and the guy who reminded him to zip up when coming out of the men's room. Now, Bobby pictured LaBarca waiting in his penthouse condo, a squat man seemingly as wide as he was tall. His nose had been badly broken and ran east and west where it should have run north and south. Bobby knew that a decent plastic surgeon could easily fix the nose but figured it was a calling card. Tough guy. Mobster. Fuck with me at your peril.

℘

Vinnie LaBarca wheezed and sneezed, his eyes tearing. "I'm living in a goddamn jungle," he yelled at Dino Fornecchio. "Get rid of these plants and fire that damn decorator."

"Okay boss," Dino said, through the screen door to the patio. Fornecchio was dark and sullen with a long neck and knobby wrists that peeked out of the sleeves of his black silk shirt. LaBarca considered him an idiot, but he was a second cousin once removed, or maybe a first cousin twice removed. If there hadn't been some blood relationship, LaBarca would have had him totally removed.

Once when Fornecchio was supposed to lay fifty grand of Vinnie's money on Penn State, he put the money down on Penn instead. "Don't you know the difference between the Big Ten and the Ivy League!" LaBarca fumed, after the Quakers failed to cover and he lost his bet.

"Oh, like you're a college man," Fornecchio replied. "Closest you ever got to Penn State was the state pen."

LaBarca would have killed him right there if not for his mother's cousin or aunt or whoever the hell the old bag was who gave birth to this retard.

LaBarca lived in the penthouse of a high-rise on the tip of Miami Beach, just a stone crab's throw from Joe's, the oldest and most famous restaurant in town. On the east was the Atlantic and on the south Government Cut where, barely a mile away, cruise ships were berthed in single file, preparing for their weekly pre-packaged excursions to various Caribbean ports.

With his bulk sinking into a groaning chaise lounge, LaBarca relaxed on his wraparound, tiled balcony that was overgrown with vines and plants and blooming impatiens in golden urns, all ordered by a prissy decorator who barely had avoided a swan dive to the pool deck thirty floors below after presenting LaBarca with his bill.

Now LaBarca's allergies were acting up. His sinuses were clogged. His head ached, and he kept hacking up phlegm and spitting it over his balcony railing into the easterly breeze, hoping it would splat on one of the sun tanned, Eurotrash club rats on the pool deck three hundred feet below.

LaBarca rocked himself out of the chaise lounge, his gut falling over his swim trunks like a bowling ball plopping into the gutter. He moved toward the balcony railing, then squinted through a fat-barreled telescope, aiming down Government Cut toward the S.S. Norway, wondering if he could hit the damn thing with a shoulder-mounted rocket launcher. He was letting the sun simmer his imagination, and in his mind's eye, he saw the vapor trail, heard the *whoosh*, and watched the orange flash, followed by streams of black smoke curling in the easterly breeze. LaBarca was wondering if he'd be able to hear the screams of the passengers on deck—probably not, the wind was against him—when dumb shit Dino slid open the screen door and told him the bookie was here.

-16-

The Foreign Team

Bobby and Scott stood uncomfortably in a hallway of mirrors. After an hour of saying "no," Bobby had grown tired of arguing and agreed to bring his son along. Now, staring into the mirrors, Bobby saw a dozen brooding images of himself ricocheting from the walls and ceiling.

"Neat place, Dad," Scott said, walking down the hallway, watching his own reflection, his sneakers squeaking on the Italian marble floor.

Dino Fornecchio led them through the apartment, toe-walking, bouncing along as if the floor were hot under his feet, each step a swagger, his dark hair greased into duck tails in the back.

LaBarca leaned against the balcony railing in the afternoon sun, his black pelt of chest hair glistening with oil. A pitcher of iced orange juice, or maybe mimosas, sat on a glass table. The sun was bright and warm, but Bobby was chilled, his hands clammy. He'd heard stories about LaBarca, everything from having pistol-whipped liquor store clerks in his youth to, more recently, extorting protection money from cargo shippers at the Port of Miami.

Before they could exchange greetings, a cellular phone rang, and LaBarca picked it up from the table. "Tony! *Mio Figlio!*

The great equalizer. Vinnie LaBarca might have been a ruthless gangster but he had something in common with Bobby. They both had sons. A break, Bobby thought.

LaBarca listened to his son for a moment, then held the phone away from his ear. "Hey Gallagher," didn't you play some college ball?"

"Penn State. Walk-on Q.B." Bobby made a motion as if throwing a pass, even though he'd never played one down at quarterback since high school. As an unrecruited walk-on, he earned his letter as a holder for kicks.

"My boy Tony's a freshman at Gainesville," LaBarca said. "No scholarship, either. He's getting the crap kicked out of him on the whadayacallit.

"The foreign team," Bobby said.

"Right. He ran up against the first string. Now, they're in winter conditioning drills, and he wants to quit the team. Give him a pep talk, yeah?"

Bobby spent three minutes on the phone with the homesick kid, a nose guard, which figured, given his father's fireplug build. Young Tony probably still had cleat marks on his chest from being run over by the Gators' first-team offensive line in practice every day. Bobby spouted a few cliches about how the tough get going when the going gets tough, and told Tony he'd look back on his freshman year with the same nostalgia as a soldier recalling boot camp. So just hang in there, and go Gators, rah, rah, rah.

LaBarca took back the phone, said a few words in Italian, then hung up and gave Bobby a friendly smack on the shoulder that momentarily displaced his scapula.

"Vinnie, this is my son, Scott."

"Hey kid, how they hanging?"

"Depends whether Dallas covers," Scott said, without missing a beat.

"Hey, me too." The gangster's smile was two rows of tombstones. "Gallagher, you got a good kid there."

"Thanks. I'm sure your boy will be okay upstate."

"Hey, don't say 'upstate.' Upstate is Raiford or maybe Eglin if the feds get you."

"Sorry, I mean at Florida."

"Yeah, he'll be fine if he don't flunk out, crack up his Corvette, or knock up any more cheerleaders. I'm just hoping to get some inside dope on injuries and game plans from him."

"Smart," Bobby said, figuring it was better than saying, *"Whoa, that's illegal."*

"Ah-choo!" LaBarca sneezed, leaving a trail of phlegm down his chest.

"Bless you," Bobby said.

"Fucking A," LaBarca said in thanks.

LaBarca wiped his mouth with the back of his hand and shifted his bulk to train the telescope down toward the pool deck. "So what's up, Gallagher?" he asked, peering into the lens.

"I couldn't lay off your six hundred large. The line moved, and I'm holding all of it."

"So?" LaBarca looked toward the pitcher, and from nowhere, Dino appeared and filled a large glass. Ice cubes clinked, but no one offered the guests a drink.

Bobby shifted uncomfortably from foot to foot. "Well, you knew I wasn't good for it. I mean we didn't discuss it, but it was sort of implicit that if I couldn't lay it off—"

"Im-pli-cit?" LaBarca rolled the syllables around on his tongue and didn't seem to like the taste. He swung the telescope away and looked directly at Bobby, his squashed nose looking even more pugnacious. "I'll tell you what's implicit. A bookie's gotta pay off when he takes a bet or he ain't gonna be taking no more bets if you get my drift."

The drift Bobby was getting was the northerly flow of the Gulf Stream where wannabe wise guys did the dead man's float. His mind raced.

"Vinnie, hear me out. I made a mistake. I shouldn't have taken the bet. I'm just doing this 'til I get my license back. I've petitioned for reinstatement to the Bar, and this was something I had to do for the money, but I'm no damn good at it. The limo business has been lousy, so I tried to go for one big score on the vig. I just want you to let me off the hook before something bad happens."

His face reddening, LaBarca leaned toward Bobby as if to get a better look. "Something bad? Like Dallas winning by more than seven."

"Yeah. Exactly."

"But something bad for you is good for me. It's not like I can go out and duplicate the bet, right. Today, I gotta give nine points, so if the Mustangs win by eight, I lose. Why the hell should I let you off the hook when I made a good bet?"

"Because I can't pay if I lose."

"I hear you got a real rich father-in-law," LaBarca said.

"Ex-father-in-law."

"So? Would he want anything bad to happen to the father of his grandson?"

"It's his fondest wish."

"C'mon, Gallagher. Families have problems, but would he want you to take a dirt nap?"

"He'd turn the first spadeful," Bobby said.

Scott couldn't believe it. Dad was fouling everything up. This wasn't the way to get to Vinnie LaBarca.

"I still haven't heard one good reason why I should cancel the bet," LaBarca said.

"Because you'll get bricked if Dallas doesn't cover the seven," Scott piped up. "The underdog is the smarter bet."

LaBarca's laugh spilled out of his stocky frame like water overflowing a tub. "The kid's a handicapper. Say, kid, do you use a system? C'mon, give me a tip."

"I like the dog when I can get more than five points," Scott said. "The *American Economist* did a study that proves you can go over the break-even point of 52.38 per cent just by following that system."

"No shit?"

"It's solid. Since you bet eleven dollars to win ten," Scott said in a grown-up tone, "you've got to win eleven bets to every ten you lose—52.38 per cent—just to break even."

"Right, because thieves like your old man take ten per cent

juice."

"Bullcrap!" Scott said. "Dad's entitled to his vig."

"Cool it, Scott," Bobby said.

"What about this underdog stuff, Einstein?" LaBarca asked. "You telling me you like Green Bay tomorrow?"

"A lot, a scabillion!" Scott said.

"Scott, let me handle this." Bobby gave his son a sharp look.

"I would, Dad, but this is too important to me."

"To you? It's my bet."

"It's my life! I don't want to get punted to some nerdy boarding school where I gotta wear a coat and tie. So, please, just let me—"

"Scott! I'm your father."

"And I'm not," LaBarca broke in. "I'm not related to either one of you, thank Christ. Gallagher, you can't even control your own kid. Ever try slapping him around?"

"No."

"Didn't think so." He fixed Bobby with a dark-eyed glare. "A bet's a bet. You gotta know that, Gallagher."

He turned back to his telescope and peered down toward the pool deck. "Hey kid, you wanna see some topless babes? Even from this distance I can pick out the real from the silicone."

"Maybe you've never heard of the letdown trend," Scott said, not willing to give in.

"You should bet against the league's highest scoring team of the prior week. The probability is that they won't cover the spread, either as favorite or underdog."

"I'm not sure Mr. LaBarca wants to hear this," Scott," Bobby said.

"Sure I do. Go ahead, kid."

Scott smiled. "If the team has two high-scoring weeks in a row, bet against them the third week, and always bet against any team that manages to score more than one hundred points over a three-game spread, especially if that team has held its opponents to nine points or less in the last two games. Dallas scored the most points and gave up the least in the playoffs. They're due to break some shop."

"To break what?"

"You know, to do something janky and shiesty, to let down."

Vinnie LaBarca regarded the boy suspiciously. "In the conference championship game?"

"The stats apply to the playoffs, too. I have the numbers on my computer at home if you want to see them."

"Are you sure?" LaBarca sounded dubious, but a note of uncertainty crept into his voice.

"Even if you don't believe the letdown theory, Green Bay is a home underdog in a big game. Betting the home dog is one of the best strategies."

"I know. I know. I've been making money on home dogs before you were born." He seemed to think it over, then stood up, wrapping a terrycloth towel around his midsection. After a moment, he said, "Nine points."

"How's that?" Bobby asked.

"The line has moved to nine. Betting Green Bay today, I'd get the home dog plus nine."

Scott knew immediately where LaBarca was headed, and he did some quick permutations. If LaBarca wanted to hedge his bet, it could be very good for Dad. But it could be very bad, too. As the men continued talking, Scott quietly figured the odds of each possibility.

❧

At first Bobby didn't understand, but then he brightened. "You want to hedge the six hundred thousand? Good thinking. Very smart. Definitely. The smart money does that a lot when the line moves—"

"You ain't gonna fuck me up the ass, Gallagher, so save the grease job."

"Okay, okay. But you do want to split the bet, right?"

Hoping, praying. *God, let him do it. I'll never break any of the*

PAYDIRT

major Commandments again.

"Yeah," LaBarca said. "I'm gonna cut you a break, Gallagher, 'cause I always liked you and you got a good kid there, even with his smart mouth. I got six hundred thousand on Dallas minus seven. Now, I'm taking six hundred thousand on Green Bay plus nine. It's a good deal for you. If the bets cancel each other out, you make sixty thousand in vig. I win if either game falls right on one of the numbers. If Dallas wins by either seven or nine, one bet is a push, and I win the other bet for six hundred thousand. Are we on?"

Bobby's mind raced. It wasn't as good as canceling the bets. He still ran the risk of losing six hundred thousand he didn't have. But now, the odds were with him. He should win sixty grand unless he was monumentally unlucky. "Of course we're on."

"Don't do it, Dad!" Scott said, raising his voice.

"Now what?" LaBarca looked annoyed.

"You could really get hammered, Dad."

"Look, Gallagher, I'm not gonna take all day with you. Do we have a bet or not?"

"Yes! Scott, keep quiet."

"But, Dad..."

"You heard me!" Bobby's voice carried a threat.

"Kid, listen to your old man," LaBarca said.

"I'm sorry, Vinnie," Bobby apologized, grabbing Scott and pushing him toward the balcony door. "We're outta here. Thanks."

"Don't mention it," LaBarca said, turning back to his telescope.

Bobby hurried through the apartment and into the elevator, hoping to get out of there before LaBarca changed his mind. Once the elevator door closed, Bobby turned to Scott and said, "I don't know what got into you in there."

Scott didn't answer, just stood there sulking.

As they exited into the lobby, Bobby laughed and said, "My boy, I think my luck has changed. The momentum has shifted. Steady breezes and sunny skies ahead."

They were inside the old Lincoln limo before Bobby realized that his son hadn't said a word since being hushed inside the

96

apartment. "Okay, what is it?"

Scott shrugged and said, "Chances are you'll win the sixty thousand. And like Mr. LaBarca said, there's a small possibility that the game will fall right on one of the numbers and you'll lose the six hundred thousand. But there's another chance that something even more skanky could happen. If the Mustangs win by eight, you've been middled. Mr. LaBarca wins his bet on the Mustangs because they'll have covered the seven, and he'll win his bet on Green Bay because he gets nine points on that one. You'll lose both bets, one-point-two million dollars."

Bobby was shaking his head. The math was right, but he wouldn't accept it. Couldn't accept it. He had a way out, and he wouldn't let the stone cold logic of the Kingsley genes defeat him. "Nobody's luck is that bad," Bobby said, praying it was true.

"It's not good for business if you care for a second whether blood is bubbling from a guy's mouth."
—Joey Browner, former Minnesota Vikings safety

"Hurt is all in your mind."
—Vince Lombardi

-17-

Lady Luck

Sunday, January 29—Green Bay, Wisconsin

Bobby Gallagher looked out of the window and thought he was flying over Siberia. The frozen tundra of the American Midwest was below him, and he shivered just thinking about those poor cheeseheads who'd be sitting all afternoon in the deep freeze called Lambeau Field, situated on picturesque Lombardi Avenue in quaint, old Green Bay. At least he'd be cocooned in the warmth of the visiting owner's suite, the sole remaining perk of having fathered Martin Kingsley's only grandchild. It was the deal he had struck with his ex-father-in-law. In return for bringing Scott to the games, Bobby got a seat in the back row of the suite, adjacent to the table filled with steaming trays of scrambled eggs and French toast.

There was an awkwardness to these mini-reunions each weekend during the football season. Bobby put up with Kingsley's animosity because Scott loved his Mustangs, and because Christine would be there. Yesterday, Bobby got his hair trimmed and spent an extra five minutes choosing his clothing, settling on a double-breasted blue blazer that Christine bought him three birthdays ago.

Bobby and Scott had left Miami just after dawn, and now, on the connecting flight from Chicago, Bobby closed his eyes and let the somnolent drone of the engines lull him into a state of half-sleep. Visions of Christine filled his mind. Along with the blue blazer he now wore, she had given him a birthday card with the photo of two polar bears, one sleeping with its head on the other. "You're my favorite pillow," the caption read.

Like the bears, they had slept entwined in each other's arms, and he remembered the warmth of her in the bed next to him, the depth of her care and affection. He pictured her now, the curve of her hips, the heft of her breasts, the scent and sheen, the steam and heat, the taste and feel of her. All he wanted was to have her back, to be a family again.

As the plane began final approach into Green Bay, Bobby stirred from his reverie, thinking he wanted something else, too.

A little luck.

He didn't care who won today's game, just so Dallas didn't win by seven, eight, or nine points. Seven and nine would be disasters; eight would be an apocalypse—one-point-two million dollars! Any other result, including an outright Green Bay victory, and Bobby would pocket the vigorish of sixty thousand dollars. It would be his ticket out of bookmaking, his first step back to respectability. Maybe he would get reinstated to the not-so-holy profession of the Bar and keep Scott in private school in Miami, and—if the gods were truly smiling—someday win Christine back.

As the plane descended, he shielded his eyes against the glare of the sun, reflected off a blanket of fresh snow. The landscape was pure Americana, boxy barns and towering silos, sturdy white houses with smoke curling from chimneys, birch and evergreen trees laden with snow. Solid towns with stout-hearted names: Sheboygan, Sturgeon Bay, Beaver Dam.

And, of course, Green Bay.

Martin Kingsley stood in front of the terminal wearing a black cashmere great coat that stopped just short of his ankles. He'd arrived non-stop from Dallas one day on his Gulfstream 5 along with Christine and the front-office personnel. Bobby could see the older man's frozen breath hanging in the hair as he smacked his gloved hands together like a boxer preparing for a bout.

From the first time he saw Kingsley, Bobby was impressed by the sheer presence of the man—tall and handsome with a mane of flowing white hair. His tanned, leathery skin made his smile all the more startling. Kingsley's visage was well known. It beamed from the game day program—"The Owner Speaks"—from society page photos at charity balls, from slick brochures celebrating the expanded Kingsley Center for abused women, and from glowing Metro page accounts of tennis courts built for inner-city kids by the generous team owner.

Ten yards away was Kingsley's silver and blue stretch limo with a miniature Mustangs helmet for a hood ornament. Vanity upon vanity, Bobby thought. His limo, like his ego, was Texas sized, and he relished the attention it garnered at fancy restaurants and plush hotels all over the league. His driver often left Dallas two days early to pick up Kingsley at the airport when the Mustangs traveled. The league had become a haven for multimillionaires who loved the spotlight more than the game. It's only a matter of time, Bobby thought, before Donald Trump buys a team and plasters a "T" or even his hair-plugged photo on the helmets.

"Scott!" Kingsley called out, as his grandson raced toward him. "How's my boy?"

"Great, Pop!"

Bobby grudgingly admitted that the boy loved his grandfather and that the feeling was mutual.

Kingsley wrapped his arms around the boy, gave him a hearty squeeze then lifted him off his feet. "Whoa! I'll pop a disk. Pretty soon, you'll be the size of a tight end."

"A quarterback, Pop. I want to be a quarterback. And a holder, like my Dad."

"You'll do better than that." The old man cleared his throat and shot a look past Scott's shoulder, showing Bobby a smile that was colder than Green Bay's wind chill. "Hello Robert."

"Martin," Bobby said, nodding.

"Speaking of quarterbacks...." Kingsley turned toward the limo and the drivers' window zipped down. Langston, his uniformed chauffeur, handed a Mustangs jersey through the window. Kingsley grabbed it and gave it to Scott.

"Wow, number seven. Craig Stringer."

The jersey had grass stains on the tail and a smear of dried blood on one shoulder.

"Stringer wore it when he threw two TD passes in the fourth quarter to beat the 49'ers," Kingsley said. "He wanted you to have it."

"Cool! Thanks Pop." Scott put the jersey on, pulling it down over his ski jacket. It hung to his knees and, for a moment, made him look like a small child.

Clever, Bobby thought. Stringer, nearing the end of his career, was dating Christine and being groomed by the old man for a front office job. Just as Bobby had been.

You want me to stare at that showboat's name plastered on my son's back, you wily bastard.

"Stringer was lucky as hell on the last pass," Bobby said. "He threw into double coverage, the ball got tipped by the corner, and Nightlife Jackson makes a fingertip grab."

"Sometimes a man has to throw into double coverage," Kingsley said. "Lady Luck belongs to those who pursue her, to those who want her badly enough. Craig Stringer is a winner."

As opposed to me, you mean,

"And winning's all that matters, right Martin?" Bobby asked. "No matter the cost."

"Careful, Robert," Kingsley warned. "You're plowing mighty close to the cotton."

"There can be honor and dignity in defeat."

"Only losers think so."

"Hey, c'mon Dad. Pop. Let's get going. It's cold out here."

With his natural instinct to resolve conflicts, Scott had become the human buffer between the two men's escalating emotions. Bobby knew he should follow his son's lead and let it go. They should all duck into the heated limo, pick up Christine at the hotel, and head to the stadium. One big, happy, fractured family like so many others. But he couldn't let it go.

"Okay Martin. No debates today on society's distorted emphasis on being number one."

"Winning isn't everything. It's the only thing!'" Kingsley boomed. "Vince Lombardi was right about that."

"Does that mean it's okay to cheat to win?"

"It ain't cheating if you don't get caught."

"Now, that's a fine lesson. Scott, don't listen to your grandfather."

"Dad, please..."

"Scott, the winners make the rules," Kingsley said. "That's all you need to know."

-18-

Freezing the Kicker

Bobby's nose went numb at the half, and he lost the feeling in his toes by the start of the fourth quarter. He hadn't brought a ski mask or a heavy coat on the assumption he'd be invited into the visiting owners' suite, as usual. But on the drive to Lambeau Field, Kingsley announced that there was no room for Bobby upstairs. He'd have to brave the cold with the cheeseheads and polar bears who lived in these arctic conditions. Scott had offered to sit outside with his father, but Bobby wouldn't hear of it. So here he was – alone – frozen out, in more ways than one.

Bobby had skipped eating on the plane in hopes of a hot buffet in the skybox. He was saved from the stadium concession stands by the generosity of some friendly Green Bay fans who invited him to join a tailgate of green-and-gold stuffed filets: steaks filled with prosciuto and cheese, garnished with yellow bell peppers.

Now, sitting high in end zone somewhere near Saskatchewan with beer and bratwurst locals who were dressed for ice fishing—rubber boots, parkas, ski masks—Bobby felt both ridiculous and frozen to the bone in his loafers, Miami-weight gray slacks, and navy blue blazer.

At the half, Dallas led 7-3 on a Stringer touchdown pass. For the time being, Bobby was ahead, too. A four-point Dallas win would split the two bets, giving him sixty thousand dollars in vigorish. But, as the talking heads on the tube might say: *"There's still a lot of football to be played, Brent."*

In the third quarter, an older couple in matching green and yellow parkas took pity on Bobby and draped a spare blanket around him, then fed him steaming coffee from a thermos. His own hands were trembling too much to risk bringing the cup to his lips. His ears were ringing and he was dizzy. Maybe it was an apparition, or maybe the beefy guy three rows in front really did strip down and bare his hairy belly for the TV cameras.

Green Bay marched down the field and appeared ready to take the lead, but a quarterback sack by the mammoth Buckwalter Washington stopped the drive. The Green Bay kicker booted a 33-yard field goal, and the Cowboy lead was sliced to 7-6. Still, it was money in the bank for Bobby who prayed that the clock would speed up, both to assure his wager and to end the game before hypothermia set in.

He looked toward the closed windows of the visiting owner's suite, imagining the festivities therein. A hot meal, mixed drinks, cushioned chairs, the benefits of privilege and class. Scott would be in there, munching popcorn, his mother on one side, his grandfather on the other. He imagined his son's happy cheers, Christine's quiet smile.

A groan from the crowd—the gasp of air after a punch to the gut—brought him back to the game. Number eighty-eight, Nightlife Jackson himself, had beaten the cornerback on a deep post and scored when Stringer hit him with a perfectly thrown pass. Bobby watched Jackson do a funky chicken routine in the end zone, looking like a long-legged Groucho Marx in shoulder pads. What was it Penn State Coach Joe Paterno admonished his players about end-zone celebrations? "Try to act as if you've been there before."

Ah, but Joe's a throwback. Nowadays, every tackle for a one-yard loss is greeted by self-congratulatory histrionics. As for Jackson, he was as gifted an athlete as he was devoid of morality. Nightlife's court appearances dated back to high school, long before the attacks on the perfume clerk and cocktail waitress. He'd grown up as a spoiled athlete, to whom few, if any, had ever said, "No."

With the extra point, it was 14-6 Dallas, and Bobby sat there stunned.

Eight points!

If the score remained the same, he would be middled. LaBarca would win both the bet on Dallas in which he'd given seven points and the bet on Green Bay in which he'd gotten nine. Bobby would owe the staggering sum of 1.2 million dollars. But there were still nearly five minutes left in the game, and...

"Five minutes is an eternity in pro football, Brent."

It only took twelve seconds. Boom-Boom Guacavera, the Mustangs' rookie kicker and a native of Colombia, had never played a cold-weather game in four years at Tulane. Today, he'd been tentative as he seemed unsure of the footing on the frozen field. Now, his kickoff was short and low, and Elroy Harris took it on the run at the fifteen, headed straight upfield behind three blockers, then cut smoothly to the left. A reserve linebacker who seemed to have the angle on him closed the distance, planted, and...slipped on the icy field. The last Cowboy who had a chance to stop him was Boom Boom, who tried the only thing he knew— to kick or at least trip Harris—as he flew by. Sneaky little bastards, those kickers. But Harris leapt over the sprawling Boom Boom and scored. With the PAT, it was 14-13 Dallas, and Bobby's fortunes had turned from minus $1.2 million to plus $60,000 in a dozen heartbeats.

He roared with the crowd at this glorious turn of events, then waited through an endless time out for the television commercial. Green Bay kicked off, deep into the end zone. Touchback, and Dallas started at its own twenty yard line. Bobby watched Nightlife Jackson trot onto the field, splitting to the right side. Wide receivers are the soloists in the sport's orchestra. Complex men, narcissists with profound egos and equally momentous insecurities.

Bobby began to feel that he was surrounded by his tormentors. Below him on the field, the prancing Nightlife Jackson. High above in the sky box, the belligerent Martin Kingsley. Calling signals was Craig Stringer, whose name was plastered on Scott's jersey and whose head had rested on Christine's pillow for the past year. Just how much can a man take?

As his face stung with the numbing cold, Bobby's mind drifted. Maybe he could have done things differently two years ago. Maybe he could have buried his self-respect in the red clay of Texas. Why didn't he balance his morals against his checkbook and keep playing Kingsley's game?

He'd had his fifteen minutes of fame—actually three minutes twelve seconds on the local news—and even received a mention on ABC's Nightline. Kingsley publicly fired him the next morning, conveniently forgetting that Bobby had already quit, then filed disbarment proceedings that were so airtight he didn't even have to bribe a judge.

The past twenty-six months of Bobby's life leapt at him like a mugger pouncing from a dark alley.

Disbarred.

Divorced.

Bankrupt.

The disgrace he could handle. His entry into the *nouveau pauvre* meant little. Losing Christine was crushing. The day he committed professional suicide, he had returned from the news conference harboring the delusion that his wife would be proud of him. Like many a reformed sinner, Bobby's heart burned with self righteousness and zealotry. To hell with being a corporate lawyer. He would now work for victims' rights and demanded that she quit her job, renounce her father, and join him in a storefront office assisting battered women, evicted tenants, and homeless veterans.

"Have you lost your mind?" she asked, stunned.

A cheer from the crowd stirred Bobby. After nibbling away for two first downs, the Mustangs were stopped cold—damn freezing cold—on third and seven. They would have to punt, and Green Bay would get the ball back with just over two minutes remaining, trailing by one point.

"Let's see what Green Bay can do in the two minute drill, Brent."

Bobby tried but could not let his heart feel even the faintest joy. Regardless whether Dallas held on to win by a point or whether Green Bay marched down to win with a dramatic field goal or touchdown, the two bets would be split, and he would pocket the sixty thousand in vigorish. With Green Bay in possession of the ball and the clock winding down, there seemed to be no way Dallas would win by the dreaded seven, eight, or nine. Even if Green Bay turned the ball over, Dallas would simply run out the clock and win the game, 14-13.

So why can't I enjoy the moment?

He didn't need expensive analysis to answer the question. He only needed to think of this morning when Kingsley's limo picked up Christine at the hotel. She was wearing a charcoal gray pants suit, a silken blue scarf and a leather jacket with a fur collar. Her blond hair peeked out from beneath a fur hat, and her pale cheeks glowed pink in the cold. She was as beautiful as he'd ever seen her.

Then, in front of God and his ex-father-in-law, Bobby shook hands—*shook hands!*—with his ex-wife, mother of his son, the woman who had shared his bed in endless nights of fiery lovemaking. Awkwardly, self-consciously, he pumped her hand as if he were an insurance salesman about to explain the benefits of whole life. He had felt like such a fool.

Now, as the bundled multitudes stood shouting, exhorting Green Bay, he stomped his feet, trying to restore circulation. The cherished home team was chewing up yardage but was out of timeouts with a minute forty seconds remaining.

For Green Bay, the game clock ticked unmercifully fast, the sand pouring, not trickling, from the hourglass. A pass brought the ball into Dallas territory, but the receiver failed to get out of bounds, and precious seconds ran off the clock, draining the team of its blood, drop by drop. An incompletion and then another short gain on a sideline pass, and the clock stopped with thirty-nine seconds left. Another incompletion, a pass for a first-down, and then a pass deflected for an incompletion. Fifteen seconds remaining with the ball on the Cowboy forty-one yard line, too far for a field goal, and still a point behind.

On the next play, with all his receivers covered, Joe Curry, the Packer quarterback scrambled out of the pocket and scurried down the field, an inelegant runner picking his way through fallen bodies, stiff-arming a linebacker, hip-faking a safety, finding a path down the sideline, finally lunging out of bounds at the Cowboy twelve, stopping the clock dead with four seconds left.

The crowd erupted with hoarse cheers. Green Bay hurried its field goal unit onto the field for what should be the winning kick. Though pandemonium raged around him, to Bobby, it didn't matter. Whether the kick succeeded or failed, LaBarca would win one bet and lose the other. Whether Dallas lost 16-14 or won 14-13, Bobby figured to make his $60,000 in vigorish on LaBarca's losing bet. It would be Bobby's largest score ever, and it would take him out of the hole. He'd pay Scott's tuition. He'd get on his feet.

Green Bay's field goal unit lined up for what should be the winning kick, a 29-yard chip shot. He recalled his own days as a holder, remembering blowing into his cupped hands to keep warm on a road game at Boston College. Before Green Bay snapped the ball, Dallas called time out, an old ruse that seldom worked. They were trying to freeze the kicker. A fitting term, given the weather, Bobby thought. The idea is to rattle the little guy by making him think about the magnitude of his undertaking. Meanwhile, the folks at home are urged to buy beer and the folks in the stadium are fighting off frostbite.

While he waited, Bobby pulled out his cellular and dialed a number. When he heard a familiar, raspy voice at the other end, he said, "Hey Cantor! How's the weather down there? It's beautiful up here. Too bad for you didn't book the bet."

-19-

The Kick of a Million Dreams

Martin Kingsley chewed on the ice in his gin and tonic. Earlier in the game, his mind had drifted. He had thought of the scarred and dangerous Houston Tyler. His extortion. His threats. The five million, chicken feed when you're flush, an impossible amount of cash when you've pledged everything to the friggin' banks that have cut off your credit.

But now, Kingsley's only concern was football. His suit coat was off and his sleeves rolled up. The skybox was overheated, and he felt feverish. All he had worked for, all the dough he had spent on rookie bonuses and veterans' multi-year packages, on egomaniacal free agents and scouts and nutritionists and weightlifting trainers and even a damn ballet master to teach the D-backs body control, all the boasts about bringing the Lombardi Trophy to Dallas, were about to go down the drain. When the timeout ended, that hundred-sixty-five pound piss-ant soccer player from Colombia would send the Mustangs back home and take his own team to the Big Dance with one scythe-like swing of his leg.

"We gotta block that kick," he muttered under his breath.

"There's a gap between the center and the right guard," Scott said, peering through binoculars. "I saw it on the two field goals they kicked earlier."

"What?"

"Dad knows everything about the kicking game. He taught me to watch how the linemen interlock their legs on the kicks when they come up out of their three-point stance. That's how they form a protective shield in front of the holder. But the Green Bay center is slow getting back. His right leg never locks with the guard's left leg." ·

Kingsley grabbed the phone before Scott had finished talking. The line went directly to the bench where Frank Morrow, the director of game day operations, wore a headset for the singular purpose of fielding his boss' calls. Sometimes, the phone wouldn't ring the entire game. Sometimes, there would be an innocuous order that the defensive linemen tuck their jerseys inside their pants. Other times, Morrow would have the unhappy task of carrying a message from owner to coach. "Mr. K would like you to run the end-around with Jackson." Coach Chet Krause would curse, spit, and then run the play.

Now, Kingsley ordered the middle overloaded just off the center's right shoulder, the Banzai middle formation. As the teams lined up for the kick, Kingsley raised his binoculars. Focusing on the center of the Mustangs' defensive line, he gave his last order of that day, this one muttered softly, but directed from Olympian heights to his eleven employees, pawing at the frozen earth like angry stags. "Block that son-of-a-bitch, you overpaid bastards!" he demanded.

✍

Make it, Bobby urged, under his breath. Though the kick wouldn't affect his bet, he wanted Dallas to lose. Let Kingsley wallow in utter despair. Let him know how it feels. The old man put all his cash and whatever heart he had into the team. Making it to the Super Bowl—and winning it—was his number one priority. To be stopped a game short would be unbearable agony.

Bobby would be sorry for Scott, though. The kid told him he'd be rooting for the Mustangs to win by less than seven, a result that would make both grandfather and father happy. That was just like Scott, always looking out for everyone else, trying to achieve peace through compromise.

Please block the kick, Christine Gallagher prayed. She gripped Scott's hand and watched him biting his lower lip, totally engrossed in the game. She'd spent much of the day studying her son. Three weeks since she'd seen him, and he looked an inch taller. The older he became, the more he resembled Bobby, and not just his looks. They had the same gait, the same sense of humor, the same pauses between certain words. When Scott asked her a question and cocked his head waiting for an answer, she could swear it was Bobby. Her ex-husband would always be with her, she thought, one way or another.

What was it about him, anyway? Why did she still have feelings for her ex? Chemistry, she supposed. She'd read in one of the women's magazines that we each have a subconscious sense of smell, and we're drawn to others who have the scent we lack. Whatever it was, all the senses worked with Bobby. When they fell in love, they laughed and played and shared everything, including a finely honed notion that the world was their amusement park. How did it go so wrong?

If Bobby hadn't gone to work for her father, maybe it could have been different. But Bobby's self-indulgent kamikaze act was unforgivable. Her father's investigators told her that now he was involved in illegal gambling. She'd be forced to use the information against him in the court case that would determine where Scott would go to school and who would be the primary custodian. She did not look forward to the hearing, but she intended to do whatever it took to win. It was a lesson learned from her father.

She wanted Scott to take advantage of his natural aptitude for mathematics. Sure, she'd miss him desperately, but the boarding school in Massachusetts offered advantages not available in either Miami or Dallas. They had Harvard professors, for crying out loud! Someday, Scott would thank her. So would Bobby. Another one of Daddy's lessons: grit your teeth and do what you know is best.

Poor guileless Bobby. Sometimes he was so exasperating she wanted to grab him by the collar and shake him.

If only you had some of Daddy's toughness...and if only he had some

112

of your tenderness.

Now she was dating Craig Stringer, heartthrob of Texas, and a pretty fair quarterback to boot. After fifteen years, it was his last season, given his gimpy knees and a desire to move into the front office. With his income from endorsements and his investments, Craig didn't need to work, but he told Christine that his dream was for the two of them to run the team together someday.

There was only one thing that was missing with Craig, but she could rationalize that. Maybe you only get that once in life. It's something you can't plan or control or call up on demand. It's hidden somewhere in the senses, that buzz of excitement and flood of feelings, a blend of sight and sound and, as the magazine would have it, smell, too. Okay, so she didn't have it with Craig, and she had it with Bobby. But that's over, right?

❧

The crowd was on its feet but quieted itself in homage to the home team's attempt to make the winning field goal. The Green Bay center, Chuck Stynchula, bent over the ball, cradling it in two hands. Stynchula was thirty-six years old, and his right knee had more tracks than the Union Pacific. Six surgeries left him with a permanent limp but an ability to scrape out a living in the pits once he ingested sufficient pain killers and was wrapped in several dozen yards of tape and supported by titanium braces. The offensive line dropped from a two-point stance to three points as the holder called out the signals. From the moment of the snap count, the center, the holder, and the kicker would have 1.3 seconds to accomplish their interdependent tasks.

The holder barked "set-set-set" and Stynchula, looking at the world upside down between his legs, snapped a perfect spiral to the holder, then raised his head and brought his right leg a step backward. Automatically, he searched for the guard's left leg, trying to lock up, hoping to push the Cowboy rushers to the outside of the cup, but Buckwalter Washington, who was blessed with what coaches call quick feet, lunged straight and low, driving a wedge between the two offensive linemen. T.J. Moore, a cornerback who had nearly made the Olympic team as a high jumper slipped past Washington's ample backside and jumped into the gap Buckwalter had just created between Stynchula and the guard. Moore took two steps and leapt high with one hand extended, a graceful cherry-picking leap which left him suspended while the kicker's leg swung through the ball.

∽

Bobby Gallagher saw none of the action on the interior of the line. He kept his eyes on the holder, in fine appreciation of the unrecognized talent of such men. He noted that Stynchula's snap was perfect and that the holder, a backup quarterback, made a smooth catch, spun the laces forward and placed the ball down at just the proper angle.

From the corner of his eye, he saw a Cowboy defender – T.J. Moore – leaping, and it occurred to him that Moore had invaded two yards or so behind the line of scrimmage.

Oh shit!

The *thwack* of the ball striking Moore's hand could be heard over the hushed crowd. The ball tumbled end-over-end and appeared to be headed out of bounds.

Damn, Bobby thought, watching the blocked kick careen toward the sideline. Dallas will survive by a point, and I'll have to put up with Kingsley's gloating.

At least, I'll still win sixty grand.

Suddenly, Nightlife Jackson, on double duty as a defensive back, sped into Bobby's line of vision. He jumped high, speared the errant kick with one hand just before it crossed the sideline. He caught the ball in full stride, a fluid, effortless play of such beauty and grace as to belong to the special preserve of the supremely gifted athlete. Jackson accelerated down the sideline past the Mustangs' bench, his cohorts waving their arms toward the Packer end zone, windmilling him home.

The scene was surreal, the stadium in numbed shock, only the voices of the Cowboy players and their scattered fans breaking the silence.

The sole pursuer was the kicker who gave half-hearted chase to the sprinting Jackson. The game, after all, was over. Except for the bettors.

Dallas had won the game the instant Moore's hand touched the kick, but now Jackson carried the Vegas point spread, as well as the football, down the sideline. Falling farther behind, the Green Bay kicker gave up, shaking his fist in disgust at the fleeing Jackson. Looking back over his shoulder, Jackson slowed to a dancing, knife-twisting waltz at the twenty, then high-stepped into the end zone where he boogied, pirouetted, and feigning a faint, toppled over backwards as if knocked unconscious by his own sheer brilliance.

Bobby watched, reeling from the ramifications.

No! No! No!

-20-

Middled

Kingsley jumped to his feet, a roar exploding from his chest. "How 'bout them Mustangs!" He turned to hug Scott, lifting him off his feet. "You did it, my boy! He turned to the others and bellowed: "My grandson called the play! He's a genius. We're going to the Super Bowl!"

"And then Disney World," somebody called out from near the bar.

Christine squealed with joy, laughing and crying at the same time. Kingsley released Scott and grabbed his daughter. They hugged fiercely. Friends and team executives crowded around to slap Kingsley on the back and share the purest moment of sheer ecstasy and exhilaration.

Only Scott did not join in the celebration. He blamed himself.

Oh Dad, I'm so sorry.

The scoreboard showed 20-13 Dallas, and the kicking unit was taking the field to try the PAT. Scott didn't need the calculator to do the math. With the extra point, his father was stuck in the middle of the two bets, and he'd done it to him.

Even if the Mustangs blocked the field goal attempt, I never thought they'd run it back for a touchdown. Aw Jeez, I should have kept my big mouth shut.

Scott had suffered despair before, of course. When his parents sat him down to explain, oh so calmly, that they were divorcing but that they both loved him and nothing would change—yeah right—he had hit bottom. He loved them both so much. Dad was a cool guy who took him everywhere and treated him like an adult.

Mom was neat, too. Okay, she worried about him too much, but that was a Mom thing. She couldn't help it.

For as long as he could remember, they were all gooey-eyed toward each other. Touching all the time, embarrassing him at Little League, sitting there in the stands holding hands, kissing after he got a hit or even reached first base on some stupid error. He pretended they were someone else's parents or recently released patients from a mental hospital who had arbitrarily chosen to root for him. Mainly, he figured they were a little goofy, but that was okay.

Why the hell did they split up? He knew it had to do with Dad working for Pop, that they disagreed about the way to do things, but why didn't Dad just get a different job? He remembered the argument with Mom at the end, right after Dad went on TV. It was the only time he ever heard her raise her voice to him. "You didn't have to make a spectacle of yourself! You didn't have to humiliate my father and me. Or did you?"

Yeah, Scott figured, he did. Right after it had happened, he'd asked Dad why he was so mean to Pop. "Because I had to get my balls back," his father said. Scott didn't understand it then, but now that he was older, it was starting to make more sense.

Now, more than anything, he wanted to help get his parents back together. If Dad could get out of debt and clean up his act, then maybe things would work out.

I should be helping him, but look what I've done!

જી

Bobby did the addition and subtraction even before the Mustangs made the PAT. Fourteen plus seven equals twenty-one. Final score 21-13. Twenty-one minus thirteen equals eight.

Eight points!

Dallas would win by eight, and he'd be middled. Vinnie LaBarca cleaned his clock on both bets. One million, two hundred thousand dollars.

"The kick is up. It's go-o-o-d! What a game, Brent."

In the millisecond it had taken T.J. Moore's fingertips to slap a football out of the air, chaos had replaced order. Suddenly, Bobby was cold again, frozen to the core. He felt as if his knees were locked and he'd never be able to stand. The Packer faithful, quiet as Quakers in church, filed sadly to the exits while Bobby sat in his seat, his mind a vague, cloudy wasteland.

Suddenly, a jarring sound stirred him. His cellular. He punched a button, figuring the Cantor was calling him back. "Jeez, Saul, can you believe my bad luck?"

"I believe it, asshole," Vinnie LaBarca said with a liquid laugh that sounded like he was hacking phlegm. "One-point-two million clams! Now pay me my fucking money."

-21-

Global Settlement

Monday, January 30—Miami

Why not ask your ex-father-in-law for the money?" Angelica Suarez asked. Bobby Gallagher jerked the wheel and nearly drove the limo off the bridge and into the Miami River. "You're kidding, right? I mean, after all I've told you, you can't be serious."

"Sure I am." Angelica was Bobby's client, and he was hers. Which is to say she was Bobby's limo customer and was also his divorce lawyer. "I'll bet he'd give you the money."

"He hates my guts. Just yesterday, he tried to give me pneumonia."

"*Ay, Dios Mio!* Bobby, where are your lawyerly instincts. Liking you or hating you is irrelevant. Martin Kingsley would probably want to pay you off as part of a global settlement."

The Lincoln rattled across the bridge, headed into Little Havana. Bobby pulled over to the curb where a man in a filthy white guayaberra tried to sell him *coco frio*, an ice-cold coconut out of a cooler. For two bucks, he'd clip one end with a machete and jam a straw inside.

Bobby was irritated and tense, his nerves tight as baling twine. He should be spending the day either trying to scrape up a million bucks or packing his bags for Bora Bora. Jeez, how much farther could he fall?

Just how far was it from LaBarca's penthouse balcony to the pool deck below?

Bobby wondered whether he should spend the day trying to

collect the money, which was impossible, or fabricating excuses, which were implausible? As it turned out, he couldn't do either one. The early phone call from Angelica Suarez reminded him that he was due in court. Now, after the hearing, his lawyer's suggestion of a "global settlement" with Kingsley baffled him. The court appearance was only round one in Christine's motion to send Scott to boarding school in Vermont. No decision yet, with more hearings to come. The notion that Scott could be so far away terrified Bobby.

Stopped at the curb, Bobby slipped the gear shift into park, then turned around and faced Angelica, who leaned back with her legs crossed, sipping a Perrier in the old limo's spacious but shabby passenger compartment. She gave Bobby the impression that she wouldn't mind being waited on for the indefinite future.

"What are you saying, Angie? Settle what? I'm not in litigation with Kingsley."

"Really? Then what just happened no more than fifteen minutes ago when the Honorable Seymour Gerstein gave you a week to show cause why he shouldn't honor a Texas order compelling Scott to pack his bags for Berkshire Prep for the start of second semester?"

"Just like I told the judge, Scott should be with his parents. If Chrissy wants him one semester in Dallas, that's fine because I'll get him one semester here. But to ship the kid off to New England for nine months is cruel and unusual punishment."

"For you or for him?"

"For both of us! Jeez, Angie, you don't have any kids, so you can't relate."

"That condition can be remedied," she said, her tone flirtatious.

He chose to let that comment drift on the tide without netting it. "Like I also told the judge, Scott's my life."

Angelica was silent a moment, as if testing the weight of her words before dropping them. "Bobby, please don't take this the wrong way, but maybe it's time you got a different life."

"What's that supposed to mean?"

"You're thinking of Scott in egocentric terms. It's *your* loss if he goes off to this fancy prep school. Sure, you'd miss him, but maybe the prep school is the best thing for him."

"Jeez, I can't believe you said that. Even Chrissy was reluctant at first about boarding school."

"Which means her father's fingerprints are all over the plan."

"Maybe so, but the case is still between Chrissy and me."

"No, it's not. And neither is the Bar proceeding. You may have slept with Christine, but you were married to her father. He's the one who wants to skin your hide."

"Even if you're right, I still don't get it. How do I settle anything by asking for a seven-figure loan? What do I have to give?"

She didn't answer, and he thought about it a moment. A Metro bus wheezed to a stop next to them, its brakes squealing, black noxious exhaust rolling over the limo. Another street peddler appeared alongside, this one hawking roses with a life expectancy equal to your drive-time home. Bobby tried to focus on his lawyer's advice and his unanswered question.

"What do I have to give?" Only one thing. No, she couldn't mean that!

Angelica Suarez was biting her full lower lip when Bobby glared at her in the rearview mirror. Her eyes were a dark brown so deep as to almost be black. Her skin was burnished bronze from weekends on the boat in Biscayne Bay. Her black hair was pulled straight back and held with a silver barrette. He had seen that hair loosened and flowing over her bare shoulders. It had been an evening of *paella* and too many mojitos, and they had ended up in bed. In the morning, he had awakened, dreaming of Christine.

"Counselor, you're not telling me to give up Scott."

"You wouldn't be giving him up. You'd be setting new primary custody provisions and visitation guidelines."

"That's lawyer double talk. You mean Chrissy would have him full time, except she'd send him off to school in New England, and I'd get him on alternate holidays."

"Maybe it's for the best."

"Bullshit!"

He started up the limo and pulled into traffic. Her office was three blocks away.

"I'm just asking you to consider it," she said. "Kingsley can use his connections to get the Texas Bar to reinstate you. If that happened, Florida would follow suit. You'd have options you don't have now."

"I wouldn't have Scott!"

"Face facts, Bobby. You won't have him anyway."

Each word, spoken ever so softly, exploded like a grenade. "What are you saying, that we're going to lose?"

"Would you rather I kept the truth from you? We're losing big time. You're in violation of a direct court order from Texas. You've been disbarred. Unless the complaining party, who happens to be your ex-father-in-law, pulls some strings to get you reinstated, it's a lost cause. If you were paying me, I'd say you're wasting your money."

The anger smoldered inside Bobby. He was furious at all of them, at Christine for divorcing him, at Martin Kingsley for impoverishing him, at his own lawyer for forsaking him.

"We're here," Bobby said, double parking on General Maximo Gomez Boulevard, just outside Angelica's office, which occupied the ground floor of a two-story building that also housed a palm reader, a *medico clinica*, and a *farmacia*. He got out and went around to the back, opening the door and avoiding her gaze as if he were the hired help.

"Bobby. I wish it were different. I wish I could do something for you." She put her hand over his, but still, he refused to meet her eyes. "Jesus, I even wish you didn't still love your ex-wife, but that's the way it is. Call me when you have a chance to think it over."

But he'd already thought it over. He used the old strategy of putting himself in his adversary's shoes. What would Martin Kingsley do if the situation were reversed? What had he said yesterday in Green Bay?

"Sometimes a man has to throw into double coverage."

The old bastard was right. Never give up, regardless of the odds.

Bobby would battle to the end, with or without Angelica's help. He'd try the case himself if he had to, appeal if he lost, and appeal again after that. He'd file every motion known to the legal system and a few he'd make up. The thoughts of fighting the good fight seemed to invigorate him.

Five minutes after dropping Angelica off at her office, Bobby was driving east on Coral Way when the cellular rang. Now what? What could possibly go wrong today that already hasn't?

"Be at my apartment tonight," LaBarca said. "Seven o'clock,"

"With the money?"

"No, with a bouquet of roses. Of course with the money, dickwad!"

-22-

Bobby's Posse

Bobby spent the better part of the afternoon at the Fourth Estate, a saloon on North Bayshore Drive near the soon-to-be demolished Miami Herald building. He had stepped into the cool environs of the Club, pausing a moment to let his eyes adjust to the darkness. The Club was a dimly lit serious drinking place straight out of the sixties, complete with a jukebox packed with ballads. No skylights, blonde wood, or California ferns. In fact, the only thing growing was mold on the bathroom tile.

Bobby was still blinking when he heard a familiar scratchy voice competing with Sinatra crooning that he'd done it his way.

"Over here *boychik*. Sit down. Let's schmooze."

After a moment Bobby found Goldy Goldberg sitting at a red Naugahyde banquette with a few of his cronies in the faint light of a faux Tiffany lamp. The old bookmaker looked at the world through thick prescription sunglasses, even in the dark saloon. Goldberg hadn't changed in appearance since Bobby's father placed bets with him thirty years earlier. With his pale, translucent skin that reminded Bobby of fine stationery, Goldy could have been fifty or eighty or anything in between. He wore a baggy brown suit with a green bow tie that resembled racing silks and was in his familiar pose, cradling a glass of cold seltzer in both hands.

How long ago was it, Bobby tried to remember, when Morris Goldberg—Goldy to friends and probation officers alike—got him the job slopping out the stalls? Bobby figured he must have been about Scott's age.

His real job, of course, was relaying information to Goldy,

everything from jockey and trainer scuttlebutt to which horses had sore knees. But most fun of all was climbing an olive tree just outside the perimeter fence and watching the races with binoculars, calling down the winners to Goldy as they crossed the finish line, practicing a melodious chant as if he were calling the stretch run at the Florida Derby.

"Down to the wire they come...and it's...Blood Orange by a nose! Romeo's Revenge second, and three lengths back, the game but outclassed Crackerbarrel for the show!"

Armed with the information, Goldy would race across the street to a pay phone— no cellulars then—and using a phony name, he'd get down a bet with a rival bookie.

Is this illegal?" young Bobby once asked as Goldy returned, out of breath, to their surveillance post.

"What, past-posting a bookie?" Goldy replied, surprise in his voice. "Maybe it ain't exactly kosher, but it ain't illegal either."

Now as Bobby settled into the booth, Goldy made a *cluck-clucking* sound like a mother hen. "One stinking play and it all goes to hell. I'm sorry, kid."

A chorus of sympathetic murmurs ran around the table. They had all heard the story of Bobby's disaster in Green Bay, Saul (the Cantor) Kaplan spreading the news like a virus through the betting community. Jose Portilla whispered some condolence in Spanish. Bobby had rescued Portilla from bankruptcy when his ill-fated fast-food restaurant, Escargot-to-Go, went belly-up. Now, the short, chubby chef operated El Pato Loco, The Crazy Duck, and was making money. Picking up the hint, Philippe Jean-Juste chanted something in Creole and dabbed his index finger in holy water— actually bourbon and water—making the sign of the cross on his forehead. Jean-Juste was a sometimes Santeria priest who would have gone to jail for animal cruelty if Bobby hadn't successfully argued that freedom of religion permitted his client to behead goats in a public park. It was one of his last cases before The Florida Bar, following Texas' lead, stripped Bobby of his license.

"Tough going, Bobby," said Murray Kravetz, self-consciously

adjusting his hairpiece. Kravetz was the eleven p.m. sports anchor on Channel 9, a great job if you wanted to drink all day and still possessed the ability to pronounce Ndamukong Suh when your lips are numb.

"Getting middled is a bookie's nightmare," Goldy said, shaking his head. "So, what are we going to do to help our friend here?"

For a moment, no one spoke, and the only sound was the clinking of glasses at the bar, and the mournful wail of Tony Bennett who wanted to pick up the pieces of someone's heart. Then Portilla suggested they go en masse to the Bahamas and knock off a casino with loaded dice. After another round of drinks, Jean-Juste said he would sacrifice two chickens, a goat and a pig and pray to the god Oshun that Bobby would win this week's Florida lottery. Kravetz claimed he knew a way to rig the ping-pong balls and fix the lottery, which sent Portilla into a soliloquy on various scams he'd run before going straight, including selling waterfront property in land-bound Ocala, and other cons, stings, and swindles, all of which could be used to raise dough for Bobby.

"Thanks guys," Bobby said, when they'd finished their alcohol-sodden meanderings. "I appreciate it. But there's nothing you can do."

"Don't underestimate us," Kravetz said. "All together, we've totaled a couple centuries of degenerate conduct."

"He's right, Bobby. Call on us any time," Portilla said.

"I will put a curse on this LaBarca if you say the word," Jean-Juste said.

"Good luck, *boychik*," Goldy concluded, clasping a hand around his shoulder.

-23-

Playing Jeopardy

Bobby entered the gilt-edged mahogany door to LaBarca's penthouse condo. This time, he had left Scott home. Outside, it was a cool and moonless evening with an ocean breeze. Inside the darkened apartment, the blast of central air could have made a side of beef shiver. The marble floors seemed frozen, the post-modern chandelier resembled a quiver of icicles, the chrome and glass furnishings seemed as barren as an alien landscape. Yet still, Bobby's palms were sweaty.

He was here to bargain for time. He would find a way to pay every cent, but with everything that's been going on, he needed some understanding, too. Hey, Vinnie LaBarca was a loving father. He'd understand, right?

LaBarca's errand boy, the creepy Dino Fornecchio, led him into the sunken living room, an area dominated by an aquarium and a large-screen TV. Bobby watched as a lionfish, gills flaring, trailed a smaller tropical fish like a cop on surveillance.

Vinnie LaBarca sat in a leather recliner in front of projection TV that nearly filled one wall. He was watching a rodeo on ESPN2 with the sound turned down. "I'll take the bull for a thousand," he said without looking away from the screen. "You want the rider, Gallagher?"

"Nah. I lost two hundred bucks once betting against a kangaroo in a boxing match against a Philly middleweight. I don't wager against animals, play poker with guys named Slim or eat at restaurants called Mom's."

When dealing with LaBarca, Bobby thought, it was best to talk the talk. He only hoped that after tonight, he could still walk the walk.

On the screen, a mangy bull with its testicles in a cinch bucked and heaved as the cowboy held on with one hand. Bobby felt his own privates tighten empathetically. A moment later, the bull tossed its rider ass-over-elbows, and LaBarca thrust his fist into the air in triumph.

"Sit down, Gallagher." LaBarca kept his eyes on the screen, where the cowboy fell trying to run away from the still-furious bull. "Stomp his ass!" LaBarca yelled, but two rodeo clowns quickly distracted the bull, and the cowboy scampered over a barrier to safety.

LaBarca put a tissue to his nose and blew, the sound of a tugboat horn. "Damn allergies," he said as he wiped. "My head feels like it's filled with seaweed."

"You oughta check the air conditioning ducts for algae," Bobby said.

"We check them once a month," the mobster said, "but only for FBI bugs."

"So how's Tony doing?" Bobby asked, trying for a little father-to-father camaraderie.

"Quit school, the lazy punk," LaBarca said. "Asked me to set him up in the video poker business offshore. I wanted him to have a different life than me. Funny thing is, he wants in. All these years I thought I was protecting him, shielding him from the life, and now, all he wants is to be part of it."

"Life's weird that way," Bobby said.

"Ain't it, though." LaBarca turned to face him head on. "So, Gallagher, where's my friggin' money?"

"I don't have all of it." Bobby placed a short stack of wrinkled hundred dollar bills on the coffee table.

"Jeez, I never thought you'd lay down on me." LaBarca did a quick count on the currency and coughed up a laugh. "You owe me 1.2 million and you bring me three grand?"

"It's a show of good faith," Bobby said, feeling a shudder run through him.

Don't let him see your fear.

"It's an insult," LaBarca said, shaking his head in disbelief, then hacking up some phlegm. "If word got out that you could stiff Vinnie LaBarca..." He closed his eyes in sad contemplation of losing his reputation as a fearsome killer.

"I would never stiff you, Vinnie. I just need more time."

"Time is what you ain't got. Time is a boa constrictor squeezing the breath out of you." He rubbed his crooked nose, and Bobby thought he could hear the cartilage snapping. "What the fuck am I gonna do with you?" LaBarca leaned over the glass coffee table and swept an arm across the stack of hundred dollar bills that Bobby had brought as a peace offering. The money – all three thousand dollars of it – went flying. "I don't want table scraps, dickwad!"

Bobby's last shreds of dignity prevented him from getting on his knees and scooping up the bills. "The Super Bowl's in two weeks. I can make some money, put a dent in the debt."

"Only dents are gonna be in your skull."

Bobby's imagined what it would feel like to be tossed overboard from LaBarca's boat, bound and gagged, weighted down with concrete blocks. He wondered if his body would drift north in the Gulf Stream or just settle at the bottom, and he thought of all the sharks he'd seen while fishing as a boy. He wondered, too, what his last thoughts would be, but then knew immediately that they'd be of Christine and Scott, just as they are each night as he drifted off to a shorter sleep.

"I'll get you the money. All of it. Day after the Super Bowl."

Bobby didn't know how he'd do that, but he had to say something.

LaBarca looked off into space as if contemplating great issues, then turned back to Bobby. "I always liked you, Gallagher, so I'm gonna cut you a break. I'm gonna be your banker. I'm gonna give you time to pay."

There was a soft squishy sound as LaBarca sucked a wad of phlegm into his mouth from his nasal passages, then swallowed

"Whatever it takes, Vinnie, if you give me time, I'll get it."

"Plus the juice! You bookies get your vig, and I get the juice. Two per cent a day, and because I like you, simple interest instead of compounded daily. So, that's 14 per cent interest..."

"A hundred sixty-eight thousand dollars," Bobby said.

"Round it up to two hundred g's for my trouble. You owe me a million-four the day after the Super Bowl. And that's it. No more credit, no more Mr. Nice Guy," LaBarca said. "You hear me?"

"Yeah. No problem, Vinnie."

"All right, get outta here. 'Desperate Housewives' is coming on the satellite in ten minutes."

"I don't know whether I prefer Astroturf to grass. I never smoked Astroturf."
—Joe Namath

"Joe Namath, you're not bigger than football! Remember that!"
—Vince Lombardi (shouting in his sleep as he lay dying in hospital)

-24-

The Owner, the Lawyer, and the Gangster

Tuesday, January 31—Miami Beach

Five Days until the Super Bowl

Not bad for a country boy. No, not bad at all, Martin Kingsley thought.

An fifteen-hundred dollar a night bungalow by the pool, a shimmering blue thread of water one hundred fifty feet long that seemed to stretch right to the beach. Not that anyone was swimming. There were a few pretty boys lounging in the shallow water, some leggy, short-haired European model types in bikinis dipping their toes along the edge. A chess set with Alice in Wonderland pieces four feet high sat on the lawn amidst towering palms, mirrors leaning against tree trunks, and a kitchen table with mismatched chairs.

Bizarre, and what a hoot for the son of a West Texas wildcatter. He was waiting for three visitors but only two had shown up. His plans had been meticulous and, he chuckled to himself, damn clever. He would destroy Robert Gallagher, would crush him into dust, watch him blow away with the Texas tumbleweeds, or more appropriately here, the Atlantic sea breeze.

Kingsley wouldn't do it for revenge, of course. He was above that, he told himself. He would do it for Scott. God, how he loved that boy. What potential the child had. But if he stayed with that loser of a father, who knows what would become of him? Kingsley shuddered, picturing a grown-up Scott sitting in a cage at a racetrack, dispensing two-dollar tickets, living in a rented room, never fulfilling his potential. A small timer like his old man.

The boy's a genius for Christ's sake, and it's my job to take care of him, to mold his life in a way his father can't. And his mother won't.

Sad to say, but Christine is too soft. Too much sentiment, just like her mother, bless her memory. No matter, I'll handle it. I'll handle everything.

Kingsley sat on a white-cushioned chair inside his all-white bungalow—white orchid in a white pot, white TV, white fridge, white linens on the white platform bed—watching the surreal scene outside his window.

Toto, we're not in Lubbock anymore.

He wondered what his father, the sun-baked, squinty-eyed Earl Kingsley, would have thought of the Delano Hotel. The man who never could scrape the grime from the seams of his hands would have figured he'd been transported not to Miami Beach, but to another galaxy.

Not that his father couldn't appreciate extravagance. He loved the finer things if they were the largest and most expensive things. Subtlety was not old Earl's strong suit. When he had money, which is to say when the oil flowed and the dice were charmed, he built the biggest house in Dallas, a monstrous combination Greek Parthenon and Southern plantation with pillars the size of giant redwoods. He'd imported artists from Italy to paint the Kingsley version of the Sistine Chapel on the ceiling of the giant rotunda. There, among euphoric visions of angels and puffy clouds was an oil derrick and a set of football goalposts. Though Earl Kingsley had never set foot inside a college classroom, he was a rabid follower of the University of Texas Longhorns and regularly slipped hundred-dollar bills to the fleetest and strongest of their so-called student-athletes.

As if the mansion were not sufficiently blasphemous in itself, Earl went on to offend the city's Baptists by proclaiming that "God hisself would have built this house if he had the money." Earl had the money but not the pedigree. He'd claimed to have been born so far west in Texas that the sun knocked a brick out of the fireplace every time it set. His hands were too callused, his humor too gruff for the folks at the Ashbrook Country Club. Earl Kingsley was not to be a part of the charity balls and coming-out parties. It only made him work harder, earn more, and spend more.

Martin Kingsley knew from early childhood that his father adored him. He remembered one Christmas when his father had the Union Pacific build a miniature railroad in the huge backyard of the mansion. There was a working steam engine, two cars and a caboose that huffed and puffed through a tunnel, across a bridge, and around a man-made mountain. It could hold young Martin and half a dozen friends. Only there weren't any friends. Martin rode the train himself, and when the neighbors complained about the noise of the steam whistle, he tooted louder and longer, especially when close to the property line. Closing his eyes now, he could still hear the whistle. Hell, now he wanted to toot it louder than ever. He wanted to get even with everyone who ever insulted his old man.

Hey, look at me. I'm Earl Kingsley's son. Look at what I've built, you bastards!

Martin also knew very young that his father was a man of excesses. Earl Kingsley drank too much, gambled too much, spent too much. When his luck ran out, one disaster after another drained him. The wells went dry; his commodities trading went belly up; and the dice kept staring back with snake eyes.

The country clubbers—safe with their inherited T-Bills and trust funds—sneered that Earl was "all hat, no cattle." One night, a drunk and depressed Earl Kingsley stuck a twelve-gauge shotgun in his mouth and left it all behind.

Martin wished his father could see what he had become. Rich, sure, but accepted too. Martin had made his first grubstake in land development and parlayed that into oil and gas, and then a go-go savings and loan which folded, but not before he'd pocketed millions. He'd invested in fledgling pharmaceuticals and computer software companies, and everything paid off. But he was always highly leveraged, asset rich and cash poor. He could never have bought the team without picking up Houston Tyler's stock dirt cheap, then pledging everything to the banks in return for the loan.

Unlike his father, Martin had the schooling and polish and a key to the members' locker room at Ashbrook. Like his father, he gambled, too, but for different reasons. With connections to wise guys in Las Vegas, he was tipped to point-shaving in college basketball, horse dopings, and fighters who planned to visit the canvas in the first round. The sheer act of winning, not the rush of adrenalin that comes with risk, juiced Martin Kingsley. He feared losing everything as his father had done and liked nothing so much as a sure thing. He dreaded only that which he could not control. The flip of a coin, a field goal attempt into a cross-wind... the explosion of a pump at the Texas City refinery.

Seven men dead and one ghost back from the grave.

Houston Tyler had been right.

He went to jail for my crimes.

For all his years tromping through the mud and muck of the oil fields, Tyler was still naive, an innocent. In a way, he was like Robert Gallagher, Kingsley thought, seeing only black and white, hopelessly blind to shades of gray. The prosecutor had offered Tyler a plea to reckless endangerment—a hundred thousand dollar fine and ninety days in jail—but he wouldn't take it, despite Kingsley's urging.

"I'm innocent, Martin, and you damn well know it," Tyler had said.

But the jury didn't know it, and at trial, Tyler had refused to point the finger at his partner.

What do you do with such a man? Kingsley wondered.

For one thing, you take him at his word.

"I'll do to you what was done to me. I'll burn you, Martin."

That son-of-a-bitch, emerging from his past like a serpent from the mist, threatening everything he had built. There is nothing so dangerous as a self-righteous man who has been wronged, Kingsley thought. What was he going to do about the lousy five million dollars Tyler demanded be paid the day after the Super Bowl? Kingsley didn't have the cash and his line of credit was overdrawn. He could sell assets, of course, but what did he have that wasn't pledged to the banks?

Yesterday, just before Kingsley had boarded the Gulfstream – liened from nose to tail – Tyler had called him at Valley Ranch. "You got room for me in that hotel suite in sunny Mia-muh?" his ex-partner asked.

"What?" Caught off guard, his heart pounding like a drowning swimmer's, Kingsley didn't know what to say.

"I suppose not, Martin. You're probably gonna have lots of fancy parties with caviar and drinks on silver trays. You always threw a good party, the costs be damned."

"What is it you want, Ty?"

"I'll be there, Martin, looking over your shoulder. Like those banks did to us when we were up to our ass in debt, I'll be keeping a close eye on the collateral. My good eye!"

He cackled with laughter, and the line clicked dead. The bastard wanted to frighten him, and he did a good job, Kingsley admitted to himself. The scratchy voice coming from that scarred throat rattled him, made him feel as if crows were pecking away at his spinal column.

Kingsley had been edgy on the flight to Miami, and once here, he struggled to relax. It would not be easy. He had to come up with the money, and as of yet, he didn't have a plan. But there was something else to be accomplished in the next dozen days, too. He had to destroy Robert Gallagher, and that plan was in full gear.

ଔ

The woman lawyer had been the first visitor to Kingsley's pool side bungalow that fine morning. The ocean breeze fluttered through the diaphanous white curtains as they'd shared a pitcher of grapefruit juice, eggs Benedict for Kingsley, a fruit cup for her. Cuban, he figured, dark and sultry like the Mexican women he had known since his wife's death, but taller and leaner with impenetrable eyes.

When Angelica Suarez had filed her appearance with the court in the custody/visitation case, Kingsley's investigators started digging. Now, Kingsley was confident he knew more about the woman than Gallagher did. He knew what videos she rented and what magazines she read. He knew what she ate for dinner and how many bottles of wine—Chardonnay and Chianti—were tossed into the recycling basket each Tuesday. He knew where she shopped, how much she spent, and—thanks to her charge account at a Little Havana *farmacia*—what day of the month her period began.

Even more important, Kingsley knew she had bought her own building in Little Havana and was behind on the mortgage payments. She had a 10-year-old niece with dyslexia, whose mother – Suarez's sister – was in drug rehab. The lawyer's credit cards were maxed out, and she was stressed out from too little sleep and too many clients who didn't pay their bills. Including one Robert Gallagher who traded limo service for legal work. And maybe slipped her some sausage on the side, judging from a Saturday surveillance that turned into an all-nighter.

Now Angelica Suarez sat on the chair across from him and smoothed the fabric on her black dress, which contrasted starkly with the white surroundings. A string of white pearls at her neck had an antique look, maybe smuggled out of Havana by her *abuela*. She had prominent cheekbones and an aristocratic bearing and could probably trace her heritage to Spain, Kingsley thought.

"I wouldn't be doing this if I didn't think it was in Bobby's best interest," she said as Kingsley poured her coffee from a white pot. "He needs to get on with his life."

"Fine with me. I don't care why you're doing it."

"We would lose the case anyway. If we could win it, I never..." She let her voice trail off like a dying breeze.

He smiled to himself.

We all rationalize, don't we? Do it every day. Hell, I can rationalize not replacing the pumps at the Texas City refinery.

"Are you sure he's coming?" Kingsley asked.

"He'll be here at eleven, but I can't guarantee he'll take your offer."

"You don't have to. Your job was to deliver him and recommend settlement. I'll do the sales job."

He slid a plump envelope across the table, and she placed it inside a Gucci briefcase without bothering to open it and count the bills.

"I hate what you've done to him," she said, getting to her feet, her eyes welling with tears.

You can put 'em in foxholes and courtrooms, but sure as shooting, they'll cry at the slightest provocation.

"He's a good man," she continued, "and I just hope you let him get a new start."

"That's up to him, lady."

℘

Kingsley sat down for a television interview while he waited for the second visitor. The team owner was getting more ink than Chet Krause, the Dallas coach, which was fine with both of them. Krause was an x's and o's guy who distrusted the press and could never figure why they needed comments every damn week when it all boiled down to the same thing: if we block and tackle better than they do, we'll win. Kingsley, on the other hand, never met a microphone he didn't want to fondle.

Although he had a personnel director, a head coach and ten assistant coaches, Kingsley never failed to take credit for the strategy that won games and the trades that brought enough talent to the team to make it to the Super Bowl. The pre-game hype and hysteria were just beginning. Once the team arrived, the media feeding frenzy would really begin. In the meantime, he would manipulate the press as he always had, kneading the reporters egos as a baker works his dough.

⍦

Outside the bungalow, a photo shoot was setting up around the pool. Kingsley watched from his patio as a photographer and several assistants fussed around three apparently anorexic young women in a low-cut cocktail dresses who were standing in the extraordinarily shallow end of the pool, the water barely covering their toes. An earnest young man in baggy shorts and t-shirt spritzed water on their golden bosoms. Again, Kingsley wished his father could be here to behold the wonders of such a strange place.

A moment later, his second visitor arrived, a stocky man with a bent nose and an unfriendly sneer. Kingsley welcomed the gangster and led him into the living room of the bungalow. He smiled to himself, imagining Bobby's fear in dealing with Vinnie LaBarca. What an able cast he had chosen for this little charade, Kingsley thought, and so far, all the actors had played their roles to perfection. Wouldn't his ex son-in-law shit a brick if he knew how he'd been played?

That's right, Robert. You're a puppet and I pull your strings.

"You want to take a walk, get away from all these fruitcakes?" Vinnie LaBarca asked, gesturing past the open patio door toward the pool.

"I'm not sure it's a good idea for us to be seen together," Kingsley said, pulling the white curtains closed. "The Commissioner frowns on owners associating with known gamblers."

LaBarca laughed. "Right. He's gotta say that, but if it wasn't for betting, who'd give a shit about a game between a couple cellar dwellers in December?"

Outside, hotel guests in chaise lounges pretended not to stare at the models in the pool.

"So how's our boy?" Kingsley asked, watching the scene through the window.

"He's in a hole so deep he can't see the sky," LaBarca said. "A million four with interest."

"And he thinks you'll break his legs if he doesn't pay?"

"Break his legs, hell. I'd make him disappear. I got a reputation to protect."

"I like your attitude, Mr. LaBarca. You're a winner."

Everything would be so much simpler with Bobby Gallagher out of the picture, Kingsley thought. He could raise Scott himself, mold him into a man. Hell, he had always wanted a son. He let the thought roll around for a moment, then stored it away, the knowledge that Bobby Gallagher's life hung by the slimmest of threads and he held the shears.

That was a treat to be savored later. For the moment, he wanted to enjoy the glorious scam that put Gallagher in debt to him. It was a combination of skill and the old Kingsley luck. He'd been feeding LaBarca inside info of injuries and game plans for years, and a week ago, he called in the debt, telling the gangster to make the first bet with Gallagher. It was a no-lose proposition. If LaBarca lost the bet, he would have challenged Gallagher to try and collect it. Win, he'd force Gallagher to pay. Once the spread moved on the game, Kingsley told LaBarca to double down, and with luck, he middled his hapless ex-son-in-law.

Like making the eight the hard way.

So far, everything had gone according to plan. Hell, better than that.

"Thanks Mr. Kingsley, and remember, you can call me any time you need an electrician."

"How's that?"

"When you want to put somebody's lights out." The mobster's sharp laugh sounded liked the howl of a coyote.

"I'll keep it in mind," Kingsley said.

An exasperated cry went up from the pool, "Too harsh!" The photographer, a skinny man with a ponytail stomped his feet and gesticulated wildly with his light meter. "Damn this tropical sun!"

"It's been a pleasure doing business with you, Mr. LaBarca,"

Kingsley said formally, sliding the second envelope of the morning across the table. This one was larger, legal-sized, and stuffed with even more cash.

"Hey, the pleasure's all mine. I never got paid to place a bet before. I just wish it had been my money up." He took the envelope, opened it and riffled through the first stack of hundred-dollar bills. He paused a moment and seemed to consider some quiet thought before speaking. "Mr. Kingsley, I'm a man who likes to return a favor. I got a real good hunch on the Super Bowl if you want to hear it."

Kingsley shook his head. "I've got to be careful. Laying down a bet myself is too risky."

Besides, the Commissioner's been on my ass about cutting corners on the salary cap, fudging injury reports and tampering with players and coaches under contract elsewhere, so I've got to watch my backside.

"Too bad," LaBarca said, "because I've got the skinny on the game."

"Even if I wanted to take a ride, I don't like the spread. My Mustangs are a four-point favorite. Hell, if we beat the Pats by a field goal, I'd still lose the bet."

"What if it wasn't a gamble?" LaBarca asked, a conspiratorial smile creasing his face.

What's he saying? This isn't some college kid shaving points in a Wednesday night basketball game. This is the Super Bowl with everybody in the world watching.

"What are you telling me? That you know my Mustangs will cover?"

"Dead solid certain. It's a lock."

"Chet Krause tells me he thinks the Pats have better personnel and are better coached, and he ain't just being humble. He also says they're hungrier."

"They could be starving. Wouldn't make any difference."

"But how can you be sure?" Kingsley pressed him.

"Trust me, you're better off not knowing."

Martin Kingsley would not trust Vinnie LaBarca any farther

than he could throw Buckwalter Washington, and the defensive lineman had an ass the size of Arkansas. Still, the possibilities were intriguing. God, how he wanted to win the Super Bowl, and how he'd love to win a huge bet.

Five million dollars had a nice ring to it. A nice round sum to pay off Houston Tyler.

But an owner of a pro team can't consort with bookies or even go to a legal sports book in Vegas or the islands. He'd taken a huge risk dealing with LaBarca on the conference championship game. Now, unlike his father, he didn't want to push his luck. Still, how could he pass it up?

The wise guys have gotten to somebody. An official, a key player for Denver, but who? And how?

"You're certain?" Kingsley asked again.

"I'll be surprised if they score a single touchdown."

Somebody on the Denver offense. Jesus, that could be anyone from an offensive lineman who'll jump offsides on fourth and goal to the star quarterback, Mike Skarcynski.

"You're sure?" Kingsley pressed him for what seemed like the tenth time.

"You could bet your life on it," LaBarca replied.

No, he wouldn't do that. But it had become something other than a bet. For all the world, it looked like a business transaction without risk, a chance to pay off Houston Tyler and savor his team's victory at the same time. These next eleven days, Kingsley felt certain, were going to be the best time of his life.

-25-

Affianced

Bobby had been walking out the door of his Coconut Grove cottage, headed for a dreaded meeting with his ex-father-in-law, when the phone rang. Scott had answered—"Hey, it's Mom!"—and quickly fabricated a story that he was home because there was no school in Miami today in celebration of Jose Marti's birthday. Playing hooky was a no-no with Christine. After speaking with her son for several minutes, she asked for Bobby, and he knew at once from her tone that something was wrong.

"I wanted you to know first," she said, sounding both apologetic and guilty. "Craig asked me to marry him."

"Craig Stringer? The quarterback with capped teeth the size of garage doors, the drunk I got off when he rode his Harley up the escalator of Nieman Marcus, the guy who's banged every groupie in the NFC East. That Craig Stringer?"

"He was going through a phase."

"I'll say. His bourbon and Vicodin phase. He's a pill popper, Christine. When he got busted for DUI with his pockets full of vikes, I had a friendly doctor write an ex-post-facto prescription in return for two box seats."

"Craig was playing with a shoulder separation and turf toe that turned his foot the color of an eggplant. He was in constant pain."

"*I'm* in pain! Lots of people are in pain, but they don't become junkies."

"He had a problem and sought help," she said, sounding more like a defense lawyer than Bobby ever did. "It was a courageous thing to do."

"What's so courageous about checking into a thousand-dollar a day spa?"

"You're behaving irrationally, Bobby. You're striking out at Craig because of your feelings for me. If you'd just get on with your life..."

I would, if I had one. You and Scott are my life.

"Craig Stringer, I just can't believe it," he said, sorrowfully. He felt as if his chest were a barrel tethered by steel straps that tightened with every breath.

"Craig's changed, matured. I like to think I've been a good influence on him. I've helped him overcome a lot."

"Why not help me? I'm the one who needs it."

"Oh Bobby," she said, with what he hoped was longing but feared was pity. "You only know Craig from your work. Off the field, at home, he's quiet and thoughtful and sensitive. Do you remember when his horse stables burned down and all those thoroughbreds were killed? He was heartbroken."

"He cheered up quick when the insurance paid off for those nags."

"See Bobby, there you go. You're making light of someone else's loss. You have a great capacity for angst but little compassion for others."

"That's not fair, Chrissy. Craig Stringer was losing his shirt in the horse business. The fire was a windfall that got him out of debt. I feel bad for the barbecued ponies but not for your All-American boyfriend. He's a guy who gets all the luck and my wife, too."

"You've changed, Bobby. You've become harder."

"Your father will do that to a man."

"Let's not start with that."

She was right. There was nothing in that for him. "You said Stringer asked you to marry him, but you didn't tell me your answer."

"At first I said to wait until after the Super Bowl. I didn't want him to have any distractions, and the press would be all over him, but he insisted on an answer, really became so agitated I was worried about his ability to focus during the next week. He gave me a ring, which I won't wear until after the game, but I did tell him yes, I'll marry him."

"Am I hearing you right? You told this gridiron Lothario you'd marry him because you were afraid he'd overthrow a receiver if you turned him down?"

"Our relationship has been progressing. We've grown very close. We have similar interests. Craig would make an excellent executive in the franchise."

"Love!" he shouted into the phone.

"What about it?"

"Are you talking about a corporate merger? Where's the word, 'love?' I haven't heard you say you love him so much your heart aches for him."

The words were no accident. That was the inscription on her first anniversary card to him. *"Bobby, I love you so much my heart aches for you. My body trembles at your touch."*

"There are many different kinds of love," she said, echoing her father's words. "Besides, you know I want another child."

"Volunteers can form a line behind me."

"Bobby, please."

He felt as if a knife were being twisted in his gut. Why had she called him?

Am I supposed to rescue her from this catastrophe, show up at the church like Dustin Hoffman in "The Graduate" and whisk her away?

"Don't do it, Chrissy. You don't love him."

"I'm going to marry him," she said, then slammed down the phone. In his mind's eye, Bobby pictured her sobbing, but he quickly realized that the only tears he could be sure about were his own.

-26-

The New Bet

An hour after hanging up with Christine, Bobby stood in front of the Delano where the valet parkers looked at his scarred and dented limo as if it were a four thousand pound cockroach. Parking at the hotel was sixteen bucks, and it usually took twenty minutes for these young Adonises in white shorts and shirts with epaulets—cruise ship cabin boys—to get your pride and joy back to you. Bobby was a heavy tipper of bone-weary waitresses who got the order straight and bartenders who drew his beer with no head, but he made a mental note not to reward these callow youths.

He almost didn't show up at all. Bobby hated groveling in front of his ex-father-in-law and would never have done it except Angelica Suarez insisted she'd quit if he refused to take the meeting. Now he wondered...

Just how do you borrow a fortune from someone who hates you?

Once inside, he saw Martin Kingsley in the high-ceilinged lobby where tourists and celebrity wannabees made an effort not to gape at the mismatched, funky furniture. A man in plaid Bermuda shorts half reclined, half sat on a metal bed draped in faux fur, then gave up and rolled off. Nearby, a tiny woman nearly disappeared into an oversize sofa with a towering winged back. The place was way beyond funk. It was in a league of its own, post-modern trendy, hey-look-at-me-Alice-in-Wonderland-on-crystal meth design.

Kingsley stood in the dead center of the lobby surrounded by a gaggle of reporters who scribbled notes or fooled with mikes. His ex-father-in-law was the image of a successful businessman in his jet-black Armani suit, white-on-white shirt and gold cuff-links.

Only the flowing mane of white hair and the lizard cowboy boots gave any hint of Texas.

"I'm not Joe Namath, so I won't guarantee a win," Kingsley said with his politician's smile. "But I'll tell you this. It'll be a hard-fought game on both sides, and nobody will turn off their sets early. We're gonna sell a lot of beer, and you can quote me on that."

C'mon, the reporters prodded, hoping for a prediction, some enticing headline.

"Well, I'll tell y'all this," Kingsley relented, slathering on the accent as thick barbecue sauce. "Them Pats better be ready 'cause we're planning to open a can of whup ass."

The reporters scratched at their pads, the cameras rolled, and Kingsley parried a few more questions, praising his all-world receiver Nightlife Jackson, reminding the scribes that only the genius of the G.M.—Kingsley himself—allowed the Mustangs to steal him from the Forty-Niners for a tight end with bad knees and two low-round draft choices.

"The Mustangs are America's dream, America's team," Kingsley sang out. He was on a roll, loving the sound of his own voice.

Bobby marveled at the man, the heavyweight champion of hype. God, how he loved to be the center of attention.

After all questions were patiently answered, Kingsley patted a few backs as the reporters drifted away, then glanced toward Bobby, adjusting his smile as if it were a party mask. "Robert, my boy, so pleased you could come."

"Hello Martin. Thanks for seeing me."

"Anytime." Kingsley wrapped his arm around Bobby and guided him through the patio restaurant and past the pool to his bungalow.

"Have you ever seen such a bunch of weirdos in your life?" Kingsley whispered, gesturing toward the pool deck. "Jesus, in the bar last night, you couldn't tell the men from the women. I'll just be glad when we can play some football."

"Four days," Bobby said, aware of the ticking clock. Each day he owed Vinnie LaBarca another twenty-four thousand dollars in interest.

"Right. Four days until the Big Dance. By God, I love it! I thought I loved seeing an oil well shoot its wad like a giant cock, but this...this, I gotta tell you, sets the heart a-thumping."

Bobby was surprised that the old man seemed so friendly. When they were inside the bungalow, Kingsley motioned Bobby into a white cushioned chair, then drew up a chair next to him. A basket of mangoes, papaya, and star fruit sat on the table between them.

"Now Robert, what can I do for you?"

∽

Kingsley made all the appropriate sounds, *cluck-clucking*, at Bobby's bad fortune, frowning with concern at every misadventure. He strained not to overdo it. His ex-son-in-law was not stupid, after all.

"How much do you owe this LoBorco?" he asked, purposely mangling the name.

"A million four."

Kingsley exhaled a long whistle. "That's a helluva herd of cattle."

"Yeah."

"I think I can help you out of this jam," Kingsley said.

"You can?" Bobby said, a bit too eagerly.

Kingsley studied him, the wolf measuring the soft belly of the lamb. Robert Gallagher, the man he had once groomed to fill his ostrich-skin boots, was offering himself up to the slaughter.

"Robert, would you agree it's time for us to settle our differences, begin behaving like a family again?"

"Yes. Yes, of course. I never wanted us to be enemies. I just couldn't go on violating my principles and—"

Kingsley silenced him with a wave of the hand. His ex-son-in-law was adrift in heavy seas and would grab the first line thrown to him. "No use replaying that old game film. Let's look to the future. Would you agree that I love my grandson very much?"

"I've never doubted it, Martin. And Scott is nuts about you."

Kingsley smiled. The drowning man beckoned, begging for the rope. "And you'd agree I always have had his best interests at heart?'

"In your own mind, I'm sure you do."

Unfurling the line now, swinging it overhead.

"And believe it or not, Robert, I have no animus for you, either. I want to help you."

"Yeah?"

He wants to believe. Let the lifeline fly, dangle it just within his reach.

"I'll take care of your debt to Mr. LoBorco."

"You'll loan me the money?"

Sounding hopeful and wary at the same time. Time to allay his fears.

"Hell, no! It's a gift. Consider the debt paid in full."

Not a very generous one, though, because I don't have to pay him a dime.

"And I'll help you get your law license back."

"You'll pay the money *and* support my petition for reinstatement?"

Wanting to believe it, praying that it's true.

"I've got quite a bit of pull where that's concerned. Consider it a done deal. It's time you got back to doing what you're good at, because Lord knows, you're a lousy bookie."

"Martin, I don't know what to say. I..."

"There's just one thing," Kingsley said, drawing a file out of a brown leather briefcase. The papers were neatly typed and stapled to a blue-backing emblazoned with the name of a Dallas law firm. "We really ought to resolve all the issues between you and Christine. Now, you and I both know that Scott will never reach his full potential going to a second rate school in Miami."

Bobby's head snapped back as if he'd taken a sharp jab to the chin. "Meaning what? I won't have him shipped off to some boarding school."

"Not some boarding school. Berkshire Prep, the best. Scott's

All-Pro material when it comes to brains. He's a math genius, Robert. Now, Christine is busy as hell in her work, and you'll be busy putting a practice back together. What I'm proposing is that you concentrate on your lawyering, Christine on the team, and I'll look out for Scott."

He slid the papers toward Bobby who glanced quickly through them, then turned to Kingsley with eyes as cold as a glacial lake.

"Give up my parental rights! Limit my visitation to holidays like some out-of-town uncle? Are you out of your mind? I won't agree to any of it. Not for a million-eight or eighteen million. I'll take my chances with Vinnie LaBarca before I'd sell you my son at any price."

Forgetting just how close to drowning he is.

Kingsley managed a smug smile, as if he expected the reaction and was not ruffled by it. Inside, his anger smoldered. The man was such a fool. "I'd make Scott my heir, give him every opportunity money can buy. He shouldn't be hitched to a dead mule like you, Robert. Frankly, you're not the best role model in the world."

"And you are? You don't even know there are some things money can't buy."

That claptrap again! Kingsley felt his rage building like water behind a dam. His ex-son-in-law was such a horse's ass. "Like your principles, I suppose. The principled lawyer who became a principled bookmaker."

"You're right. I was a whore, a liar, and a cheat. I was trying to be just like you."

The chump wasn't going for it! I'm offering salvation, and he's turning it down!

"Damn you, Robert Gallagher!" Kingsley was shocked the weasel still had any fight left in him and was bitter that his plan was not working. "Who are you to talk to me like that? What have you ever done? You didn't even play the game! You crouched on one knee and held the ball for the kicker. You've always been an anonymous, faceless nobody who got his picture in the papers only when he ratted on his own clients. You're washed up as a lawyer and can't make a living as a bookie, and your self-righteousness disgusts me. I'll take Scott from you one way or the other and some day thank me for it."

Kingsley felt his face turning a blustery red as if steam had just blown out of him. It was a relief to tell Gallagher what he really thought instead of pretending to care about the prick. Thinking now he'd turn LaBarca loose on Gallagher. If he's floating in the Bay, who'll raise Scott then?

"You can't intimidate me, Martin. You could once, but no more. And another thing, your team was lucky as hell to cover the spread in Green Bay, and I was unlucky as hell to get middled. I think your Mustangs are gonna get the shit kicked out of them in the Super Bowl, and I hope they do."

A smile sailed across Kingsley's face like the brim of a ten-gallon hat. "Talk's cheap, Robert. If you had any money, I'd ask you to put it where your big, stupid mouth is."

He said it without thinking, surely without a plan, but it came to him then, a way to turn mud into oil, bullshit into gold. It had nothing to do with the litigation. Hell, his lawyers would win in court eventually. Gallagher was finished, washed up, and Scott would have to look to his loving grandfather for stability and support. This had just been a way to speed up the inevitable. But now, another thought was forming, another problem to be solved.

Maybe Gallagher's stubborn rectitude had just become a blessing, Kingsley thought. Maybe he could parlay Gallagher's ruination into a way to solve his own financial problems. The germ of the idea was multiplying rapidly, and like most of his ideas, it had a dollar sign attached to it. The dollar sign stood directly in front of the five million dollars that Houston Tyler wanted paid the day after the Super Bowl. So neat and clean. He'd win the bet, pay off Tyler, then tell LaBarca to toss Bobby off the highest building in Miami.

"How would you like to take a bet on the Super Bowl, Bobby?" Kingsley asked.

ⓔↄ

At first, he didn't think Kingsley was serious. Bobby was too angry to pay much attention anyway, his heart banging away like a hammer pounding rocks. Who did the old man think he was? Trying to buy his son as if he were a mineral rights lease. Now Bobby was on his feet, preparing to leave, barely listening as the crazy bastard was yammering about a bet on the Super Bowl.

"If you're so sure my Mustangs will lose, or at least won't cover the spread, take some action on it."

"Are you nuts? I'm not gonna do business with you."

"Well, you're a bookmaker, aren't you? I'm giving you a chance to get even. I'll take Dallas minus four for five million dollars."

Bobby wasn't sure he heard correctly, so he stood dead still and asked Kingsley to repeat it. After he did, Bobby said, "Martin, if I had five million dollars, I wouldn't be here. I'd have paid off Vinnie LaBarca and would be winterizing my yacht."

"I know that, Robert. I'd expect you to lay it off, go partners with some of your bookie friends. Let's say I lose, I'd owe you what? Five point five million with the vig, right?"

"Yeah."

"And if you bring that in to a syndicate of bookies and Dallas fails to cover, what would be your share?"

"Probably twenty per cent."

"One-point-one million, including the vig," Kingsley said. "You'd have a helluva start paying off your debt."

Bobby nodded. He'd love to take the bastard's money. He'd love to see Dallas lose the game and Kingsley lose the bet. Plus, if he paid one-point-one million, more than three-quarters of the debt, he could buy time from LaBarca. There were hockey and the NBA playoffs coming up and March Madness. He could make more money, pay down what he owed. But what if Dallas covered? What if Kingsley won the game and the bet? He'd probably be dead the next day.

Bobby suddenly felt dizzy, his body rocking like a boat in a swell. He sat down and tried to think clearly. Maybe it would work. Maybe Kingsley's giant ego had just saved him. He could get healthy on Super Bowl Sunday if someone would back the bet. An amazing array of prospects spun in his head.

He'd fight to get his Bar license back.

He'd beat them in court and keep Scott at home.

He'd win back Chrissy from that born-again hambone quarterback with the plastic smile. Maybe they'd even have another child. Suddenly, there were more possibilities than grains of sand on the beach. Now who could he get to back the bet?

"The Super Bowl is to compulsive gamblers what New Year's Eve is to alcoholics."
—Arnie Wexler, former executive director, New Jersey Council on Compulsive Gambling

-27-

A Bet With "Intervention"

Wednesday, February 1

Four days until the Super Bowl

Sometimes he acts like such a kid, Scott thought, as he let his father ramble on excitedly, rehashing several scenarios in which Dallas would lose to Denver or simply fail to cover the four-point spread.

"It's time for Stringer to have a bad game," Bobby chattered, hopefully, "plus the Dallas O-Line is getting old, and Buckwalter Washington looks too heavy to me."

That's so lame, Dad. Stringer's on a hot streak, the Mustangs are the most experienced in the league, and Washington is so big, the Denver O-Line couldn't move him with a fork lift.

The limo was stopped at a traffic light on Biscayne Boulevard. They were on their way to meet Uncle Goldy, a bookie with enough contacts to lay off a five million dollar bet. But would he?

The light was green, but a cop held up traffic as a parade of marchers protested conditions on some Caribbean island that Scott hadn't yet studied in geography. And here was Dad, jabbering away, believing he's going to get lucky and beat Pop, as if luck had anything to do with it.

How many times have I told Dad that the answers are in the numbers if you know how to look at them?

Scott wanted to help his father, but how? He'd already crunched the numbers, and now it was too late.

How can I help you once you've bet on the wrong horse?

"Your grandad, bless his dark heart, has walked right into this one," Bobby said, drumming his fingers on the steering wheel like Charlie Watts on the drums. "If only Goldy will back the bet..."

He let his voice trail off, counting his mythical winnings already, Scott thought.

The marchers turned onto Flagler Street, and the cop waved the limo through the intersection. When they reached the turn onto the MacArthur Causeway headed for Miami Beach, Bobby announced happily, "I can feel it, Scott. My luck's about to change. The law of averages is with me."

"That's a mathematical fallacy, Dad," Scott said. "An example of innumeracy."

"Huh?"

"The math version of illiteracy, the inability to deal with simple numerical concepts."

"Thanks a lot, son. I'm just saying I can't keep losing forever."

"Sure you can. The law of averages doesn't change. If a coin comes up heads a hundred times in a row, there's still a fifty-fifty chance it will be heads again on the hundred and first."

"Yeah, so?"

"So you have to look at the teams, not at your losing streak. Defense and the running game wins Super Bowls, and the Mustangs are better in both. They also have the league's best turnover ratio, a better field goal kicker, and Craig Stringer is playing the best ball of his career. Not only that, they've covered the spread all but three games, which is the mark of a championship team."

Bobby quieted down as they passed the seaport, the cruise ships all gone from their berths, merrily steaming to island ports. Scott looked at his father, his forehead knitted in thought. He's changed, Scott thought. Ever since the divorce, Dad's been going downhill. He looks older and his belly has gotten soft, and he's not as much fun as he used to be. Suddenly, Scott was angry and sad at the same time, angry at his mother and grandfather for grinding Dad down, and sad that he couldn't do anything about it.

Sorry you're feeling bonked, sorry I had to tell you're gonna lose, but Jeez, Dad... somebody has to tell you the truth.

Scott was still trying to figure out how he could help his father when they pulled into a parking space just behind Goldy's ancient yellow Coupe de Ville.

cs

Bobby could hear the old man slurping his soup before they reached the booth. Bent over his bowl of chicken-in-the-pot, Goldy Goldberg was dressed in a dapper seersucker suit and wore a red-white-and-blue bow-tie over a white shirt. He was a small, spare man with thick prescription sunglasses that had slipped down a notch on his nose. As he stared into the soup bowl, his pale skin seemed a jaundiced yellow under the glare of the fluorescent lights.

Bobby had silently rehearsed his pitch, but now he was suddenly nervous and full of doubts. What if Goldy wouldn't put up the money? There was nowhere else to turn.

"My favorite ex-lawyer and my favorite 12-year-old," Goldy greeted them. "Scott, are you getting ready for your Bar Mitzvah?"

"We're not Jewish, Uncle Goldy."

The old man shrugged. "And I'm not your uncle. But then, nobody's perfect. You want to eat a little something?"

"Sure," Scott said.

Goldy turned to Bobby. "How about some chopped liver on a garlic bagel with onion?"

"Why don't I just go straight to the Maalox and skip the preliminaries?" Bobby replied.

"Suit yourself, but you don't look so good. Food can cure a lot of ills."

Bobby ordered coffee for himself, and a reuben and cream soda for Scott.

"The older I get, the earlier I eat dinner." Goldy attacked a piece of chicken bobbing in his soup like a life raft at sea. "Then I fall asleep even before they start the night games on the Coast."

He looked up long enough to discover that Bobby wasn't listening. "Okay, *boychik*, what can I do for you?"

Bobby walked Goldy through it, the old man listening while slurping up noodles from his spoon. Scott kept quiet, letting his father make his spiel. There were half-a-dozen patrons in the ancient Collins Avenue delicatessen whose walls had blown-up photos of Frank Sinatra, Dean Martin, and Sammy Davis, Jr. staring down at them. Like Goldy, Bobby thought, throwbacks to a by-gone age.

Bobby tried to put some excitement in his voice, though Scott had dampened his mood. Now Bobby watched for Goldy's reactions and all he got was a grim frown and his own reflection from the dark glasses.

Damn! He's not buying into it.

"Let me get this straight," Goldy said when Bobby finished. "You need someone to put up five million dollars."

"In cash," Bobby said, "to be placed in escrow."

"*Oy vey.*"

"I prepared the contract myself. Kingsley's worried about getting paid if he wins, so he insisted on the escrow. The money will be held by First Florida Bank. So will two per cent of Kingsley's stock in the team, which covers the five-point-five million he's risking. He takes Dallas minus four. If we win, I want twenty per cent of the total, including the vig, one-point-one million, which almost covers what I have to pay LaBarca the day after the Super Bowl. You'll get three-point-four million. If we lose, you gotta pay the whole bet, five million."

The old man took off his sunglasses and blinked, his heavy-lidded eyes as sad as a beagle's. "I don't like it."

Bobby felt panic bubbling up inside him like water in a boiling spring. "C'mon Goldy, you're a bookie. The line is four points. What's wrong with making the book?"

"What's wrong is that I'd be putting up five million to win three-point-four. That's be fine if I needed some heavy wood on Dallas to balance the books. But it's just the opposite. Too much money is coming in on the Mustangs. They're the glamour team, plus more people like the favorites. So I can't get a splitter because I don't have enough money coming in on Denver, and I can't lay it off because every book in town is overloaded with Dallas money, which means I'd be bankrolling it myself. It's *meshugeh*."

"You're talking as if we'll lose. We're gonna win!" Bobby bellowed, loud enough for a blue-haired woman to turn around in the next booth.

"You'll pardon me for saying so, Bobby, but you're not the best bookmaker in the world, or even in this booth."

"C'mon Goldy, I know football."

Goldy narrowed his eyes and lowered his voice. "What specifically do you know about this game that leads you to think Denver will cover the spread?"

"I just feel it in my bones, that's all."

"Not enough *boychik*."

Bobby felt his heart sink as if into a muddy lake. Without Goldy, he was lost.

"Bobby, we've known each other a long time, haven't we?" Goldy said, his voice tinged with sadness.

"Since I was a kid. You gave me my first job."

"And later," Goldy said, "when you came home from Texas with no wife and no profession, like some *shlepper*..."

"You taught me how to make book. I haven't forgotten all the things you've done for me."

"It goes both ways," Goldy said. "I won't forget how you got the case dismissed when that *momzer* U.S. attorney indicted me, and you didn't charge me a dime."

"How could I take money from you, Goldy?"

"That's why it's hard to say no to you. I love you like you're my own son, but Bobby, you got no *kop* for bookmaking, no head for the numbers, the odds, the instincts you gotta have. So when you come to me like this..."

The old man raised his hands as if there was nothing he could do. They sat silently a moment, the only sounds the restaurant clatter of dishes on counters and the murmur of voices at other tables.

Suddenly, Bobby felt exhausted, the dejection pinning him to the booth, as if gravity had increased tenfold. Men on death row had brighter futures.

No, strike that, Your Honor. Men on death row have the same future.

Goldy pushed his plate aside, patted his lips with a napkin and turned to Scott, who looked as if he might cry. "I'm sorry, *bubeleh*," Goldy said. "You know I'd do anything for you and your Dad."

"I know, Uncle Goldy," Scott said, choking back the tears.

"So tell me if I'm wrong. Put in your two cents worth."

Scott shot a look toward his father, and Bobby tried not to show his concern, but his heart was flopping like a trout on the line.

Help me, Scott! Help me.

He'd always taught Scott to tell the truth, but just now, he prayed for a white lie. His son was a tow-headed portrait of innocence with a shred of corned beef glued to his lip by a dab of melted cheese.

"I think Denver is a good bet," Scott said, eyes on his sandwich. "The Mustangs are due for a letdown."

"Aye, the kid's not as good a liar as his father," Goldy cried out.

"No, Uncle Goldy, I mean it. We can win the bet."

That's my boy, Bobby thought. It hit him then, the realization that the feelings between them were mutual. Of course! Why hadn't he realized it before? You get back what you give. He always knew he would do anything for his son, but he was just learning what his son would do in return. A surge of emotion flooded over him like a warm, tropical wave.

Goldy replaced his spoon on his plate and studied the boy. "*Nu?* Tell me about it. Are you using your algebraic formula of good defense stopping good offense? Is it a particular match-up on the lines? Why won't Dallas cover?"

"Oh, they will, Uncle Goldy. Dallas is the better team, and without some intervention, they won't have a letdown. They'll win and cover the spread."

"What are you talking about?" Bobby asked, confused. "You just said Denver was a good bet."

"Intervention?" Goldy mused. "What does that mean?"

Goldy and Bobby waited. Scott leaned close over the Formica tabletop and shot glances in both directions. As far as Bobby could tell, there were no spies among the octogenarian clientele.

"To win the bet," Scott whispered, "we're gonna have to fix the game."

"What?" Bobby recoiled, astounded.

"We can fix the Super Bowl so that the Mustangs don't cover."

"*Sha! Shtil kind,*" Goldy sputtered. "Hush child! We don't even joke about those things. Besides, it can't be done. No one's ever gotten to a referee. No league player has ever been accused of throwing a game or shaving points. You can trust the game more than your banks or politicians or any of our institutions."

"There's another way, Uncle Goldy."

The old man looked at him suspiciously. "How?"

"Dad and I know the Mustangs. I mean, we really *know* them."

"So?"

"We can't bribe them or make them throw the game, but we can still make them lose."

❧

Bobby looked at his son and read his mind. Okay, so maybe he didn't really know precisely what Scott was thinking, but he knew where he was headed. It was like that with Christine. When they were on the same wave length, they finished each other's sentences. The bonding process. Two people who are so close begin to think alike. Husband and wife, father and son.

"I think I know where Scott's going with this," Bobby said, "and it might work."

"You want to fill me in?" Goldy asked.

Bobby and Scott exchanged glances. "Give it a try, Dad."

"Scott's hung around Valley Ranch and the practice fields and the hotels," Bobby said. "He's listened to the players and the coaches. I've handled their legal problems. Together, we know their weaknesses. I can tell you right now who'll be violating curfew, who'll be doing drugs, who'll be chasing women."

"And I know who's superstitious and who loses his play book and who falls asleep in squad meetings," Scott said.

"They have vulnerabilities," Bobby continued, picking up the beat. "Craig Stringer's likely to leave his best work in a cheerleader's hotel room. Nightlife Jackson could get arrested. Buckwalter Washington could gain twenty pounds at the hotel snack bar."

"So you're just gonna hope they get in trouble?" Goldy sounded skeptical.

"No, we're gonna lead them into trouble," Bobby said.

"Together, we know how to get to them," Scott added.

"You're sure about this?" Goldy's interest was rising.

"You bet," Uncle Goldy.

"Hold on second *boychik*. You're talking about sabotaging your grandfather's team."

"So?" Scott's face was a portrait of blue-eyed innocence.

"What Goldy means," Bobby said, "is that you've been a Mustangs fan since the day your Mom brought you home from the hospital and decorated your crib in silver and blue. You love the Mustangs."

"Sure I do, Dad, but not as much as I love you."

PART THREE

The Big Dance

-28-

Even Cheerleaders Get the Blues

Thursday, February 2

Three Days Before the Super Bowl

Let the madness begin. Christine Gallagher surveyed the surreal scene outside the stadium where a radio station had set up a ten-foot high heap of cow manure. A man who won a drawing—or had he lost?—was about to leap into the fetid pile of crud from a diving board in hopes of rooting out a pair pf fifty-yard line seats to the game. The bullshit would be thick inside the stadium too, she thought, as the interminable press conferences had begun.

The hoopla and hype, fueled by a media blitz, had spread across South Florida. Overhead, a plane pulled a banner advertising an all-nude Super Bowl Cruise, featuring the talented lap-dancing ladies from Club Plutonium. There were street festivals, bay cruises, blimp rides, private jets, and theme parties with rivers of bloody Marys and mountains of stone crabs. Outside the stadium were corporate tents for manufacturers of soft drinks, athletic shoes, muscle cars, and even a little elastic bandage that goes across the nose and is supposed to prevent snoring, a handy device in the event of a typical Super Bore of a game.

A paean to capitalism run amok, Christine thought, then chased away the heretical notion. She was, after all, the marketing director of a Super Bowl team. With contract renewals coming up for the team's official soft drink, shoes, cars, sports drinks, candy bar, bank, and phone carrier—everything but jock itch powder—a victory could boost rights fees by millions of dollars a year.

Showing her credentials to a security guard at the press gate, Christine passed a pit full of alligators and crocodiles attended to by Miccosukee Indians in colorful garb. Entering the stadium, she wondered vaguely what other rapacious reptiles she'd be dodging all week.

On the field, more than two thousand reporters from two hundred countries jostled each other and moved in little clusters, like herds of well-fed sheep, from one player. The reporters, bobbing and weaving, tried to avoid bumping their heads on hundreds of video cameras, peering like cyclops, at the Mustangs, dressed out in uniforms without pads. There was a pecking order here, Christine knew, with the largest clump of sheep surrounding number seven, the quarterback who was as quick with the quip as he was in hitting the tight end over the middle. Now, the reporters circled Craig Stringer, alternately taking notes on small pads, then looking up to ask questions, their heads bobbing like bidders at an auction.

"I know you fellas like baseball," Stringer was saying to a Japanese camera crew, "but it's an undisputed fact that football players are smarter. In baseball, they got a diamond showing them where to run, and still, they gotta have coaches at first and third base telling 'em which way to go. If not, some fool would get a hit and run all the way to the right field wall."

The Japanese interviewer dutifully nodded while others in the cluster scribbled notes.

"Has football gotten too big?" a pretty young TV reporter asked.

"Heck no," Stringer replied, smiling for the cameras. "If God didn't intend man to play this ole game, why would he have shaped testicles like footballs?"

The TV gal was rendered speechless, and the others—lacking a philosopher or urologist among them—also remained silent, so Stringer rolled on, extolling pro football's charitable contributions and other good works. "The game brings together black and white and brown, men and women and whatever."

Murray Kravetz from Channel 9 squeezed through an opening between a Dutch photographer and a Sports Illustrated reporter, adjusted his toupee, then slipped a microphone under Stringer's nose. "Craig, you've been criticized for throwing the long ball too much. Any chance, you'll go more to your backs in this one?"

Stringer gave the old reporter an icy stare. "I wonder if y'all ever heard the definition of a sportswriter. It's someone who would if he could, but he can't, so he tells those who already can, how they should."

A ripple of laughter ran around the ring of reporters, and Stringer turned his back on Kravetz. The quarterback surveyed the throng surrounding him, spotted Christine, gave her the thumbs-up sign, then turned his megawatt smile back to the reporters. He was smooth, a marketing director's delight, Christine thought. He was driven to succeed in everything he did, and she liked that.

Naked ambition and he looks great naked, too.

But sometimes she wondered what lurked behind the perfect smile and twinkling eyes.

How does he really feel about me?

Christine had been aware from an early age that she was damn near irresistibly attractive to men. She had the looks, the brains, the personality. But, she also had the burden of money, and that attracted more than a few suitors by itself. The money made no difference to Bobby. If anything, he didn't like it. They'd both been struck by the lightning bolt, the thunderclap of love, and that's all that mattered.

But what about Craig Stringer? What was his agenda? What did he really want, a loving wife or a boost to the next level of business success? She couldn't read him.

And how do I really feel about him?

She didn't know. She set a personal deadline. By the final gun of the Super Bowl, she would decide whether to go through with it, whether or not to marry Craig. Sure, it sounded silly, but she worked best under pressure. She'd already semi-accepted his proposal but told him not to tell anyone until after the game, and she kept the ring in the little black velvet box.

I didn't even try it on.

It had upset Craig, of course. And what would a shrink say about her unwillingness to test the feel of the ring on her finger? Not a damn thing, because a shrink would never hear about it, she told herself. A Kingsley doesn't need help from anyone else. Hadn't her father taught her that?

But when Craig showed me the ring, why was my first thought of Bobby?

Before she could answer the question, she spotted her ex-husband, press credentials looped around his neck, wearing khaki shorts and running shoes and a Channel 9 polo shirt.

What's he doing here?

Christine watched Bobby float around the periphery of reporters who surrounded Nightlife Jackson, just next to the crowd around Stringer. Nightlife looked relaxed with a silver and blue 'do rag on his head, his gold earring sparkling in the Florida sun as he extolled the virtues of the South Beach clubs. The weasel. Christine prayed that he wouldn't victimize any star-struck young women on this trip, but what could she do about it? Her father had told her that she couldn't solve all the world's problems, and maybe lately, she'd stopped trying.

She sneaked out of the horde of quote-hungry journalists just as Stringer was thanking God for his good fortune—"I gotta give a big hand clap to the head coach upstairs"—then followed Bobby from a distance. He seemed to be scanning the crowd, looking for someone. Christine edged her way behind a heavyset TV cameraman and watched Bobby without being seen by him.

Behind her, Nightlife Jackson was regaling the press with easygoing humor. How different his public persona was from his private one, Christine thought. A daytime charmer, a nighttime slasher.

"Any predictions, Nightlife?" someone from the back of the crowd asked.

"We're gonna smash, trash, bash, and crash 'em. Denver will

be screwed, tattooed, and barbecued and ah'm gonna get me a championship ring."

"He oughta get a home-confinement bracelet," a reporter deadpanned. Christine recognized him as a wiseguy from ESPN.

"Hey Nightlife," the ESPN guy called out. "Is it true you majored in basket weaving in college?"

"Nah," the player replied. "That was way too tough. I studied broadcasting."

There were a few laughs, and Christine watched Bobby move away from the rat pack, heading toward the crowd around Buckwalter Washington who was describing his eating habits which included a dozen big Macs after practice. Bobby seemed to listen a moment and moved on, still not seeing Christine behind him.

She watched him approach the corral of reporters circling Chet Krause. The coach was dispensing his usual platitudes in a Texas drawl, worrying that his players were "tarred" from full contact practices and didn't seem to have the usual spring in their legs.

Cameras whirred and clicked, and utterly bored reporters duly recorded their banal notes. Christine watched Bobby move away again.

Who's he looking for? And why do I even care?

ↄ

Don't y'all go calling us cowgirls," Shari Blossom was saying to a semi-circle of reporters, all male, all staring at the cleavage rising from her push-up bra underneath the blue shirt tied at her midriff. Her white shorts were cut into a V so far below the navel as to require regular waxing sessions. Completing the outfit were white boots and a white bolero vest festooned with silver stars. She chewed a pink wad of bubble gum as she spoke, occasionally cracking it between her molars. "We're the Dallas Mustangs Cheerleaders, and don't be fergittin' it, honey."

She winked at a paunchy, sweating, balding reporter, who furiously scribbled notes as if Shari Blossom, co-captain of America's

Sweethearts, were disclosing the precise location of the Holy Grail.

"We're not cowgirls. We're not bimbos, hoochies, or Hooters girls. We're the pick of the litter and as American as apple pie. Or apple tart." She winked again and wiggled her hips.

The reporters nodded at the imparted wisdom and jotted more chicken scrawl in their little notebooks. Bobby studied this ripe peach of a woman, this symbol of healthy, innocent sexuality and, for a moment doubted his plan. Would Shari help him? Could she carry it off? Was he crazy putting so much trust in her? His life would be riding on those long, sun-tanned legs.

He'd known enough of the cheerleaders to realize that they were more than prancing, boob-jigglers with wide-eyed smiles. Although they might not have Ph.D.'s in astrophysics, they were savvy and sophisticated about men. They'd partied with Saudi sheiks and Texas oilmen, made commercials and personal appearances, and traveled the world. Shari was brighter than she'd let on, and if anyone could get close to Craig Stringer, she was the one. Besides, at this point, Bobby didn't have any other options.

It had been Scott's idea, though the kid tried to make his father think it was his own.

"Who's the most important player on the Mustangs?" Scott had asked him that morning.

"Easy, Craig Stringer."

"Absolutely. He's the bomb, but what does he do off the field?"

"Chase your mother, apparently."

"No, I mean, what are his weaknesses?"

"He's vain and arrogant, but those are probably considered assets in his line of work."

"C'mon Dad, get stoked. You were the team lawyer. What shaddy stuff has he been into?"

"Booze, women, drugs, the unholy trinity."

"Right! So..."

"So," Bobby said, picking up the pace, "he can probably handle one. Maybe he can handle two. But can he handle all three during the most pressure-packed week of his life?"

"What do you think, Dad?"

"I don't know, but there's a sweet Texas belle who might be able to find out," Bobby said.

"Hiya Boy Scout!" Shari called out, spotting Bobby in the crowd. "Long time, no see."

True, Bobby thought. He hadn't seen Shari since he'd walked her out of a Dallas courtroom, acquitted of a shoplifting charge. He couldn't claim much credit as it was Shari's testimony, or maybe her leopard print mini-dress that did it, the judge buying her story that the pearls from the Nieman Marcus jewelry counter must have been swept into her purse by "an act of God." On the way back to Valley Ranch that day, Shari allowed as how Bobby was her hero, a knight in a shining Benz, and she'd be oh-so-thrilled to show her gratitude if he wanted to stop by her apartment that night.

He politely declined, citing legal as well as marital ethics.

"You've never cheated on your wife?" Shari had asked, incredulous.

"Never have, never will."

She had looked at him suspiciously. "Most married men I know got two-toned ring fingers and fergit their wives names after a couple bourbons."

"Not me."

"Then you'll just have to be Shari's little Boy Scout," she said, leaning over in the front seat of the Mercedes to give him a peck on the cheek.

Now, Bobby gave her a wave and a Texas, "How-dee!"

"Be with you in a jiff, sugar," she said, turning back to her admirers and blowing a pink bubble with her gum.

Bobby watched her now, doing her blonde Barbie Doll shtick, the essence of Texas womanhood. She stood five feet nine, had ice blue eyes, a year-round parlor tan, and blonde hair parted in the middle and fluffed up at her shoulders. She wore her trademark pink terrycloth headband as if ready for three hard sets of tennis. According to cheerleader mythology, Shari would reward a man with a souvenir headband if he scored in her four-poster bed, rather than in Mustangs Stadium.

Her bare midriff showed a taut set of abs from daily workouts in the gym and her breasts were perfect globes, thanks to a the handiwork of a multi-millionaire plastic surgeon favored by Dallas socialites as well as cheerleaders. Her lips were slick with gloss and red as dewy raspberries, her eyes wide with seemingly innocent sensuality. A practiced sensuality, Bobby thought. This was a young woman, no more than twenty-five, whose entire being was devoted to the way she looked and the pursuit of pleasures given and received.

He'd long ago come to the conclusion that some seductive women are catnip, others are cats in heat. Shari was both. She could be cute and cuddly, the girl next door, or an outrageous vamp, frank about her desires and abilities. Either way, she was cherry pie ala mode, a rich confection for dessert.

"Mah head's just spinning from all your questions," Shari cooed at the journalistic posse, "so If you gentlemen are through, I'm gonna go talk to an old friend."

The reporters looked as if they could stay all day, but taking the hint, they moved off toward the team's weight-training coach to gather some profound quotes about squats and bench presses.

"Jim-mee!" Shari squealed, throwing her arms around his neck. "How are you?" she asked, giving it that peculiar Texas twang, *"Hah har yo-uu?"*

He hugged her and picked up the scent of hair spray and pink bubble gum. "Just great, Shari. What about you?"

"Plum wore out, Bobby. After seven years of bouncing and jiggling, I got a bum knee, a herniated disk, and pre-menstrual stress three weeks out of four."

Bobby worked out of her clinch. "Jeez, I'm sorry."

"Even cheerleaders get the blues, hon."

"You fixin' to quit?" he asked, finding her accent downright contagious.

"Not 'til a rich, handsome gentleman pops the question."

Bobby steered her toward the sideline. "Can we go somewhere

and have a drink?"

"Why sure, honey! Are you ready to take me up on an old offer?"

Bobby leaned close and spoke into her ear, long blond strands of hair tickling his nose. "I need to talk to you about Craig Stringer."

"Now why would you want to talk about a feller who thinks he's the only rooster in the barnyard?

"I know the two of you used to be close..."

"That's one way of putting it. If he'd be tense on the night before a game, I'd relax him. He'd pretend it was somethin' more than that, and I was just a rookie, fresh out of Galveston High, so I was a little starry-eyed and believed everything he said. It took a while and a bucket full of tears, but I finally figured out Craig would always be AWOL, After Women Or Liquor."

They approached the tunnel under the west end zone. In just three days, Craig Stringer and his teammates would come roaring over the same patch of grass where they now walked. Eight days that meant life or death. "Is Craig still popping pills?" he asked, suddenly. Sometimes the best approach with a witness is the element of a surprise.

Shari didn't blink. "Is Dr. Pepper sweet? 'Course he is. He just hides it from Coach Krause and Mr. K."

"You're sure."

"Tammi told me his bathroom looks like the Rexall store."

His look shot her the question. "Tammi?"

"She's a rook from Denton who's pulling Saturday night duty in Craig's hotel room. As he gets older, Craig likes his girls younger. Gets more applause that way."

Now came the difficult part. Bobby was as tense and jittery as a horse at the starting gate. He didn't know if he could trust Shari, who looked at him with her photogenic smile, waiting. What if she turned him down and ran to Stringer, exposing the plan? What if she reported him to league security? His nerves felt like exposed power lines, snapping like whips, crackling with hot sparks. "Do you think you could sub for her?" he asked. "There's ten thousand dollars in it for you if it works."

She turned off her smile as if hitting a light switch. "Don't insult me, Bobby! Ah turned down fifty thousand dollars and a diamond necklace from an A-rab prince who wanted me to do splits for him in his castle in Abu Dhabi. Ah've given a lot away, but ah've never sold it."

She pouted at him. The approach had been all wrong. He felt his face redden and suddenly felt feverish.

"I'm sorry, Shari. I didn't mean—"

"Ah don't go to bed with anyone unless ah've got the itch."

"I'm know, I know, but he's an old lover of yours. It's not like I'm..."

"Pimping?"

"Yeah."

"What makes you so damn interested in improving Craig's sex life?"

He'd been expecting the question and had worked on the answer, which unlike many statements he'd made as a lawyer, was at least a half truth. "He's been seeing Chrissy."

"Ah git it!" Shari cried, showing a smile of perfect teeth the color of fresh cream. "This is about your ex. She's still got her brand on your hide, don't she sugar?"

"I guess so," he said, sheepishly. "They're semi-engaged, and I want to break them up."

"And ah thought Craig would chew off his own leg before he'd get caught in the matrimonial trap, but he's always lookin' to improve himself, and Christine Kingsley's just another step on the ladder. Now what can Shari and her pink headbands to do help?"

Bobby took a deep breath and sang it out. "Christine doesn't know what she's getting into. I need proof that Stringer's popping pills, drinking and womanizing again...and I'll need it all videotaped."

"Video!" Her eyes flashed with what he thought was anger.

Now I've gone too far. Damn, I'll lose her.

"So ah could be on 'Hollywood Tonight!'"

He realized he'd mistaken her enthusiasm for anger.

"Hell yes. You could get your own TV series."

"You think I could get a book deal like Paula Barbieri?"

"Maybe. Did you ever sleep with O.J.?"

"Who didn't, honey?"

"So what do you think?"

"Ah think you're a smooth talker who could sell fur coats in hell."

"Will you do it? And will Craig go for it?"

"Hell yes, sugar! Any old night. Craig still comes sniffing around, but ah've given him the stiff arm the past two seasons. Been there, done that, and to tell you the truth, he ain't that hot. We won't be needing any extended play videotape. With Craig, it's always the two minute warning, then he's running the hurry-up offense."

Bobby laughed and let some of the tension go.

"What's so funny, honey?"

"I'm just glad to learn there's one thing I can do better than Craig Stringer."

Christine watched Bobby and Shari disappear into the shadows of the tunnel. She fought the urge to follow them, a dozen thoughts buzzing in her mind.

What was Bobby even doing here? She had checked with the media relations director. Bobby was listed as an assistant to Murray Kravetz at a local Miami TV station and would have press credentials for the game. What was he up to? And why had he sought out Shari Blossom? Christine tolerated the cheerleaders because they made money for the team, but their image as pretty playthings offended her feminist sensibilities. The girls were always polite to her face, but she knew they called her "the Axe" behind her back because she was always trying to cut team expenses.

There was something about Shari Blossom that bothered her. No, *everything* about Shari bothered her, she now thought. Shari was a throwback, a woman who wiggled her ass to get what she wanted. She also held the all-time cheerleader record for the most times per season that her top came untied during the Rockettes-like high-kick maneuver. Each time, her boobs would come bouncing out to the delight of the hooting Billy Bobs. And, each time, after receiving dozens of letters from the Southern Baptist churches, Christine would summon Shari into the office.

"I'm awfully sorry," Shari would say, reaching for sincerity like a soap opera understudy. "Next time, ah'll tie the top on tighter."

"Funny, Shari, " Christine would reply. "I always figured you learned a slip knot from some sailor passing through Galveston."

Christine had heard rumors that Craig was involved with Shari before they started going out, but he denied everything. "Chrissy baby, I never touched one of those girls. I believe in their illusion of innocence."

"Craig, if you could throw the football as well as you sling the bullshit," she said, "you'd already be in the Hall of Fame."

"You can get anybody you want to coach the team. The only guy I want you to get for me is that guy with the whistle."

—Gangster Frank Costello, in reply to a promise that the Washington Redskins would hire a famous college coach if Costello would invest in the team

-29-

The Lake of Fire

Martin Kingsley drummed his fingers impatiently on the table top. He was sitting at a café on Lincoln Road, waiting for the lights to be adjusted so they could get on with taping a Super Bowl spot for Fox Sports, and as usual, it was hurry up and wait. Television, Kingsley fumed, was one big waste of time. If he didn't enjoy the spotlight so much, he would say to hell with all those morons waving microphones at him.

From the corner of his eye, Kingsley saw a figure in black move through the throng of tourists in shorts and pastel shirts at the sidewalk cafe. The figure disappeared, but a moment later, Kingsley felt a tapping on his shoulder.

"Hello pardner," Houston Tyler breathed into his ear.

Kingsley jumped. "Jesus! You startled me, Ty. What are you doing here?"

"Working on my suntan," he said with a sickly smile that twisted his purple scar into a crescent. He was wearing black denim jeans, black cowboy boots, a black leather belt with metal studs and black silk shirt with silver buttons. He looked like a bald Zorro without the mask, and Kingsley was aware of people staring.

"You want tickets for the game?" Kingsley asked, hoping to get rid of him. "If you'll stop by the hotel later—"

Tyler barked out a laugh. "Why the hell would I want to watch a bunch of overgrown men jumping on top of each other for three hours?"

Kingsley didn't have an answer. The sudden appearance of this madman had jarred him. "I just thought as long as you were in town..."

"I came to watch you, Martin, and to collect my due. Super Sunday. I just don't want you to forget."

Tyler reached into his shirt pocket and withdrew a fat cigar with a tapered tip that looked like the Cuban Diplomaticos number two. "Doctor told me to stop smoking, but if I'm in Miami, how the hell can I resist?" He pulled a long-stemmed wooden match from the same pocket, lifted a leg and struck the match on the heel of his boot, then set the flame to the cigar. After a deep pull, he exhaled white smoke into Kingsley's face. "Care for one, Martin?"

"No, I quit."

"Good for you. When I was in prison, I dreamed of good cigars and fine brandy. Hell, it was so real, I could smell it and taste it. But then, in my dream, I'd sip the brandy and it tasted like vinegar. I'd put the match to the cigar, and it exploded in my face and caught me on fire. I'd just lie there, unable to wake up, watching my nose and lips melting in the flames."

Tyler was threatening him, Kingsley thought, and enjoying it.

"Fire's an awful purgatory, Martin. Luke said it in the Good Book: 'I am tormented in this flame.' It's the bottomless pit of Revelations. It's a boiling lake of fire."

"What the hell are you talking about?" Kingsley felt nailed to his chair, petrified like the biblical pillar of salt.

"We're headed there, Martin, you and me both, for all eternity. The only question is when."

"We're ready, Mr. Kingsley," an associate producer called out from a tangle of cables and lights.

"In a minute," Kingsley said. He turned to his ex-partner. "I'll have your money, Ty."

"I know you will, Martin. You'll scrape and claw your way up the cliff to keep your toes out of the boiling sulfur, but that tide will keep on rising." He turned and disappeared into the crowd.

❧

Hours later, Kingsley sat across a table from Vinnie LaBarca. He'd called the mobster just minutes after wrapping the TV spot. Something from their last conversation kept gnawing at him like a squirrel at an acorn. He had asked Vinnie LaBarca how he could be so sure Dallas would cover the spread.

"Trust me, you're better off not knowing."

But he just had to know. Someone was crashing the Big Dance, and he didn't have a clue. Could someone on Denver be taking a dive in the Super Damn Bowl? Jeez, that would be like Rommel laying down for Patton.

Now, Kingsley and LaBarca were sharing stone crabs and secrets in a private room at Joe's on South Beach. Vinnie was spearing some meat from a claw and talking at the same time, telling Kingsley to relax.

"It's all taken care of, a done deal," Vinnie said.

It had better be. A psychotic ex-partner was waiting to use a flame thrower on him if it didn't work.

"I feel like we're in this together, Vinnie, and I'm just not good at being a silent partner," Kingsley said.

LaBarca toyed with his French fried sweet potatoes and seemed to think about it. He was wearing a beige Armani suit with a peach t-shirt underneath, a Miami Vice look popular 25 earlier. His face softened, and he said, "Awright, awright, it's ain't complicated. It all goes back to jocks betting, an old story. Hey, remember Paul Hornung. The league doesn't know what to do with guys who bet on the games. You remember Art Schlichter, the Colts QB suspended for gambling? He was a compulsive, so what'd they do? They sent him to a rehab clinic in Las Vegas. He liked the town so much, he moved there!"

"I don't get it. What's that have to do with—"

"Bear with me. Now, there's another old story, too. This one goes back to the Black Sox scandal, maybe even back to the Olympic games in Greece for all I know. Players throwing games or shaving points. Kentucky basketball in the fifties, Boston College in the seventies, Northwestern in the nineties. Now you combine these stories, and what do you get?"

"What?"

"You get Mike Skarcynski."

"The Denver quarterback?"

"Yeah. He's a compulsive gambler. He already had a bookie when he was a sophomore at Pitt. Would hit the race tracks, too. Gambled away his signing bonus, got some psychological treatment, was caught betting with a bookie on League games two years ago."

"I never heard anything about it."

"His lawyers worked out a deal the Commissioner. He hadn't been betting on Denver's games, so the Commish gave him a hush-hush talking to, no press releases, no nothing but a warning. Now here's where it get's good. If he's ever caught betting on a pro football game again, he'll be suspended for a year, and if he's ever caught betting on one of his own games, it's life! Out the door. Whoosh!"

Vinnie made a soaring motion with a fork full of creamed garlic spinach.

"I still don't get it," Kingsley said. "You got him to bet on the Super Bowl."

"Nah, he's done all the betting he's gonna do this season," LaBarca said with an undertaker's smile. "I got him to throw the Super Bowl."

"What!"

LaBarca leaned over the table, closing the distance between them. He spoke in a whisper even though no one else was in the room. "Like I told you, he's a gambling junkie."

"I get it," Kingsley said. "He owes you money, and you're holding his chit."

"Hell no. He's a great gambler, cleaned house a couple of weeks early in the season, probably won three or four hundred thousand for the year."

"Then, how..."

"He uses a bookie in Boston who's a Denver fan and would

never do anything to hurt the QB, but he's gotta lay off some of the bigger bets with a guy in Atlanta who works for me, and one day the Atlanta book is throwing his weight around and says, 'you know who you been losing to?'"

"And he tells your guy it's Denver's quarterback."

"Yeah, and my guy has to come to me to cover the bets, so he's pissed that he's dropping a bundle to someone who shouldn't be betting anyway and whose information on injuries and inside stuff is better than ours."

"And you decide to take Skar down?"

A waiter came into the room and cleared the table. Both men declined the offer of key lime pie. Kingsley's appetite was whetted, but not for dessert.

"I buy some insurance," LaBarca said, when the waiter had left. "When the bets get even bigger, my guy tells the Denver bookie to have Skar deal directly with him. We record the calls, then when Skar wins a bet, I have a guy video the hand-to-hand transfer of money. The video's so good you can see Ben Franklin's pictures on the bills. So what I'm saying is that I got Mike Skarcynski's pecker in my pocket."

"He's agreed to..." Kingsley couldn't even bring himself to say it. The possibilities sent waves of excitement through him like the torrent of crude oil in massive strike.

"I convinced him that it's better to lose one Super Bowl," LaBarca said, and get to play another six or seven years, than to be disgraced and unemployed for the rest of his life."

"Then it's a lock," Kingsley said.

"That's what I been telling you."

"I should get some more money down on the game," Kingsley said aloud, but more to himself than to LaBarca.

"Every last cent you got," Vinnie LaBarca said.

☙

Later that night, the paperwork with Bobby Gallagher was

completed. Kingsley laid out 5.5 million bucks without putting up a dime. He escrowed two per cent of the team's stock, which covered the bet because the team was worth far more than $275 million, indicated by the transaction. In reality, there was no market for a minority interest in the team, so the stock was essentially worthless until the team was sold, and Kingsley had no plans to sell it.

Even if he lost the bet and the two per cent, a family trust would still own ninety-eight per cent. On Christine's thirty-eighth birthday, just 10 days away, 49 per cent of the stock now in trust would go outright to her. The Kingsley family would control ninety-eight per cent of the stock, no matter what, and a two per cent minority shareholder could not expect dividends, profits, or even free popcorn, as long as Martin Kingsley was running the show. He had snookered Robert Gallagher again, win or lose.

But I'm not going to lose, Kingsley thought. He would win and get rid of both burrs under his saddle. Let Houston Tyler take his money and crawl into the night to die. Kingsley didn't want to see his deformed face again. But Bobby Gallagher was something else again. Kingsley wanted Bobby there when the clock ticked down to zero, when every drop of blood was drained from him. There is nothing quite so satisfying, Kingsley thought, as looking into the eyes of a man you have vanquished.

-30-

Samson and the Philistines

"What we've got here, Your Honor, is a jurisdictional dispute," J.B. (Jailbreak) Jones was saying in his best basso profundo voice. "While the Texas court clearly retains jurisdiction over all matters pertaining to custody and visitation of the minor child, Mr. Gallagher has tried an end run, or a flea flicker if you will, in a bald-faced attempt to hornswoggle my client and rustle this case from Texas to Florida. Well, Your Honor, as we say back home, that dog won't hunt."

Christine watched her lawyer huff and puff and spout a gusher of Texas-sized cliches, all the while embellishing his drawl with flourishes and curlicues as he tended to do whenever in front of a judge or jury. They were in the chambers of the Honorable Seymour Gerstein in the Miami-Dade County Courthouse as Christine pressed her case to have Scott returned to her care and control.

Bobby sat across from her at the conference table, looking mournfully like a hound that had been banned from the house. Next to him sat his lawyer, an attractive Hispanic woman, and Christine couldn't help but wonder if there was anything going on between them. From time to time, when Bobby became agitated, the lawyer patted him gently on the arm, and Christine felt a pang of jealousy.

Oh, damn you, Bobby Gallagher! Why can't I get you out of my mind?

Carrying Christine's spear into battle was Jailbreak Jones, a man whose enormous girth nearly matched his grandiose ego. He wore a brown plaid three-piece suit, incongruously with a Western string tie. Seated at the conference table, just back from the lunch recess, Jailbreak's stomach threatened to burst the buttons of his vest. The scalp of his bald head was pink, as were his jowly cheeks. A brown Stetson sat on the table next to him.

As Jailbreak bellowed in indignation at the judge, Christine reflected on just how much she loathed being here. She didn't want to hurt Bobby any more than she already had.

Poor, misguided Bobby. I know you love our son, and you think you're the best Dad to ever place a new ball glove in your son's crib. But Daddy is right. You'll hold Scott back.

All she wanted was what was best for her son. Let him maximize his potential. Not that she didn't have second thoughts about shipping her son off to Berkshire Prep. The separation would be heart-wrenching, but hadn't her own father sent her to boarding school after her mother died? She had cried at the airport the first time she made the Dallas-to-Boston trip, but never again. The experience had made her stronger, more self reliant. Or was she just rationalizing now? Did it make this decision easier? Would she feel less guilty working weekends or coming home at nine p.m. if Scott were half the continent away instead of waiting for her latest dinner meeting to end? She didn't know.

Life was growing more difficult every day. Not her work life. That was challenging, of course, but manageable. You set goals and then surpassed them, a straight ascending line on a flow chart from where you are to where you want to be. There were no straight lines, however, in relationships. Relationships—man and woman, mother and son—were complex, contradictory, and constantly changing. There were no road maps to lead the way.

The litigation had gotten out of hand. It began as a dispute over Scott's schooling, but her father and her lawyer had shaped it into an all-out assault on Bobby, a mechanism for restricting his time with Scott. She'd argued with them, but in the end, the two men wore her down.

"Robert has no one to blame but himself," her father told her. "He likes to think he's Samson tearing down the Philistines' temple, but he's just a horse's ass crapping in his own stall."

There was nothing they wouldn't do to defeat Bobby and disgrace him. Her father waged what he called a two-front war, fighting over Scott and trying to keep Bobby from getting back his license to practice law. A private investigator had snooped in Bobby's trash, followed him to the laundry, and eavesdropped on his cellular calls.

"If I have to destroy that self-righteous prick to save my grandson, I will," her father told her.

It had become a battle between the two men for control of her precious child. She just wanted it to end.

Now she was listening to Jailbreak Jones proclaim that Bobby was a low-life scumbag who should be thankful that his ex-wife and father-in-law were willing to take on all parental responsibilities. "Alternatively, Your Honor, if this Court has jurisdiction," he sang out, "we will demonstrate on the merits that Robert C. Gallagher, a disbarred lawyer, a criminal who earns his living through illicit means, a malcontent and a miscreant, is an unfit parent, and that, while he may be entitled to certain visitation with the minor child, he should no longer enjoy the benefits of split custody, joint custody, or any control whatsoever of the boy's activities."

She looked across the table and saw the hurt in Bobby's eyes.

I'm sorry, Bobby. I'm sorry for everything.

"We have photographs of Mr. Gallagher at the racetrack in the company of known gamblers," Jones rumbled on, "some with extensive criminal records. And who does this man drag along to race tracks, taverns, gambling dens and pool halls? The minor child! The man is not a father. The man is a disease!"

Pool halls? For God's sake, Scott loves to play pool with his Dad.

Bobby's face turned red and he fidgeted in his chair. Christine closed her eyes and tried not to listen to her own lawyer, tried to wish herself into another time and another place. The anguish engulfed her. Part of her wished she had never met Bobby Gallagher, but that was ridiculous. If there'd been no Bobby, there'd be no Scott, and she loved her son with all her heart. Part of her wished she'd never divorced Bobby, but that was ridiculous, too. She had to choose between Bobby and her father. Once Bobby became the avenging angel of justice, at least in his own mind, the two men were mutually exclusive players in her life.

I had to choose Daddy. Didn't I?

Her father had insisted that she retain Jailbreak Jones, the most famous criminal lawyer in Dallas. Christine had wanted to use a female divorce lawyer, a friend from the Kingsley Center, but her father was adamant.

"Jailbreak saw me through my darkest days," Martin Kingsley had told her. "I'd trust him with my life, or even more important, my grandson's future."

Years earlier, just after the Texas City refinery explosion, Jailbreak Jones had practically become a member of the family. He was at her father's side during press conferences and appearances before the grand jury. How she had feared for her father's well-being then. Everything was at stake, his wealth, his health, his sanity. Publicity after the accident was devastating to Martin Kingsley's reputation. Seven men died at the refinery, and the newspapers blamed her father for cutting corners on safety. A federal investigation turned up dozens of workplace hazards and OSHA violations. On a tour of the burned-out shell, the Secretary of Labor called the place a "death trap for the innocent, a money machine for the guilty."

Her father had assured her that his only sin was allowing Houston Tyler to run the plant. Grand juries were impaneled. Victims' families sued. Reporters camped out on their lawn. Her father was on the verge of bankruptcy, indictment, and mental breakdown. He had fallen into a depression so deep it was as if he were lost in a thick, dark forest that the sun could never reach.

It seems like a lifetime ago.

Now, thanks to skillful lawyering—Jailbreak's—and solid business advice—hers—Daddy was posing for the cover of TIME this very morning. But still Martin Kingsley could not relax, could not enjoy his success.

"It's a long, hard climb up," he always told her, "and a damn quick fall down. I could lose everything in a heartbeat."

It was true, she thought, for all of us, particularly those who live as close to the edge as her father. The higher the peak, the steeper the precipice. A slip of the accountant's pen might draw the attention of the I.R.S.; a shadowy spot on an X-ray might foretell an excruciating death. We are so fragile, hurtling along, vaguely hoping the train doesn't jump the tracks.

"What about it, Ms. Suarez?" the judge asked. The Honorable Seymour Gerstein leaned back in his high leather chair, a spare man with rimless eyeglasses perched on his nose. Christine and Jailbreak Jones sat on one side of the conference table that formed a "T" with the judge's desk. Bobby and his lawyer sat on the other side facing them. Christine had watched the body language earlier when Bobby and Angelica Suarez had entered chambers. Bobby held out the chair for his lawyer, and she had smiled sweetly at him. Then later, when he became overwrought at something Jailbreak had said about his "unsavory" character and the fate of "the minor child," Ms. Suarez placed a calming hand over his. Was it Christine's imagination or did her hand linger a moment too long?

And damn it! Why do I even care?

"Scott Gallagher is now a resident of Florida," Angelica Suarez said. "He is enrolled in school here. His friends are here. His loving father is here. In addition, there are grave doubts as to whether the Texas court sufficiently retained jurisdiction. If we turn to the language of the order..."

She droned on for a while in that lawyerly way, picking at words here and commas there. Christine wondered about her. No wedding band, nails well manicured, an expensive business suit, Chanel perhaps. She had a gorgeous head of dark hair which she had pulled back into a bun for her court appearance, but Christine could picture her in a cocktail dress, hair down, someone Bobby would find exotic and enticing.

At least she called my son by his name, not "the minor child."

Sitting next to the judge, a young stenographer pecked away on her machine, recording every word. This is what it comes to,

Christine thought. A marriage, a child, a life. We record what our formerly beloved has done and said, then paint the deeds and words on a canvas in the harshest colors possible. There will be a winner and a loser—cheers and tears—just like a football game. Trial by combat, battle by attrition. It was all so depressing.

The man I loved sits across from me, a stranger, or even worse, an enemy. How did it come to this?

Finally, the judge nodded to his court stenographer and began reciting in a senatorial timbre: "This court finds that Texas has jurisdiction over the subject matter hereof and the parties hereto. There is before me an order of the Texas court compelling the Respondent, Mr. Gallagher, to return the child to the care and custody of Ms. Gallagher for enrollment in the Berkshire Academy in Massachusetts, and thereafter to return to Dallas. I have no choice but to enforce it, and if I may say so, I would enforce its provisions on the merits even if I were free to ignore its clear dictates."

෴

The anger smoldered inside Bobby like a spreading fire. He refused to look at Christine or her lawyer. He suddenly felt exhausted, spent. A sharp, hot pinprick of pain worked its way into his skull like a drill bit. He had invested so much of himself into his son, and now they were taking him away.

Damn! But what could I expect? My lawyer had warned me.

The judge turned to Angelica Suarez. "Counselor, I suspect you may appeal my ruling, and though I'm ruling against you on the threshold jurisdictional question, you may make a proffer of what your evidence would be on your client's fitness as a parent."

"That won't be necessary, Your Honor," Angelica said.

"What!" Bobby hissed in her ear. "Don't give up a chance to get our case on the record. We can't let the accusations against me go unrebutted on the appellate record."

She leaned close and shook her head. "That's irrelevant to jurisdiction."

"But not to the way judges decide cases," Bobby insisted. He was stunned by her decision not to protect the appellate record.

The judge waited a moment until attorney and client ceased arguing. "Alternatively Ms. Suarez, you may take a limited amount of testimony for the record."

"Put Chrissy under oath," Bobby said in a loud whisper. "Ask her if Scott loves me, if he loves spending time with me. Subpoena her prick father. Prove this is a vendetta against me."

"There is no testimony to elicit at this time," she replied to the judge.

Bobby's hands trembled like branches in a gale. Anger had turned to numb disbelief. Why was his lawyer abandoning ship? Why had everyone turned against him?

Jailbreak Jones was exchanging pleasantries with the judge about the fine bone fishing in Florida and had His Honor ever hunted wild bore? Christine was looking at Bobby, but he avoided her glance, shamed by his defeat. Angelica Suarez was packing her briefcase, seemingly in a hurry to leave the chambers.

"I'm not planning to appeal," Angelica Suarez said to Bobby in a low voice.

"Dammit! That's not your decision." His voice was loud enough to stop the conversation between the judge and the Texas lawyer. Jailbreak Jones looked directly at Angelica, smiled and nodded. It was not the smile of a victor to the vanquished, Bobby thought, but rather a congratulatory look. She turned away from him.

Now what the hell was that all about!

Bobby stood up and confronted his lawyer. "What the hell's going on?"

"It's best for you to put all of this behind you," Angelica said, trying to calm him.

"That's not your decision either!" he shouted, then stormed out of chambers.

"Hookers love the Super Bowl. Thousands of affluent men hit town. Not just beery football fans with their faces painted, either. In January [the Super Bowl site] is jammed with successful guys who feel like showing off, a city full of Charlie Sheens. The typical ticket holder is an executive or star salesman on a company-paid holiday. After a year of corporate war he may want a cocktail. He may want to loosen his tie and his wallet, roll down his limo window, do a little shouting, maybe even do his part to help make Super Bowl week the best prostitution week of the year.

—"Sex and the Super Bowl," by Kevin Cook, *Playboy*

-31-

Born Loser

A pulsating laser beam played across the spurting fountain in Bayfront Park. A string ensemble plucked away at Mozart, the delicate notes floating on the soft, salty air from the bay. In another part of the park, a Jamaican steel band banged away while closer to Biscayne Boulevard, the Junkanoos from the Bahamas performed their drums and brass routines. Neon lights flashed in the palm trees like madcap Christmas decorations, casting an eerie glow on the swaying fronds. Barechested Bahamian bartenders presided at torch-lit chickee huts, dispensing rum-filled coconuts and icy margaritas to thirsty patrons. Waitresses in colorful sarongs carried trays of fried alligator, Bimini bread, Haitian conch salad, Cuban *media noche* sandwiches, and Jamaican jerk chicken.

Billed as "A Caribbean Fantasy," the Super Bowl media party was a cozy little gathering for three thousand reporters, photographers, TV producers, team administrators, league officials, network executives, current and former players, corporate sponsors, salesmen-of-the-year, party girls (amateur, semi-pro, and Hall of Fame material) and various other freebie glomming wannabe-VIP's and hangers on.

And Bobby Gallagher.

Bobby was not here to party, although he did have a double date in mind. He was with Shari Blossom. Somewhere in the happy horde was the quarterback with the toothy smile and his quasi-fiancee, the former Mrs. Christine Gallagher. He had to find them and pull a switch. He had to hook up Craig with the voluptuous and willing Shari, get them into bed, videotape the whole shebang, plus find evidence of Stringer's continued drug use.

Is that all? Why not invent cold fusion in my spare time?

Scott's idea, which had once seemed brilliant, now seemed ludicrous. What if Craig were no longer attracted to Shari? What if he was truly in love with Christine?

Why not? I am!

Bobby forced himself not to become overwhelmed with the task. When he was a practicing lawyer and the sheer scope of trial preparations seemed daunting, he would focus on one small task at a time. Outline the points you must prove and organize the evidence to establish each point. Now, the small task was simply to find the lovebirds.

Despite the surroundings and the overall mood of gaiety and laughter fueled by free booze and food, Bobby was hardly in a festive mood. After the disastrous court hearing, he had driven to his cottage in Coconut Grove while he waited for Shari's phone call to come pick her up. It was a four-beer wait. He sat in his postage stamp backyard, slumped into a lawn chair with broken straps, listening to a mockingbird, missing Scott already, even though he was still here, hanging out tonight with friends from school.

He would never give up Scott. Nothing was that important, not even his own life.

But that was a battle for another day. He still needed to win a five-million dollar bet just to stay healthy enough to fight for Scott. Murray Kravetz had done the research, and Bobby was convinced he would be killed – or at least maimed – if he failed to pay off Vinnie LaBarca. LaBarca's rap sheet was peppered with arrests for mail fraud, loan sharking, racketeering, and extortion in recent years. In his youth were numerous assault and batteries and one attempted murder. Eighteen arrests but only one conviction, a plea to a reduced charge, so the mobster had spent only eighteen months in prison.

"But that ain't the worst stuff," Kravetz told Bobby. "He's been a suspect in half a dozen disappearances, but no bodies were ever found. Guys who owed him money, business partners in the vending business, that sort of thing. It seems like some guys who go fishing on LaBarca's Hatteras never make it back to shore."

Thinking of LaBarca chilled Bobby to the core, but not because of the pain or the eternal darkness that he feared awaited him. His only thought was of Scott. What would become of his son without him?

Bobby was late arriving at the party, having gone to pick up Shari at her hotel, then waiting another hour as she applied her blush, shadow, eye liner, lip gloss, and various other potions and lotions, and then tried on and discarded seven different outfits, all of which displayed her cleavage to a degree that could get her arrested in certain small Southern towns.

"Does this one do anything for you, sugar?" Shari had asked, tying a gold lame halter top under her breasts.

"You know damn well what it does for me," he told her. "Me and every other man you ever met."

"If that's the way you feel, Bobby, why don't we just party right here?

"Because there's work to do."

She pouted and let him get a glimpse of a breast in profile, nipple erect, as she tied and re-tied her top. Some women, he decided, practiced their megawatt sexuality so often and so hard that they were unable to turn off the electricity.

"I'm disappointed, Bobby. I was figuring you might end up with my headband tonight."

"And all this time, I thought the headband story was just part of the legend."

"It is and it ain't. Half the men in Dallas got pink headbands hanging from the rear-view mirrors, but they're just dreaming. What the public sees is pretty much an act. It's really a look-but-don't-touch show, and I'm gonna keep it up 'til I find what I'm looking for."

"Which is what?"

"A man who loves me with all his heart and all his soul. A man who'll carry the torch through a monsoon and fight off lions and tigers in the jungle for the woman he loves." She cocked her head and looked at him with eyes crackling with mischief. "A man like you, Bobby Gallagher."

ও

Bobby and Shari were making their way through the throng of people at the outdoor party. Everyone was eating and drinking twice as much as they would if they were paying. Bobby said hello to Murray Kravetz, who wore a Channel 9 windbreaker, and couldn't say hello back because his mouth was stuffed with Brazilian *rodizio* sirloin, cooked rare, freshly sliced from a skewer bulging with a bloody chunk of beef the size of cow's hip. Bobby scanned the crowd for his accomplices. There was Goldy, dancing his own version of the rhumba with Gloria Vazquez, a retired clerk at Hialeah's hundred-dollar window. Goldy motioned with his arm, imitating a quarterback throwing the ball, then nodded in the direction of Bayside, a collection of waterfront shops and restaurants. Bobby steered Shari that way in hopes of finding Craig and Christine.

They worked their way down the path, which was lighted with flaming torches and crowded with partygoers. At a kiosk, Bobby spotted Jose Portilla roasting whole pigs on a rotating spit. Jose wiped his forehead with a towel and gestured down the same path. Another sighting. They headed that way, passing Nightlife Jackson, who moved at the center of a chirping, cooing flock of South Beach models in mini-skirts and hot pants, some of the young women taller than the defensive back, at least in their platform shoes. The park was abuzz with music and laughter and the joy of people being just where they want to be, secure in the knowledge that they are the chosen ones, permitted to guzzle free booze and rub shoulders with those society has deemed celebrities.

"Gallagher!" the voice boomed behind him.

Bobby turned to find Martin Kingsley, surrounded by his entourage, two bodyguards in blue blazers, his PR flack, a couple of front office flunkies, and three Dallas newspaper reporters. "What the hell are you doing here!" Kingsley demanded.

Bobby pointed to the laminated press credentials which hung from a chain around his neck. "I'm a member of the Fourth Estate, which makes me a guest of the league."

"We'll see about that." Maybe it was the glow of the torches, but Kingsley seemed to be turning red as he turned and scowled at Shari. "Young lady, if you value your employment, you will not consort with this man."

"Ah wouldn't dream of consorting with him," she said meekly. "After all, ah barely know him."

Kingsley motioned to one of the bodyguards, a beefy, crew-cut steroid freak whose neck threatened to burst the buttons on his shirt. "This man was fired from the Mustangs organization and is *persona non grata* at league functions," Kingsley said, raising his voice for the benefit of his worshipful entourage. "He's a disbarred lawyer and a known gambler. Get league security to put him under surveillance."

"While you're at it, Crew Cut," Bobby told the bodyguard, "tell them your boss is a known asshole. Have them send a proctologist right over."

Kingsley stood as still as if encased in a block of ice. "What did you say?"

Bobby closed the distance between them and jabbed an index finger under the older man's nose. Crew Cut moved closer and stood with his arms bent at the elbow, knees flexed, bouncing on his toes, glaring at Bobby with eyes hard as little black buttons.

"Martin, you're not in Dallas," Bobby said, "and I've got news for you. You'll never get your hands on him. I won't let you twist him into a clone of your sick self."

Kingsley's laugh was as cruel as a land mine. "You lost the case just like you've lost everything else! You don't know how to play hardball. You were born a loser and you'll die a loser. You should have taken my offer. You should have given me Scott and gotten your life back."

"He *is* my life, you arrogant son-of-a-bitch!"

"Then you're a dead man," Kingsley said, spitting out the words like poisonous seeds, "because I'm taking him away from you."

Bobby felt the rage in the pit of his stomach, hot and deep as a stab wound. His next movement was not volitional and he was scarcely aware of doing it. It was just a reflex, a drawing back of the arm, the balling of the fist, the pivot of the hip, the snap as his fist shot forward. The punch had too much loop to it, and Crew Cut, graceful as a tiger, took a step between them, deflected Bobby's fist with his forearm, then buried a short right hook into Bobby's gut.

A burst of air exploded from Bobby's mouth before he felt the pain. He dropped to one knee, gasping for breath that wouldn't come, feeling his stomach heave, threatening to hurl hor d'oeuvres all over his loafers. He heard Shari scream, a first rate, girly-girl horror flick scream. Through a cloud of pain, he was aware of the big man looming above him. Bobby's lips felt fat as sausages as tried to say something, but he had no air behind it. Then, he made a gurgling sound and out came, "Fuck you, Tarzan."

Suddenly, the man leaned down and ferociously boxed his ears with two open palms. The thunderclap rang into the depths of Bobby's brain, his skull pealing like a bell struck by a sledgehammer. He sprawled to the ground, fireworks lighting up his closed eyelids, pain surging down his spine. He felt as if he were drowning in turbulent waves, unable to move his limbs.

"Should I punch his lights out, Mr. Kingsley?" the man said, the words echoing faintly in some distant metal drum.

"No! Don't touch him!"

A woman's voice.

But not Shari. The voice was filled with anxiety and concern. How long had it been since he'd heard that in any woman's voice?

"Daddy! Tell him to stop! Now."

Christine!

"All right," Kingsley said. "That's enough, Kyle." He turned toward his daughter. "He attacked me, Christine. I could have him prosecuted for assault."

Suddenly, Bobby was aware of the scent of jasmine. Christine was crouched on the ground next to him, appearing from the dark night like an angel of mercy. She held one of his hands, then brushed the hair off his forehead and placed a palm to his cheek. Tears brimmed in her eyes, and she asked if he was all right. He could barely hear her through the chapel bells ringing in his ears, which seemed to grow louder by the second.

"I'm fine. First rate. Tip top." From her facial reaction, he realized he was shouting. He also realized he was lying as his head throbbed with every heartbeat. She said something to him, but he couldn't catch it. She seemed to repeat it, but again, he couldn't hear.

A moment later, Bobby was aware of being helped to his feet by a pair of strong hands. He turned to see Craig Stringer wearing a cowboy hat and a shit-eating grin. Stringer said something, too. It could have been, "You okay, pardner?" or "Your ocelot pooped" for all Bobby knew. He heard a mush of voices as if a tape recording were playing too slowly. Several feet away, Christine was wagging her finger at her father. Off to one side, Craig was talking to Shari. She said something that made the quarterback smile. He said something that made her laugh. Bobby wished he could hear them.

Now, Kingsley had his hands on Christine's shoulders, a real father-to-daughter Norman Rockwell pose, but she was shaking her head, not buying whatever he was selling.

That's my Chrissy. You're too smart not to wise up to that phony.

He could still feel the warmth of her hand against his cheek. Maybe if Crew Cut would stomp his head, he'd get a kiss from his ex-wife. He began to pick up snatches of words and phrases as the pealing bells began to subside. Christine had convinced her father to leave before the TV cameras showed up. She'd get Bobby out of there and smooth things over. He gave his daughter a forced smile and left, taking his entourage with him.

Christine returned to his side. "I'm sorry, Bobby. I'm sorry for what happened in court today and I'm sorry for this. Do you need a doctor?"

Great. He could hear again. "Nah, he just knocked the wind out of me with a sucker punch, then hit me when I was down. In a fair fight, I could've—"

"Gotten killed," she said. "Look, we should talk. Do you want to come back to my hotel?"

Only as much as I want to breathe.

Bobby's eyes flicked toward Stringer who was regaling Shari with one of his tales of last-minute heroics.

"Craig's got curfew tonight," Christine said. "He's got to get back."

Perfect. He couldn't have planned it any better, though if he had, he would have omitted the five-Tylenol headache.

"Great," he said, then turned to the pride of Galveston, Texas. "Shari, can you fend for yourself tonight?"

"Sure, sugar," she cooed. "Ah been off and on since I was fifteen."

"Nobody in football should be called a genius. A genius is a guy like Norman Einstein."
—Joe Theismann, TV commentator and former NFL quarterback

"It isn't like I came down from Mount Sinai with the tabloids."
—Ron Meyer, former Indianapolis Colts head coach

-32-

Happily in Pain

Christine's room at the Fontainebleau had an ocean view, and on this cloudless night, the moon was as full as Bobby's heart. Moonbeams streaked across the black water, paving a shiny path from the hard-packed sand along the beach, through the gentle shore break to the endless horizon. The wind plucked at the curtains covering the sliding screen to the balcony. Bobby looked out at the shimmering water, tasted the scent of the sea breeze, and smiled at his good fortune.

Hit me again, Crew Cut. Hell, punch out my lights every day at high noon if it'll get me between Chrissy's sheets.

Bobby was propped up on two pillows in the king-size bed watching Christine fluttering at the vanity. She was rummaging through a pink cosmetics case, looking for aspirin, making feminine sounds, asking what she could do to ease his pain.

You could crawl into bed with me.

"I think I should just rest here a while," he said.

"You don't have double vision, do you? You could have a detached retina. Do you want an ice pack? And what about your neck and spine?"

She spoke rapidly, as if she were an ER nurse running through her triage checklist.

"It's just a headache," he said, trying to sound brave, as if it hurt like hell, which it did, but that he was man enough to bear it, which was problematic.

"What kind of headache? Is it a sharp pain or a dull, thudding pain?"

Christine was always more of a detail person than he was.

"It's like the cast of 'Stomp' is rehearsing in my cerebellum."

"Are you sure you don't want a doctor?"

"I'm fine," he said, wincing in a cheap ploy for sympathy. "Thanks Chrissy. It means a lot to me that you care."

"Of course I care! I never stopped caring. I just stopped being able to live with you."

She found the aspirin, then knelt in front of the mini-bar, opening it with a key. Her blond hair was swept straight back off her forehead and held with a barrette. She was wearing a black silk wrap dress tied at the waist and trimmed in white. The dress stopped several inches above the knee. Bobby watched her movements, the flex of the muscles in her calves, the slope of her neck, as she craned her head to see inside the bar, the delicate motion of her hands. He could watch all night.

"Apple juice or orange juice?" she asked.

"How about some Jack Daniels juice?"

She brought him a handful of aspirin, a glass filled with ice, and a miniature bottle filled with the luminous amber sour mash whiskey. Sitting on the edge of the bed, she poured the liquor over the ice, then motioned for Bobby to open his mouth. Daintily, she placed three aspirin on his tongue and handed him the glass.

He wanted to kiss her hand, to suck her fingertips, to gobble her up, but restraining himself, he sipped at the Jack Daniels, tossed his head back, and swallowed the pills. He could scarcely believe this was happening. How long had it been since he'd been alone with her?

He had dreamed of moments like this. Okay, not exactly like this, the dreams not including his getting mugged as a prerequisite to landing in her bed.

They sat silently a moment, then Christine ran a hand through his shaggy hair. "I sometimes forget what a devilishly handsome man you are, Bobby Gallagher."

"I never forget how beautiful you are," he said.

Her hand lingered, and she gently caressed his cheek. "I'm

sorry, Bobby. I'm sorry all this happened, but I don't know what I could have done differently."

She swung her legs up onto the bed, then lowered her head onto Bobby's chest. A feeling of warmth spread over him. The pain in his head had become bearable. The ache in his heart had not.

As she nuzzled against his chest and wrapped her arms around him, he stroked her hair. He could feel her warm breath against his neck. She drew her knees up, tucking into the shape of question mark and curling her body into his. They had often fallen asleep this way, her head on his chest, their bodies intertwined. He felt lightheaded, intoxicated. It was the first act of intimacy between them in more than two years. Was it really happening? Maybe he'd been knocked unconscious. Maybe he was hallucinating. Maybe he was dead.

"Breathe," she said.

"What?"

"You're holding your breath."

He let out a gasp of air, inhaled deeply, then laughed. "I guess I thought if I breathed, I'd wake up and find this was just a dream."

She raised up on an elbow and looked down at him. They were within kissing distance, but neither would make the move.

"I wish we could start over," she said, "but nobody gets that chance."

"I regret having hurt you. I behaved childishly and didn't accomplish anything. Nightlife still got off, and your father hasn't changed a bit."

Outside, the wind was picking up and tore at the flimsy curtains that billowed across the sliding door to the balcony.

"Don't start in on that, please Bobby."

"I won't. But you know it's true. If it hadn't been for your father—"

"Don't blame him!" she said with a harshness that stunned Bobby. Christine hoisted herself up and sat on the edge of the bed, peering at him from the perch of a nurse, not a lover. He knew from the look on her face that he had broken the mood. "Bobby, please. You know where that will lead."

She was right. She was always right. But just the thought of Martin Kingsley invading this private space he shared with Christine, infuriated Bobby.

"I don't know what makes me angrier," Bobby said, clenching his jaw tight, trying to will himself from saying more, from stepping into the quicksand, "that your father drove us apart or that he's trying to take Scott from me."

"I know you love Scott," she said. "I know you wouldn't do anything purposely to hurt him, and I hate to do anything that will limit his time with you, but we have to look out for his best interests."

"*We?* Do you mean you and me or you and your father?"

He didn't like the sound of his own voice, petulant and accusing.

"Daddy only wants what's best for Scott, too."

Bobby tried to control himself. He tried to preserve the moment that was slipping away, but he lost the battle with his own fiery instincts, his knack for self-immolation prevailing over reason.

"Is it best for me to be out of the picture?" He fought against the shrillness in his own voice. "Is it best for me to lose all parental rights?"

"What are you talking about?" Her forehead was wrinkled, her look both puzzled and angry at the same time.

"Your old man tried to buy me off. He offered to pay off a gambling debt of mine if I'd get out of Scott's life."

"I don't believe it, Bobby. Daddy knows I would never want that."

"He doesn't care what you want! He doesn't care what Scott wants! He's a megalomaniac who wants to control everyone around him. He's immoral and corrupt! He's even betting on the Super Bowl."

"How would you know that?"

"Because the bet is with me! It's for five million dollars."

"Oh right! I think your brains got rattled tonight. Where would you get five million dollars? Why would Daddy bet with anybody, much less you?"

"It's a long story," he said.

She bounded off the bed and backed away, putting distance between them. Her look was one of complete puzzlement, as if she didn't even recognize him. "You're lying to me, Bobby. You never did that before, ever."

"I'm not lying, dammit!"

"Daddy might cut some corners, but he wouldn't bet on the games. It's a major violation of league rules that could cost him the franchise."

"When will you learn that your father doesn't follow any rules except his own!" He shouted the words, and the noise jump-started the headache, which had all but faded away.

"You're obsessed with him, Bobby. Your hatred of Daddy has poisoned your mind, made you paranoid."

"Then forget about me! Go run to your pretty-boy quarterback, if you can find him, if he's not shacked up with half the cheerleading squad and sailing the high seas on a Vicodin buzz."

Like so many times in the past, he immediately regretted what he had said. He wanted to cut out his tongue with rusty garden shears.

"You're so spiteful, Bobby! First Daddy and now Craig. Have you fallen so low that you have to attack everyone who's accomplished more than you have?"

"There aren't enough hours in the day or arrows in my quiver to do that," he said, sorrowfully.

"So why attack Craig? You're the one hanging around with Miss Headband. I saw you at Media Day. I don't know what you're up to, but whatever it is, if I know you, you'll get into more trouble."

"I may have been with Shari, but Craig's the one who's chased her from Plano to Tijuana and back."

"Why are you so hateful?"

"Because I hate having lost you. I understand your loyalty to your father, I really do. I've always known that you're blind to his dark side. But Craig Stringer? Why are you with him? Because he needed you to cure his addiction? Because he was upset when his stables burned down?"

"Don't mock his pain, Bobby. He even lost Temptation. God, how he loved her."

"Yeah, yeah, I remember. The only filly he never cheated on."

"You should have seen how he cried when she died."

"He cried because the insurance company wouldn't pay off until his lawyer sued. The tears stopped when Craig pocketed four million in insurance payments."

"Damn you, Bobby! Get out of here!"

"Don't make me leave. My head hurts. I'm dizzy."

"Is that a cheap plot for sympathy?"

"No, it's true." He felt faint and sick to his stomach. He didn't know if it was from being boxed on the ears an hour earlier or falling on his sword just now.

"I don't care! Leave!" She scooped up a glass from a tray on a chest of drawers and hurled it at him. Her aim was high and to the left, and the glass crashed into a framed print of white herons legging it through an Everglades slough. If Craig Stringer threw the football as inaccurately on Sunday, Bobby had a chance to win the bet.

"I'm leaving," Bobby said, hopping out of bed, his temples throbbing. "But someday, you'll see I'm right. I've been right about everything."

"Sure I've got one. It's a perfect 20-20."
—Duane Thomas, former Dallas Cowboys running back, when asked about his IQ

-33-

All Life is Timing

Friday, February 3

Craig Stringer backpedaled while scanning the field in front of him. His right hand cocked behind his ear, he whipped the arm forward. The ball rocketed toward the sidelines, an apparently errant pass. Suddenly, Nightlife Jackson who had been streaking upfield from his wide receiver position, planted a foot in the turf and cut hard toward the sidelines without losing any of his sprinter's speed. He turned his body back toward the quarterback and raised his arms and the ball was there in a tight spiral, settling into his hands. He had run to the spot where the ball was supposed to be, had cut and turned at the correct millisecond in time, and there it was. Craig Stringer had thrown the perfect pass at the precise moment to the exact spot.

"Timing!" boomed Martin Kingsley. "All life is timing."

"And practice," Coach Chet Krause added. "We've run that play about a thousand times since two-a-days in August."

Several reporters stood around the sidelines, searching for news angles, as the Mustangs went about their drills. Kingsley had declared the first thirty minutes of practice open to the press. Then, the pesky reporters would be shooed away, and the team would work on new plays and formations. At the moment, Kingsley was a happy man. He was on the verge of his greatest triumph. He could feel the Commissioner's Trophy in his hands, could imagine himself being doused with champagne in the locker room, being interviewed live, his face appearing in hundreds of millions of homes around the world, the President calling to congratulate him. The victory would clean up several other loose ends. He'd win the bet, pay off that maniac Tyler, and go home a hero, taking Scott along. Christine would marry Craig Stringer and would forget all about her ex-husband. By the end of the game on Sunday, Gallagher would be a broken man. No career, no wife, no child.

Busted, disgusted, and can't be trusted.

Kingsley still hadn't decided whether to let LaBarca use him as chum on a deep-sea fishing trip. Maybe just a thorough thrashing to whip the piss and vinegar out of him would do. Revenge is a sweet meat, indeed.

He'd spotted Gallagher earlier, hanging out with Murray Kravetz, the local sportscaster with the bad toupee. At first, it aggravated Kingsley that his ex-son-in-law was here, but on second thought, to hell with it. Let the prick see the Mustangs juggernaut up close. Let him get trampled in the hooves of the stampede.

On the field, the offense continued to work on its passing game. Craig Stringer hit the tight end over the middle after pumping once as if he were throwing long. On the next play, he went deep, hitting Jackson in mid-stride for a thirty-yard gain.

"Stringer looks sharp," one of the reporters said.

"Sharp?" Kingsley replied. "Hell, he's a saber honed to a fine edge. He's a polished diamond, a laser beam. I'd bet you he gets three hundred yards passing, at least, but the Commissioner won't let me bet."

The reporters chuckled. Kingsley had seen Stringer in the locker room, and his future-son-law hadn't looked so good up close. Red-rimmed eyes and a leaden look as if he'd been up all night. Kingsley just hoped he wasn't popping pills again. But the QB was practicing great all week, and today, he was drilling the passes through defenders' arms outstretched arms right into the receivers' hands.

"How about a prediction?" someone else asked.

"I'd tell you what I think, but then Denver would be putting the clippings up on the locker room wall. I learned a long time ago to save my breath for breathing and not to put my jaw in a sling because I was apt to step on it."

"What about reports that Skarcynski has a sore arm?"

"I don't know anything about it," Kingsley said, shrugging. What else could he say?

He doesn't have a sore arm. He's so scared shitless, his asshole puckers up when he throws the ball.

"We want to beat their best with our best," Kingsley said, trying to sound sincere. "I'm sure when that whistle blows, Skarcynski will forget all about what ails him. Do you remember the time Jack Youngblood played with a broken leg? Just taped a couple of aspirin to it and played a whale of a game."

He was on a roll, basking in the light of a tropical winter day. Everything he had worked so hard to accomplish was about to come to fruition.

❧

You got them? You got them on video?" Bobby couldn't believe it was true. His night had been such a disaster. Did Shari Blossom rescue him? "What'd you do, Murray, hide in the closet?"

"Not exactly," Murray Kravetz said. "I was on the balcony most of the night. A triple feature fuckfest with two intermissions."

Bobby's heart was hammering like a hummingbird's. This could be what he needed. Even sleepless, Craig Stringer was a helluva quarterback. But how would he be after Christine lowered the boom? Bobby couldn't wait to show her the tape and prove he'd been right.

Just look at your sensitive, horse-loving Casanova now.

There's no way she'd tolerate the bum's infidelity. She'd toss the ring back at him, and he'd see his meal ticket float away. A two-bagger, a way to foul up the Mustangs and get Christine back, too.

"How did you get it? Did they leave the lights on?" Bobby asked.

"Nah. Stringer made her turn out the lights."

"Do you have a low light camera?" Suddenly, he was worried. Murray was not adept at getting his facts straight or doing his homework. If he had been, he wouldn't be stuck on the weekend slot at a local station for twenty years.

"Hey, this ain't the CIA," Kravetz said, self-consciously adjusting his toupee. He wore a Madras sport jacket that went out of fashion long before several of the Mustangs were born and he kept an unlit cigar in his mouth. "I was lucky to have one of the station's camera's overnight. The tape's a little dark. To tell the truth, it's very dark, but you can tell there's some serious screwing going on, I mean, you can hear Stringer shouting "Hallelujah" and Shari says his name, but the video looks like a couple of black cats at the bottom of a coal mine."

"I've got to see it," Bobby said.

Okay, so maybe Kravetz wouldn't get the Oscar for best cinematography. But with the audio—Shari and Stringer had distinctive accents—Christine would get the drift.

℮/૩

Practice was over, and the players were giving impromptu interviews, so the press room was empty when Bobby tried to hustle Christine inside.

She pulled away from him. "What do you want?"

He figured he had five minutes to convince her, five minutes to change his life. "Bear with me, Chrissy, please. There's something you've got to see."

She regarded him suspiciously. "What is it?"

She was wearing a long, A-line dark skirt that emphasized her height and a short-sleeve jersey. Her Super Bowl credentials hung around her neck, competing for space with a simple strand of white pearls. He grabbed her by the elbow and guided her toward an editing booth.

"Don't pull me," she said, twisting out of his grasp. "What's your big hurry?"

"You've got to see this now. Our future depends on it."

"Our future is in the past," she said.

"I refuse to lose you to that phony, Bible-quoting bull slinger."

"You lost me all by yourself with no help from Craig or anyone else."

Bobby refused to let her resistance discourage him. He guided her into a small editing booth with two monitors and a control panel with a jumble of wires. He popped a video cassette into a slot, pushed a button and waited. A sizzle of static criss-crossed on of the monitors, which then went to black and then color bars. Then Murray Kravetz' TV baritone could be heard in a whisper. "The place, a balcony of the Fontainebleau, the date, February 2, the event, the Super Bowl of Fornication. Now, let's get up close and personal with our contestants."

"Bobby, what is this?" Christine protested. "Did you drag me in here to see some stupid porno film?"

In that moment, the screen came to life with a blurry creaminess. A second later, a woman's naked body was visible from the waist down.

"That's Shari Blossom," Bobby said.

"Really?" Christine asked, archly. "How would you know?"

"Aha," Kravetz whispered on the tape as Shari's tapered blonde bush filled the screen. "Now here's a commercial for Gillette that could really sell some shaving cream."

"Bobby, this is disgusting!" Christine said. "You're acting like a college sophomore."

"Hold on. This is important."

"Why? How?"

"As we say in the law, 'I'll tie it up, Your Honor.'"

The audio track rumbled as Shari opened the sliding glass door to the balcony. "There we are hon," she cooed to someone in the room. "Just feel that salt air. Ain't it refreshing?"

She turned and twirled her pink headband around her hand, directly in front of the camera, then headed toward the bed, pausing a second to give a little butt wiggle.

"Oh, for God's sake," Christine muttered.

Okay, okay, so Shari isn't Meryl Streep.

A man's bare legs flashed across the screen in the background, then disappeared. "Shari, turn out the lights," said the faraway male voice.

"There!" Bobby shouted. "Did you hear that?"

"Yes. So what?"

"Did you recognize the voice?"

"No."

Bobby did, or thought he did. Of course, he knew who it was, and that made it easier. But Christine couldn't tell. Maybe the sound was too distant and was competing with the slap of shore break and noises from the pool deck bar far below the balcony.

"Aw sugar, doncha wanna see my face when I come?" Shari sang out in a little girl's voice.

"I think I'm going to be sick," Christine said.

"Already seen it," the man said. "Your eyes roll back like you got a concussion from a helmet-to-helmet collision."

"Did you hear that?" Bobby asked, excitedly. "He's talking football."

"So?"

"So, it's Craig Stringer!"

She let out an exasperated sigh. "Bobby, there are eighty thousand football fans in town plus all the players. That's not Craig."

The screen went dark and Shari's voice could be heard, but her pout only imagined. "Oh, all right, party pooper, but I know garage mechanics from Galveston who are more romantic than you."

After that, there were a number of sounds. Bed sheets rustling, bedsprings groaning. A feminine, "Don't stop now!" A masculine throaty growl. A few intermixed shouts and whoopty-dos, and finally silence. Then, after a moment, with his voice rising and falling in the sing-song of a country preacher, the man called out, "The lips of a strange woman drop as a honeycomb, and her mouth is smoother than oil."

"What's that you're saying, sugar?" Shari asked.

"It's from Proverbs. Read your Bible, girl."

"That's Stringer!" Bobby shouted. "You know it is. It's your home-fried, holier-than-thou theology expert who thinks he's the fourth member of the Trinity."

Christine pursed her lips, and her forehead wrinkled in thought.

C'mon Chrissy. You know I'm right.

"Proverbs or adverbs, I still don't get it," Shari said on the tape. "How can I be strange to you, Craig?"

"There! There it is! She called him *Craig!*" Bobby hit the stop button. Now he had the proof. "Do you want to hear it again? It's Craig! Craig the country boy, Craig the preacher, Craig the quarterback, Craig the unfaithful."

He wanted to hug Shari Blossom for coming through. He wanted to scoop Christine up in his arms and comfort her in her time of need. But most of all, he just wanted a reaction from her.

"Let me hear it again," she said, calmly.

Does nothing perturb you? C'mon Chrissy, show some emotion.

He rewound the tape several seconds and played it again. Christine closed her eyes and listened to that voice, the voice that must have whispered endearments into her ear. What must she be feeling? Shame? Anger? Despair?

I'm here for you, Chrissy. I've always been here and I always will be.

For a moment, Bobby thought he had her. For a moment, her eyes flickered with doubt about her fiancee. But we all are capable of repressing what we fear is true, he knew. We are all capable of seeing what we want to see. Her eyes flared to life like golden tigers. "Bobby, you're despicable! My father was right about you all along."

"What are you talking about?"

"Do you think I can't spot a scam? I saw you with Miss Pink Headband at Media Day and then again at the press party. I don't know who you have playing the role of Craig. Maybe it's you with that god-awful impression of a Southern accent, or maybe you recruited one of your low-life friends from the race track, but it's not Craig. He wouldn't have been there. He wouldn't have done that. It isn't him."

"Yes it is. I swear on a stack of that bastard's Bibles."

"Tell me," she said calmly. "Is it possible for you to sink any lower?"

Without waiting for an answer, Christine turned and rushed out of the editing booth.

"No," Bobby said to himself, watching her go. "This is as low as it gets."

"If Jesus were alive, he'd be at the Super Bowl."
—Norman Vincent Peale

"If Jesus were a football player, he'd play fair, he'd play clean, and he'd put the guy across the line on his butt."
—Barry Rice, former football player, Liberty University

-34-

That Voodoo You Do So Well

Murray Kravetz claimed that his second cousin Morty was a ham radio operator with the skills of a computer hacker. "He could jam the signals transmitted from the Dallas bench to Craig Stringer's helmet," Kravetz said excitedly, self-consciously touching his toupee. "Then, we send in our own plays, really screw them up, make 'em quick kick on third and long."

"Nah," Bobby said. "If the play doesn't make sense, Stringer will just call his own or check off at the line of scrimmage. At most, they'll get a delay of game penalty."

"Okay," Murray said, stirring his rye whiskey with an index finger.

"*Stupido!*" fumed Jose Portilla, the chef, shaking his head. "Really dumb, Murray." Dressed in a white cook's smock stained with duck grease, he gobbled honeyed peanuts by the handful, unmindful that his bulging belly was hanging over the tabletop.

"All right, already," Kravetz said. "I'm just trying to help."

"Let him alone, Jose'," Bobby said. He was nursing a Samuel Adams beer and looking glum.

Bobby had brought his cronies into the plan. Figuring that none of them had done an honest day's work in years, he hoped they could come up with some scam that could tip the game toward Denver.

It was a desperate move, he knew, and already he was regretting the idea. For a bunch of losers, the guys were incredibly competitive.

"If you prayed to the warrior god Zarabanga, you would have a better chance of winning," said Philippe Jean-Juste, looking up from a glass of Scotch on the rocks.

"Oh great," Kravetz moaned, "the ex-con witch doctor has an idea."

"I never went to jail," Jean-Juste said. "The deity Olorun protected me."

"Actually, it was Judge Irving Fishbein," Bobby said. "He bought my argument that the First Amendment allowed you to behead goats in Bayfront Park."

They were all crammed into a red Naugahyde booth at The Fourth Estate, conjuring ingenious schemes to torpedo the Mustangs, and with each round of drinks, the plans became more fanciful and less likely. The only perfectly rational person there, Bobby thought, was his son. Scott was unusually quiet, occasionally swiping sips of his father's beer, but mainly focusing on his own burger and fries. Bobby sank further into depression as he listened to one bizarre plan after another.

Who are these guys?

Other than Goldy, a successful bookie who had never filed a tax return and kept his mattresses stuffed with cash instead of springs, they were born losers, the gang that couldn't bet straight. They would be considered half-wits, nitwits, or lunatics by nearly everyone else, he figured.

But they're my best friends. Jeez, maybe my only friends. So what does that make me?

"I could slip Ex-Lax into their food at the Fontainebleau," de la Portilla offered. "I know a *sous chef* who would let me in for a small bribe."

"*Oy vey,*" Goldy said.

"You can't be serious," Bobby said.

"I could make them crap their guts out the day of the game," he added.

"Gross," Scott said, chomping on a bacon cheeseburger with onions.

Chagrined, de la Portilla hunched over the table and dipped a tortilla chip into a bowl of salsa.

"You are all lost," Philippe Jean-Juste said as he swirled his Scotch, the ice cubes clicking like dice at a craps table. He was a tall, slim black man with a shaved head and the sing-song accent of the islands. He wore an immaculately pressed white linen suit over a black silk shirt open at the collar. Around his neck was a beaded necklace studded with cowrie shells and pennies, the jewelry of a Santeria priest.

"I saw in the paper Stringer's leading a team prayer meeting tonight," Kravetz said.

"He's a born-again hypocrite," Bobby said.

"I will disarm his Eleda, his guardian spirit," Jean-Juste said, squeezing his eyes closed, as if communicating with the gods. "I will place a spell on him that will cross his eyes and strike him dumb."

"Why not just make him color blind?" Bobby suggested. "Maybe he'll throw to the guys in the blue jerseys."

"The only curse I know is in Yiddish," Goldy said. "*Zoll vaksen tsibiliss in zein pupik!* Onions should grow in your navel."

"If you make light of the gods, the orishas may use their black magic on you," Jean-Juste said. "I am offering my help. Do you want it or not?"

"Of course I want it," Bobby replied.

"Good. Now, this Stringer. Is he a religious man?"

"Yeah, he worships himself," Bobby said.

"The kicker Boom-Boom Guacavera is religious," Scott said. "He's into that voodoo, just like you, Mr. Jean-Juste. He nearly got thrown out of the Fontainebleau for sacrificing a rooster on his balcony."

"It's not voodoo," Jean-Juste said, offended. "I practice Santeria and make offerings to Olorun and his orishas, his emissaries to mankind."

"You leave cakes on the courthouse steps is what you do," Kravetz said.

"The cake sweetens a judge's disposition when I am unfairly brought before the court.. A dead lizard with its mouth tied shut will silence an unfriendly witness. It is all quite logical when you think about it."

"This is more complicated," Bobby said. "We need Boom Boom to miss his field goals."

"I am also proficient in the witchcraft of Palo Myombe. So, if you want a magic spell, a nsarandas curse, just tell me."

"Let's forget the curses," Bobby said. "I'll just take a good 20 knot crosswind when Boom Boom lines up to kick."

"I could do that," Jean-Juste said, but Bobby just waved for the check and got up to leave.

-35-

Pre-Game Jitters

"Jeez Dad, you can throw better than him," Scott said, watching Mike Skarcynski bounce a pass to the tight end.

"Your Mom can throw better than that," Bobby replied. "Hey Murray, what gives?"

Murray Kravetz lowered his voice into an unintentional parody of a color announcer. "Looks like pre-game jitters to me, Bobby."

"That's so Captain Obvious," Scott said.

"Plus he's gripping the ball too tight, hanging on too long," Kravetz continued in his basso profundo tones. "Aiming, instead of throwing."

"Thank you, Brent Musberger," Bobby said.

They were at Denver's' practice, courtesy of Murray Kravetz. Scott knelt on one knee and aimed his Nikon with the long lens at the quarterback. A photographer's press pass, procured of Murray, dangled from his neck. Bobby listened to the *click-click-click* as Scott snapped off several shots. On the field, two assistant coaches clapped their hands and blew whistles.

"Maybe we can analyze Skar's throwing motion and help the dude," Scott offered.

Bobby wondered what else could go wrong. Denver's veteran quarterback looked like as skittish as one of Craig Stringer's spindly-legged foals. Even though it was a no-contact drill, Skarcynski had a case of the happy feet, stutter-stepping before releasing the ball, throwing off the wrong foot.

"His fundamentals are all out of whack," Bobby said, dejectedly. "His footwork is messed up, there's a hitch in his throwing motion, and his timing with his receivers is way off."

"Just nerves," Kravetz said, hopefully. "He'll settle down."

On the opposite sideline, Denver head coach Harry Crenshaw shook his head disgustedly while huddling with his offensive coordinator.

It was a glorious South Florida day with a soft breeze from the ocean, a deep azure sky with puffy white clouds casting shadows as they scudded across the field. The humidity had fallen, and the colors—the green grass, white yard lines, blue practice jerseys— were as clear as fresh-cut flowers. It was a day to luxuriate in the sheer act of being alive, of breathing in the sweet air...but Bobby was as melancholy as autumn waiting for the winter snow.

"Something's wrong," Bobby said as the trio—sportscaster, bookmaker, and son—moved out of the knot of reporters and across the practice field. "Skar's been in the league half a dozen years. No way he should be feeling that kind of pressure."

"It's his first Super Bowl," Scott said. "He's stoked to the max. Maybe he'll settle down."

"I don't know," Bobby said, feeling powerless. "What good will it do if we foul up Dallas but Denver can't score?"

No one answered. Scott snapped off a few more photos, and Kravetz scratched some notes on his pad. This would be the last Denver practice open to the media, and they wanted to check on their team, which at the moment appeared incapable of beating Slippery Rock State.

Bobby had considered stealing the Mustangs' playbook and delivering it to Denver's coaches but had rejected the idea. Denver had tapes of all the Mustangs' sixteen regular season games plus the playoffs, so there was nothing new to be gathered. Besides, he doubted that Harry Crenshaw, the dean of the league's coaches, would even accept the tainted gift. It would have been too much like cheating. When Bobby stopped to think about it, he felt the sharp pangs of a guilty conscience.

I'm trying to fix the Big Dance, tampering with Americana.

If he succeeded, it would rank up there—or down there—with

the most egregious sports sins of the century. Like the Black Sox scandal or point shaving in college basketball.

Say it ain't so, Bobby.

He could rationalize it. Martin Kingsley was a crook who didn't deserve to win.

But who in the name of Vince Lombardi appointed me the sport's avenging angel?

No one. It wasn't some universal good he sought. No, to be truthful about it, he wasn't corrupting the country's biggest sports event for some notions of higher justice. He was doing it to save his own skin and to protect Scott from the tentacles of the boy's avaricious grandfather. He would do anything for Scott. He would do anything to win...which, upon reflection, was a sobering thought.

So just what is the difference between Martin Kingsley and me?

☙

Crossing the field, Bobby paused to watch the long snapper rocket hard spirals between his legs to the holder, who spun the ball around and held it at the proper angle for the field goal kicker to blast a long one through the uprights. The least appreciated play in football did not escape Bobby's notice. Like so much of life, perfection came from precise repetition and hard work.

The snap, the hold, the kick.

Each should be identical to the one before and the one after, as alike as sparrows perched on a line.

"At least the kicking game looks solid," Bobby said.

"It's easy when there's no rush coming," Kravetz replied.

"Yeah," Bobby agreed. "That's why it's so strange that Skarcynski can't hit the broad side of a barn. They're playing touch out there. What's gonna happen in the game?"

"Hey Dad," Scott said, "isn't that Mr. LaBarca?"

Bobby looked into the lower stands. Dressed in a warm-up suit was a stocky man in sunglasses. Two other men in sport coats with open-collared shirts flanked him.

"I don't know," Bobby said, squinting into the sun. "I can't see him from here."

Scott raised the Nikon with the telephoto lens and peered through the viewfinder. "It's him, Dad. Plus that dweebis Dino Fornecchio and someone else I've never seen."

"What the hell's LaBarca doing here?" Bobby asked.

"Maybe checking on his investment," Kravetz said. "What do you think, Scott?"

The boy didn't answer. Instead, he steadied the camera and pressed the button, and Bobby heard the *click-click-click* over the shouts from the field.

ℒ⃝

Goldy bit into his sandwich, his false teeth crunching through the onion, chopped liver squishing out of the garlic-studded bagel. "The Schlemiel," he said, pointing at the image in viewfinder of Scott's digital Nikon.

"That's his name?" Bobby asked, confused. They were sitting in a booth at Goldy's favorite deli. For a guy with five million dollars on the line, Goldy Goldberg seemed remarkably calm. But the old man looked ancient tonight and more fragile than Bobby had remembered. The folds of skin at his neck were gray as toadstools, and the seersucker suit hung loose and baggy on his wire hanger shoulders.

"The guy in the picture. Shecky Slutsky, a bookmaker from Kansas City," Goldy said. "They call him 'The Schlemiel.'"

"What's he have to do with LaBarca?"

"Wrong question, *boychik*," Goldy said. "What's he have to do with Skarcynski?"

Bobby signaled the waitress for a cup of coffee. "I don't know, what?"

"Slutsky's cousin Izzy Berg is a bookie in Atlanta. Now, he's a real *schlemiel* or maybe even a *shlimazel or shmegegge*. Instead of being happy to balance the books and live off the vig, he takes positions."

"Like a bartender who's an alcoholic," Bobby said.

Goldy nodded and licked chopped liver from his fingers. "Izzy Berg lays heavy wood on glamour teams, always bets the home team on Monday nights regardless of trends, bets against the Super Bowl champ the first month of the next season, all the cliche bets that can go wrong and usually do."

"So?" Bobby asked. The waitress poured Bobby a cup of coffee and he wrapped both hands around it but made no effort to take a sip.

"Izzy is the bookie who took Skarcynski's bets when he played for the Falcons. The Commish gave Skar a private reprimand and that was the last anybody heard of it."

"I don't get it. What's that have..." He stopped himself, because he did get it. It took a moment, just like the old Lincoln, which picked up speed several seconds after hitting the accelerator. "Izzy lays off bets with the Schlemiel, who's hanging out with LaBarca who's at Denver practice with that ape Fornecchio. They're showing muscle to Skarcynski. Oh, jeez, don't tell me Skar's betting again, and they've gotten to him."

"Who knows? But *boychik*, you better find out."

Bobby sat there, brooding like a forlorn ghost. "I'm sorry, Goldy. It's your money that's up. I'm sorry I did this to you."

"You didn't do nothing to me. Hey, I been around a long time. Remember in '72 when the Dolphins won the Super Bowl?"

"How can I forget? They went 17-0."

"No, they went 14-3 against the spread, which is what counts. With all the hometown money coming in on the fish, I couldn't balance the books. I lost my shirt and my Bermuda shorts, too. But I came back. With the vig, a smart, cautious bookie can't lose. I'm a rich man, Bobby, so don't worry about me."

"But Goldy, I—"

"Feh!" Goldy said, hushing him. "All right, it don't look so good, but that ball's not round. It bounces funny sometimes. Now, from what I hear, you got enough problems with your ex, so you worry about that. Take care of Scott. He's a good kid. Don't lose him, Bobby."

The two men sat in silence a moment, huddled morosely in the booth. Bobby was spent, his heart a cinder within a fire that consumed him. Not only was he bringing an avalanche down upon himself, but upon those he cared about as well.

If I'd gotten a regular job, maybe they couldn't have taken Scott from me. If I hadn't turned to my old friend, I wouldn't be costing him a fortune.

"Goldy, I love you like a father."

"You're a good kid, too," Goldy said.

On the drive back across the causeway to the mainland, Bobby squinted into the bloody fireball of the sunset dipping into the Everglades to the west. Behind him, a slice of moon was rising over the ocean. Why, he wondered, did that luminous sliver of pearly white remind him of the blade of a scythe?

"I believe in America, the flag, freedom and the fact that people have had to die over the years so that we can do what we're doing right now."
—Kevin Greene, Pittsburgh Steelers linebacker at Super Bowl XXX

-36-

Room Service

It cost Bobby a hundred bucks to get Skarcynski's room number from the bell captain. Bobby waited in the lobby until just after the midnight curfew, took the elevator to the ninth floor, and stood in front of the door for a moment, planning what he would say. First, he'd flick open the leather wallet, flash the phony FBI badge, and scowl like a parson.

"Agent Mahoney here, we had reports of players gambling on the Super Bowl."

Or something like that.

He'd put the fear of the feds into the quarterback and hope it cut deeper than fear of Vinnie LaBarca. He'd get Skar to fess up and convince him that the only way to beat the guys extorting him was to beat Dallas. He'd give a pep talk that would make Knute Rockne blush.

"Show them you can't intimidate Mike Skarcynski. Besides, what are they gonna do? Tell the commissioner you placed a few bets. You'll be the straight arrow who stood up and refused to dump the Super Bowl. You'll be a hero."

He leaned close to the door and heard the faint sound of the television. Taking a deep breath, he rapped three times, hard enough to sting his knuckles.

"Yeah?" came a voice inside the room.

"Special Agent Mahoney, Federal Bureau of Investigation."

He heard the chain rattle, then the door swung open, and Bobby was staring into the sullen face of Dino Fornecchio. "Mahoney baloney," he said, his voice as friendly as the crepe on a coffin.

"What the fuck are you doing here?"

The open wallet still stuck in his hand, Bobby was speechless. Fornecchio tore the fake ID away, glanced at it, then barked out the laugh of a Doberman pinscher. "Scott G. Mahoney, F.B.I.?" Fornecchio's pock-marked face creased into a cadaverous smile that revealed small pointed teeth, sharp as stalactites. He was more wiry than muscular, but his long arms were thick and bony at the wrists. His entire being exuded malice and danger. "Uh-oh, I'm in trouble now," Fornecchio said. "Elliot Fucking Ness is here."

Terror gripped Bobby. He felt a sweat break out on his face. "Uh, sorry, I must have the wrong room."

"You got the wrong fucking city, dickhead! You got the wrong fucking planet."

"Who is it?" a male voice asked from somewhere inside.

"It ain't nobody, Skar," Fornecchio said.

In the next instant, he tossed the ID back into Bobby's face. As Bobby blinked and tried to catch it, Fornecchio grabbed him by the collar and dragged him into the room, letting the door slam behind them. Then, the sinews of his neck standing out like the cords of a block and tackle, he banged Bobby's head against the wall as if hammering nails—*whap, whap, whap*—rattling a framed Winslow Homer print of swaying palms on a Caribbean island.

"You ain't nobody, are you bookie?" Fornecchio hissed in Bobby's face, his breath smelling of cigarettes and pepperoni.

"No," Bobby agreed. "I used to be somebody, at least I thought I was." Pain rang through his skull like thunderclaps. The fear weighed on him like a marble tombstone.

Fornecchio loosened his grip slightly but kept Bobby pinned against the wall, their noses nearly touching. "So what the fuck is a nobody like you doing here impersonating a federal officer?"

Out of the corner of his eye, Bobby saw Skarcynski. The quarterback was wearing shorts and a T-shirt and eating a slice of pizza.

Thank God. With a witness here, he won't...

"Skar, go take a dump," Fornecchio ordered. "You don't wanna see this."

"Whatever," the quarterback said and disappeared into the bathroom, carrying the pizza carton with him.

"I just wanted an autograph for my kid," Bobby said.

How lame! C'mon, think your way out of this.

"Great, maybe I'll get Skar to autograph your cast when I'm through with you." Fornecchio showed a smile like the blade of a serrated knife, then slammed a knee into Bobby's groin. Bobby doubled over, his hands folded over his crotch. Electric pain shot through his body. Sparks flashed behind his eyelids. Tears welled, then flowed uncontrollably. His stomach heaved, and he was nauseous.

"All right," he whispered between sobs. "I'll just leave."

"Sure you will. The only question is whether you go down the garbage chute or over the balcony. Get up!"

Bobby struggled to straighten up, but before he could reach his full height, Fornecchio grabbed him again by the shirt collar and dragged him deeper into the hotel room. "You still didn't answer my question, bookie. What the hell are you doing here?"

Bobby remained silent, and Fornecchio wrapped a hand around his throat and squeezed. Bobby gagged and croaked out a sound.

"What'd you say, shyster?" Fornecchio asked, loosening his grip.

"I can't answer if you're choking me," Bobby said.

Thinking won't work. Look for an opening and...

"I know what you're doing," the punk said. "You're snooping around after your bet, aren't you? I saw you at practice the other day. You're shitting razor blades about Skarcynski."

"Yeah, you're right."

"Too late, bookie. You bet on the wrong horse, and this race is over."

"Look Dino, I want you to tell LaBarca something for me."

Buy time, now. Get your wind.

"I ain't your messenger."

"No, please. It's important."

"He don't want to hear nothing from you except the sound of currency as it goes through the counting machine."

"He'll want to hear this."

Fornecchio relaxed a moment, stepped back, and folded his arms over his chest. Bobby had been waiting for the moment. Mustering what little strength he had left, he straightened and fired a left jab. The punch had too little hip and shoulder in it to have the snap Bobby wanted, but it caught a surprised Fornecchio squarely on the nose, which burst like a squashed plum into a fountain of blood.

"Fuck!" Fornecchio yelled, covering his nose with a hand, blood spurting through his fingers. "You broke my fucking nose!"

Bobby brought his hands together, laced his fingers, then swung upward and hammered Fornecchio on the point of the chin. He flew over backwards, bouncing off one wall, careening into the bedside table, then toppling to the floor. He lay there gasping, opening and closing his mouth like a beached snapper, praying for high tide.

Bobby stood over him, his knuckles stinging. "Tell LaBarca he can scare me, but he can't stop me."

Fornecchio didn't reply. Couldn't. He was out cold.

From the bathroom, Bobby heard a flushing sound. "Everything okay out there?" Skarcynski yelled.

Bobby went to the bathroom door, tried the knob, found it locked. "You don't have to do it, Skar. LaBarca's bluffing you. You might as well play your heart out."

"He'll cut my heart out," Skarcynski said through the door. "Now leave me alone."

It wasn't working. LaBarca's creepy associate was babysitting the quarterback, putting him under wraps. He was too scared even to listen.

"Listen to me," Bobby said. "They'll never go to the Commissioner. It will bring too much heat on them. Bookies never rat out on the bettors."

"I can't risk it," Skarcynski said. "Now, get outta here and lemme alone."

On the floor, Fornecchio was stirring, groaning and cursing at the same time, his face gray as lava. On his way out of the room, Bobby reached for the ice bucket, then dumped its contents—cubes and frigid water—on the fallen man.

"Three of my wives were good housekeepers. When we got divorced, they kept the house."
   —Willie Pep, featherweight boxing champion

-37-

Roadkill

Friday, February 3

Two Days Before the Super Bowl

Judge Seymour Gerstein studied the legal documents and twitched his nose, rabbit-like, nearly tossing his rimless glasses overboard. "You filed a motion for rehearing?" he asked, peering over the top of his reading glasses.

"Yes, respectfully Your Honor, I would submit that the Court's prior ruling should be set aside," Bobby said. He employed his bootlicking, lawyer-to-judge tone, in which a clever advocate delivers the message: *"you blew it, asshole"* without offending the court. "It is not in the interests of my son to be shipped off to a boarding school."

"And where is your lawyer?" the judge demanded, shooting a glance at the grandfather clock in the corner of his chambers. Next to him, the court stenographer, an older woman with eyeglasses on a chain, waited for Bobby's answer.

"I've discharged Ms. Suarez," Bobby said. "I'm representing myself."

I've fired her from my life, too.

She'd been calling Bobby, wanting to get together, but he had neither the time nor the inclination. Ever since the night when Christine had nursed his injuries in her hotel room, his thoughts were only of her, and Angelica seemed to know it.

"Do you know why you're fighting this case so hard?" she had asked him.

"Because I want my son."

"Because it's the only way to keep in contact with your ex-wife. It's sick, Bobby, but you don't see it. When will you face the fact that she's gone? She doesn't love you! You'll never get her back."

After Bobby had pulled the sword from his stomach, he told Angelica good night, then burned rubber pulling out of her driveway.

Bobby returned his attention to the judge who was shaking his head unhappily.

"You know the expression about having a fool for a client," Judge Gerstein said.

"Yes, Your Honor, but even a fool could win this case."

Or see which way to rule.

"I've only granted a handful of rehearings in twenty-two years on the bench, so you've got your work cut out for you, Mr. Gallagher."

"I understand, Your Honor." Bobby knew the odds were against him, but this was his only hope. An appeal to the Third District would take a year, and Scott would be long gone. Here was a chance to get the trial judge to overrule himself.

"Very well, then," Judge Gerstein said. "Now, who's this handsome lad?"

Next to Bobby, Scott squirmed in his seat. Bobby had wanted to bring him to the first hearing to demonstrate their closeness, but Angelica told him it might backfire. Judges don't like to put kids in the cross hairs of their parents' big game rifles.

"Your Honor, this is my son, Scott."

"Any objection?" the judge asked, turning to the other side of the table.

"Please allow me to consult with the boy's mother," Jailbreak Jones said, turning to Christine, whose face was tightened up like a spring. Jones wore a beige suit with shoulder piping and a string tie with a silver clasp. Next to him, a stack of poster boards leaned against the table, covered mysteriously with a black cloth.

Bobby stared out the window at the downtown skyline. In a dozen high-rise office buildings, he imagined, lawyers at this very moment were fabricating their evidence, salting their briefs with false accusations, and billing their time at outrageous rates.

"There's no need to put the minor child through this torture." Jones glared at Bobby with the same disapproval he might use for a pedophile kindergarten teacher.

"Scott is a material witness," Bobby said. "I'd like the Court to take his testimony."

Across the table, Christine looked stricken.

"This is a rehearing, not a trial *de novo*. It's completely improper to take evidence." Perched on the edge of his chair like a vulture on a limb, Jones seemed to consider a notion before continuing. Bobby had been a trial lawyer long enough to know that the Biggest Mouth West of the Pecos was changing gears.

"Upon reflection, Your Honor," Jones continued, a smile stretching his thin lips, "we welcome the re-opening of evidence at Mr. Gallagher's request."

Uh-oh. What now?

"We will demonstrate that the father has exposed the minor child to lowlifes, felons and miscreants, to professional gamblers and bookmakers, and that the father himself is a bookmaker." With a wave of a hand, he theatrically swept the black cloth from the stack of poster boards, and held up the first one, a grainy black-and-white photo blown up to gargantuan size. "Exhibit A, Your Honor. The father, the minor child, and a convicted felon mingling in a saloon."

"That's my Uncle Goldy!" Scott piped up, and Bobby hushed him with a gentle hand.

"Your Honor, that's Goldy Goldberg," Bobby said," a lifelong friend. We were in the Oceanside Deli eating dinner."

"I had a Reuben," Scott said.

"Goldy's like a member of the family," Bobby said.

"A crime family!" Jones boomed. "The man has a rap sheet as long as the reins on a forty-mule team. This disbarred lawyer who calls himself a father consorts with criminals in the presence of the minor child."

"I like to hang with Dad," Scott said.

"We have affidavits," Jones said, without taking a breath. "We have files from the county sheriff, the city police, the state Department of Law Enforcement, the FBI..."

What, no CIA?

"The boy would be better off in an orphanage than with this sorry excuse for a father," Jones concluded.

"Bullshit!" Bobby boomed. "That's complete crap, and this flannel-mouthed windbelly knows it."

"Mr. Gallagher!" The judge glared at him, his cheeks reddening. "I won't tolerate that! One more outburst, and I'll hold you in contempt. If that is the kind of language you use in the presence of your son, it's no wonder you're in such trouble today." The judge adjusted the spectacles on the bridge of his nose, straightened in his high-backed leather chair, and nodded toward Jailbreak Jones. "All right, both of you. Talk's cheap. Let's hear some evidence."

കൗ

The rest was dreamlike. Foggy and detached, Bobby felt as if he were floating above the conference table, looking down on the rest of them, listening to the babble. Isn't that what it's like when you have a near-death experience?

Jailbreak Jones droned on, thumping his drums, bellowing with indignation. He introduced his evidence, and the judge *tut-tut-tutted* and looked at Bobby, first with displeasure, then shock, and finally a blistering anger.

Bobby tried to defend himself, but he was in a daze. The voices in the room overlapped, his own words echoing like distant thunder. He seemed paralyzed. He tried to concentrate on what was being said, Jailbreak's voice rising and falling with the cadence of a country preacher, slathering on accusations like butter on biscuits.

Bobby glanced at Christine, whose forehead was knotted, her

eyes filled with pain.

And pity! The same look she'd give a dog run struck down crossing the highway. Is that what I am...roadkill?

౪

When it was over, when they were through hacking away at his limbs like loggers at a tree, the fog began to clear. The judge sat silently a moment, spun around in his chair and stared at the ceiling. In the moment of quiet, Bobby listened to the cough and rattle of the air conditioning and looked outside the window where the black turkey buzzards, ugly as death, floated effortlessly in the updrafts between the downtown skyscrapers.

"I don't take this action lightly," Judge Gerstein said, whirling around to face the litigants and their attorneys. He spoke directly to the stenographer whose fingers banged away at her machine, recording the words for posterity and the appellate court. "I'm going to grant your petition for rehearing, Mr. Gallagher and vacate the prior order, but I'm afraid this is a Pyrrhic victory for you. Based on the evidence submitted, it is the judgment of this court that you are not a fit and proper parent for custody, joint custody, or even liberal visitation. Your actions have had a deleterious impact on the minor child, and if continued—"

"No, they haven't!" Scott called out. "Dad's fun. He teaches me a lot of neat stuff and he needs me. I mean, I need him, too. He's my Dad."

"Young man," the judge said sharply. "Be quiet when an elder speaks. Please look to your mother and grandfather as role models, and not your father."

"Bullshit!" Bobby shouted for the second time that morning.

"You're in contempt, Mr. Gallagher!" the judge fired back. "That will cost you five hundred dollars, and if you repeat it, you'd better have packed your toothbrush in that attache case because you're looking at thirty days in the stockade."

Bobby fought the urge to leap up and pull down the floor-to-ceiling shelves of law books, burying all of them in useless words. Despair howled in his ears like a winter wind. He had lost Scott.

"It is the further judgment of this court," the judge continued, "that Robert Gallagher be stripped of all parental rights, and that full custody and all decisions regarding the minor child shall be forthwith vested with the mother, Christine Kingsley Gallagher. Mr. Gallagher shall be entitled to limited visitation upon a strict schedule to be promulgated by the domestic relations child welfare unit, said visitation to take place only in public facilities such as the courthouse or court liaison offices, and only in the presence of licensed counselors from H.R.S. or the comparable agency in Texas. No overnight visitation will be permitted until such time as Mr. Gallagher demonstrates a

change in attitude, lifestyle, and fitness as a parent. We'll set a report date for further proceedings in six months."

With a bang of his gavel, the judge dismissed them and said good day.

Jailbreak Jones cleared up his files. Christine motioned to Scott to come with her.

The boy looked at his father who nodded, gave him a squeeze on the arm, and let him go.

"I'll be outside," Scott said, hurrying out of chambers.

The judge and stenographer walked out, too, leaving Bobby and Christine alone with the whir of the air conditioning and the ticking of a grandfather clock.

"I'm sorry, Bobby," Christine said. "This isn't what I wanted."

"You could have stopped it. You could have said 'no' to your father."

"This never would have happened if you'd just let Scott go off to boarding school."

"So it's my fault!"

"Yes, it's your damn pigheadedness. It's what led to our breaking up and all of this. You've lost everything, but you blame everybody but yourself."

"And you've won everything. Your father must be very proud.

You've turned out to be just like him."

Bobby grabbed his briefcase and fled.

"When we won the AFL Championship, a lot of people thanked their wives. I'd like to thank all the single girls in New York. They deserve just as much credit."
—Joe Namath before Super Bowl III

-38-

Temptation

Am I interrupting anything?" Christine asked, when Craig Stringer opened the door to his hotel suite.

"Nah. Just watching Sports Center." He was wearing grey shorts, a Mustangs

t-shirt, unlaced Nikes, and somehow managed to look like a teenage boy instead of a pro football player nearing the end of his career.

She entered the living room of the suite, unusually neat and orderly for a man, much less a football player. The large-screen TV was on, and there was Craig, his smile filling the screen, elaborating on reaching the pinnacle, grabbing his dream, and a few other cliches that filled the endless hours of Super Bowl mega-coverage.

"Do you think my hair's too long?" he asked, studying his image on the tube. They both sat on the sofa in front of the TV. Outside the penthouse windows, the blue Atlantic stretched to the horizon.

"Your hair looks fine, Craig."

"Yeah, but maybe I should fly Pepe in from Dallas, get it styled before the game. Afterwards, there'll be a lot of interviews."

"It won't matter if your teammates give you a champagne shower first."

"Good point. Didn't think of that."

"Or if you lose."

"Hey Chris! Don't even joke about that." He turned his attention back to the screen. "After the game, I'll have public appearances all over hell and half of Georgia. You think the Today show has a stylist for the guests?"

It occurred to her then that he hadn't kissed her when she came into the room, and that she hadn't kissed him. She had come straight to the team hotel from the courthouse. He was wrapped up in the televised image of himself, and guilt-stricken, she was swimming through a lake of her own misery.

"Forget about your hair," she said. "I need to talk to you."

"Sure Chris. Fire away." He used the remote to mute the sound but kept his eyes on the screen where he seemed to wink at the camera.

"The judge stripped Bobby of all his rights to Scott," she said. "He can't even visit our son unless it's in a courthouse."

"Great!"

"It's not great! It's terrible."

"Hey, knock, knock. Anybody home? You won! That's what it's all about."

"No it's not. For all his faults, Bobby loves Scott, and Scott needs him."

"What are you all tore up about? Where's that old killer instinct? You can't ease up in the fourth quarter. That's when you roll up the score."

"This isn't a game. All that matters is what's best for Scott."

"You're too soft, Christine. I'm glad the judge cracked down. Now you've got control."

"You sound just like my father."

"Hey, nothing wrong with that. Your Pop's the King."

It hit her then. The man she was engaged to marry was a cheap copy of her father. The realization chilled her heart, parched her soul. Craig Stringer wore his arrogance and insensitivity as proudly as his number seven jersey. Everything in life was a competition, and opponents were to be crushed. Wasn't that Daddy's philosophy? Well, they'd succeeded. They'd crushed Bobby.

With my assistance. What have I done to Bobby and to my son?

"Anyway, I gotta go," Craig said. "Practice in half an hour." He tied the laces on his Nikes, waved and smiled his ESPN smile. "See ya later, Chris. There's some beer in the fridge and jars of cashews in the cupboard."

⁓

Christine sat there, unaware of the passage of time. The TV played silently, an auto race on now. A breeze from the ocean whipped through the open balcony door and rustled the drapes. On this bright sunny day, she felt gray and heavy, thick and sullen. She believed herself to be the perpetrator of a great wrong. She'd inflicted pain on a man she had loved—maybe still loved—and she'd hurt her son in the process.

Though hardly a religious woman, she wondered if she did not deserve some divine retribution. But then, maybe God didn't have time to trifle with misdemeanors.

More time passed, and she discovered that she'd been crying without even realizing it. Finally, she stood and walked to the bathroom. Her makeup was ruined. She splashed cold water on her face, then scrubbed at her skin with hotel soap. She rinsed again, then reached for a towel, her eyes still closed.

What she grabbed felt like a towel, but it was too small. Before she opened her eyes, she knew what it was, and her heart ached with the knowledge. It was as if someone plunged a knife deep inside her, then yanked it up and around like a child's jump rope.

In Texas, she knew, there were many icons. An oil derrick set against a barren landscape, the legendary Alamo, longhorn cattle. There were the pecan trees, the mockingbirds, and the bluebonnets. To the men of Texas there was one more, and she held it now, gripping it fiercely in both hands, trying to tear it in half, but the pink, terrycloth headband – symbol of cheerleader Shari Blossom – held fast.

Bobby never would have done this, she thought. For all his faults—his stubbornness, his self-righteousness—he never would have been unfaithful.

Damn you, Craig Stringer!

He had denied ever being involved with Shari Blossom, even in the past. She should have trusted her instincts. Craig was a born womanizer. Everybody knew it. She had known it but she would change him. What monumental ego! A flood of emotions washed over her, equal doses of anger and humiliation. Did everybody in the organization know about it? Did those boob-heavy cheerleading twits laugh about her behind her back?

Oh Bobby, you were right. Why didn't I listen to you?

She dropped the headband, and trembling with rage, paced through the suite like a tiger in a cage, from the bathroom to the living room to the balcony overlooking the ocean. Feeling feverish, she stood there a moment, letting the breeze cool her. Along the beach, sea birds dipped and whirled, crying like angry children. Christine felt a tear track down her cheek to the corner of her mouth where she tasted its saltiness. After a moment, she came back inside, mustering the courage to walk into the bedroom. Once there, she stared at the king-size bed, crisply made up by housekeeping, a cover of red and pink hibiscus flowers. What acts of betrayal occurred beneath that floral cloak? What lies were told between those sheets?

On the night stand was a framed photo of Craig astride Temptation, his leopard Appaloosa. She'd been a magnificent horse with striped hooves, a beautiful spotted coat, and a pleasant disposition. Christine had loved that horse nearly as much as Craig did. She had cried when Temptation died in the barn fire and cried now, in mourning for the death of something else. Then, incongruously, she laughed. It was Temptation's photograph, not hers, that decorated Craig's bedside. There was something darkly amusing about the revelation that he loved his horse more than he loved her.

Oh, how she had been fooled. Craig had shown such deep sensitivity and vulnerability when Temptation died that Christine was drawn to him in a nurturing mode.. He was an emotional wreck, needy and open to her love.

That's why I fell for you, you big creep.

She studied the photo now. Rider and horse, both mugging for the camera, Craig's smile even more horsey than Temptation's. Maybe she didn't notice it before, but weren't Craig's teeth ridiculously big?

She knew that she was employing a defense mechanism, finding flaws in the man who had just violated her trust, and in so doing, ended their relationship. She didn't need to do that. There was only one flaw in Craig that mattered: he cared only about himself. He satisfied his own pleasures and took whatever he needed from whomever would give it. She felt used and abused. And stupid!

In that moment, she decided she was through with love. Look where it had gotten her so far. A husband who self-destructed before her eyes and a semi-fiancé who wanted to set scoring records on and off the field. Suddenly, she needed to talk about it. She wished she could turn to Bobby, but how could she, after what happened in court today? Alone, adrift, she needed to talk to a man, but no, not Bobby.

☙

Daddy was at practice with Scott, but she would wait for him in the quiet of his hotel suite, five floors above Craig's. Daddy had taught her strength and self-reliance, but there was only so much she could do alone. He would understand.

Her father had given her an extra key to his suite, and as she let herself in, another thought came to her. With the game two days away, Daddy would insist that she put off any explosive scenes with Craig. She imagined what he would say.

"Darling, you can't be upsetting Craig's fragile ego right before The Big Dance."

She had no illusions about her father's reaction to her plight. He would put the game ahead of her feelings because they were, after all, only feelings. They weren't real, like a glistening trophy you can park on the mantle.

But how could she ignore what had happened? How could she

smile and pretend that she loved that fake, that womanizer Craig Stringer, just so he won't be upset and throw into double coverage?

As she closed the door behind her, a sound came from the suite's second bedroom, which had been turned into a study. "Daddy?" she called out.

No answer.

It could be housekeeping, someone tidying up while listening to an iPad to drown out the drudgery of the task.

She headed through the living area, a 1960's sunken room with white leather sofas, an aquarium with tropical fish, and a gas-lit fireplace, useful in case of snow in Miami Beach. A plaque on the wall boasted that Frank Sinatra, Jacqueline Kennedy, and Muhammad Ali had all stayed in the suite, though presumably not at the same time. From this height at the top of the hotel, the ocean, viewed through floor-to-ceiling windows, was a calm sheet of aquamarine.

As she neared the study, she saw a shaft of light under the closed door. "Hello," she called out. "Anyone there?"

She stopped and listened a moment, but there was only the white noise of the air conditioning. Telling herself it was foolish to be alarmed, she turned the knob and opened the door. A man sat at the desk, reading a sheaf of papers, his scarred face hideously lit by a desktop lamp. Calmly, he looked up and nodded, as a priest would to parishioner. "Howdy, Christine," Houston Tyler said. "Why don't you come in and sit for a spell?"

-39-

A Member of the Family

Christine did not sit down. Instead, she walked closer to the desk, hardly believing this was the man she had known nearly all her life. When she was a small child, she thought he was a member of the family. The Tylers were constant guests in the Kingsley home. Her mother played golf with Corrine, and the two men were partners for nearly 20 years until the Texas City refinery fire tore them apart and sent Houston Tyler off to prison.

Her memories of her father's partner were strange and conflicting. There was the broad-shouldered man who laughed uproariously and gave her piggy-back rides in the swimming pool. There was the profane, hard-drinking man who cursed her father in language she'd never before heard. And there was the weeping man who comforted her after her mother died.

But the man sitting in front of her was none of those. His head was shaved and loose folds of skin hung from his goose-slim neck. His skin was the color of warm milk, and when he smiled, a purple scar that ran from cheekbone to scalp slid into the folds of his face. His left eye was chalky white and seemed to look in an entirely different direction than the right. She felt herself staring at his scar.

"Guess I don't look too pretty," he said.

"It isn't that. I just never expected to see you in my father's room. What are you doing here, Mr. Tyler?"

"Hell, Christine, you can call me Ty. You used to call me Uncle Ty, remember?"

"Does my father know you're here?"

"Hell no, and he wouldn't like it one bit. Your old man would like to see me dead."

"I'm sure that's not true. He was very sorry about what happened to you."

Tyler growled his disagreement, the sound of water gurgling down a pipe. "I'll say this for your Daddy, though. He was always a good record keeper. Me, hell I never wrote a memo in my life. Hated meetings and business lunches. I'd just tromp around in the fields and find the oil so your Daddy could dicker over mineral rights and sew up the deals that would make us rich. Or at least make one of us rich."

"Mr. Tyler, what's going on?"

"Here, look at this," he said, holding up a file folder. "Your Daddy carries around some interesting reading material in his briefcase. Player contracts under negotiation, loan extensions, licensing agreements, and then there's—"

"You have no right to be going through his things." She closed the distance between them and snatched the file away. On top was a legal document with "Escrow Agreement" written in fancy script. She hadn't seen it before and had no intention of reading it, but the "party of the second part" caught her attention.

Robert C. Gallagher.

The "party of the first part" was her father.

The escrow agent was her father's bank.

The subject of the escrow was two per cent of the stock in the Dallas Mustangs.

What in the world!

"You still wrinkle your forehead when you're thinking just like you did when you were a little girl," Tyler said. "Well, what do you think about all that legalese? I ain't no Philadelphia lawyer or even a Corpus Christi lawyer, but it seems to me your father's bet the farm on a football game."

Her first thought was that it was a forgery, an elaborate fake. Maybe Houston Tyler brought the document here. Maybe he was setting Daddy up. But she recognized both signatures. What had Bobby told the night he was beaten up at the party?

"Your father doesn't care what you want! He doesn't care what Scott wants! He's a megalomaniac who wants to control everyone around him. He's immoral and corrupt! He's even betting on the Super Bowl."

She had laughed at him and asked how Bobby would know.

"Because the bet is with me! It's for five million dollars."

She had called him a liar. Dismissed everything he had said about her father and Craig. She'd been such a fool. For the second time today, she felt betrayed. First by her fiancé, then by her father. Her throat was constricted, her windpipe tightening up. Her limbs felt stiff and brittle, as if they might shatter like the stems of wineglasses.

"Looks like your Daddy's fixing to win himself five million dollars," Tyler said.

"I don't know anything about it." She wondered what other secrets Daddy and Craig shared,

Oh Bobby, I need you now!

"I'm glad to see that Martin's getting creative, seeing how he owes me the five million dollars that's in the pot. I just wonder what that old fox is gonna due if he loses."

-40-

Run Bobby, Run

The house was simply too quiet.

It had only been hours, but how he missed his son. What would it be like next week, next month, next year?

If there is a next week.

Bobby lay in a hammock strung between a red poinciana tree and a scraggly palm in the backyard of his cottage just off Tigertail in Coconut Grove. It was an old Cracker house made of Dade County pine with a sloping tin roof and a ragged coral rock wall surrounding the property. The mesh hammock was torn in several spots, and Bobby threatened to tumble to the ground like a fish slipping out of a net. He reclined in the darkness, listening to the night birds, sipping his third Samuel Adams, thinking it was time to take action. But what?

The Super Bowl is fixed, but the wrong way. Denver's quarterback is throwing the game!

Even worse, he'd lost his son, who at this very moment, was with his grandfather at a Fox network party. Bobby didn't have a prayer of getting back his law license or Christine. Come Monday, when he couldn't pay Vinnie LaBarca, he was a dead man.

And so he found his plan. A simple one-word plan. Run.

Run Bobby, run.

Pago Pago, Bora Bora, Abu Dhabi. Poetic names of exotic places blew into his head on steady trade winds. Why not go? He'd get word to his son, somehow, once he was safe.

He hoisted himself out of the hammock, tossed the empty beer bottles at an open trash can, hitting one out of three. With the sound of broken glass and his own shattered thoughts still ringing in his ears, he entered the cottage, which would have fit neatly into the garage of his old house in Dallas. Christine's house now.

Christine. Will I ever see you again?

૮╱ა

Bobby headed west on Tamiami Trail, the old two-lane road that cuts through the Everglades. He'd drive to Tampa and get a flight from there. Maybe he was being paranoid, but then again, why risk flying out of Miami and being spotted? With LaBarca's connections, who knows what he might come up with if he started checking the international flights?

But what if LaBarca had him under surveillance? When he pulled the limo out of the gravel driveway just after ten p.m., wasn't there a car at the end of the block that took off after him? And now, staring back into those headlights, isn't it the same car?

He thought about Dino Fornecchio. Wouldn't he love some payback? Bobby knew he'd been lucky in Skarcynski's hotel room. He'd caught Fornecchio off guard. But now, the punk would be ready and armed.

Bobby hit the accelerator, and the old limo whinnied like a spavined nag, backed off, then sped up. The car behind him fell back, picked up speed, closed to within two car lengths, then flicked its high beams.

Oh shit.

Bobby floored it, and the big Lincoln engine seemed to remember its childhood, because it roared to life and in a moment, the speedometer was flicking between eight-five and ninety. Behind him, the other car kept pace. On both sides of the road, canals ran parallel to the pavement, the water black and still in the night. Somewhere beyond the canals, sawgrass towered eight feet high, but on this moonless night, Bobby couldn't see past the reach of his headlights.

The car behind him tooted its horn twice and gave a right turn signal. They wanted him to pull over. No way! He flew past a strand of Brazilian pepper trees, standing sentinel, casting shadows in the glare of his high beams.

Ahead, a lone pair of headlights, appeared, headed eastbound. In a moment, a huge tractor trailer blew by them, the limo shimmying in its wake. Again, it was just the two cars, screaming westward on the old road. Bobby hoped he didn't hit a stray alligator and flip over into the canal.

He squinted against the glare of the high beams in his rear view mirror. Then, suddenly, they were gone. It took a second to realize that the car had pulled into the left lane and was crawling up on him. Were they going to ram him? Were they going to push him into the black water and watch him drown?

He thought of Scott and of Christine. How did he muck up everything?

He shot a look to the left as the car pulled alongside. He expected to see a window come down, a gun barrel come up.

He inadvertently pulled to the right and his wheels slipped onto the berm. He hit the brakes, too hard, and fishtailed, the rear of the limo sideswiping the other car. He spun the steering wheel to the left, over-correcting, fishtailed right, then spun out of control, the limo's tires shrieking on the pavement as it turned one hundred eighty degrees, sliding across the road, crashing sideways into a strand of red mangrove trees. He came to a sudden, hard stop, the limo pointed back toward Miami, as if intent on returning him home. The tangled mangrove roots and limbs, intricate as a spider's web, had broken the slide, though not without caving in the passenger side of the limo.

He took inventory of his body parts. All seemed to be in the right place. Not even a whiplash, but his left shoulder ached where it had banged into the driver's side door. He was just getting out of the limo when the other car pulled to a stop on the other side of the road, angled to throw its high beams in his face. He heard the door slam and then his name called out.

That voice! Out here?

He squinted into the lights and shielded his eyes with a hand. "Is that you?" he asked, hoping.

"It's me," Christine said.

လ

An hour later, he could still feel the warmth of her cheek against his. She had thrown her arms around his neck and hugged him fiercely, her fingers digging deeply into his shoulder blades. He hugged her right back, the tension and fear draining from him.

Now, back in his cottage, suddenly filled with sound and light, they sat on the old sofa of Haitian cotton, remembering, talking, pouring out a flood of feelings.

"I'm sorry for everything," she said. "It's my fault for letting my father run my life and run you out of it."

"No. I mishandled it, Chrissy. I made ultimatums. I didn't give you a choice."

"Is it too late to..."

"No! We can do it."

"You were right, Bobby. You were right about Craig and about my father. You were right that Scott would be better off with you than under Daddy's control. And you right about something else, too."

"What's that?" He looked deep into her green-gold eyes, praying she would say it. His heart was choking. He had loved her when she returned his love, and he had loved her when she didn't. He had loved her through the nights of wine and honey, and he had loved her when pricked by angry thorns. He never stopped loving her and never would.

"What you said to me in Green Bay," she said.

"Something about how cold it was," he replied, pretending he didn't remember, wanting to hear her say it.

"No. You said, 'I still love you, Chrissy, and you still love me.'"

"I know the first half is true," Bobby said.

"It's all true. I repressed what I felt. I let my anger overcome me, but nothing could extinguish what I felt. What I still feel."

Bobby was a jumble of emotions, laughing and crying at the same time, the rain falling and the sun shining, a rainbow of feelings. In this instant, he knew, his life had changed. With Chrissy's love, there was new hope.

He didn't know if she moved toward him, or if he moved toward her, but in a second they were in each other's arms. He felt feverish as if he'd been hit with heatstroke. He kissed her with a hunger and desire that he could scarcely remember he possessed. She kissed him back, greedily, biting at his lower lip. Their hands tore at each other's clothing. He felt a surge of heat moving through him. He wanted to devour her.

Their lovemaking was urgent and laced with torrents of emotion. Chrissy sobbed, her tears dripping on him, as she straddled him from above. As their coupling grew frantic, their bodies joined, an animalistic roar came from deep inside him.

Moments later, as she lay on his chest, listening to the beats of his heart, Bobby said, "You want to try this again, but a little slower this time?"

"Maybe in the morning," she said. "We've got work to do now."

"Work?"

"We've got to figure out how to beat the Mustangs in the Super Bowl," Christine said.

രാ

It was after one a.m. and Christine was sleeping when Bobby, wearing gym shorts and nothing else, walked onto his front porch, carrying a cold Samuel Adams. It was a cool night, and he shivered as he sank into an old chaise lounge with broken straps.

He wanted to think things over. He had told Christine everything, the first six hundred thousand dollar bet with Vinnie LaBarca, how he got middled in Green Bay and lost 1.2 million – now 1.4 million with interest – and then fronting the five-million dollar bet with her father to try and pay off the first bet.

Christine said she wanted to sleep on it, that in the morning she'd have a plan. Just like that. Bobby wasn't skeptical, even for a moment. If anybody could think through a problem—awake or in dream land—it was Chrissy. He sipped at his beer, listened to the cries of a neighborhood mockingbird, a male, calling for its mate. He was at peace.

He saw it then, a car parked down the street two houses away. It had been Chrissy in that spot earlier tonight, but who was this? The vanity light was on, then clicked off. Okay, so someone was in the car. Probably nothing, no reason to be paranoid. He squinted into the darkness but couldn't make out the model.

He stepped down from the porch and started padding barefoot that way. The car's engine turned over and it pulled away from the curb with its lights off, screeched through a U-Turn, and headed toward U.S. 1. It was too dark to make out the driver or read the license plate, but Bobby was close enough to I.D. the car. It was a white Infiniti, just like the one Angelica Suarez owned.

-41-

Cutting the Knot

Saturday, February 4

Day Before the Super Bowl

The screeching of the neighborhood parrots jarred Christine awake. She was disoriented. She was on her side, the warm breath of a man on her neck. It took a moment for her to realize it was Bobby, and they lay there in the spoon-to-spoon position, bodies touching. Sun streaked into the bedroom from an open window. Bobby stirred next to her, his heavy breathing still so familiar even after all the time apart.

So much had happened in the last twenty-four hours. But so much more remained to be done. Was there time? Could they do it? Bobby had made a mess of everything, but she blamed herself for his plight. She should have protected him from her father two years ago. She could have run interference for him, like one of the Mustangs' offensive linemen. Maybe she could still do it, but now, she'd have to run straight over her father.

Christine had fallen asleep weighing the benefits and risks of a dozen different plans. She prayed for one that could rescue Bobby without sinking Daddy. But it wasn't possible. There was a one-man life raft in a sea of sharks, and this time, Bobby would get the rescue line.

"'Morning sweetie," Bobby said, thickly, stretching and opening his eyes.

"Good morning. Do you still own a business suit?"

"Two, trial lawyer sincere blue and funeral director charcoal gray."

"Wear the gray. You'll blend in with all the Gulfstream jet crowd from Ford, Coca-Cola, and Apple."

"What are you talking about?"

"The Commissioner's party. We're going to need to get into the VIP room."

"Do you think we have time to party?" he asked, rolling onto his back and cracking his knuckles over his head.

For an intelligent man, she concluded, Bobby could be such a dolt. She watched a thought slowly cross his face like a wagon train plodding across the old West.

He made a clucking noise with his tongue. "I don't believe it. You want me to go public? "You want me to do what I did in Dallas two years ago?"

"The Commissioner and all the owners will be there," she said. "So will the corporate bigwigs, all the sponsors, the financial backbone of the league. We're talking billions of dollars eating hor d'oeuvres under the palm trees."

"You think they want to hear from me?"

"You can bring it all down. You can destroy everything they've built. If the quarterback of a Super Bowl team is throwing the game and the owner of the other team makes a multi-million dollar bet, the game is corrupt and everything they have is a sham. They'd have to move quickly to clean it up. League security has strong ties to the FBI. They could protect you from LaBarca and your testimony could send him away."

"You make it sound so simple."

"It will be once you tell the Commissioner everything."

"What if I can't get to him?"

"Then you'll go up on the stage, take the mike from Justin Timberlake and tell everything to five thousand of the Commissioner's closest friends."

"I'm serious, Chrissy. What if he doesn't believe me?"

"I've seen the escrow agreement. I'll corroborate your story."

257

Bobby propped himself on an elbow and looked at her with his sad, brown eyes. "You would do that for me? Do you know what that would do to your father?"

"Of course I know. He'll lose the franchise."

Saying it aloud brought it home to her. She had just made a choice, this time with her heart. Love had so many meanings. There was the burst of romantic love. There was the reservoir of love of a mother for her child which, like a deep well, will never run dry. And there is this, the love that comes with a price. To savor it, you must slice the Gordian knot of your entanglements cleanly in two for they cannot be untangled. This is the love that requires the abandonment of one love for another, and she would do it fully and recklessly.

"Not just the franchise," Bobby said. "This will destroy your father. He'll be disgraced. He could even go to jail."

"I know all of that."

"There'll be no turning back. Don't do it unless you're sure. Don't do it because you feel sorry for me. Don't do it unless you're sure about this. Don't do it unless–"

She silenced him with a long, lingering kiss. When their lips finally parted, they looked into each other's eyes.

"I'm sure," Christine said.

℃

For a man on top of the world, Martin Kingsley was irritable and out of sorts. He'd yelled at the publicity director, threatened to fire the special events coordinator, and nearly strangled the tickets manager. And all before lunch.

The only one who hadn't aroused his ire was his grandson. Scott was playing catch with one of the assistant coaches on the finely trimmed grass of Sun Life Stadium. The boy had moped around all day yesterday after the hearing, pleading with him to undo what the judge had done. He'd told Scott that it was the judge's decision, and there was nothing an old wildcatter from Texas could do about it. He gauged Scott's reaction, figuring he didn't buy it. The boy picked over his dinner, sulked until bedtime, but then today, the sun shone again. The kid had a ball in his hands and was playing.

Kingsley marveled at the resilience of children. Once he brought Scott to practice, the boy lit up like a Neiman-Marcus window. Hell, what red-blooded American boy wouldn't want to be here on the day before the Super Bowl, tossing a ball with America's Team?

He wished he had the same powers of recuperation. The victory in the courtroom had tasted sweet yesterday, but this morning brought indigestion with his Western omelet. The Cuban lady lawyer had called him just after eight, claiming that Christine had spent the night with Gallagher. Kingsley had stormed to the elevator and down to Christine's room. The bed had been turned down by nighttime housekeeping and had not been slept in.

Damn you, Robert Gallagher! Why don't you just crawl under a rock and die?

The thought of his daughter sleeping with his mortal enemy enraged Kingsley to a degree that nearly cost several Dallas employees their jobs. How could a man enjoy the fruits of all his labors if his piss-ant, shyster ex-son-in-law kept crapping all over his shoes?

Kingsley weighed his options. He could have Vinnie anchor Robert to an offshore reef. What were the ramifications? He'd still get paid on the bet, because the money was in escrow, but if Robert disappeared, it could bring unwanted attention. Still, he could weather that storm.

Kingsley walked toward Scott who was standing at the thirty-five yard line. Nearby, Craig Stringer was on one knee, taking long snaps and holding the ball for Boom Boom Guacavera, who was loosening up his leg with a series of dead-solid perfect field goals.

"Hey Craig!" Scott shouted. "Once you spin the laces to the front, you gotta tuck your right hand in your crotch so it doesn't distract Boom Boom."

"Yeah?" Stringer asked, grinning. "Who says?"

"My Dad."

"How many years did your Dad play pro ball little fellow?"

"None."

"That's what I thought. You tell your Dad to keep his hand in his crotch, and I'll keep my hand in your momma's."

Scott appeared startled, then walked away, looking at the tops of his sneakers.

Son-of-a-bitch! Insolent prick, talking to Scott that way.

Kingsley had to restrain himself from taking on his star quarterback right there. If that cocky bastard wasn't facing the biggest game of his life in 24 hours, Kingsley would rattle him upside the helmet right here and now.

What the hell was going on? Everything should be perfect, but it's falling apart.

Kingsley watched Stringer turn his attention toward the center, who was looking at the world upside down between his legs. Stringer barked the signals, and the center fired a tight spiral. Stringer easily caught the ball with both hands, thumbs together. He brought the ball to the ground with the index finger of his left hand on top, spun the laces away from Boom Boom, and sure enough, he left his right hand dangling there, fingers wagging. It was a small point, but Scott was right. And so was the boy's father, goddamn it.

Kingsley wanted to say some encouraging words to Scott, to console the boy, but there was something he had to do first. As for Stringer, who wasn't quite the gift to womanhood he thought, that would have to wait until after the game.

I'll squeeze your balls 'til you sing soprano. And that's if you win!

Kingsley walked off the field and into the entrance to a tunnel behind the end zone. He wanted some privacy. His thoughts turned back to Robert Gallagher. His hatred of the man seemed to scald his throat with bile.

Pulling a cellular phone from his pocket, he punched out a number, and when a man answered, he said, "Vinnie, it's time to do that electrical work we talked about."

"How's that?" the mobster asked.

"I need you to turn out somebody's lights."

-42-

The Last Days of Pompeii

What they would do tonight would forever change America, Bobby thought. The Super Bowl being synonymous with America or at least Americana. All the glitz and glam, all the hype and show biz aside, it's still what we're all about. Striving to be number one. Winning fair and square, and all the other cliches. They're cliches, Bobby thought, only because they're true.

But Vinnie LaBarca and Martin Kingsley were sharks feasting on the carcass of the American dream.

Bobby was sorry he'd even attempted to fix the game himself.

I sank to Kingsley's level, and I drew Scott into it.

He vowed to be a better father and a better husband, if only he got a second chance.

These thoughts came to him as he was sucking on a stone crab claw, and Christine was urging him to hurry up.

"We have work to do," she said, over the noise of the Jamaican steel band.

"Uh-huh," he said, loading his plate with cold shrimp the size of grappling hooks.

Bobby thought the scene resembled the last days of Pompeii. They were just a few miles from downtown Miami on the grounds of the Vizcaya mansion, which was supposed to look like an Italian Renaissance castle, but tonight, resembled the setting of a Roman bacchanalia.

A mountain of stone crabs sat atop a glacier of chipped ice. Nearby was a sushi table, Japanese chefs with hands as deft as a wide receiver's, molding the little treats. Tubs of chilled gaspacho and spicy cerviche rounded out the tables of cold foods, along with the requisite guacamole and salsa. Alongside were the hot tables with snapper in mango chili sauce and a dozen roasted meats. At the end of the line, past dripping ice statuary shaped like goal posts, were the cornucopia of tropical fruits—papayas, mangoes and carambolas—and the requisite caramel flan and Key lime pies.

Slinky models in floral wrap skirts and halter tops handed out drinks while bands played from three stages on the lawn and gardens amidst marble sculptures, vine-covered gazebos, and fountains with frogs spouting water into the velvet night air. Not that the Super Bowl folks could leave well enough alone. Bobby and Christine had entered the party through pink marble gateways that belonged to the original mansion, then crossed a stone bridge that ran through a pseudo-plain of Everglades sawgrass that had been installed by the league. They passed a man-made marshy hammock and walked around an alligator pit complete with Miccosukee gator wrestlers. Several Ford executives, or maybe they were with American Express—who can tell with white guys in suits?—were huddled around a stage where an old Cuban man hand-rolled cigars, and a dark-haired woman with a red hibiscus in her hair handed them out.

Christine guided Bobby away from the food and the music, but not before her ex snared a margarita from a tray. "Let's blend into the crowd."

"You're too beautiful to blend in anywhere," he said, meaning it. He had always thought her to be magnificent in black, and tonight, in a sleeveless black crepe chemise with a white satin collar, she managed to look both sexy and regal.

"C'mon, pay attention to business. We've got to get into the VIP room."

"That shouldn't be hard for you. Your father's on the list."

"So are you. If the guards see your face, they're supposed to throw you into Biscayne Bay."

They moved from the gardens to the stone patio just outside an enclosed loggia. A red velvet rope closed off the door to the loggia though they could clearly see into the room through a wall of ten-foot high stained glass. Inside, the Commissioner, team owners, network bigwigs, and corporate CEO's were sitting down to dinner. No buffet tables there, but rather fine china and silver and white-gloved waiters.

"I'm going to need another drink," Bobby said, reaching for a glass from a passing tray.

"Enjoy your margarita, sir," said the young woman holding the tray.

"Lateesha!" He hadn't recognized her at first, hadn't really looked at the tall black woman with beaded corn rows and developed shoulder muscles

"Hello, Mr. G. Enjoying the party?" She flashed a big smile.

"Absolutely. Christine, say hello to Lateesha. Before the Bar pulled my ticket, I helped Lateesha out of a little problem."

"An ex-boyfriend who couldn't take no for an answer," Lateesha said. "You know the type?"

"Do I ever," Christine said, playfully.

"Meanor!" boomed a voice behind him. Bobby turned to see Nightlife Jackson in a purple suit that buttoned up nearly to his throat. He turned on a smile that was long on teeth and short on sincerity. "I've missed you, man!"

"Hello Nightlife," Bobby said, evenly.

"Ms. Gallagher." Nightlife nodded respectfully toward Christine, who didn't acknowledge him.

"And who's this foxy fox," he said, turning to Lateesha.

"Lateesha, this is the mouth of the South, Nightlife Jackson," Bobby said, trying to ignore Christine's stiletto heel that was digging into his instep. "Be careful. He's a hound who likes to tree the foxes."

"I recognize his pretty face," Lateesha said. Balancing her tray of drinks in one hand, she shook his hand with the other.

"Oh momma, you've got a grip!" Nightlife howled, feigning pain.

"Lateesha's a personal trainer," Bobby said.

"I could use some training, up close and personal," Nightlife said with a serpent's smile.

"Then you've come to the right place," Bobby said.

"Bobby!" Christine's glare could have withered crabgrass.

"C'mon, Chrissy. We've got work to do." Bobby led her toward the house. Behind them, Nightlife was asking Lateesha what time she got off work.

"Bobby, are you crazy! That man's an animal. How could you encourage that woman to—"

"Lateesha can take care of herself," he said. He was going to explain but standing six feet in front of them on the steps outside the VIP room was Peter Constantine, the Commissioner of the National Football League. He was a tall, graying man in his fifties, who looked like a corporate lawyer, which he'd been. He was holding a drink and talking to two men Bobby recognized as a team owner and a network play-by-play announcer.

"Mr. Commissioner!" Bobby blurted out, realizing at once he was too loud. He sidestepped a stone urn and closed the distance in two steps with Christine following. "There's something you've got to know about the Super Bowl."

Constantine laughed and shot glances at his two companions. "And I thought I already knew it all."

"You don't! It's being tampered with. Gamblers are involved. Mobsters are extorting Skarcynski."

"Calm down, Bobby," Christine whispered into his ear. "Go slowly."

"How's that?" Constantine appeared alarmed. "Who are you?"

"A crackpot!" It was Martin Kingsley, in a black sharkskin suit and black boots, breaking into the circle. "I apologize, Pete. This is my ex-son-in-law. He's a disbarred lawyer with severe emotional problems."

"Kingsley's involved!" Bobby shouted, gesticulating wildly at the team owner. "He's got a five million dollar bet on the game. He's probably in on the extortion plot.. He'd do anything to win."

"I remember you now," the Commissioner said, appraising

Bobby as one would a lizard on the bathroom tile. "You're the fellow who cracked up and went on television a couple of years ago."

"He didn't crack up," Christine said, elbowing her way in front of Bobby, as if to shield him from harm. "He did what was right."

Kingsley's face reddened. "You'll have to forgive my daughter, Pete. Love is blind, as they say."

Kingsley took Christine by the arm and tried to lead her away.

"Don't touch her!" Bobby warned, moving toward Kingsley,

Suddenly, Bobby felt a hand gripping his shoulder. "Is there a problem here?" It was Mr. Crew Cut, or Tarzan, or whatever his name was, Kingsley's security thug who had boxed his ears. The guy had hands the size of hubcaps. He was dragging Bobby one way, while Kingsley was hauling Christine the other.

"Daddy, let go!" she pleaded.

"This is for your own good, darling."

"Bobby!" Christine called out to him, but now a second man had a grip on Bobby's other arm, and he was being hustled behind the caterers' tent that backed up to the seawall running along the bay. Suddenly, they were in darkness, the tent blocking out the lights from the party, the water dark and forbidding behind them.

"Hello asshole," the second man said, his voice hissing like water dousing a fire.

"I owe you some pain. Big time."

Bobby couldn't make out his face, but he recognized the voice. The angry, ugly voice of Dino Fornecchio.

-43-

A Magic Carpet of Moonlight

In her thirty-seven years on earth—thirty-eight as of next Thursday, Christine had never yelled at her father. No teenage tantrums, no adolescent alienation. The perfect child for the loving father.

Now, standing among his heavy-hitting brethren, the fraternity of wealthy team owners, she leapt at him, beating his chest with both her fists. "Where is he!" she screamed. "What have you done with Bobby?"

Kingsley backed up but she stuck to him like a burr to a horse's mane. Absorbing the blows as she continued to strike him, the blood seemed to drain from his face, and his eyes grew wide. "Calm down! You're hysterical. I've never seen you like this."

"Damn you! Where's Bobby?"

Conversation around them stopped, and hundreds of startled faces stared. Christine didn't care. Her heart was drumming like the wings of a bird. She pushed him with both hands to his chest, and he continued retreating until they were off the limestone terrace and in the shadows of a row of statues. In a moment, she had him pinned to the towering figure of Minerva, a marble goddess of wisdom.

"You've lied to me, Daddy! I know all about your bet with Bobby. I know everything."

"You don't know the half of it."

"What does that mean? What else have you done?"

"It's all been for you," he said. "I've brought Robert Gallagher to his knees for you and Scott. How do you think he got into this mess?"

"He told me all about it. He lost a big bet to a gambler named LaBarca."

"It was me! LaBarca was my beard. I dug a hole for that shyster ex-husband of yours, and he jumped right in. Now, I'm here to turn the last spadeful of dirt."

"No, no," she said, crying. "How could you?"

"I'm proud of what I've done for my family. I'd do it again. That man has caused us nothing but trouble."

"I love him. Scott loves him."

"Listen to me, Christine. He's not the one for you. He doesn't have what it takes."

"I've listened to you!" she wailed. "All these years, I've done everything you wanted. I've tried to please you. God, what I've done! What I've given up! Not only did I sacrifice my husband, I've given you my son!"

"You did the right thing, but now that bastard has misled you. He's mixed you up. I'll take care of you, and I'll take care of Scott."

He tried to put his arms around her, but she swatted him away. "No! I'll take care of myself, and Bobby and I will raise Scott."

"I won't let you do that, and neither will the judge."

"What are you going to do? Sue me?" The anger boiled up inside her like soup in an iron kettle.

"I'll do what I've always done," he said, his eyes a steely blue. "Whatever it takes. If you're consorting with that felon, if you're behaving irrationally, then maybe you should go away for a rest somewhere. Get some treatment. I'm sure the judge would see it my way."

"What are you talking about?"

"Custody of Scott. I've had Jailbreak look into it. When both natural parents are unfit, a grandparent is the next logical custodian."

"You'd do it, wouldn't you?" Tears ran down her cheeks like two flowing brooks, all the strength seemed to seep out of her bones. The hurt pierced her heart. Her father had been everything to her.

That he could turn on her, that he could threaten to take Scott was unthinkable.

He looked at her now with a triumphant glare. She'd seen he same look in business deals when her father had the upper hand, when he was about to squash his opponent like an insect under the heel of his boot. This was just another deal, another game to be won. She had become the enemy, another foe to vanquish.

"Bobby was wrong about you," she said, walking away. "You're an even bigger bastard than he knows."

ɷ

Bobby's ankles were banging off the rough steps of the stone bridge as he was dragged along the seawall behind the mansion. Crew Cut had him under one arm, Dino Fornecchio under the other. After crossing the bridge, they went up a second set up steps and into a stone gazebo at the water's edge. A sliver of moon rose over Biscayne Bay, lighting a path across the dark water straight to the seawall.

"Stop here," Fornecchio said, and they both released their grips.

"Now what the fuck am I going to do with you?" Fornecchio asked. A white bandage was taped across the bridge of his nose, and his voice had a heavy adenoidal twang. He pulled a handgun from a holster inside his suit coat and waved it in Bobby's face. "I never killed anybody in such a scenic place before."

"That would be smart, Dino," Bobby said, struggling to stay calm. "Why not dump my body in the VIP room when they're having their Key lime pie? I'm the guy who just told the Commissioner the game is fixed by gamblers and that Kingsley's involved, and the last two guys I'm seen with work for Kingsley and the biggest gambler in town. Why not take an ad in the Herald saying who killed me?"

That seemed to stop Fornecchio a moment, and Bobby frantically tried to think his way out of the jam. He fought to control his panic, resisting the urge to run like a rabbit in front of the dogs, wondering if Fornecchio would put a bullet in his back. He tried to focus on his surroundings, to plan a path of escape. In the distance, a yacht chugged across the bay, and water slip-slopped against the seawall from its wake. Here he was, on the verge of death, and the rest of the world continued at its own pace, oblivious to his and a million other tragedies.

"Maybe you ought to call Vinnie before you do something that'll piss him off," Bobby said, buying time. In his heart, he knew LaBarca could order him killed as easily as he ordered linguine with clam sauce

"You think all I do is take orders from him?" Fornecchio asked, angrily.

"I think when you take a shit, you ask him for permission to wipe."

Growling like a hungry Doberman pinscher, Fornecchio jammed the barrel of the gun against the tip of Bobby's nose. "You broke my nose, asshole. How would you like me to shoot off yours?"

"Good thinking, Dino. There are only about two hundred security guards on the other side of those hedges. Why not shoot yourself in the foot at the same time?"

Fornecchio drew back the hammer of the gun, the metallic click seemingly as loud as a gunshot itself.

"Hey, wait a second, Dino," Crew Cut said. His neck seemed ready to burst the top button on his banded collar shirt. His arms were so thick they hung away from his body like a gorilla. "I didn't bargain for this. I gotta check in with Mr. K if you're gonna go ballistic."

Fornecchio's stupid face lit up like a neon sign. "If this prick tried to get away, you think Kingsley would mind if we messed him up?"

"No," the big man, said warily.

"Didn't think so."

"So?"

Hold him!" Fornecchio demanded, and Crew Cut, used to

following orders, grabbed Bobby from behind, looping his arms through Bobby's armpits. "Hold him up straight."

Propped up, Bobby braced for what was coming. Fornecchio threw a hard right that landed squarely in Bobby's solar plexus, knocking the wind out of him. His stomach heaved once, twice, and then, he gagged and vomited straight onto Fornecchio's shoes.

"Oh shit!" Fornecchio shouted. "My wing tips! I'll never get the crud out. You're gonna lick my shoes clean, asshole, then I'm gonna inflict some pain on you."

Bobby heaved again, and this time he hurled even farther. Fornecchio stepped backward but the splash caught the cuffs of his suit pants. "You dirtbag!"

"Hey, Dino," Crew Cut said, "this smell is making me sick." He released his grip on Bobby and turned his head, trying to suck in some clean air.

Through a haze of tears, Bobby saw the path of moonbeams stretched across the bay. The light seemed to beckon to him. He got to his feet, sidestepped Fornecchio who was shaking off his pantleg, and raced to the open face of the gazebo that sat at the water's edge. He knew from fishing in the bay that the water was exceptionally shallow along the seawall. Concrete waste from repairs to the mansion formed a rocky ledge just inches below the water line. He would have to clear the ledge.

With his last step, he shot into the air in a racing dive, extending as far as he could, praying he would make it.

In a second, he felt the splash of surprisingly warm water and the tangle of sea grasses, but he had just cleared the ledge. As he kicked off his shoes and began swimming furiously away from the seawall, he heard the shout behind him.

"Get him!" Fornecchio yelled.

"I can't swim," Crew Cut replied.

"Goddamit!"

Bobby looked back over his shoulder just in time to see Fornecchio jumping off the seawall, feet first. He went up about two feet in the air and came straight down, his shoes banging the ledge like a sledgehammer breaking rocks.

Bobby heard Fornecchio's scream, the sound carrying across the water, a keening, high-pitched wail of pain.

"I broke my fucking ankles!" Fornecchio yelled into the night.

చౌ

From her car, Christine called Bobby's house, then his cell. No answer. She tried the Fontainebleau to see if he'd left her a message. Nothing.

Twenty minutes later, she was in the hotel, on her way down the corridor, when she heard a commotion behind a closed door several rooms from her own.

Nightlife's room!

Approaching the door, she heard a woman's scream, then a thud, and the crash of furniture.

Oh God, now what?

She had forgotten about Lateesha. Damn it, Bobby! What have you done now?

She banged on the door. "Open up! Nightlife, open the door!"

Behind the door, there was an indecipherable sound. It could have been a cry of pain or exultation. Then another crash. Glass maybe, a lamp falling to the floor. Then, Nightlife's voice, "You bitch!" And a sharp female cry.

"Open the door!" Christine screamed. "Police! Security! Help!"

Down the corridor, a young black woman was pushing a housekeeping cart. "Yes, ma'am, can I help you?" she asked, in the lilt of the islands.

"Your key! Open the door. A woman's in trouble in there."

The housekeeper put her ear to the door just as a muffled shout came from the room. She hurriedly slipped a card key into the slot and opened the door.

Christine threw the door open. The room was a shambles. The writing desk was overturned, a lamp lay smashed on the floor. The bed coverings were balled up in a corner, and the mattress had slid off the bed. Lateesha stood in the center of the room, her dress torn open in front nearly to the waist. On the floor lay Nightlife Jackson, moaning, one hand clutching his groin, the other arm twisted at an unnatural angle away from his body.

"Omigod," Christine said. "Are you all right, Lateesha?"

"Hell no, I broke a nail," she said, examining the pinky of her right hand.

"How did you...?" Christine gestured toward the fallen man, who made no effort to get to his feet.

"Oh, he's not too much. Didn't Bobby tell you?"

"Tell me what?"

"I'm a three-time national karate champion. That's how I met Bobby, sort of. This ex-boyfriend of mine kept hanging around like a flea on a dog. He still had a key to my apartment, and I woke up one night to find him in my bed all hot and bothered. I lost it and let him have it. Not like it was unfair of me, unloading on him. He teaches martial arts at the Y and outweighs me by eighty pounds, but he's the one who ended up in the hospital, and I'm the one who got charged with assault and battery."

Nightlife rolled to one knee and said in a whisper, "Call a doctor, please."

"What happened?" Christine asked.

"Nightlife seemed to think I was a piece of meat he could have a slice. I told him he'd be wearing his balls as earrings if he didn't take his hands off me, but he didn't listen. Why don't men ever listen?"

"I truly don't know," Christine said.

-44-

Aces and Jokers

February 5

Super Bowl Sunday

Christine lay in Bobby's bed restlessly tossing from side-to-side. She had called the police to report Bobby missing, but the dispatcher said to wait 24 hours to see if he showed up. They were awfully busy with all the people in town.

Christine had picked Scott up from her father's hotel suite where the boy was watching "Cheerleader Gang Bang" on pay-TV. He argued it was a football flick, but she made him turn it off anyway, and they headed across the causeway to the mainland.

She wanted to get as far away from her father as possible, and she figured that Bobby would come home sooner or later.

If he was okay. But what happened to you, Bobby? What have they done to you?

Scott was sleeping soundly in his room, while Christine listened to the palm fronds slapping the tin roof of the cottage. She watched the digital time display flick from 3:11 to 3:12 on the clock radio. She had dozed earlier, but her sleep was like a cocked pistol, and she kept awakening at every sound.

A ceiling fan whirled endlessly above her head, and she tried to let the *whompeta-whompeta* of the motor lull her back to sleep. No luck. She buried her head in the pillow, which smelled faintly of Bobby, and she remembered their lovemaking. Was it only the day before?

Oh, Bobby. Where are you? I need you.

At first she didn't hear the tapping at the window, and then, she thought it was a light rain falling. Then she heard Bobby's muffled voice.

"Chrissy, it's me."

She opened the window, and Bobby hoisted himself into the room.

"Thank God you're all right. Bobby, I was so afraid."

He hugged her, and she noticed that his clothes were dripping water. "What happened to you? You looked like you swam here."

"No. I swam to the Rickenbacker Causeway. I hitchhiked here. Or rather, I walked here. You'd be surprised how many people won't pick up a barefoot guy who's soaking wet at one o'clock in the morning."

She wrapped her arms around his neck and gripped him fiercely, and he lifted her up. She wrapped her legs around him, their bodies joined, his nooks into her crannies. They fit perfectly together, like the pieces of a rock carefully split by a sculptor, then slipped together into a singular, smooth piece. With her eyes squeezed shut, she felt a tear tracking down her cheeks. This is what she wanted. Her son and the man she loved...together again.

Bobby told her about Dino Fornecchio, and how he got away. Christine told him that LaBarca was working for her father, and how he'd been set up. Then she told him about Lateesha kick boxing Nightlife's testicles from Miami Beach to Opa-Locka, and they both smiled.

"Who says there's no justice in the world?" Bobby said. "How badly is he hurt?"

"Doc Joyner says he has a broken clavicle and separated shoulder, to say nothing of very blue balls. He won't even suit up."

"Excellent," Bobby said.

"What? What is it?" She saw the shadow of a thought crossing his face. It was a look she knew as well as a sailor knows the sky.

"I've got to make a call," Bobby said.

❧

Vinnie LaBarca awoke in slow, ponderous motion, like a diver emerging from the depths. When he opened his eyes, his head was a bucket of sand that shifted with every movement.

Goddamn sinuses. Goddamn allergies.

He also realized that the humming electrostatic ozone machine that was guaranteed to knock all the dust motes, mildew, and airborne crud out of his apartment was a twelve-hundred dollar ripoff. It was supposed to cleanse the air but couldn't re-circulate a fart. He made a mental note to take the machine back to the Bal Harbour shop where he bought it, and stick the salesman's hand into the fan.

Finally, he realized that the phone was ringing. Now what? He'd already been awakened once, that dickwad Fornecchio calling from the hospital.

He picked up he phone and said, "This better be fucking good."

"How many points is Nightlife Jackson worth?" a man's voice asked.

"Who the fuck is this?"

"C'mon Vinnie, Dallas is favored by four. What should the line be if Nightlife doesn't play?"

"Gallagher? Is that you? When I find you, I'm gonna tear off your arms and beat you to death! I'm gonna chop off your head and piss down your neck! Do you hear me Gallagher?"

"Nightlife's scratched. Physically unable to perform. It'll be announced at a press conference at ten a.m. The game will either go off the board or the line will move to what, dead even, pick 'em?"

LaBarca saw where Gallagher was going, but how could he trust him? "Are you shitting me, Gallagher?"

"Nope. I've got the Mustangs' marketing director here with me right now if you want to check."

"If you're talking about your ex-wife, she ain't the best character witness."

"Then just assume I'm right. How much is Nightlife worth?"

"In my book, a touchdown. Christ, he plays both ways, and he's the best player on both sides of the ball. He's a combination of Deion Sanders and Jerry Rice, and his backups are both journeymen."

"So why don't you put everything you've got on Denver?"

"You know damn well why, and I don't say anything on any phones unless I know who's listening in."

"You won't do it," Bobby said, "because you know Skarcynski's gonna be throwing the ball to the cheerleaders."

"No fucking comment."

"But you control that. Whatever you bet on Dallas is at risk now. Maybe Denver will cover even with Skar tanking it. Now, if you tell Skar to take the gloves off, they should easily cover the spread and may even win outright. Let Skar play and put everything you got on his team."

"Go fuck yourself, Gallagher, and if I see you anywhere near the stadium, I'm gonna..."

The beep of call waiting broke his concentration. Now what? Damn modern technology. You can't even threaten to poleax some bum without being interrupted. At three-thirty in the morning for Christ's sake.

"Yeah," LaBarca said, clicking onto the new line.

"Your half wit associate let Gallagher get away," Martin Kingsley said, angrily.

"No shit," LaBarca said.

"Well, do something about it, goddamit!"

"Who the fuck do you think you're talking to?"

"You don't scare me! Do you know what I have riding on this game?" Kingsley said. "I got into it because of you. It's a lock, you said. Now Gallagher is shooting off his mouth and jeopardizing everything. You were supposed to take him out of commission but what happened? Jesus H. Christ, it's the morning of the game, and all hell's broken loose."

The old man sounded strung out. What a fucked up family. "Mr. Kingsley, I don't know what you're talking about, and I don't talk business on the phone, if you get my drift."

"Goddammit, find that bastard. If he sets foot in the stadium, shoot him in the kneecaps!"

"You've been watching too many movies, Mr. Kingsley. I'm trying to be polite here, and I'm taking into account that you're under a lot of strain..."

"You're goddamn right I am."

"By the way, is Nightlife Jackson out of the game?"

There was nothing but the buzz of the telephone line until Kingsley said, "How did you know that?"

LaBarca clicked back to the other line. He had underestimated the lawyer. Somehow he managed to knock the star player out of the Super Bowl the night before the game. "Okay Gallagher, you're on to something. But It ain't solid. Besides Nightlife, you got any more tricks up your sleeve for today?"

"I've got two or three aces I haven't played yet."

"Good, 'cause I think Skarcynski's gonna have the game of his life."

❧

At four a.m., Kingsley reached for the ringing phone in his hotel suite. The noise did not disturb him. He'd been drinking bourbon ever since he got the news about Nightlife, and a warm buzz filled his head. He wasn't sleeping and halfway expected a call. Maybe LaBarca intending to apologize, to say, "sure Mr. Kingsley, I'll take care of it." Maybe it was Christine, calling in tears to say he was still the most important man in her life and that she now appreciated everything he'd done for her.

Putting down the glass of Jack Daniels, he picked up the phone and said, "Kingsley here."

"'Morning pardner," rasped Houston Tyler. "I figured you'd be awake. Heard you had a little trouble at the party last night. Also heard you lost one of your thoroughbreds for the game."

"How the hell did you know that?"

Christ, bad news travels like a tornado down here.

"You want to know what's going on in a hotel, hang around with the housekeepers, Martin."

"I'll remember that."

"I hope this little setback doesn't jeopardize anything," Tyler said.

"Don't worry, Ty. It's money in the bank."

"Good," he said, then clicked off.

Kingsley finished his bourbon, then summoned his security chief from the next room. The burly, crew-cut George Brauninger was an ex-cop who was thrown off the force for excessive brutality in making arrests. There were even stories about a missing witness in an Internal Affairs investigation, a witness who turned up too dead to testify.

Just days ago, in Kingsley's presence, Brauninger had flattened Gallagher, and the memory of it gave him some pleasure now. But earlier tonight—yesterday really—Brauninger had let Gallagher get away. His security cheif was a man who took pride in his work, and Kingsley knew he was humiliated.

"You let me down," Kingsley said, when Brauninger came to his suite.

"I'm sorry, Mr. K. It won't happen again."

"I know that, George. And you can make it all up today. Gallagher will be at the game. He's got a press box pass and a sideline pass."

"You want me to detain him, Mr. K."

"Permanently, George."

"I want to make sure I understand you, sir."

"Oh, I think you do."

"Yes sir, Mr. K, I do."

⁓

Scott pretended there was nothing special about it, nothing special at all, his Mom and Dad having breakfast together on Super

Bowl Sunday, Dad making the coffee, Mom slicing grapefruit. So here they were, all gooey, just looking at each other, but only a total dipstick would make a big deal out of it.

"You want some more French toast, Scott?" his Mom asked.

"Sure. Dad always burns it."

"So that's the thanks I get," Bobby said.

"Maybe we'll re-assign the household chores," Christine said. "I'll do breakfast, your Dad will cut the lawn, and you'll wash the dishes."

"So I guess we're staying here?" Scott said, suppressing his emotions, keeping the joy under wraps.

"This seems like a good place to live," Christine said. She glanced around the old kitchen with its dropped ceiling, flourescent lights, and avocado green appliances. "It could use an update, though. And why are the front windows covered with sheet metal? Is the neighborhood that dangerous?"

"Hurricane shutters, Mom. Dad forgot to take them down last Fall."

"I didn't forget," Bobby said without much conviction. "With El Niño, you never know."

Christine wrapped both hands around her coffee cup and took a sip before speaking. "Another rule in the house will have to change. No TV while we eat."

"Aw, Mom, it's Sports Center." Scott shot a look at the 13-inch Sony on the counter. A Super Bowl preview was on with the sound muted. "It's the best show on television."

Scott saw his father looking at the screen, his jaw muscles tightening. They were showing highlights of the Mustangs eight-point win over Green Bay. It was the game in which Dad was middled, pounded flat by skanky luck. The memory was already as rusty as a bike left in the rain.

Jeez, it seems like I was just a kid then. So much has happened.

"What other aces?" Christine asked, pouring orange juice for Scott.

"What?" Bobby said.

"On the phone, you told that gambler you had two or three aces you hadn't played yet."

"Oh."

Scott could see his father's mood change. The happiness that he must have felt—that all three of them felt at being together—was melting away.

"I don't have any aces," Bobby said. "Just a couple of jokers. I needed LaBarca to turn Skarcynski around, and it looks like he'll do it. But even that may not be enough."

"Well, think about it, Bobby. The game is hours away. What else can we do?"

"Nothing. With Skarcynski trying his best and Nightlife out, the odds are definitely improving. There's no guarantee, but with a little luck, Goldy and I will win 5.5 million dollars. Which your old man won't pay."

"So you'll end up with two per cent of the team's stock," she said.

"For which there's no market.".

"Sure there is."

"Meaning you?"

"Meaning us." Christine laughed, the sound of chimes tinkling in the breeze. It was just about he best sound in the world. "Oh, Bobby, think about it. Do you know what Thursday is?"

"Of course, I do. I've never forgotten your birthday, even when we were apart."

"My *thirty-eighth* birthday! The stock that's held in trust comes to me outright, forty-nine per cent of the team! Bobby, if the Mustangs don't cover the spread, you and I will own fifty-one per cent. We'll control the team!"

"Wow," Bobby said. "I'm in love with a woman of substance. CEO of the Dallas Mustangs."

"And you'll be G.M.," Christine said.

"Hey, Scott, how'd you like to coach the special teams?" Bobby asked.

"Groovalicius," Scott said, keeping his eyes on the TV where

ESPN was profiling the two Super Bowl quarterbacks.

"It's what we talked about years ago," Christine said. "We could clean it up, do everything you wanted Daddy to do."

"Are you going to fire Pop?" Scott asked.

"Let's just say it'll be time for Daddy's retirement," Christine said.

"Two per cent," Bobby said, almost to himself. "Your father never thought he was putting up control of the team."

"He thought he'd win the bet," Christine said.

"Sure, but even if he lost, he never thought you and I would join up."

"We make a great team, pardner," Christine said, laughing again.

"Only if the Mustangs don't cover the four point spread," Scott said, tossing cold water on their bonfire.

"Yeah," Bobby said. "It's not a lock. Look, no matter what I told LaBarca, the Mustangs are damn good, even without Nightlife. I hate to admit it, but Stringer is the better quarterback, even when Skarcynski's trying his best."

Christine rested her chin on one hand, deep in thought. Scott had seen the look so many times, usually when there was a problem that needed solving.

"So what can we do, Bobby?" she asked. "Do you have any more of those voodoo curses you were telling me about?"

"No, and I wouldn't do it, anyway."

"Why not, Dad?" Scott said.

"Trying to foul up the game was a mistake. Let them buckle up their chinstraps, look across the line at each other, paw the turf, and go at it, man to man. See who's tougher, smarter, and better. It's chess with muscles. It's the American way."

"You just sound a little cornball," Christine said.

"And very old school," Scott added. "Like civics class."

"It's just a game, Bobby. The fate of civilization doesn't depend on who wins."

"Not on who wins but on how it's played," Bobby said. "It's

all about the drive for excellence, teamwork, and relentless effort against overwhelming odds."

"And corporate greed, hype, and gluttonous excess," Christine said.

"That too. That's why it's so damn American. But when the whistle blows, the distractions don't matter. For three hours on one day a year, we're all brought together. Kids believe in the Super Bowl long after they know there's no Santa Claus. It's become part of the fabric of our society and it shouldn't be meddled with any more than the Rocky Mountains should be leveled or the Great Lakes filled with sand. Let them play. We're not going to monkey with it. It would be wrong. It would be..."

He couldn't seem to find the word.

"Un-American?" Christine helped out.

"Bogus?" Scott suggested.

"Sacriligious," Bobby said.

Christine laughed. "Football as religion. Perfect."

"The game is our secular religion," Bobby said. "Super Bowl Sunday is Christmas. The stadium is the church, the coaches the priests, the players—"

"Altar boys?" Christine teased.

"All right. I'm getting carried away, but I'm still not going to mess with it."

"Even if it meant saving your own skin and getting the team away from my father?"

"It wouldn't be right," Bobby concluded.

"There's Craig!" Scott pointed at the television screen.

Sure enough, there was number seven in cowboy garb, riding a spotted horse.

"Must be an old video," Christine said. "That's Temptation, his favorite Appaloosa. That coloring is called the leopard pattern."

On the screen, a grinning Craig Stringer sat astride a white horse with dark spots.

"See that big spot on her haunch," Christine continued. "Craig always said it looked like the map of Texas. You can't see her

hooves, but they're striped, like she's wearing old-fashioned socks."
Christine grew silent a moment. "God, Craig was heartbroken
when she died in the fire with the rest of the horses."

Bobby stood and started clearing the breakfast plates. "Luckiest
thing that ever happened to him."

"What!" Christine nearly dropped her coffee cup.

"Stringer was overextended. The race horses were eating up
his capital along with their oats. Did you know he had to sue the
insurance company to get paid?"

"He told me the company was just playing hardball."

Bobby laughed. "Yeah, they tend to do that when somebody
burns down their own barn."

"Arson? Are you saying Craig killed his own horses?"

"It's not me saying it. It's the insurance investigator. They just
couldn't prove it. Stringer won by claiming the fire started in the
barn by spontaneous combustion."

"What's that, Dad?" Scott asked.

"Spontaneous combustion happens when you rub a million
dollars in horseflesh up against a four million dollar insurance
policy."

Scott laughed, but Christine scowled at Bobby. "I'll never
believe that," she said. "Craig might be vain, arrogant, and selfish,
but he'd never do that, not to Temptation."

On the screen, Stringer and his late Appaloosa were replaced
by a commercial for a beer that will apparently attract bikini-clad
young women to play volleyball on the beach.

"That was his defense," Bobby said, "and it worked. But
knowing Stringer, I think that's the proof that he did it. If he'd
taken Temptation out of the barn that night and just killed the
other horses, it might arouse suspicion. So he sacrificed the horse
he supposedly loved to prove that he didn't do it. It's just like Craig,
superficially clever but thoroughly cold and calculating."

Christine looked at the television, studying Craig Stringer's face,
as if she could divine the truth behind the plastic smile. "That's so
Macchiavellian. I can't believe it. He hasn't ridden a horse since the

fire. He says he can't bear to have any reminders of Temptation."

"He probably feels guilty," Bobby said. "Maybe he even dreams about her. Nightmares of getting stomped to death."

"Omigod, you're right!"

"What?"

"Craig told me he dreamed about Temptation. Not getting stomped, but riding her across a stream. It's too deep and she drowns while Craig swims away."

"Fire into water. Wouldn't Freud have a ball with old number seven?" Bobby said.

"Maybe we can use it somehow," Christine said. "Maybe between now and kickoff, you can get to him and—"

"No," Bobby said. "Weren't you listening?"

"There's a lot we could do, Dad.. Maybe we tell Denver's D-Line to yell 'Temptation' when Craig is calling signals. Maybe we do something with the horses in the halftime show. Maybe we start a fire under the bench, I don't know."

"For the last time, no!"

"Your father's right," Christine said.

"But you just said—"

"We're not going to tamper with the game," she said, firmly.

"Okay, okay. Whatever you guys say."

"Good," Christine said. Then, as Bobby turned toward the dishes in the sink, she winked at her son. "We'll never do anything your father forbids, okay Scott?"

"You got it, Mom," he said, winking right back.

"It would be easier to bribe the President of the United States and the entire Senate and Congress than to fix a Super Bowl."
—Sonny Reizner, Las Vegas bookmaker

-45-

Super Sunday

Yesterday's ice sculptures had become today's dirty dishes. All the stone crabs, smoked shrimp cakes, and Swedish meatballs had been eaten. All the street festivals, Fortune 500 shindigs, blimp rides, bay cruises, alligator wrestles, and golf tournaments were over. The sports page blather and TV yackety-yack had wound down, the commentators seizing on "focus" as this year's Super Word: "The team that keeps its focus should win today."

The bookies, hookers, and hucksters had finished their business, though pickpockets, souvenir hawkers, and scalpers were still working the parking lots and access roads. The schmoozing, networking, freebie glomming, and manufactured gaiety were coming to an end with the last of the pre-game bashes. All the gaudy TV spots were in the can, ready to be unwound at forty-five thousand dollars a second.

It was time for The Game.

Super Sunday for America and a super day for me, Bobby thought. Denver had a decent chance of covering the four-point spread. He had his wife and child back, and his heart was a cup overflowing with infinite possibilities. He and Christine could end up owning the franchise and running the team. Scott would bask in their love and thrive. The boy could become a physicist or the best oddsmaker in Vegas, it didn't matter. Sun Life Stadium was filling up, seventy-five thousand fans by kickoff, but it seemed unusually quiet to Bobby during pre-game warm-ups. Too many corporate bigwigs, too few true fans. Too many helicopters buzzing like mosquitoes, dropping off celebs and wannabees at the "corporate hospitality village," a classic oxymoron. Too many limos—more than one thousand—lined up outside the stadium, including one sad, sagging Lincoln that Bobby had piloted with Christine and Scott in the back. And too many quiche and Chardonnay fans in the party tents surrounding the stadium, too few boilermaker and bratwurst guys inside.

Bobby wore chinos and running shoes with a Channel 9 windbreaker and figured he looked liked he belonged on the sidelines, which is where he was, the appropriate credentials dangling from a chain on his neck. Christine and Scott were in Kingsley's suite, and Bobby couldn't help wondering what the wind chill factor was between father and daughter. On the field, pre-game warmups were almost completed. Under the stands, Christina Aguilera was warming up her vocal cords to warble the National Anthem.

Bobby watched Mike Skarcynski head toward the tunnel with the rest of the Denver offense. Back to the locker room for a few minutes before kickoff. He'd been sharp in warm-ups, tossing bullets to the wide receivers. "Go get 'em, Skar!" Bobby yelled, just a short down-and-out from the QB.

Skar responded with a thumbs-up sign. "Gonna rope those Mustangs!"

"He'd better," a voice said.

Bobby turned to find Vinnie LaBarca. "I only got a sideline pass for pre-game, so I'm going up to the club seats. You got everything under control, Gallagher?"

"Nothing to control. You hedge your bet?"

"And then some. I need the Pats to cover." LaBarca blew his nose into a handkerchief with the sound of a foghorn. His eyes were rimmed with red. "Damn allergies."

"We're on the same side today," Bobby said. "We both want Denver to win or lose by less than four."

"Right. So what else you got going? Did you poison the Mustangs' pre-game meal? You gonna stick a hypodermic full of barbs in Stringer's ass on the way out of the locker room?"

"Nothing like that, Vinnie. We're just gonna let them play."

"What! You said—"

"C'mon Vinnie, it's a beautiful day. The sun is shining. A breeze is blowing."

"Yeah, blowing pollen and melaleuca shit right up my nose."

"Let's enjoy the game the way it was meant to be played."

"Who gives a shit about the game? I don't care if the ball is inflated or filled with feathers. I just wanna win."

"And maybe you will."

"You better hope so. If Denver don't cover, I'm looking for you to make it good."

"Hey, that wasn't part of the deal."

"The deal is what I say it is. Right Dino?"

Bobby turned to find Dino Fornecchio, both ankles in casts, an aluminum cane in each hand. "Fucking A," Fornecchio said, aiming the tip of one cane at Bobby's midsection as if it were a gun.

Bobby laughed. "Maybe you haven't noticed, Vinnie, but your tough guy can't even unzip his fly without help."

"You bastard!" Fornecchio swiped at Bobby's knees with his cane but missed and nearly fell.

Bobby was no longer scared. Amazing. Assured of Chrissy's love, he had confidence now, and the world looked took on a different look. The winds that once seemed poised to blow him away were cooling breezes. Vinnie LaBarca had once seemed so menacing, but look at him now, a red-nosed clown, sniffling into his handkerchief. As for Fornecchio, he couldn't find his dick with both hands.

"I owe you, asshole," Fornecchio said.

"I'll put it on your tab," Bobby said, then headed for the tunnel under the stands. He felt liberated, his life a rubber ball that keeps bouncing higher and higher instead of losing momentum. He was a new Bobby Gallagher, and it felt great.

"This feels like my lucky day," he said aloud.

"Then I'd hate to see your unlucky day," said the man's voice behind him.

What the hell? Bobby turned. Standing in front of him, legs spread, arms dangling at his side, was Crew Cut, burly and menacing in a nylon windbreaker. He had a thick neck and tiny, pink pigs' ears. Before Bobby could say a word, a punch was coming at him. He tried to duck, but all he saw was a giant fist blocking out the light, following his movement. He felt it then, an explosion that started at his chin and rocketed into his brain, thunderclaps of noise and blinding fireworks of pain. As he fought to keep his balance, Bobby realized he was staggering back one step, then two, and he had the sensation of falling down, but before he hit the ground, the world had already faded to black.

⁂

Both teams must have been feeling the pressure, Christine thought, because the first quarter was played with the sloppy ineffectiveness of an exhibition game. Dallas fumbled on its first possession, but Denver squandered the opportunity by consecutive holding penalties followed by an intercepted pass. They exchanged punts twice, and finally, Craig Stringer put together a drive that resulted in a field goal by Boom Boom Guacavera. At the end of the first quarter, Dallas led, 3-0.

Until today, Christine had never paid much attention to the game itself. Not that she lacked knowledge of the sport's subtleties. If she took the trouble to watch a rookie offensive lineman just before the snap, she could predict run or pass from whether he leaned forward or rocked back in his three-point stance. She appreciated the cleverness of a passing play that created a mismatch with a fleet running back being covered by a lead-footed linebacker, and she understood the raw courage it took for a punt returner to face a Pickett's charge of onrushing tacklers.

But usually, she was content to ride with the general ebb and flow of the game, enjoying the moments when her father and her son joyfully high-fived each other.

Today was different.

Today she watched every play through binoculars, gritting her teeth when Dallas made a first down or got the benefit of a questionable penalty. She and Scott sat in Siberia, the last row of the suite. Just before kickoff, her father had looked right through her and asked Scott to join him in the front row.

"That's okay, Pop. I'll stay here with Mom."

"C'mon Scott, who's going to help me call the plays?"

Scott shifted uncomfortably in his chair. "Sorry Pop, but I'm rooting for Denver today."

Kingsley could not have looked more shocked if his grandson had announced he was a cross-dressing, communist drug dealer. The old man's face came apart at the seams, his jaw muscles quivering, a tic pulsating above one eye. "It's sinful, Christine, to turn a child against his grandfather."

"No, the sin is trying to take the child from his father and mother."

"There'll be a day of reckoning," he said, icily. "There'll be a judgment day."

"It's today, Martin," she said, using his given name for the first time in her life. It was the final break, she knew, and it filled her with pain.

At the sound of his own name coming from those lips, Kingsley blinked rapidly as if unexpectedly slapped by a dinner companion. Without another word, he turned and headed for his seat in the front row.

It all came back to her in a flood of conflicting emotions. Her father had been everything. He had doted on her and treated her like a princess, and even now, after she had peeled away the gilt-edged wrapping that had hidden who he was, even after the disillusionment, she knew that she loved him still. But that only made the pain worse.

℘

Bobby was vaguely aware of a man's voice, and then a crackle of noise. It took a moment to realize the man was speaking into a walkie-talkie, then listening to a reply. Maybe it was his imagination, but the scratchy reply sounded like Martin Kingsley.

Bobby opened his eyes and tried to flex his neck. His head was a sack of cement, and his jaw seemed to be attached to rusty hinges. He could barely open his mouth to lick his parched lips. Several little men were inside his skull banging cymbals in a very poor rendition of the *1812 Overture*. When the cobwebs cleared, he realized he was sitting on a bare concrete floor, his hands cuffed behind him. A maze of wires and cables criss-crossed overhead and plugged into dozens of panels. He could hear the crowd noise and what sounded like distant music.

"Do you know where you are?" Crew Cut asked. The bastard was standing at a small window overlooking the field.

"An electrical closet, somewhere in the press box," Bobby said.

"So far up, you can barely see the field. In case you're interested, and I know you are, Dallas is ahead, ten zip, at the half. There's some show horses down on the field and a bunch of Disney characters lip-synching. It's the most sorry shit you've ever seen."

Somewhere on the other side of the electrical panels a door opened, then closed with a harsh metallic clang. He heard footsteps on the hard floor. "Hey!" Bobby called out. "Help me! "Help!"

"No one can hear you up here, except God hisself," Kingsley said, rounding the corner and looming above Bobby. He turned to Crew Cut. "Good work, George."

"Where's it going to end, Martin?" Bobby said, his words thick, his jaw aching.

"First you broke league rules, now the criminal laws. You can't go on. It's over. You're going to lose the franchise when word gets out."

Kingsley looked at him with such a cold hatred that Bobby felt a chill go up his spine. "Still trying to reform me, aren't you Robert? If I was you, I'd be more worried about my own hide, because from up here, you're the one who looks like the frog in the frying pan."

"What are you going to do, Martin, kill me so you don't have to give up two per cent of your stock?"

Kingsley's laugh was a series of clicks, like a ticking bomb. "Two per cent? You must think I'm stupid, Robert. I know what you're cooking up. With you twisting everything around and turning Christine against me, you're after control of the team. That's been your plan all along, hasn't it? You've known me a long time. Do you really think I'd let that happen?"

"Killing me won't stop it. My two per cent will go to Scott."

"Precisely, and within a month or so, I'll be the lawful guardian of Scott and Christine will be hospitalized and medicated."

A bolt of red-hot anger shot through Bobby. "You bastard! Chrissy will fight you with everything she's got."

"The poor child will be distraught after your suicide. I don't know how effective an advocate she'll be."

"Suicide?" Bobby asked, ice water rushing through his veins.

"What would a man with a history of instability and self destructive behavior be likely to do? Hell, you looked like you were cracking up last night at the Commissioner's party. Who would be surprised if you did a swan dive off the back of the press box?"

Kingsley's eyes were as dead as pieces of stone, and Bobby had no doubt he was serious.

"Do you think that will get your daughter back?"

"Maybe not today or tomorrow, but eventually. You're the one who drove her away, and when you're gone, when she realizes that she hitched her wagon to a dead mule, she'll come back. I'll raise Scott to be ten times the man you ever were. I'll raise him to be like me, and she'll thank me for it."

"You heartless son-of-a-bitch!" Bobby struggled against the handcuffs. He wanted to leap at Kingsley, to smash him into the electrical panels and fry the man's brains, but he could only get to his knees, his hands still locked behind his back.

"Hey!" Crew Cut yelled. "Where do you think you're going?" He kicked Bobby in the ribs and sent him sprawling.

"Wait till right after the final gun, George, when people are pouring out of here. It'll be dark, so just take him up top and give him the heave ho into the parking lot. Then come down to the locker room and have some champagne."

"I wish to hell I'd never said the damn thing. [Winning isn't everything; it's the only thing.] I meant the effort. I meant having a goal. I sure as hell didn't mean for people to crush human values and morality."
—Vince Lombardi

-46-

Shades of Gray

Halftime was a blur to Christine. First, the field was covered with Disney characters, singing syrupy songs. Then the Petaluma show horses high-stepped and pranced across a specially made tarp so that a diving wide receiver wouldn't get a facemask full of poop in the third quarter. Finally, there were the Black Eyed Peas, Usher, Slash, and Madonna.

"Damn halftime show is lasting longer than most guys' playing careers," said one of the guys from personnel.

Her father had disappeared just after the half ended. He'd been whispering into a walkie-talkie, then walked out of the suite with a crooked grin in place, slapping backs and exchanging "howdys" with friends and league officials. He came back just before the second half kickoff, looked down at Christine and said, "Do you know the difference between Robert and me?"

The words swirled through her head. *Integrity, honesty, sensitivity.* But she didn't answer.

"I'm a man who always does what has to be done," he said, answering his own question. "Nothing's changed about that, and it never will. Someday, you'll appreciate it, and you'll know it was for your own good and for Scott's."

After he'd taken his seat, Scott said, "What did Pop mean?"

"I'm not sure." The father she once knew so well had become a mystery, full of threats and innuendos.

"Is it bad to do what has to be done?"

"Not if it's the right thing."

"But Pop...?"

"He always thinks whatever he wants is the right thing. And it isn't."

On the field, Denver had received the kickoff and ground out three first downs. The ball sat astride the mid-field stripe, sneaking a peek at Dallas territory.

"What are we going to do, Mom? The Mustangs have the spread covered."

"We'll wait until the fourth quarter. Your father will be angry if we go through with it."

"I know, but it needs to be done and doesn't the good outweigh the bad?"

"I think so, Scott, but morality is funny. We'd be breaking the rules, and your Dad believes in sticking with them. When we used to play tennis, he'd give me every shot that was even close to the line. What you and I are going to do isn't black and white. It's like so much of life, a shade of gray. Does that make sense?"

"He's open!" Scott yelled, his eyes on the field.

Christine turned just in time to see the two Denver receivers crossing in the center of the field. One of the Dallas cornerbacks got tangled up and fell, and as a receiver broke open, Mike Skarcynski lofted a high, soft pass that nestled into his receiver's hands at the twenty. He ran untouched into the end zone, lifted the ball high in the air as if offering it as a sacrifice to the gods, then slammed it into the turf.

"Where's the flag!" Kingsley screamed from the front row. "Illegal pick! Where's the goddam flag? Dammit, they never make that call! We're getting screwed, blued and tattooed by the refs."

Others rumbled about the unfairness of it all. Had Nightlife Jackson been in there at cornerback, he never would have fallen down.

"Hell, he would have intercepted the pass," one of the loyalists said.

"Jeez, it's like losing two players, Nightlife being out," another whined. "Our best cornerback and our best wide receiver all rolled into one."

After the extra point, Denver was only three points behind, and Christine felt some relief. "Maybe we won't have to do anything," she told Scott. Even though trailing 10-7, Denver was one point up on the four-point spread. If the game ended this way, Bobby would win his bet.

After the kickoff, Dallas began a methodical march down the field. The offense seemed more determined as often happens after the other team scores. With Nightlife missing, Coach Krause was calling more running plays, and the Mustangs chewed up yardage and the clock, finally petering out at Denver's twenty-nine yard line. After Craig Stringer overthrew an open receiver on third and nine, Boom Boom Guacavera lined up for a forty-six yard field goal attempt.

"Make it, you little wetback," one of the P.R. guys ordered.

"Yeah, keek a touchdown," another said, mocking the foreign kicker who wasn't fully aware of the game's terminology.

Miss it, Christine prayed.

"He's gonna nail it," Scott said. "In warmups, he was hitting from sixty yards out. I've never seen him so strong."

Stringer barked signals from his position as the holder, and Christine could not help but think of Bobby. He was so proud of having played college football, even if all he ever did was hold for the kicks. "I never dropped one," he told her many times. "Never even bobbled a snap in three years." Now, she thought, he held her heart in his hands.

Don't drop it Bobby.

With the serenity that comes from endless repetition, Stringer cleanly handled the snap, swung the laces away from the kicker, and placed the ball on the ground in precisely the right spot. Boom Boom kept his head down, planted his left foot, and swung his right leg as smoothly as a championship golfer wielding a three iron. The ball rocketed through the uprights with a good ten yards to spare.

"Attababy!" Kingsley yelled from down front.

"He tucked his free hand away, just like I told him," Scott said, regretfully. "He gave me grief, but he did it. Mom, we gotta do something."

"Not yet," Christine said.

After the kickoff, Denver bogged down and punted after one first down. With the ball once again in their hands, the Mustangs tried banging away with running plays but with little success. Christine kept glancing at the clock as the teams played conservatively and traded punts, and as the seconds ticked down like a beating heart, Dallas led 13-7 at the end of the third quarter.

ℰↄ

This game should be called the Snore Bowl," Crew Cut said. "Jesus, there's no offense, and I bet the over."

"How much time is left?" Bobby asked. His knees were stiff, and his wrists were numb from being locked behind his back.

"Still early in the fourth quarter. Dallas ahead by six.

"How about letting me watch through the window?"

Crew Cut shot a look at him.

"What am I going to do? Spoil your day by diving through the glass and committing suicide early?"

"All right. Get up here, but if you try any shit, I'll stomp you right here."

Bobby struggled to his feet and stretched, flexing his shoulders, feeling the inside of his swollen jaw with his tongue. Then he joined Crew Cut at the small window. overlooking the field from a height Zeus must have observed mankind. The electrical closet was five stories above the highest row of seats, even above the press levels and the luxury suites.

Somewhere below him, Bobby thought, Chrissy and Scott were watching the game, oblivious to his plight. While he'd been sitting there, contemplating his own mortality, he decided he was not afraid to die. What ate at his gut was the thought that he would never see Chrissy or Scott again. He imagined the pain they would feel. Then he vowed to fight. If he had a chance, he would claw his way out of here.

"Damn, Denver's moving," Crew Cut said.

Bobby watched as Skarcynski dropped back, avoided a sack by sidestepping Buckwalter Washington, then calmly stepped into the pocket and hit a wide receiver twenty yards down the field.

"That fat-assed Washington is sucking eggs," Crew Cut said. "He's gassed."

"He's been pigging out at buffets since the first round of the playoffs," Bobby said. "Looks like he gained fifteen pounds."

With a first down on the Dallas thirty-two yard line, Skarcynski peered over his line at the Dallas' defense where Washington scratched at the turf like an angry stag. Just before the snap, the linebackers moved up, filling the gaps between the linemen, knees bent, bouncing on toes, prepared to pounce like jaguars through the slightest crack in the offensive line.

"Gonna blitz!" Crew Cut shouted.

"Get rid of it quick," Bobby urged Skarcynski, as if he could be heard through the window, several stories above the field, and over the din of seventy thousand voices.

Skarcynski backpedaled into the pocket, and with an avalanche of Mustangs flailing at him, calmly flipped the ball underhanded to Shamar Pitts, the running back, who had feigned blocking for the quarterback.

"Shovel pass!" Bobby screamed, igniting the ache in his damaged jaw.

"Oh shit," Crew Cut said.

There is a sublime moment in football, Bobby thought, when an offensive play works on the field just as it was diagramed on the blackboard, when the "o's" are arranged as precisely as the stars in a constellation and the "x's" are scattered in useless disarray. Once the linebackers had committed to an all-out blitz, the defense was outnumbered on its side of the ball. As he crossed the line of scrimmage, Pitts headed upfield behind a phalanx of blockers who picked off the remaining corners and safeties. He scooted into the end zone untouched.

"TD!" Bobby cheered, trying to raise his shackled arms like an official and nearly tearing his shoulders out of their sockets.

Crew Cut slammed his fist into the window. "Bullshit!"

After the extra point, Denver led 14-13. It would not last, though, as the pace of the game had just changed. Falling behind seemed to ignite the Dallas' offense. Stringer led them down the field in six plays, scoring himself on a quarterback draw from the eight, making it 20-14 Dallas. Now, it seemed that the offenses had taken over, much to the delight of the fans.

With five minutes left in the game, Skarcynski began another drive, bringing Denver down the field with a deft mixture of runs and passes, tossing a 12-yarder to his tight end for the score and with the PAT, a one-point lead once again, 21-20..

"Looks like you might win the over after all," Bobby said.

"I don't care about that," Crew Cut said. "It's just twenty bucks. All I want is for the Mustangs to win."

"Why?"

"What kind of a question is that? They're my team. Always have been, even before I worked for Mr. K. Always will be."

With the time remaining now crucial to the game, as it is in life, a sense of urgency filled the stadium. Players hustled quicker back to the huddle. Fatigue was forgotten, and linemen fired out of their stances with ferocious purpose. Great waves of noise rolled through the stands along with a sense that the finale of the game would hold surprise and excitement.

Stringer guided Dallas into Denver territory yet again, needing a field goal to take the lead but a touchdown to cover the point spread. After three first downs, the drive stalled, and with just over two minutes left, Boom Boom Guacavera lined up for a long field goal that would give the Mustangs a two-point lead.

"Jesus, the line of scrimmage is the thirty-eight," Crew Cut said as the teams broke the huddle for the kick. "That makes the kick..."

"Fifty-five yards," Bobby said.

"Oh shit, he'll never make it. They should have gone for the first down."

"I wish you were right, but he'll make it," Bobby said. "He was banging them in warmups, and he's had the best week of practice of his life. He doesn't think he can miss."

Holding his breath, Bobby watched as Stringer barked signals while crouched just over seven yards behind the center. The snap came back high and wobbly, and Stringer stretched overhead, coming off his knee to catch it one-handed. He smoothly came back down and placed the ball on the pre-ordained spot. Boom Boom's powerful leg swept through the air with a motion as immutable as the pendulum of a grandfather clock, and he connected solidly. Bobby watched as the ball sailed end-over-end, descending as it crossed the goal line, looking as if it wouldn't make it, fluttering toward the goalpost where it bounced off the crossbar and fell over.

"Good!" shouted Crew Cut. "Holy shit! Good by a public hair."

Bobby gritted his teeth. It was a mixed blessing, a bittersweet symphony. Dallas led 23-21 but still hadn't covered the spread. Denver would get the ball and try to get in position for a winning field goal. Unless they turned the ball over and Dallas scored again, Bobby should win his bet.

But who'll be there to collect? A lawyer for my estate?

To hell with it. He wanted to live long enough to see Kingsley lose the bet, but nearly as important, he wanted Denver to score again. He wanted them to win the game, over and above the point spread.

After the timeout and the requisite commercial, Dallas kicked off and the crowd roared, even corporate CEO's appreciating the artistry and courage of the twenty-two gladiators. Watching the ball fly toward the returner, Bobby was struck by a revelation about the power of the game. Here he was, kidnaped and beaten, likely awaiting his own death, and he was cheering for a football team.

I must be crazy.

Not only that, the guy who would kill him was cheering, too, though for the other team. He'd seen something like it in sports saloons, two men who didn't know each other—a banker and a truck driver maybe—men who would never exchange hellos on a city street, huddled together like praying monks, as they dissected the strategy of going for it on fourth and one.

Sports distracts us, Bobby knew. It makes us forget our own problems as we throw our hearts and souls into something utterly meaningless on a cosmic scale. But it also brings us together. At the moment, he and Crew Cut were not captive and captor. They were just feuding fans. But in a few minutes, Bobby knew, the game would be over and unless he came up with a plan, the final whistle would signal his final breaths.

-47-

A Knock on the Door

Martin Kingsley could not hear the voice on the phone. In the owners' suite, the team officials and corporate sponsors were hooting and hollering and noisily congratulating him, but every word, whistle and cant sounded like the executioner's song.

Don't these morons know we haven't covered the spread? Don't they know that winning isn't enough!

He was yelling into the phone at Chad Morrow, the Mustangs' director of game day operations. Just as he did at the NFC Championship Game in Green Bay, Morrow was standing behind the bench, relaying messages to Coach Krause from on high. "You heard me!" Kingsley yelled. "When we get the ball back, tell Krause not to sit on it. We need another score."

"But sir, there's no reason to—"

"Do you hear me! Do you goddam hear me?"

"Yes sir."

But before the Mustangs could think about moving the ball, they had to get it back, Kingsley knew. On the first play after the kickoff, Skarcynski had an open receiver over the middle, but Buckwalter Washington batted down the pass at the line of scrimmage. The play took them to the two-minute warning and another television commercial.

While all the other Cowboy fans—at least the ones who didn't bet—praying that the clock would tick away—Kingsley tried to will it to stop. When play resumed, Skarcynski hit a short pass over the middle, then brought his team to the line of scrimmage without a huddle. On a quick count, he rolled out of the pocket, took his time and launched a rainbow down the sideline. His wide receiver made an acrobatic catch in Dallas territory barely getting his second foot in bounds. First down Denver at the Dallas forty-six.

God damn it to hell!

Suddenly, the point spread wasn't all that mattered. Denver could move into field goal range and win the game! But then, football can be a baffling game, and the oblong spheroid doesn't always bounce straight. After an incompletion and a quarterback sack that had the Mustangs' fans going wild, Skarcynski tossed a bullet to across the middle to his tight end, who reacted a fraction of a second too slowly. Late in bringing up his hands, the ball ricocheted off his shoulder pads and straight into the hands of a Dallas linebacker. Interception at the thirty-eight with fifty-three seconds left.

We have the ball back! We can score again and cover!

Pandemonium in the stadium. The Dallas faithful were on their feet, confident in victory. Denver fans moaned and shook their heads. Kingsley, however, was on edge.

What if Morrow didn't deliver the message? Or what if Krause doesn't follow orders? What if just runs out the clock? We win the game, and I lose the bet.

With the clock stopped for the change of possession, Kingsley bolted from his seat and headed toward the door that led to the concourse. He was consumed with one thought.

My Mustangs must score!

Either a field goal or a touchdown and they'd cover the spread. He'd win five million dollars and get Houston Tyler off his back and out of his life. He was already at the elevator when it occurred to him. There were two empty seats when he passed the last row of the suite. Where were Christine and Scott?

※

The horses whinnied and high-stepped nervously from side-to-side in that peculiar equine show of discomfort. Nostrils flared, eyes darted, ears perked at every thunderous sound from above, the noise increasing as the game reached a crescendo of its own.

"Where is she?" Scott asked.

"Right in the middle of the Petaluma show horses," Christine said.

They were in the cavernous staging area beneath the north stands. There, amidst the groundskeeping tractors and the half-time floats were the sixteen horses from the famed Petaluma troupe and one Appaloosa mare with distinctive leopard spotting.

When she came up with the idea this morning, Christine doubted she'd have time to carry it out, but she found an Appaloosa stable in Davie, west of Fort Lauderdale. Once there, she found Temptation. Or at least an Appaloosa mare with similarly striped hooves, the white sclera around the eyes and a black-on-white leopard spotting. She didn't have Temptation's two-tone mane, but a quick Clairol rinse took care of that, and a fast application of black spray paint added the distinctive map of Texas on her haunch.

"Will Craig really think this is Temptation?" Scott asked.

"That or her ghost."

But would he really? Christine didn't know. She hoped that, at first glance, he'd be fooled. "He'll be focused on the game," she said, "and what he'll see will be so out of place that his brain won't have time to think it through. Maybe he'll think he's hallucinating, but that should be enough to break his concentration."

"C'mon Mom, we don't have much time. You better change now."

"Okay, lead her up to the tunnel. I'll meet you there in a minute."

∞

At first Bobby thought the rapping sound was just part of the raucous cacophony from the stadium. Ahead 23-21, the Mustangs had intercepted the ball at their own thirty-eight yard line. They would run out the clock, he was sure, and win the game, but not cover the spread. He and Christine would own the team...if only he was still breathing.

Suddenly he recognized the sound as a fist knocking on the metal door to the electrical room.

"Godammit, open the door!"

The West Texas accent sounded just like Kingsley. But now? Here? With the game on the line, Bobby thought.

Crew Cut tore himself from the window and must have been thinking the same thing. "Jesus, Mr. K., it's the play of the game. What are you doing up here?"

He threw open the door, and a man dressed all in black burst into the room. He was bald and had a chalky pallor, made even paler by the purple scar that covered one side of his face. Emaciated and old, he would have seemed feeble except that at that moment, he was swinging a tire iron at Crew Cut's head.

The startled big man stumbled backwards and raised an arm. The tire iron crushed his wrist with the sound of a machete decapitating a coconut. Crew Cut wailed and brought his arms down, tucking the wounded wrist into an armpit. The tire iron swung again, this time connecting with the man's right knee. Crew Cut toppled to the floor, screaming. The man in black was on him then, pressing the iron to his throat, then looking up at Bobby.

"I do a pretty good imitation of the bastard's voice, don't I?" the man asked. "Hell, I've heard him give orders so long I even hear him in my sleep."

"Who are you!" Bobby demanded.

"Where are the keys to your cuffs?"

"Right pants pocket," Bobby said, motioning with his head toward the fallen Crew Cut.

The man dug out the keys, unlocked Bobby, then cuffed the moaning Crew Cut to an exposed pipe.

"Why are you doing this?" Bobby asked.

"I'm the only man in the world who hates Martin Kingsley more than you do," the man said.

"You're Houston Tyler! But you're wrong. I don't hate him. I feel sorry for him." Bobby rubbed his wrists and worked the blood back into his hands. "Thank you, Mr. Tyler. Thank you very much."

"You're welcome. I didn't want Martin to get the better of you."

"Where is he now?"

"I followed him out of his suite, figuring he was coming here, but he took the elevator down to the field. I suppose he wants to get his face on the TV."

"No," Bobby said. "He wants to call the plays."

-48-

The Snap, the Hold, the Kick

Martin Kingsley couldn't see a damn thing until he bulled his way past the security guards and sideline photographers. By the time he got to Chet Krause, the team had run one play, a two-yard plunge by the fullback. Denver called time out to stop the clock with forty-six seconds left, and Craig Stringer trotted over to the sidelines to consult with the head coach. "Just take a knee," Krause said. "They're down to their last time out. Make 'em use it now."

"No fucking way!" Kingsley boomed, breaking in. "Chet, didn't you get my orders?"

"I got 'em Martin," replied the lantern-jawed coach, "but I figured you'd had too many margaritas."

"Godammit, listen! We gotta score again. Craig, throw the down and out so the receiver can get out of bounds and stop the clock."

Stringer's eyes flashed back and forth from the owner to the coach.

"Craig, you'll do no such thing. This game is already won and I won't risk a turnover. I don't know what the point spread is, Martin, and I don't give a shit. We play to win, not to satisfy your drinking buddies who've bet on the game."

"It's not them, you horse's ass! It's me! Now, do as I say."

"Hey guys," Stringer said. "We're gonna get a delay of game penalty if you're not on the same page pretty damn quick."

"If you don't get at least three points, Craig, I'm putting you on waivers, but only after I have both your kneecaps broken," Kingsley said. "If we score, you get a five hundred thousand dollar retirement bonus and you become general manager of the team. Stock options, six million dollar salary, expense account, you name it."

"You got it," Stringer said, buckling his helmet and running onto the field.

Chet Krause turned away in disgust, and Kingsley moved down the sideline to stand at the Mustangs 40, the line of scrimmage. "Don't do it, Martin," said a voice behind him.

He turned to find Bobby walking toward him, brandishing a sideline pass to a security guard. "What the hell are you doing here?" Kingsley demanded.

"Watching you become a spectacle. Jesus, Martin, your face was just on the Jumbotron and on every TV set in the world. Everybody saw you arguing with Krause. What do you think the commentators are saying? If Stringer throws the ball now, everyone will know you've got money riding on the game. You can't do it."

"Why? So you can win the bet?"

Before they could answer, a gasp when up from the crowd. The two men turned to see Stringer rolling out to his right and firing down the sideline to a wide-open receiver who had caught the secondary playing up for the run. The pass was complete at Denver's thirty-seven where the receiver stepped out of bounds. The clock stopped with thirty-one seconds left.

"Way to go!" Kingsley yelled.

"It's not the bet," Bobby said. "I want to preserve the institution of football."

"You hypocrite! You're the one—"

They were interrupted by a second roar from the crowd. After faking a handoff to the fullback, Stringer dropped back and tossed a short pass over the middle. The tight end grabbed it, broke two tackles, then dragged a defensive back to the sixteen-yard line. Now, crazily, both teams attempted to call time out. Denver had to stop the clock in order to have enough time to score if they ever got the ball back; Dallas needed to stop it to have a chance for a field goal. The referee decided Denver had signaled first and ordered the time out charged to the defense. Nineteen seconds left.

"You tried to sabotage my team, you bastard," Kingsley said.

"I shouldn't have done it," Bobby admitted. "I shouldn't have become just like you. But now, you've won the game fair and square, so be happy about it."

"Screw you! All you care about is the bet."

"I care about the game. Don't destroy it. Too many institutions have been ruined. We don't trust the White House or Congress or the media or even our churches. Let us have something to believe in. Let us have football."

"You can have it on my terms," Kingsley snarled.

Time was back in, and now Stringer used a quick count and a two step drop before snaking a pass toward the end zone. The wide receiver on the right side was running a post pattern, streaking straight down the field, then cutting hard left to his left. He broke open just beyond the goal line, and Stringer's pass hit him squarely in the hands, but the ball squirted out like a wet bar of soap and fell harmlessly to the ground. Kingsley let out a groan as if he'd been knifed in the gut.

"Eleven seconds left," he said, shooting a look a the stopped clock. "I don't want to risk a sack or turnover. "Turning toward the bench, he waved his arms and yelled, "Field goal unit, get your asses in there!" Turning back to Bobby, he said, "Thirty-three yards. This is a chip shot for Boom Boom."

"It's crazy, Martin. Run out the clock. This will ruin you."

"Fuck you," Kingsley said, "and the horse you rode in on."

As Stringer broke the huddle and took his position with one knee on the ground seven yards and change behind the center, another gasp went up from the crowd, but this time it had nothing to do with the play selection. As Stringer barked the signals, a spotted horse with a rider dressed in flowing black silk and a black mask galloped onto the field, headed straight for the kneeling quarterback.

⁊

Zorro, Christine thought.

I look like Zorro.

Her senses took in everything as the horse broke from the tunnel. The first two security guards let her pass, probably figuring she was part of the post-game festivities. A uniformed Miami-Dade cop wasn't so sure. "Whoa there!" he ordered. But Christine tugged at the reins and guided the bogus Temptation around him. The horse whipped its mane, which cracked like a rug snapped into the wind, then leapt over the Mustangs' bench, knocking over a table of Gatorade and scattering the players who stood at the sideline, ready to celebrate the victory that was already assured.

She noticed the strange sound coming from the stands, a communal catching of breath, a soft whooshing wind that turned to laughter and cheers as the horse galloped past the line judge and directly toward the twenty-two men on the field. As she closed on them, the crowd suddenly grew silent, as if someone had turned off the TV set, and she could hear the horse's breathing and the clomp of its hooves on the grass.

Craig Stringer looked up then as the horse bore down on him, looked up from his kneeling position, and through his face mask, his face appeared to freeze, his mouth open, his eyes wide in terror. Then his features seemed to melt, like a block of ice perched close to a flame. Christine tugged hard on the reins, and the horse halted, reared on its hind legs and whinnied, the sound as accusatory as a lover's lament, the cry crawling up Christine's spine like a saw blade shrieking against iron. The horse, she thought, sounded just like Temptation.

Stringer emitted a high-pitched scream, then ducked and covering his helmet with both hands, as if the horse would crush him with its striped hooves.

Suddenly, Christine was aware of a piercing whistle. The referee ran toward her, followed by several uniformed police. She dug her heels into the horse and headed for the end zone. None of the policemen made a move to block the path of fifteen hundred pounds of horseflesh, and she flew out the stadium exit, streaking toward the horse van at the far end of the parking lot.

❦

What in the name of jumping Jesus Christ is going on!" Martin Kingsley fumed.

"All those years of horse riding lessons just paid off," Bobby said.

"The hell does that mean?"

"Nobody ever listens to me," Bobby said, shaking his head. At first, he was angry. He had told Chrissy not to mess with the game. To Chrissy, he thought, there was something larger at play.

This was the ultimate act of rebellion against her father.

The referee signaled timeout, then jogged from sideline to sideline to confer with the head coaches. The clock still showed eleven seconds remaining and wouldn't start again until the ball was snapped. Stringer removed his helmet and trotted straight for Kingsley.

"I don't think we should go for the points, Mr. K.," he said. He was as pale as the papers his lawyers filed against the insurance company for the dead horses, Bobby thought.

"What the hell's wrong with you? You look like you've seen a ghost."

"It doesn't seem right. I mean, the game's won."

"Not my game! Now, get the hell back in there and give him a good hold. Boom Boom can make this one in his sleep."

Stringer pulled his helmet back on and trotted back toward Dallas huddle.

Kingsley turned angrily to Bobby. "Goddammit! You were behind this, weren't you? This was some cheap stunt to throw off Boom Boom, wasn't it?"

"No. We were going to sacrifice a live goat at midfield to get to Boom Boom."

"I knew it! Well, tough luck, because he'll still make the kick. A 33-yarder is a gimme for that little cricket."

Bobby watched Stringer as the Mustangs came out of their huddle. Usually, the quarterback would just move to his spot, drop into the knee-down stance, and call the signals. But now, he was looking around the stadium, his eyes stopping on the end zone where Christine and steed had disappeared into the tunnel. Was he worried the horse would come back? Or maybe a stampede of the other horses he burned to death. What fiery winds were blowing through his mind?

"Christ, Stringer, get into your stance!" Kingsley yelled.

The quarterback did it then, hurrying to the spot, dropping to one knee. In the entire stadium, Bobby thought, there might be three or four among the multitudes who took note of what he saw. The Dallas special teams coach would have noticed and maybe the assistant coaches in the press box working the phones to the bench. Boom Boom would have seen it, but it was too late to do anything about it because Stringer was already barking signals.

Stringer had lined up a yard short!

Boom Boom had marked the spot for him, walking back eight yards from the spot of the ball, then toeing the ground a foot inches in front of that. Seven yards, two feet, the precise distance. But Stringer was a yard closer to the line of scrimmage.

One yard. Three feet. Thirty-six inches. It could be the distance from the earth to the sun.

Bobby's hopes soared. So much could happen now. Used to a longer distance, the center could snap the ball high. Even with a good snap, the defensive linemen would be one step closer to blocking the kick. Or it could distract Boom Boom as he approached the ball. So much in the kicking game required the same position, the same movements, time after time. The entire sequence—the snap, the hold, the kick—should take no more than 1.33 seconds, or the kick will likely be blocked. One little variation, and...

Before Bobby could think it through, the center snapped the ball. He must have made the adjustment because—damn it!—the snap was perfect. Stringer brought up both hands turned in slightly, with thumbs together, as he'd done a thousand times, as

Bobby himself had done hundreds of times.

The long snap was true, hitting Stringer in both hands. But the ball thudded off his palms. One bobble, two bobbles, then he snared it. Boom Boom had already taken two steps, planting his left foot, and his right foot had begun its arc when Stringer finally had control. He rushed the ball down, clumsily tilted toward the kicker, laces facing the oncoming foot. Boom Boom stutter-stepped and threw his entire motion out of whack. His foot hit the top of the ball and sent it hard and low toward the line of scrimmage where it smacked the right guard in the buttocks and shot skyward, hooking back toward Stringer.

A startled roar went up from the crowd.

"Oh Christ no!" Kingsley raged.

"How about that?" Bobby laughed. "How about that!"

For a moment, the field resembled a basketball court with all the players fighting for a rebound. Stringer leapt high and deflected the ball, sending it end-over-end, and keeping it in the air. One of Denver's linebackers got a hand on it and tipped it toward the sidelines where Marcus Ingram was waiting. Ingram was a defensive back who had been released by the Mustangs when Nightlife Jackson started playing on both sides of the ball. Denver picked him up, paid him league minimum, and had him playing second team cornerback plus duty on the special teams.

Ingram wasn't very good at pass coverage, and he hated physical contact so much he couldn't tackle a shoplifting grandmother. What he could do was run. Unless the horse returned to the field, Marcus Ingram was the fastest living thing within the sidelines.

When he saw the ball nestle into Ingram's hands, Bobby let out a whoop. He quickly scanned the field. Only Craig Stringer was between Ingram and the goal line. Ingram flew down the sideline, cut inside, leaving Stringer grasping at air, his legs tangled. When Ingram reached the goal line with Denver's fans screaming deliriously and the Mustangs fans looking on in stunned disbelief, he didn't spike the football. Instead, he calmly trotted to the official who was signaling the touchdown and flipped the ball to him.

Then he dropped to one knee and crossed himself.

"Amen!" Bobby shouted.

Kingsley didn't say a word. His face knotted up like burls on a slab of pine, he stood frozen in place. Denver came out to kick the meaningless extra point, and when it sailed through the uprights, the final score was Denver 28, Dallas 23.

"You lost, Martin," Bobby said. "You didn't just fail to cover the spread. You lost the game, a game that had already been won. Everybody in the world saw you do it. And they know there can be only one reason why. You bet on the game! What do you think the papers will say tomorrow? What do you think the Commissioner is saying right now?"

One of the network cameras was jammed into Kingsley's face, and a jitterbugging sideline reporter thrust a microphone under his chin. "Mr. Kingsley, why the field goal try? Why risk it? Did the point spread play any role in—"

Kingsley swatted the microphone away and took a swing at the reporter. "Get the fuck out of my face!" he yelled on live television.

The reporter backed off, still speaking into his mike. "Obviously, the Mustangs owner is upset. He may not answer my questions today, but you can be sure that the Commissioner will have his own in the next few days."

On the Dallas bench, the players moved away from Kingsley, then with heads down, slouched off toward the locker room. In the center of the field, the winning players were diving onto each other, piling into a mosh pit of Denver beef. Kingsley dropped into a crouch and ran his hand along the ground, the way Bobby figured he must have done on so many dirt fields where he would drill for oil. Tears tracked down Kingsley's face, slowly at first in tiny rivulets, then gushing like a fountain.

"You're balling like a little girl," Houston Tyler taunted, coming up alongside the two men. Turning to Bobby, he said, "Hell, Martin never shed a tear when seven men were killed at the Texas City Refinery, but lookee here. He loses a game and a bet, and he's wetting his pants."

Kingsley turned to look up at the cadaverous man. "I don't have your money, Ty."

"What do I care? I won't live long enough to spend it, and seeing you like this is worth more than five million dollars."

"You don't want the money?" Kingsley got to his feet, drew a handkerchief from a pocket and wiped his eyes. "What the hell does that mean? I lost everything betting on this game just to pay you off, and you don't want the money."

"I wanted to see what you would do, Martin," Houston said, hacking out a cough. "You never understood that money don't mean nothing. I thought there was a chance you'd self destruct, but frankly, I never knew how big the bang would be."

"You bastard," Kingsley said, more with resignation than anger.

"Even now, I wonder if you've learned your lesson," Tyler said. "All that matters is how you live your life. Did you do more good than evil? Did you earn people's respect? Is the world a better place for your having lived? I've asked myself those questions, and I don't like the answers. Now it's your turn. Know this, Martin. You'll live out your years just like me. You'll be a pariah, an outcast."

Tyler walked away, fading into the crowd.

"I underestimated you, Robert," Kingsley said. "I never would have thought you could have pulled off something like this."

"I couldn't. But there are people who care about me who could. And you, Martin, you were your worst enemy."

"Go ahead, Robert. Have your say. Gloat about it."

"I have nothing more to say. You're old and stubborn, and even now, you can probably justify everything you did."

"I did it all for my daughter and grandson."

"I'm sure your believe that, Martin. It's helps you mask just how selfish you really are. You didn't do it for anyone but yourself. Somewhere your wiring got crossed and you re-wrote all the rules to suit yourself. You had to win at all costs. You had to crush everyone in your path. Look what it's come to, Martin. You lost your daughter, your grandson, and your team."

"For someone with nothing to say," Kingsley said, "that's a

mouthful. You done?"

"Yeah, except for this, Martin. You're fired."

"The greatest accomplishment is not in never falling, but in rising again after your fall."
—Vince Lombardi

Epilogue

Togetherness

Friday, May 4—Irving, Texas

Goldy's eyes swept across the oversize office, taking in the framed team photos, trophies, and game balls from victories past.

"Nice," Goldy said, "but what's with the two desks?"

"Chrissy's the CEO, and I'm the general manager. For the first two months, we kept running in and out of each other's offices all day long. Finally, we just moved in together."

A wide smile cracked Goldy's leathery face and he put down the cup of tea Bobby had served him. "You're a happy man, eh Bobby?"

"I wake up every morning and think I must be dreaming. Chrissy and I have never been closer. Scott is a delight. I have great friends like you, and we're molding a football team we can be proud of, both on and off the field."

"All life is three-to-one against, *boychik*, but you beat the odds."

"I owe you a lot, Goldy."

"That's the *emmis*. You still owe me a bundle for backing your bet."

"Now that Chrissy and I own 51 per cent of the team, that's no problem. You want a check?"

"Either that or next season you can give me some tips. Injury reports, game plans, that sort of thing."

"Aw Goldy, you know I can't do that. We're doing everything straight. Fifty per cent of the profits go into the shelter for abused women and scholarships for inner-city kids."

"I know, I know. Like every reformed sinner, you're a pain in the *tuches* with your righteousness. Meanwhile, did I tell you they're making a movie about Vinnie LaBarca?"

"What?"

"Sure. HBO is doing the story of his life, 'Diary of a Mobster.' Should be on the air about the time he gets out of Eglin, which will be about 24 months. And guess who says hello? Your old girlfriend. She says if you'd have asked, she would have married you."

"What? She knows I'm marrying Chrissy."

"She means she'd have performed the ceremony. She's a judge now."

"Angelica Suarez? No way."

"Yeah, a couple of circuit court *momzers* got convicted of bribery, and there was a big push to find some judges with ethics."

"So the governor appointed Angelica?"

"They wanted a minority woman, too."

"Goldy, in Miami, Cuban-Americans are the majority."

"Don't blame me. I'm just telling you the news."

"Okay. Anyway, thanks for coming all the way here. Chrissy will be happy to see you, and Scott loves you almost as much as I do."

"I wouldn't miss it for anything. After all, how many times are you going to marry the woman?"

"Twice, Goldy. Only twice."

"Yeah, but who ever heard of a bookie getting married on the first Saturday in May? It's the Kentucky Derby, for crying out loud."

"I'm not a bookie anymore, Goldy."

ço

Bobby was grilling chicken on the gas barbecue and arguing with Scott when Christine joined them on the backyard patio.

"Hi Scott. Hi sweetie," Chrissy called out.

She came to Bobby and they kissed gently. "Hello, my once and future wife."

"I love you, too, sweetie."

"I'm gonna hurl chunks," Scott said.

"Sweetie," Bobby said, "will you tell our son that we're not making him personnel director of the team?"

"Listen to your father," Christine said, glancing at the grilling chicken. "Better lower the heat, honey."

"You offered me the job, Dad. How can you back out?"

"I meant after you graduated from college, or at least junior high."

"Didn't I help in the draft?" Scott said, turning to his mother.

"A lot," Christine said.

"Didn't I come up with a radical mathematical metric system by position?"

"You did that, too,"

"And didn't we steal Lavar Long out of Penn State in the third round because of me?"

"Okay, okay," Bobby said. "You can be the assistant personnel director after you finish your homework."

"I want a written contract," Scott said. "I'll have my lawyer call your lawyer."

"You're pushing it, kid," Bobby warned him.

That seemed to quiet Scott for a moment, and Bobby turned to Christine. "All ready for tomorrow?"

"I've been ready all my life," she said, dipping a finger in the barbecue sauce and tasting it. "What about you? You have seventeen hours and thirty minutes to back out."

"No way. I want a long-term contract, just like our son."

When Christine didn't smile, Bobby gave her a long, inquiring look. Between lovers, he had learned, words are often unnecessary.

"We got a telegram today from Daddy," she said, answering the unasked question.

"We?"

"Actually, yes. Wedding best wishes, that sort of thing."

"Is he still in Saudi Arabia?"

"Bahrain. He says he's on the verge of a huge oil strike and he's in tight with the sheiks."

"Where's Bahrain?" Scott asked.

"Outside the jurisdiction of a federal grand jury," Bobby said. He turned to Christine. "Are you okay?"

"It's just a strange feeling. He's still my father, and I still care for him."

"Nothing wrong with that." He gestured toward the window ledge leading to the kitchen where a glass pitcher sat, sweating. "Say, are you thirsty? I made the margaritas."

"Not tonight, Bobby."

Their after-work ritual always consisted of a kiss followed by a margarita. So she was bothered by the telegram, he thought. How bittersweet to have a wedding without your father, no matter what the history. "Do you want to talk about it?" he asked.

"No, it's not that. I'm fine, really."

"Uh-uh," he said, unconvinced.

"Guess who I ran into in the doctor's office today?" she said, changing the subject.

Bobby didn't know. He didn't even know she'd been to the doctor.

"Who?" he asked, trying to mask his concern, which now extended to her emotional and physical well-being.

"Shari Blossom. Or I should say, Shari Stinger. She and Craig are very happy. I think they were in love with each other for years, but neither could let down their guard and admit it."

"That's great," Bobby said, "but why were you at the doctor's? Are you sick?"

"Anyway, she's pregnant. Twins! Can you believe it?"

"A pair of little Stingers. If they have her brains and his teeth, they'll be little beavers."

"Bobby! Be nice."

"Okay, but why were you at the..."

Omigod.

It struck him them. Of course. They'd been trying, after all.

"My OB-GYN," she said, with a smile like sunlight on a spring day.

"Why were you at the OB-GYN?"

"Why do you think, silly?"

"Oh wow! Holy cow! Oh boy!"

"Or girl," she said.

"Oh, Chrissy!" A thousand thoughts swirled through Bobby's head. His life had become a sweet potion that overflowed the glass, and he was drunk with happiness and excitement. "Scott, get your mother a chair. Chrissy, are you too warm? Too cold? Do you need anything?"

"Bob-by," Christine sang out, melodiously.

"Yes?"

"Relax. And don't burn the chicken."

"Right. The chicken. Scott, do you have anything to say to your mother?"

"Sure, Dad. Hey Mom, I'll give you two-to-one I'm gonna have a sister."

#

AUTHOR'S AFTERWORD

If you enjoyed "Paydirt," please try some of my other sizzlers. "To Speak for the Dead," "Night Vision," "Fool Me Twice," and "Impact" are all number one bestselling Kindle thrillers. "The Road to Hell" is a number one hot-selling short-story anthology, which is being offered briefly at 99 cents for the entire compilation.

TO SPEAK FOR THE DEAD

"Move over Scott Turow! Mystery writing at its very, very best."
—USA TODAY

The first of the award-winning Lassiter series, "To Speak for the Dead," set new standards for the modern legal thriller.

A doctor in love with his patient's wife...
A fatal mistake during surgery...
Accident? Malpractice? Or murder?

Defending a surgeon in a malpractice case, Jake Lassiter begins to suspect that his client is innocent of negligence...but guilty of murder. Add a sexy widow, a deadly drug, and a grave robbery to the stew, and you have the recipe for Miami's trial of the century.

"To Speak for the Dead" introduced the world to Jake Lassiter, the linebacker-turned-lawyer with a hard bark and a tender heart.

An international bestseller, my debut novel was named by the *Los Angeles Times* as one of the best mysteries of the year.

All author proceeds go to the Four Diamonds Fund, which supports cancer treatment and research at Penn State Hershey Children's Hospital.

Sample or purchase "To Speak for the Dead" from Amazon: **http:// amzn.to/vRIi7p**

NIGHT VISION

Ahead of its time, "Night Vision," the highly praised sequel to "To Speak for the Dead" predicted the danger of homicidal stalkers on the Internet.

Linebacker-turned-lawyer Jake Lassiter is appointed a special prosecutor when women in a sex-charged Internet chat room are targeted by a serial killer. Enlisting a brilliant female psychiatrist and assisted by retired coroner Doc Charlie Riggs, Lassiter wades into a maze of lies and corruption to uncover the murderer. Soon, Lassiter finds himself on the trail of a psychopath from the mean streets of Miami to an insane asylum in London and the very streets where Jack the Ripper once stalked his prey.

"Mystery writing at its very, very best. Jake Lassiter is my favorite new character in fiction."
—Larry King, *USA Today*

Sample or purchase from Amazon: **http://amzn.to/rtzoZy**

FOOL ME TWICE

Murder to Go: From Miami to Aspen. A witness is dead and Jake Lassiter is the prime suspect. If he doesn't find the killer, he'll face a murder charge. A bloody trail of evidence leads to an abandoned silver mine under the Colorado ski slopes and an explosive finale.

"Delicious."
—*Los Angeles Times*

"Take one part John Grisham, two parts Carl Hiaasen, throw in a dash of John D. MacDonald, and voila! You've got Jake Lassiter."
—*Tulsa World*

Sample or purchase as either an ebook or paperback: http://tinyurl.com/3o2jzxt

IMPACT

Jetliner Crashes in the Everglades.
A Billion-Dollar Lawsuit: Negligence or Terrorism?
The Defense: Kill Anyone, Even a Supreme Court Justice, to Win the Case.

Supreme Court Justice Sam Truitt takes the bench with high ideals, lofty intentions...and a troubled marriage. If Lisa Fremont, his stunning and brilliant law clerk, doesn't get Truitt's vote in case involving a catastrophic airplane crash, she and her boss will be killed. IMPACT is a tale of seduction and betrayal, of passion and greed. Truitt, who has always followed the rules, and Lisa, who never has, join together to battle those who live by no law at all.

"A relentlessly entertaining summer read."
—*New York Daily News*

"A breakout book, highly readable and fun."
—*USA Today*

Sample or purchase from Amazon: **bit.ly/nUJGZs**

THE ROAD TO HELL

A Kindle 99-cent special.

Four thrilling short stories: "Solomon & Lord: To Hell and Back," "Development Hell," "A Hell of a Crime," and *"El Valiente en el Infierno."*

The heroes of these tales travel dark and dangerous paths as they confront devilish and powerful villains. The journeys are by land, by sea, and in one case, perhaps only in the mind. A hellishly good read!

Sample or purchase from Amazon: **bit.ly/pZRFjy**

More information on these and other Paul Levine mysteries and thrillers at http://www.paul-levine.com

ALSO AVAILABLE

THE JAKE LASSITER SERIES

TO SPEAK FOR THE DEAD: Linebacker-turned-lawyer Jake Lassiter begins to believe that his surgeon client is innocent of malpractice...but guilty of murder.

NIGHT VISION: Jake is appointed a special prosecutor to hunt down a serial killer who preys on women in an Internet sex chat site.

FALSE DAWN: After his client confesses to a murder he didn't commit, Jake follows a bloody trail from Miami to Havana to discover the truth.

MORTAL SIN: Talk about conflicts of interest. Jake is sleeping with Gina Florio and defending her mob-connected husband in court.

RIPTIDE: Jake Lassiter chases a beautiful woman and stolen bonds from Miami to Maui.

FOOL ME TWICE: To clear his name in a murder investigation, Jake follows a trail of evidence that leads from Miami to buried treasure in the abandoned silver mines of Aspen, Colorado. (Also available in new paperback edition).

FLESH & BONES: Jake falls for his beautiful client even though he doubts her story. She claims to have recovered "repressed memories" of abuse...just before gunning down her father

LASSITER: Jake retraces the steps of a model who went missing 18 years earlier...after his one-night stand with her.

STAND-ALONE THRILLERS

IMPACT: A Jetliner crashes in the Everglades. Is it negligence or terrorism? When the legal case gets to the Supreme Court, the defense has a unique strategy. Kill anyone, even a Supreme Court Justice, to win the case.

BALLISTIC: A nuclear missile, a band of terrorists, and only two people who can prevent Armageddon. A "loose nukes" thriller for the 21st Century. (Also available in a new paperback edition).

Visit the author's website at http://www.paul-levine.com for more information. While there, sign up for Paul Levine's newsletter and the chance to win free books, DVD's and other prizes.

ABOUT THE AUTHOR

The author of 14 novels, Paul Levine won the John D. MacDonald fiction award and was nominated for the Edgar, Macavity, International Thriller, and James Thurber prizes. A former trial lawyer, he also wrote more than 20 episodes of the CBS military drama "JAG" and co-created the Supreme Court drama "First Monday" starring James Garner and Joe Mantegna. The critically acclaimed international bestseller "To Speak for the Dead" was his first novel. He is also the author of the "Solomon vs. Lord" series and the thriller "Illegal."

FREE NEWSLETTER

Sign up for the free JAKE LASSITER NEWSLETTER and the chance to win signed books, DVD's, and other prizes at http://www.paul-levine.com.